Leave Me Where I Lie

By

Ellen Williamson

To Beverly

God bless you
Ellen Williamson
John 14:6
Romans 1:16

ISBN: 1-4140-6264-8 (e-book)
ISBN: 1-4140-6263-X (Paperback)
ISBN: 1-4140-6262-1 (Dust Jacket)

Library of Congress Control Number: 2004090529

This book is printed on acid-free paper.

Prrinted in the United States of America
Bloomington, IN

1stBooks – rev. 02/27/04

Dedication

In memory of my beloved grandmother, Mattie Parilee Posey Mayo, who, when I was but a child laid her heart bare to relate stories of her life to me. I re-lived, with her, the joys as well as the heartbreak of her courtship with Frank Haney and the tragedies that followed. As she told me some of the many incidents of her childhood happy, sad, or sorrowful, her expressive eyes reflected the deep emotion she still harbored in her soul.

This work is a historical novel. Where reality ends and fiction begins, the events, conversations and characters are products of my imagination. Many of the stories are true - some are fiction. The many incidents of Mattie's life as she related them to me are too numerous to detail in this book. Except for the names of my immediate family and that of Frank Haney, the names are fictitious. Any resemblance to persons, living or dead, is entirely coincidental. The places are real and still exist today.

Ellen Williamson

**MATTIE "PARILEE" POSEY
1906**

WILLIAM WADE POSEY
(circa 1900)

ANNIE JANE HODGES POSEY
(circa 1900)

JOHN ALBERT MAYO
1906

Come Not When I Am Dead

Alfred Lord Tennyson

Come not, when I am dead,
To drop thy foolish tears upon my grave,
To trample round my fallen head,
And vex the unhappy dust thou wouldst not save.
There let the wind sweep and the plover cry;
But thou, go by.
Child, if it were thine error or thy crime
I care no longer, being all unblest;
Wed whom thou wilt, but I am sick of time,
And I desire to rest.
Pass on, weak heart, and leave me where I lie,
Go by, go by.

LEAVE ME WHERE I LIE

Summer 1906

Mattie's heart pounded and her face felt flushed as she paused in the hallway and looked both ways to see if anyone was watching. Stealthily, she made her way down the hall toward the back door.

A caldron of emotions churned inside her. She did not know if she was trembling from excitement or anxiety. Or was it simply fear? She knew the anger that seethed inside her was directed at her parents. Anger for forbidding her to marry the only one she had ever loved.

She wanted to scream and curse her dead mother, to look toward heaven and shake her fist and call her, *Ma! Ma! Why? Why Ma?*

Her mother's own words echoed through the hollow places in her mind, *"He was Catholic, Mattie Parilee. That's why!"*

She had grieved, resented and hated for ten lonely years. Now happiness, joy, security, and peace beckoned her. Dare she reach for it, grasp it, pull it to her, clutch it tightly to fill up her empty life? But where was true love? She knew. It was gone forever – never to return.

Now a decision would be made, which would change the rest of her life. She hoped to sneak under the front porch to listen as John Mayo asked her father for her hand in marriage.

1

Mr. Mayo, Mattie had thought when he first hinted of marriage, *You've come to rescue me. Rescue me from this life of drudgery and loneliness. I'll soon be thirty years old and you're my last chance.* The fact that he was twenty years older than she bothered Mattie; but, what else was there? Her true love was gone forever. She had grieved long enough. John was a good man, affluent, educated, suave, a typical 'Southern Gentleman'. Did it matter that she did not really love him? She respected him greatly, but love him? He was a widower with a son the same age as Mattie and that bothered her but she shrugged it off thinking, *Oh well, that's the way it is.*

Mattie's sisters exchanged lively banter with Brother Tommy as they washed dishes and put away the food from lunch. They spoke in hushed whispers about the possibility of Mattie getting married - at last. The smell of fried chicken still hovered in the air. The leftovers on the table were covered with a freshly starched and ironed tablecloth to keep flies and dust out of what would be their supper.

Mattie was tall and slender, with fair skin, bright blue eyes and long, coal-black hair which she wore in a bun buried in a fluff of curls on top of her head. She opened the heavy, wooden back door very slowly and closed it as quietly as possible. No one seemed to hear. Although it was not a secret that she was expecting a marriage proposal, she did not want anyone to see her sneak under the porch and eaves drop on Mr. Mayo and her father. The welcoming radiance of the warm May sun bathed her face as she stepped gingerly down the steps.

She shivered somewhat to think of marrying John Mayo. How could she betray her beloved to whom she had sworn to forever be faithful? Nevertheless she had consented, "if it's all right with Pa and he doesn't object to the age difference."

John Mayo had just gone to the front porch where Mattie's father, Wade, sat in a rocking chair enjoying his chewing tobacco. He stared across the towering trees that separated him from the tiny town of Philadelphia, Mississippi.

Wade Posey had sat in this same spot for thirty years when he could get a break from his farming chores. Sunday afternoons were the most relaxing of all the times. The past week's work was reworked in his mind and the coming week's work was planned down to the hour. *"We'll do this on Monday. We'll do that on Tuesday. By*

Saturday we'll wind up with..." so it played in the thoughts of the earthy farmer. Now he sat with his feet propped up on the banister running the length of the porch. He had always considered it a challenge to spit his tobacco juice into the yard without hitting his feet. Sometimes he did. Sometimes he did not. He was a muscular man of average height with dark, bushy hair, not yet graying despite his age. His eyes, which were a hazy blue, were deep set under heavy eyebrows. A thick, bushy moustache covered his top lip.

The marriage proposal had not come suddenly. It had been preceded by "If we were to...", "If we decide to...", "Where would you like to live if we...". Mattie had dreaded the official proposal, and in a way, hoped it would not happen. She was not anxious to marry an older man, but who else was there? Most of the eligible men in the community were either related or "undesirable" in her way of thinking. She shuddered at the thought of soon being thirty and unmarried. The children in the community would giggle and whisper, "Old Maid, Old Maid." The men and women conjectured as to why she had never married and referred to her as a spinster or a bachelor lady.

She stepped out into the back yard then eased past the well where the wooden bucket hung from a rope across the roller that lowered it in the well. She shooed the strutting red rooster and half a dozen other chickens out of her way when they flocked to her.

Mattie lifted her long skirt to keep it from dragging in the red dust of the freshly swept yard then inched slowly along the side of the house, careful not to cast a shadow. She gathered her skirt and petticoats up around her trembling knees then stooped to sneak under the edge of the four-foot high front porch. A sticky spider web grazed her face and sent shivers over her. The ends of it stuck to her fingertips when she attempted to pick it out of her hair. Her black hair was pulled up neatly in a bun on the top of her head then buried in a fluff of hair that surrounded her face and neck. Her bright blue eyes were exaggerated by her dark hair and the high, ruffled collar of her homemade Sunday dress, patterned after the fashionable dresses of present day, 1906.

"Git," Mattie whispered to the old brown hound that nuzzled up to her to be petted. "Git away," she hissed but he only wagged his long, tapered tail. He put his wet nose to her cheek, which she promptly wiped with the palm of her hand.

She sat in a squatting position with her skirt smoothed over her knees she rested her chin on her knees and listened intently.

The shadow of the wisteria vine at the end of the porch gave Wade respite from the bright rays of the sun. His eyes closed briefly and his chin tried to find a resting-place on his chest as he intermittently dosed. Chewing tobacco made a pouch between his teeth and cheek. Brown juice seeped out the corners of his mouth.

"It sure is a pretty day, isn't it?" John Mayo said cheerfully as he sat in the rocking chair beside Wade. *There is no need to hold to the formality of calling him mister since there is only four years difference in our ages*, John thought.

"It shore nuff is," Wade answered, as his feet fell from the rails with a thud. His manner of speaking sharply contrasted with that of his daughter's educated suitor. "We got a good rain on Wednesday and I just walked out across the cotton patch. There's little sprouts ever'where." He leaned forward and spit across the edge of the porch, then leaned back in the heavy wooden rocker. He crossed his left ankle on his right knee then laced his fingers around his knee.

"It's going to be a good cotton year, I do believe," John replied as he settled in the other rocking chair. He ran his hands through his thinning, auburn hair, then smoothed his heavy moustache.

Wade did not bother to look directly at John, just sort of leaned his head in that direction. "All the signs point to it. Had couple 'a hard freezes to kill all the bugs and sech."

John pulled his pipe from his pocket, studied it carefully then turned the opening down and tapped it with the heel of his hand. The small leather pouch of tobacco he retrieved from his vest pocket was well worn. He loosened the purse-string tie then took his time packing the tobacco in the pipe, struck a match and held it to the tobacco. Little puffs of smoke surrounded his head as he sucked the end of the pipe patiently. Soon it was burning sufficiently. He clenched the pipe between his teeth and inhaled deeply, savoring the mild, sweet taste of his special home-grown concoction.

Wade Posey did not mind the lull in conversation. A man needs time to get his pipe drawing. Mattie, however, was becoming agitated at the silence.

John rested his elbow on the arm of the chair then started it gently rocking as he stared down the winding, tree-lined road that led to the house. In his normally sedate manner, he felt no need to rush into conversation. His refinement had a calming effect on the rugged farmer sitting next to him. John smiled as he noticed the worn indentation in the rail where Wade rested his feet. The years of foot-propping had slowly worn it away. Little flecks of brown were scattered along the rail and on the floor. Tobacco juice, John surmised.

John Mayo, a widower, was forty-eight years of age, not a handsome man, but well groomed and dressed in the latest fashion of the early twentieth century. He was slightly built less than six feet tall. His receeding auburn hair and heavy moustache exaggerated his finely chiseled nose and dark eyebrows. His soft, hazel eyes, reflected serenity and intelligence. He wore a tailored suit, which included a crisp, white shirt, vest and a black bow tie. A gold watch nested in his vest pocket, the chain draped gracefully to a buttonhole in his vest. His perfect diction and manner of speaking revealed him to be an educated man, at least for the twentieth century. He sat silently as he and Mattie's father relished the slight breeze, which filtered through the fragrant wisteria.

The driveway to the house was little more than a trail lined with huge oak trees. Pink, white and lavender petunias spilled from the flowerbeds onto the walkway. On each side of.the steps were large rose bushes Mattie's mother had put there. One red. One pink.

"Are you and your son's crops comin' along good up in Winston County, Mr. Mayo?" The first topics of conversation among the men of the area were the crops and the weather. Nothing else could be discussed until observations and opinions of both were exhausted.

"Everything's coming along very well up there, not quite as advanced as here. The little cotton plants are just beginning to crack the soil." They chatted inanely.

John's hand shook ever so slightly when he took his pipe from between his teeth. Although he was a very self confident man, asking a man for his daughter's hand in marriage was not something in which he had a lot of experience. He had only done this once before. He was a teenager at the time and he just blurted it out without making any effort to be suave and dignified. That had been thirty years ago and he was not benefiting from that experience at the moment.

"You got a mighty fine horse and buggy, there. Looks to be fairly new." Wade gestured toward the barn where the shiny buggy with the covered top glistened in the sunlight.

"I've had it for about three years now, try to take good care of it. Sure speeds up the trips into Louisville."

"Louisville? Oh, that's right, Mattie said you were working with the government to get high schools in every town."

John Mayo worked tirelessly to get community high schools. Most of the local people saw no need for the young people to go to school further than the eighth grade. Establishing high schools had been an effort in futility until some educated people started moving into the towns and opening businesses, law practices, and doctors' offices. This gave the young people incentive to be more than farmers and housewives.

"The buggy is nice for sparking too, ain't it?" Wade Posey offered with a jolly laugh.

"Well the ladies do like it and I have to say it doesn't hurt my image at all." John chuckled. "The ladies are proud to be seen in a nice buggy." John grinned broadly. *Hopefully that will soon be a thing of the past – proud ladies in my nice buggy.*

"I do admire your taste. Shows you got class." Wade ran his fingers through his bushy dark hair. "I have t' say I'm proud for my Mattie to be seen ridin' around with ye. Beats anything any of the old boys around these parts have showed up with!" He raised his heavy eyebrows and glanced at John.

Mattie shifted from one leg to the other in an attempt to get comfortable in a squatting position. The dog had made a bed in the dust under the porch as close to her as she would let him. The smell of dust and chicken feathers made her want to sneeze. She pressed her fingers tightly above her upper lip and held her head close to her knees.

The house was built on pilings some four to five feet high in the front so she had ample room to change positions. *Wish I had brought something to sit on. Didn't know it was going to take them so long to get around to the subject at hand. Which just so happens to be me!* She felt impatient and was getting more than a little bit aggravated.

6

"Just get to the point, Mr. Mayo," Mattie said in a whisper but she wanted to scream it at him. She hated all this beating around the bush. She began to perspire and fanned her nose with her fingers. *I wish I had brought my fan.*

"Mr. Posey, speaking of Mattie Parilee…" John cleared his throat. "I was wondering if you had any objections to the two of us, I mean, what I wanted to say was… I wanted to ask you if you would let me, or…uh…give me Mattie's hand in marriage?"

"Oh Pa, please say no, make some excuse, ask him to wait a few months or something." Mattie whispered only loud enough for the dog to hear. He wagged his tail as if she were talking to him. She noticed that her eyes were beginning to tear and a lump was in her throat. She slowly inched closer to the front of the porch.

What is the matter with me? She chastened herself harshly. *I should be proud that such a well-to-do gentleman wants to marry me. He is a Godsend.* She dabbed the tears off her cheeks with her fingers. God help me love him, she prayed silently. Even if my heart's not in it, help me to love him. Another tear escaped from the corner of her eye. She let it slide down her face then wiped her tears on her petticoat. *I haven't cried in a long time, and I am not going to start now*, she resolved. She attempted to shrug off her despondency.

"Just say yes, Pa. You might as well say yes."

Silence. Wade cleared his throat and shifted in his chair. An eternity of silence.

Silence means consent, at least that was what John had always heard – now he was not so sure. *What will I do if Wade objects to the marriage? Maybe I had better change the subject until he can collect his thoughts. This silence is deafening.* "You sure have a nice piece of property here - big farm, nice home."

"Yep." The subject of his property brought Wade out of his reverie. "Me 'n Annie and our chillun worked hard over the past thirty years to build up the place. Land ain't so easy to come by, especially when a fella's young." He looked toward John. "Of course you know that," he added.

"I know what you mean. Did you pay a lot for the land thirty years ago?" John really was not interested in what he paid for the land but that seemed to be the only subject to keep Wade talking.

Wade laughed then rested his head on the back of the chair. "Didn't pay anything for it, 'cept what I added on to it over the years, an acre here; a few acres there." He lunged back in his chair and propped his feet back on the rail.

John looked at him quizzically. He turned his head to ask Wade how he acquired the land if he had not bought it.

Wade's eyes were closed. A smile spread across his face.

"How did…"

Wade interrupted, anxious to tell how he had come by the land. "I remember the day as if it was yestiddy. My Pa…"

Memory is a wonderful thing. In a fleeting moment several years can flood the mind. However, when telling it, it can take much longer.

2

Summer 1880

"What do you mean a hundert acres of land and one of my coloreds?" Wade Posey's father yelled at him. "You're askin' for a lot to be such a young whipper snapper! You ain't even dry behind the ears and you think you can manage a hundert acres of land?!" He slung his pitchfork into the pile of hay he and Wade were loading on the wagon and faced his son expecting further explanation.

"But Pa, you always said you'd give each of us boys a hundred acres of land when we got married."

"You ain't married!"

Wade plunged his pitchfork into the ground at the toes of his well-worn boots. He yelled defiantly: "I will be if Annie Jane'll have me." His eyes narrowed and his lips tightened into a straight line.

"You ain't but nineteen years old! What makes you think you can make a livin' for a family?"

"I can if you let Josh come live with me." Wade sounded like he was starting to beg and he hated that. "Besides…"

His Father interrupted him. "I need Josh to help me here. He's the hardest workin' colored I got on this place. Do you think for a minute

I'm gonna let you take him away from me?" Leonard Posey's face was red and his glaring eyes pierced Wade's.

"He's not a slave, Pa! He can go where he wants to!" Now Wade was hot with anger that his Father had refused his request. He and Josh had made such big plans!

"He ain't goin' nowhere! You got that? And you ain't neither. If you jist gotta git married you can live here on my place and work like you're doin' now." He gouged his pitchfork into the pile of hay and slung it on the wagon.

"I want a place of my own...an...an, YOU PROMISED!" Wade shouted at his father. Anger darted from his eyes. His disappointment was evident. He had been so sure he would get the land. He and Annie had made plans and now... now... what?

"I ain't promised nothin'. I just said when my boys git to be men I'd give 'em a start in life."

"I am a man!" Wade yelled angrily as he threw the pitchfork across the field and took a step toward his father. He clenched his fist tightly, not that he would strike his father - he knew better than that. "I AM getting married and I AM taking Josh with me! The slaves have been freed and you can't keep him here against his will!" Wade's defiance and determination startled Leonard.

"Don't you talk to me like that, boy"! Leonard Posey turned to face his oldest son only to soften his attitude when he saw Wade's pale face and his fist clenched as if ready to fight. He turned back to his pile of hay in an attempt to ease the tension. "You'd best go somewhere and cool off for a few minutes, boy." He recognized some of his own hot-bloodied and short-tempered traits in his son.

With his hand still clenched in a fist, Wade whirled around and stomped across the field. He was surprised at his sudden defiance of his father. His father ruled his family and his "farm hands" with an iron fist and nobody crossed him.

"Smart alec," Leonard said aloud. "That's what happens when a man loses control. Got no control over his own chilluns or his own work hands neither. Now a days the chillun's think they can boss their Pa around. The very idea, wantin' to take Josh." He stuck his pitchfork deep into the hay and heaved a huge bundle up on the wagon. Bits of straw and dust fell down his collar and on the ground around his feet.

Leonard Posey was a hulk of a man, his bulging muscles a result of hard labor. He was practically bald with a thin moustache underneath a bulbous nose. His eyes were a deep green. Having lived during the Civil war, it was impossible for him to be completely unscathed by the attitude of the time. Even though he did not believe in slavery, he still believed the black people were somehow subservient to the white people. He could not imagine making a living on the farm without their help. The man with less than a hundred acres might make a living of sorts but not the man with a thousand acres, like himself.

Leonard had always called the black people "niggers", not that he meant it disrespectfully; it was simply what he had always heard. He, and the people of the community church had been informed of the correct terms, but somehow it just did not stick.

The visiting evangelist had come from somewhere up north to hold the annual protracted meeting the second week in July. Some wondered if he came to proclaim the saving power of Jesus Christ or if he came to "straighten out" the people of Neshoba County. At any rate, his sermons, for a large part were spent on attempting to correct the congregation's diction and attitude. Negro, he explained, meant black. "Oh, I know, the sluggish southern tongue has difficulty saying the word Ne-e-egro and it comes out nigger."

The head Deacon was the only one with the courage to defend the Southern speech, and attitude. "My papa always told me the rich Northerners brought them from Nigeria and sold them to the Southerners so that's why we call 'em niggers."

"If that were the case," the Evangelist countered somewhat self-righteously, "you would call them Niger, not Nigger."

"Oh well," the Deacon shrugged, "that's jist the way we say it down here."

With all his proffering, they were no closer to the correct pronunciation when he left than the day he arrived.

Some of the high society women did attempt to change the pronunciation but it usually came out "neegra" or "ne-e-gro". It proved to be too much an effort for most of the uneducated people so they continued to say nigger.

Leonard Posey's father, Richard, was a simple dirt farmer who never owned slaves himself but the neighboring plantation owners did. What Leonard witnessed when he was a child made him sympathetic with the slaves. He remembered vividly going with his father to one of the plantations and seeing the slaves' fed in troughs like pigs. He had seen a white man repeatedly hit a slave across the back with a leather whip. When the men talked of the abomination of freeing the "heathen slaves" Leonard secretly hoped for their freedom.

When the slaves were freed and had nowhere to go, several of them had gone to Leonard's father and asked if they could live on his farm and take his surname as theirs. They helped him work his land in exchange for a plot of land to raise cotton and vegetables for their families. Hastily built three room, shotgun houses were built for them. With the additional help, Richard planted more cotton and bought more land.

Richard Posey was fortunate enough to be able to buy a large portion of one of the plantations after the slaves were freed. The owner could no longer work the land without the help of the slaves so he sold it. Leonard eventually bought the land from his father.

With seven healthy, strapping boys, seven girls and the help of the Negro families Leonard could manage more land so he bought more and more as it became available. It took a lot of farming to provide for that many children and the Negro families. Leonard was kind to the black families but deep inside he felt they should still be submissive to him. "Not slaves", he rationalized, but still submissive. Make no mistake about it, they knew who was their boss.

Most of the black people who stayed in Central Mississippi were submissive, or appeared to be. They, too wanted to be free, to have a farm of their own, but were unable to get the resources to buy land, if, indeed someone would sell land to a black man.

Joshua Posey was the son of one of the black families that lived on Leonard's farm, so he and Wade had been buddies since they could run across the pasture to play together, which was at a rather young age. When they were very small, they referred to themselves as brothers, since they had the same last name. It took quite a bit of explaining to convince them they were not brothers and help them understand why their surnames were the same.

Wade relished telling his children about his and Joshua's antics; how he could not remember the first time he and Joshua played together. As a matter of fact, he could not remember a day in his life that he and Joshua had not seen each other at some point in the day.

Joshua's mother brought him up to the Posey house to help with the wash every Monday morning. Joshua and Wade explored the woods near the house, and played soldiers. They fashioned guns from tree limbs and battled until they were exhausted. For a snack they were often given a cold biscuit with molasses poured in a hole in the center.

Wade and Joshua worked side by side in the fields from the time they were big enough to hold a hoe handle or hold up a plow stock behind a mule. They competed to see who could pick the most cotton or who could work the fastest and hardest. They even started courting at the same time. They rode their horses together to the fork in the road then Joshua rode over to the Jasper place where his sweetheart, Louisa lived and Wade rode to Annie Jane Hodge's home two or three miles in the opposite direction.

Now the "courting" had become serious and Wade was ready to marry his sweetheart. Wade and Annie talked about it for months waiting for Wade to turn twenty. He would in two months and he was ready to get married.

"Papa won't let me marry you if we have to live with relatives," Annie had told Wade. "Ma said she wished I would wait until I'm older to get married."

"Lots of girls get married at sixteen," Wade's fingers stroked the back of her hand.

"I know. Mama was sixteen." Annie gazed into his eyes with uncertainty, wanting him to convince her.

"If I talk to Pa and he gives us some land, will you marry me?" He raised his eyebrows questioningly then squeezed her hand tightly.

"Sure, if my Mama and Papa say it's all right. It would be real nice to have a place of our own, wouldn't it?" She giggled as she imagined her own house.

"I've always heard Pa say he wanted to give his children a hundred acres when they married. If we can get the land, we can make it! We can live in a little house for a while can't we? It won't take

13

much room for two people." He glanced at the parlor door then leaned over and hastily kissed Annie on the cheek.

"I know Pa will give us the land."

In the spring a young man's fancy turns to thoughts of love.

3

The shade of a huge oak welcomed Wade so he put his forearm on the trunk of the tree and pounded his head on it. Tears of frustration brimmed his eyelids. He had been sure his Father would give him the land. After all, he had heard him brag often about the amount of land he now owned and how he would be able to give his boys a hundred acres of land so they would have a good start in life. Now he was going back on his word.

"You promised!" Wade screamed loudly to the white oak quivering in the breeze above his head. He tightened his hand into a fist and hit the tree in an attempt to squelch the tumult raging inside him. He rubbed his knuckles with his left hand and looked back across the field. Joshua was helping Leonard with the pile of hay.

Wade heard the dinner bell ring in the distance and saw the men in the hay field climb on the wagons and start toward the barn.

"I'll show him! I'll just leave and go up North!" Rebellion flared up in Wade mixing with his anger. He plopped down on the ground at the foot of the tree and pitched his hat over in the weeds.

******

"You be's asleep?" Joshua said loudly as he nudged Wade with the toes of his bare foot.

15

Joshua Posey was a tall, very dark, twenty- year-old, black man with thick, kinky hair and laughing, black eyes. His face revealed an untroubled soul and his lips smiled readily and often. His laughter was contagious. Except for the stories told by his parents of the days of slavery he was somewhat unscathed by the plight of the slaves. Although he had to work hard on the farm he had a fairly easy life. He and Wade had played and worked side by side since they were small.

Wade raised his bushy head. "Guess so. Didn't aim ta go to sleep. I just got so mad at Pa!"

"I heerd you and Mistuh Posey arguing this mornin'. He sho' ain't gonna give ye the land is he?" Joshua handed Wade a big piece of cornbread. "He ain't gonna let me go neither, is he?"

Wade bit voraciously into the still warm bread. "Why'nt you bring me a piece a fried chicken?"

"Wadn't none left. You shoulda come on t' the house t' eat dinner." He swiped perspiration from his forehead with the back of his hand.

"I was too mad. Did you bring any fresh water?"

"Yep." Joshua nodded toward the side of the tree to indicate a wooden bucket with a goard dipper in it. "What'cha gonna do? What'cha gonna tell Annie?" His six foot four inches towered over Wade.

"I don't know. Maybe I'll go up north or maybe I'll buy me a few acres of my own somewhere close around." He glanced up briefly at the broad, black face.

"What'cha gonna buy it wif? You ain't got no money." He squatted in front of Wade.

"I don't know!" Wade took a dipper full of water out of the bucket and drank thirstily. "What will you and Louisa do now that our plans are all fouled up? You still gonna marry her?" He slammed the dipper back into the bucket splashing water on the dried leaves around it. Wade looked across his knees at Joshua who was chewing on a twig of grass.

Joshua switched the twig of grass from one side of his mouth to the other. "Don't know. Guess we could move in wi' her pappy. Do ye thank there's any chance your Pa'll change his mind?"

"Don't think so. He sounded mighty certain to me." Wade took another mouth full of water, swished it around in his mouth and spewed it on a stalk of broom sage.

"You know what my pappy tole me on the way t' the house, jist a while ago?" Joshua didn't wait for Wade to answer. "He heered everything ya'll said, says he thanks Mistuah Leonard don't realize you done turnt 'nto a man. Still thanks you a chile. If'n he a'mits you be's a man it'll make him feel ole so he wants to be keepin' you a chile."

"How in the Sam-hill is that bit of profound wisdom going to help me?" Wade sneered at his friend. "How can I prove to my Pa that I AM a man?"

"I don' rightly know 'bout that; maybe you oughter ax my pappy fer some a'vice."

"Pa and Ma married when he was twenty." Wade raved on ignoring Joshua. "Why does he think I'm less of a man than he was?"

"I ain't got no answers fer ye, Wade. It's just like my pappy say, 'you can prove you be's a man by bein' a man'."

Wade looked at Joshua with a blank look in his eyes. "Sounds like a buncha dang double talk to me!" He stood up and started toward the hayfield where the empty wagons waited to be loaded again. "Bring the bucket a water."

******

"What's the matter, Leonard, too tired to sleep?" Tabitha whispered softly. "You've done nothing but toss 'n turn for the past hour."

"It ain't nothin'," he muttered as he pounded his pillow and turned his back to his wife.

"When you say it ain't nothing, I know it's something. Don't you know you can't fool me after all these years? You might as well spit it out." She continued to lie with her eyes staring at the dark ceiling.

"It's just the boy," Leonard muttered.

Tabitha laughed. "Which boy is that? We got six of them."

"William Wade. Thinks he's old enough to get married. Wants me to give him some land and help him build a house." He sounded sullen, almost like a pouting child.

17

"Why are you surprised at that? He's been courting Annie Jane Hodges for two years." Tabitha tried to reason with him.

"He still seems like a youngun t' me." He muttered. "How could he work a hundert acres of land?"

"How old were you when we married?" She waited for an answer. Leonard did not answer. "You always said you were gonna give each of the boys a hundred acres when they started their family. Didn't you?" she prodded.

Leonard flopped over to face his wife. "I expected them to be more mature than Wade is. Do you know what else he wants?" He paused long enough to pique her interest but not long enough for her to answer. "He wants Joshua to go with 'im." He raised up on his elbow to look at Tabitha's face in the moonlight coming through the open window. "Do you know what that means? I lose two workers instead of one." He plopped back down on his pillow.

"Is that all you're thinking about, losing two workers?" She tried to reason with him without losing her patience.

"Well, no, it's just that…"

"Just what, Leonard Posey?" Tabitha interrupted him, a tinge of aggravation showing in her voice. "You need to remember that Wade and Joshua are both men now and they have the same desires you had when you were twenty. Remember?" She smiled in the darkness and tweaked his chin affectionately. "They want a wife, a family, a farm of their own. I've heard the two talk since they was little bitty boys - how they were gonna get married at the same time, live side by side and raise their families. What if he takes off up North like two of your brother's boys? Do you want Wade to have as hard a time as we had getting land?"

"Well no, it's just that it's so sudden…"

"Sudden? Sleep on it, Leonard! Things'll look different in the morning." She turned her back to him and stared out the window. *Stubborn ole jackass!*

A man convinced against his will is of the same opinion still.

4

Heavy dew settled on the grass during the night. Wade's shoes and pants legs were wet by the time he rounded up the horses and mules to hitch them to the hay wagons. A mist covered all the low-lying areas making the air heavy and wet. The rising sun had not yet penetrated the fog but turned the moist air into orange and pink hues over the tops of the pine trees in the hollow down by the creek. Wade's brothers emerged from the house ready to tackle their designated chores. The younger ones drove the teams of horses while the older ones joined Leonard, Wade and the older men on the ground. Joshua, his father and brothers as well as other black farm workers joined the others at the barn.

"Climb in!" Leonard called to the workers as they arrived. They all climbed on the wagons to ride to the hay field.

Joshua and Wade's feet hung over the edge of the wagon and occasionally scraped the ground as they rode on the back edge of the wagon.

"You any better this mornin'?" Joshua asked as he nudged Wade with his elbow.

"Nope. Shore ain't, but I been thinking about what you said." He waited for Joshua to show some interest.

"Which part wuz that?" Joshua peered at him from under a dirty rag he had tied around his forehead to catch the perspiration.

"About proving I'm a man. I've decided to try working harder than I ever have to see if Pa will change his mind. I'm gonna show Pa I can stand on my own."

"Ye can't do no more poutin'."

"You're right. No more pouting."

"No holdin' a grudge agin' 'im."

"No holding a grudge."

"That'll show 'im! Show 'im how big you is on the inside!" Joshua clenched his fist and punched Wade's bicep. "Pappy said Mistuh Leonard would come aroun' if'n ye don't push 'im."

"Do you know what Ma did at the breakfast table this morning?" Wade looked over his shoulder to be sure the others on the wagon couldn't hear him. "She winked at me and said, 'you can catch more flies with honey than you can with vinegar'."

"What'd she mean by that?" Joshua's brow was furrowed in a puzzled expression.

Wade shrugged. "I'm not quite sure but my guess is she meant I'd come nearer getting the land if I'm nice to Pa instead of being mad."

******

The hot July sun soon dried the moisture out of the Mississippi air and off the plants. The hay that was moist with dew when Leonard Posey and his workers entered the hayfield at sunrise was now dry and scratchy. There had been no rain in two weeks so dust swirled from under the horses' hooves and the wagon wheels. The hay rake pulled by a mule sent a cloud of dust across the field, which settled on the men's sweaty arms and faces. A few of them pulled off their shirts to try to be cooler but the hay fell on their shoulders and necks and gouged into their skin. They worked at a fever pitch to get the hay in the barn before the next rain, never knowing when that might be. As soon as the wagons were piled to their capacity, the men climbed to the top to sit on the hay for the ride to the barn.

When they arrived at the barn, their pitchforks again picked up the hay and threw it through an opening in the loft of the barn. When the barn loft was full, they piled the hay around a pole in the barnyard.

Today, Leonard Posey did not have much to say as he worked in the hayfields. Usually a jovial man with a sense of humor, the joking and laughing did not seem funny at all to him today. He was deep in thought, he would soon be losing his son, and if he were not careful, he would lose him in more ways than one. He glanced in the direction of Wade and Joshua as they worked side-by-side, jesting with each other and talking as they worked. They had always worked well together. *It would be a shame to separate them now,* he thought. *What if they have some other plan now that I have refused them the land.*

"Quitin' time!" Leonard yelled. Some of the men took off their hats and looked at the sun in an effort to determine the time of day. The sun was still well above the horizon. There were at least two good working hours left in the day so the men hesitated to see if they had heard Leonard correctly.

"I said, quittin' time!" Leonard yelled again. "Pile on!" The men threw their pitchforks across their shoulders and gladly "piled on" the nearest wagon.

Joshua and Wade were taking the bridles off their horses when Leonard walked past them. He stopped, his eyes glued on the manure strewn barn lot.

"The dance is tonight. You boys go get your girls." He turned to walk on, then hesitated, "By the way, go on with your plans. I'll have your land deed ready on your weddin' day." He strode off at a faster pace.

Wade was surprised but then ran after him and clutched his father's arm, then turned to face him.

"Thanks Pa," he said sincerely, resisting the urge to hug him.

"Sure thing, Son," he squeezed Wade's muscular arm briefly.

"Can Josh go with me?"

"S'pose so. Seems t' me there ain't no separatin' the two of ye."

There comes a time when a man has to soften up a bit. Let go of his determination and harsh discipline. There comes a time when he has to change a "no" to a "yes" and a "later" to a "now". There comes a time when he has to loosen the grip on a treasure he holds tightly in his hand and trust it to one who will treasure it just as much as he. A grown boy is like a fist full of sand. The tighter one holds it the more it slips through his fingers, flutters through the air, gets caught in a puff of wind and is blown to, God only knows where.

5

Leonard and Wade walked the boundaries of the land that was to be deeded to Wade and Annie. They hammered stakes at the corners of the property and at key places to designate the boundaries.

True to his word, Leonard Posey handed Wade and Annie the deed on their wedding day.

Joshua and Louisa married shortly after Wade and Annie. All hands on the farm joined together to build them a house not far from where Wade and Annie planned to put theirs. The house wasn't a large one but it was warm and cozy, built in a clump of pine trees, a perfect place for newly weds. Wade had insisted that Joshua's house be nicer than some of the shacks where other Negro families lived.

Wade and Joshua stood in the shade of the pine trees behind the four-room bungalow and admired their handiwork. The smell of freshly sawn lumber still permeated the air. Louisa puttered around the house and arranged things in the kitchen, meager as they were.

Joshua stuck both hands inside the bib of his overalls and rocked back on the heels of his bare feet. "That sho' is a mighty fine little ole house you built fer me an' Lou!"

"Yeah…but I'm thinking it should be a lot bigger. I have a feeling you 'n Lou's gonna have it filled up in no time." Wade laughed at his prophecy.

Joshua laughed loudly. "Prob'ly gon' be a race 'tween the two uv us, don't ye 'magine?"

"I know one thing, I need to get me some boys on the way to help me work this hundred acres."

Joshua cocked his head to one side and gazed at Wade. The smile was gone from his lips and his eyes took on a look of seriousness. "Wade Posey, do you know how confound lucky you be's?"

"Lucky? What you talking about?"

"The land. A whole hundert acres of land to call yo' own! I be's lucky too, with the house, an' all – but - the land. Do you know how lucky you be's to have land? What's a man without land?" He continued to look deep into Wade's eyes.

Wade dropped his eyes to the toe of his boots. "I know how lucky I am. Not many men get land just given to them free and clear."

"You be mo' blessed than anything. Do you be real-l-y thankful?" His gaze demanded an answer.

"Course I'm thankful." His reply was somewhat defensive. "I thanked Pa. You heard me."

"One time just don't seem quite enough ta me. Not fer a hundert acres. What 'bout thankin' the good Lawd? Did ye thank him too?" He continued to stare at Wade's downcast eyes. Wade shuffled his feet and socked his fists deep into his pockets.

"Well, yeah…I…"

"If'n I'd a got a hundert acres give ta me, I'd be down on my knees thankin' the good Lawd ever' day. If I had twenty-five acres…or…or…ev'n one lil' ole bitty acre, I'd be on my knees praisin' the Lawd. Just one little ole acre ta call my own. One little ole acre that nobody could run me of'n."

"You will, one day. You'll have land one day." Wade tried to reassure him but in his mind he doubted that a black man would ever own land in Mississippi. At the present time it was illegal – or so everybody thought.

"I sho' hope you be's right Mistah Wade. I sho' hope yo' prophesy be's fulfilled one a these days."

Wade and Annie's house would take longer to build and would be much bigger than Josh and Louisa's.

"You'll be havin' lots a chaps and I ain't wanting to have to come up here every few years to build on a extry room," Wade's father said

23

adamantly. "We'll have plenty of help from all the neighbors so it won't take a lot longer to build a big house to begin with. You and Annie can stay with us until we get it built. We'll have a log rollin' the last of August so we can get them to Meridian to the sawmill before the cotton's ready to pick."

Leonard Posey was still in control.

Give thanks unto the Lord for He is good.

(The Bible)

6

By the first of September the logs had been sawn for Wade and Annie's house and a caravan of wagons was assembled to haul them to Meridian to be sawn into lumber.

The trip would take more than a week with relatives and neighbors lending their team of horses and wagons. The men carried quilts and pillows for camping out, along with pots and pans for cooking. The men turned the trip into an adventure. After all, they did not leave the farm very often. The crops were "laid by" meaning there was no more work needed until harvest time. The women were at home taking care of everything else.

The trip to Meridian was party time for all of them. It was a time they could talk dirty, cuss, chew tobacco, spit and drink moonshine without a dirty look from the lady folk. The young boys were old enough they could participate or not. The older men's attitudes were that the boys had to get out in the world at some point. They had to learn to hold their liquor and this was a good time.

The saloon in Meridian was the main attraction for the crowd of men. The pretty girls with their low-cut dresses and flirty eyes commanded the attention of them all, young as well as old.

The older men kept a close eye on the younger ones to keep them from over-drinking and ascending the beckoning stairs with the girls.

******

Joshua went along to drive one of the teams of horses as well as did Homer Young's two black farm hands, Roscoe and Oscar.

Since Negros were not allowed in the saloon, Joshua and Roscoe sat on the edge of the porch in the front of the saloon. They leaned back against posts while Oscar sullenly leaned against a hitching rail, trying to see what was going on inside. Leonard brought them drinks, which they sipped slowly, savoring the frothy foam on the warm beer.

"Just like when we wuz slaves," Oscar complained. "Have ta stan' outside."

"But we ain't slaves. We can leave and go sum'ers else anytime we wants," Roscoe said as he licked the foam off his upper lip.

"Just be glad we got a place to live and a place to work," Joshua added as he sniffed the glass he held with both hands.

"Mistuh Leonard seems like a mighty fine boss man," Roscoe commented to Joshua.

"Mighty fine. Couldn't want no better but from now on Wade is gonna be my boss. I'm livin' on his place now, you know. Mistuh Leonard has already built me and Louisa a purty little house right in the middle of a clump a pine trees," Joshua bragged. "How's Mistuh Homa' ta work fer?"

"He be's purty good but at times he be's mighty tough, huh Roscoe?"

Roscoe nodded. "At times he spects us to still act like we's slaves. Sometimes I thinks 'bout just runnin' off and goin up North."

"It'd probably be a whole lot worse up there. I heered the colored folk wuz slaves up there jist like down here, jist not as many of 'em. There ain't no cotton fields in the no'th, that's the only diff'ernce," Joshua informed them.

"At least we could have jobs that ain't so back breakin' as pickin' cotton. We'd get a paycheck ever' mont," Oscar said sullenly.

Roscoe nodded in agreement. "That's sho right."

"Well, why don't ya'll jist go on up 'air? You ain't tied down here. Leave yo' wife and younguns here and ketch the next train goin' no'th. Where would they stay if'n you left 'em? Mr. Homer ain't gonna let 'em stay in the house on his place if'n there ain't nobody to hep 'im work. Where would they go?"

"My wife could take the younguns and live with her Mammy and Pappy 'til I could git 'nough money to come back fer 'em." Oscar seemed to have it all planned.

"I know where her Mammy and Pappy live an' they ain't got no room for even one more set 'a toes under their eatin' table. Ain't room for another bed in that little shack," Joshua scoffed.

"That's what we all lives in - shacks." Anger was beginning to show in Roscoe's voice. "Mistah Leonard's son gives you and yo' family a fine place to live. We ain't got it so good."

"Maybe you jist needs to do a little work on the house yo'sef and not wait for Mistuh Homer to do it fer ye. Clean up 'round the place. What you thank you'd live in if'n you moved up no'th, huh?"

"Cain't be no wors'n what we lives in now," Roscoe complained.

"You needs ta talk to somebody who done been there and tried it." Joshua leaned forward and put one foot on the ground. He stared into Roscoe's eyes. "Do you know Zeke whose Pappy lives over on the Henshaw place?"

"Yeah, I knows 'im. He's up no'th.

"Not no mo'. He be's back." Joshua looked from one to the other. "I seen 'im in town back in the sprang an you shoulda heered him tell some 'a the ways the colored folks live up there."

Roscoe and Oscar were all ears. They leaned forward to hear more but it was doubtful anything Joshua had to say would quench their restlessness or the desire for adventure.

What did he say 'bout it?" Roscoe asked as he drained the last drop from his glass and glanced at the door to see if Leonard was bringing him another one.

"Well, he tole me he had a job awright. Said 'e worked in a steel mill over a flaming hot pot a steel. He tole me the heat in the cotton patch wadn't nothin' compared to the heat in there. Said he worked from sun-up to sundown. Days would go by without him see'n daylight. They wadn't 'lowed to stop fer nothin' but ta eat a bite a cold biscuit, if'n they had one to brang wif 'em."

Josh set his beer glass on the porch beside him and waved his hands as he talked.

"Zeke tole me, he said, 'Josh-a-way, there be's some mighty purty houses there but the colored folk don't lives in 'em. They lives in little shacks throwed up anywhere somebody will let 'em put it, which was nowheres 'round the white folk's purty houses. Some of the Neegros lives in ole warehouses or basements. They have no heat and liked ta froze last winter!'"

Joshua paused to take a sip of his beer. He licked his lips then wiped them with the back of his hand. "You knows what else he tole me? He says to me, he says, 'Josh-a-way, da only Neegros who lives in a decent house was the ones that had been slaves to the white folks. Even since they wuz emancipated they still lives just like they did befo' they wuz freed. Still a slave to the white folk'. He tole me they don't call 'em slaves no mo but they's still gardners, cooks, housekeepers, an' farmers. The black folk is the ones who take care a da animals, clean out da barns and do all da dirty work. They still don't get no pay fer it. They's told they's givin' 'em a place to stay in exchange for the work they do. They tell 'em they're free to go where they want to - but they ain't got nowheres ta go!'"

"Guess they could come to the South," Roscoe chuckled.

"Why would they come here? Ain't no work here fer 'em, 'cept farmin' and pickin' cotton jist like us." Oscar said louder than he intended. He glanced at the doorway to see if anyone was listening.

"Zeke tole me, he stayed in a filthy camp outside a town," Joshua continued. "Said he had to walk fer two miles to git water to drank. No cook stove, just a open fire. Sho wuz sad! He said his job didn't pay enough to buy a house - got barely enough to buy food. He jist give it up and come on home. He said the cotton fields wuz a whole lot better'n the steel mills."

"I still ain't gonna be satisfied till I try it fer myself," Oscar said stubbornly.

"Well, head out!" Joshua chuckled. "When you come back, if'n you get the money to come back, you can tell me a-a-a-all 'bout it but I ain't got no hankerin' to leave. I'm a stayin' right here in Neshoba County wid Wade Posey and breathin' this fresh Mississippi air. Me and my Lou's gonna have a dozen younguns and live right there in that cozy little house in the pine trees." He stretched his legs out on the porch and leaned his head back against the post. He tipped his glass to his lips and drained the last drop of beer into his mouth.

"Yeah, you set right here in Mississippi and you won't never have nuthin'." Oscar said as he raised his eyebrows and leaned toward Joshua.

"I might! I might buy me a little farm some day, who knows?" He smiled and ran his fingers through his thick, kinky hair. He was confident that someday Wade would help him have his own place.

"Yep, when hell freezes over! Niggers ain't 'llowed to own property and you know it! Ain't that right, Roscoe?"

"Sounds like we niggers ain't got no chance no matter where we goes," Roscoe pulled off his cap and scratched his head. "You won't never own no land, Josh-a-way. None of us will."

Joshua stared up at the banana moon and the billions of stars in the night sky. His optimism could not be squashed by two restless, rebellious mavericks. "You cain't neva' tell. I might be da firs'." He locked his fingers around the back of his head and grinned.

Leonard appeared in the light of the open door with three glasses in his hand. "You boys havin' a good time?"

"Sho nuff, Mistuh Leonard," Joshua said as he took a glass from him, thanked him and winked at Roscoe and Oscar. "I'm sho nuff havin' a good time."

Sometimes when the grass looks greener on the other side, you haven't seen the grass up close.

7

Abigail, the pretty, voluptuous blond, and Wade were in the middle of a checker game when Leonard suddenly stood up and stretched.

"Boys it's nine o'clock. I'm mighty tard from the long drive over here and it's already past my bedtime. Let's go ta camp."

The boys groaned and muttered objections but dutifully started saying their goodbyes to the ladies. Standing and walking was a bit awkward after drinking more than they were used to. Some of them staggered a bit, but somehow they managed to go single file out into the hot, sticky, summer night - all except Wade.

Abigail fluttered her eyelids at Wade and touched the back of his hand with the tip of her long, slender fingers. "Are you leaving too?" It was more of an invitation than a question.

"Naw, I think we should finish the game, don't you?" Wade said as he winked at her and smiled.

"I would like that very much," Abigail tucked her chin and looked at him seductively. Leonard Posey was already out the door.

The somewhat inebriated group advanced toward the camp near the sawmill laughing, slapping each other on the back and feeling the effects of the liquor. Leonard, Jasper and Homer led the pack, as each occasionally reached out to steady the other. They reached camp, found their bedrolls and without undressing fell on them. Most were asleep soon after they lay down.

Leonard looked around to make a head count.

"Where's Wade?" he yelled.

"He stayed to finish the checker game," George muttered.

"Checker game, my hind leg!" Leonard shouted. "I'll be back in a few minutes." He stomped off toward the saloon.

******

Abigail leaned back in her chair and stretched her arms above her head. "I'm tired of checkers, let's go upstairs." She got up from her chair and started toward the stairs.

Wade hesitated, then looked around. There was no one to see him. Buford was busy washing glasses and cleaning off tables. He pushed his chair back from the table and watched Abigail as she paused half way up the stairs. She smiled at him sweetly. Wade felt his heart start to race. He fingered the checkers, setting them up for the next game.

"You commin'?" Abigail said softly, barely above a whisper.

Wade pushed his chair back then sauntered toward the stairs.

"William Wade Posey!" a voice pierced the silence of the tavern.

Wade did not have to look to see who it was nor did he have to inquire what he wanted. He turned and followed his father out into the moonlight without bidding goodnight to Abigail.

Abigail shrugged and proceeded up the stairs.

Wade trailed his father down the street until they came to the sawmill. Leonard did not reprimand his son, no need to, he knew right from wrong, just needed a little reminder now and then, that was all.

"Pa, why don't we have a sawmill in Philadelphia?"

"I was just thinking that myself."

"You know, we could hang around here this week to learn just how it's done then when we sell the cotton, we might be able to buy the saws. What you think, Pa?"

"We shore need one back home, don't we? Me 'n you could run it. Make some good money. Course we would still need to farm."

"Let's do it, Pa, lets do it." Wade's ambition and excitement was evident. The prospect of having a business besides farming appealed to Wade.

31

"We'll look into it, boy. I can tell you're gonna be a success, 'cause you gotta eye for biz'ness. I could tell that when you hit me up for a piece of land." He chuckled audibly. Wade grinned at his slyness. "You 'n Josh had it all planned out." Leonard laughed out loud as he picked up his pace. Wade trailed slightly behind.

"Pa, -uh – Pa." Wade hesitated. "I'm much obliged to you for comin' and gittin' me back there."

"That's what Pa's are for, son, that's what Pa's are for."

More often than not, a man's got to slap his young'uns around like a mama bear does her cubs when they go pokin' their noses where they ain't got no business.

8

The wagons rolled into the house site and the men had all the lumber unloaded shortly after dark on Thursday.

Annie ran out to the barn where Wade and his father were feeding the horses. Wade pulled her to the side of the barn where his father could not see them and hugged her tightly.

Annie was of medium height, frail, thin and pale. Her eyes were a bright blue. She wore her dark hair in two braids twisted around her head. "Did you get all the logs sawed?" She asked anxiously.

"Sure did!" They're at our place ready, just waiting for the saws and hammers. We got nails and two new hammers too. We can start any time."

"Supper's ready, come on in." She hooked her little finger around his and led him to the house.

The men devoured the hot, home cooked meal. Fried chicken, fresh peas and corn, okra, squash, hot biscuits and corn bread. Annie had made a blackberry cobbler, which she served hot, right out of the oven. The younger children sat with wide eyes, listening intently to the stories about Meridian. Wade remembered Abigail and was thankful his father had kept him from ascending the stairs – stairs that would have, most certainly caused pangs of guilt to pierce his conscience for the rest of his life.

Annie pressed her hands firmly just below her breast then pushed her chair back and left the table. Wade followed her to the back porch.

"Ann, you sick?"

"I've just been throwing up a little bit the last few days. I'll be all right." She heaved over the side of the porch. "Will you get me a wet cloth and a glass of water?"

Wade rushed in the kitchen and was soon back. He pressed the cloth to Annie's cheek. "What's the matter?"

"I don't know. I may be in the family way," she said weakly, too sick to be enthusiastic.

Wade's knees grew weak so he sat on the side of the porch beside her. "How—how, do you know?"

"I just know," she answered weakly. She leaned her head against his shoulder. He stroked her hair gently.

"That's great, hon, just great. I brought you a pretty parasol from the store in Meridian."

Annie smiled; her eyes sparkled in spite of her nausea. "Let's go inside so I can see it."

A strange feeling of sadness and a sense of doom came over Annie along with her nausea. She did not dare tell Wade about it. Since she was a very small child, she would have times of extreme sadness, which seemed to her, to be followed by some sort of family trouble. She often felt she needed to warn someone about something but had no idea who to warn about what.

She once mentioned it to her Mamma but she told her not to say anything about it. "Do you want people to think you're crazy?" So she said nothing, then felt guilty when something bad happened. Now she had the same feeling but she certainly was not going to tell Wade. He might think he married a crazy girl.

9

Leonard Posey snatched the kitchen door open, stomped inside and let the door slam hard behind him. He jammed his hands deep into his overall pockets and stood staring down into the pot of peas boiling on the stove.

"What's got you so riled?" Tabitha asked. She continued to gently move the churn dasher up and down.

"If it ain't one thing it's another." He turned to face his wife. His eyes were squinted and his lips drawn. "Give one youngun something an' you have to give to another. Let one of 'em do something an' another 'spects the same thing. I'll soon be reduced to nothing but a house and a acre of land."

Tabitha stopped the churn dasher in mid-stroke. "What're you talking about?! What do you mean, 'reduced to nothing?' Which of the children?"

"It's George, you might know. When Wade does something, he wants to do the thing. The two of 'em are always in competition."

"What does he want?" Tabitha reached for the churn dasher again and started slowly pumping, her anxiety subsiding after learning her husband was referring to George.

It seemed George could get Leonard upset quicker than any of the boys. Leonard had a quick temper and often flared out at his boys for one reason or another. Lately he had been trying to think before giving a quick yes or no.

"We had to work hard to pay Papa for this land! You know how hard we had to work. You were right there 'long side a me. Now it'll soon be dwindled down to nothing."

"Will you stop your raving and tell me what you're talking about. What does George want?"

His voice started to rise in a crescendo. "What's he wantin'?" What's he wantin'!? I tell ye what he's wantin'! Land! That's what he's wantin'! A hundert acres, just like William Wade."

Tabitha smiled, her hand moved up and down with the churn dasher. Her voice was calm. "Is that all? You don't have to give it to him, you know. You're not obligated until he gets married."

"That's just it, he says he's marrin' Delvine Hodges."

"Annie's sister?" She let go of the churn dasher and stood to face her angry husband. "She's not but fifteen! What did you tell him?"

"I didn't tell him nothin'. I was so surprised I just stood and stared at him. I walked off, plain and simple, didn't yell at him or nothing. I throwed my ax down on the ground and come in here!"

"Let's get him in here and talk some sense into him!" She jerked the back door open and yelled. "George! George! Get yourself in here, right this minute!"

Leonard and Tabitha tried reasoning with George to no avail. Regardless of his age or whether his parents consented, George was determined to get married. He had an answer for every objection and stated it calmly and determinedly.

"You gave Wade his land. Why can't I have mine? You have nine-hundred more acres."

"I can't be giving the land to you 'til I know you're old enough to work it."

"I'll be nineteen next week. Lotta boys git married at nineteen. Delvine's fifteen, soon be sixteen and if Mr. Hodges don't let us git married, we're gonna elope." He stood rigidly facing his parents.

"I'm not askin' for one of your colored hands, Pa. Not like Wade got. There's plenty of 'em around and I'm sure one of Homer's hands will be glad to move off his place. They're not too happy with him any way."

He waited for a comment from his bewildered parents. They looked at him silently.

"I'm not asking you to build me a house, neither. If you'll deed me some land with some trees, I'll saw my own and build my own house. All the neighbors will pitch in like they always do." He paused for his parents to think about what he had said. They were strangely silent, staring at him without blinking.

"If you give me a hundred acres, that's a hundred acres you won't have to work." He shuffled his feet and looked from one to the other. It was obvious his father was putting forth great effort to keep from exploding. As for his mother's silence, well, he guessed she was just waiting to hear what else he had to say.

"Sure it's a big responsibility but you and Mama done it an' I can too." He stood and looked from one silent parent to the other. "If that's all, I'll get back to chopping stove wood." He walked calmly out the back door and closed it softly behind him.

Leonard turned to his wife. "Well, Tabitha, reckon we can talk him out of it?"

"We can try but if we can't we might as well consent. What do you think?"

"Guess we might as well. He could do a lot worse than Delvine Hodge."

Tabitha pulled the pot of peas to the side of the stove and returned to the chair beside the churn. "Couldn't we give him the same amount of help we gave Wade?"

"I guess so but I think he needs to work for a year or so to get a little more level headed before I give him the land."

"Sounds like a good idea to me."

Leonard stomped out the kitchen door letting it bang hard against the doorjamb.

A man convinced against his will, is of the same opinion still, Tabitha thought, still troubled about the fact that George was determined to get married. *He wants to do everything Wade does.* "Boys!" She pumped the churn dasher rapidly. Milk spurted through the top of the churn and ran down the sides.

******

Wade pulled his coat collar over his ears to protect them from the icy wind. "Are we never gonna get this roof on. It's taking a long time."

"Takes a long time to put shingles on a house this big. Especially when it's only the three of us." Leonard put more nails between his lips and fit another cypress shingle in place.

"One shangle at a time." Joshua muttered. He grinned around the nails he held in his mouth. Then in the blues rhythm of the Negro spirituals so common among the slaves he made a song of it.

"O-o-o-ne at a time, that's all ye can do.

One at a time, never two.

Hm-m-m-m, hm-m-m-m.

Pound them nails, through and through,

O-o-o-ne at a time never two.

Hm-m-m-m, hm-m-m-m.

Wade laughed. "That's a profound observation you made there, Josh. Did you come by it yourself or did somebody have to help you? I thought we were putting them on two at a time."

Joshua laughed with Wade. "Nawsuh, I come up wid it ri' by myself. Ye gots to put on o-o-o-ne shangle at a time."

Leonard couldn't help but laugh with them.

"If ye hadn't a wanted sech a big house ye'd been in it by now like me and Lou. We's all cozy in our three little rooms down 'air in that pine grove."

"It was Pa's idee to make it so big. Ain't that right?" He looked toward Leonard who was on his knees nailing.

"That's right! Make it big to start with and you don't have to keep adding on. That big hall down the middle will keep the cool breeze coming through in the summer time."

"The winter time too, if ye ask me, which you didn't." Wade added, but regretted it immediately. He did not want to get his father riled up right in the middle of putting the shingles on.

"It sho be's nice though," Joshua added to try to smooth things over. "That big ole pantry'll hold a lotta cans a mo-lasses and canned beg'tables."

"As soon as we can get Harvey to come build the chimney and we get these shingles on, ya'll can move in. We got the ceiling in the front room and the kitchen. We can do the rest with ya'll living in it."

"That won't take long if'n we'll start puttin' these heah shangles on tw-o-o-o at a time." Joshua drawled, trying to lighten the conversation.

Leonard shook his head and clicked his tongue against his cheek. "You're plumb full of mischief."

"By da way Mistuah Leonard, what'd ye d'cide ta do 'bout lettin' George marry up wif' Miz Annie's sistuh? If'n ye don't mind my axin."

"Do? Nothing I can do. There's no 'letting' to it."

"Din he gwin do it?"

"Next week." Wade answered for his father. "Pa's making him wait 'til he's twenty to get his hundred acres."

"Not even then if he don't get a whole lot more mature than he is now," Leonard hastened to say.

"He'll sho' matu' in a hurry when he gits a wife and young'uns. Me'n Lou's gettin' one sometime in the sprang."

Wade sat back on his heels and looked at Joshua. "You rascal! Why didn't tell me?"

"Didn't know it myself 'till yestiddy."

"Guess she's been keeping it a secret from you, huh?"

"Uh huh, sho' has."

Wade couldn't help think about his baby's arrival in March. "Pa do you think we'll be through with the house by the time our baby gets here?"

"Pretty near."

Leonard stopped hammering and stared at the even, neat rows of shingles that lay on the housetop behind him. It was obvious he had something serious on his mind.

Wade had noticed that his father became strangely quiet every time he mentioned the baby. "What's on your mind now?"

"Just thinking."

"About the baby?" Wade stopped nailing and looked at him. "Why do you get all clammed up every time I mention the baby?"

"I'm a little bit concerned, that's all, with Annie having to take to the bed all winter." He leaned on one knee and looked at Wade.

"I know. She's thrown up every day."

"It ain't so much that as it is the birthing pains she has every few days - and the bleeding. It ain't normal."

Wade knew the bleeding and pains were not normal but he was unaware of the severity of the complications.

Joshua slapped another of the six-inch shingles in place and pounded the nails down. "Lou tole me she knowed of a woman that died 'cause a bleedin' 'fo the chile wuz ready ta come out."

"Your Ma says she don't know if Annie's gonna make it all the way through this." Leonard hesitated. "I hate to mention it to you but you need to…to…well, you need to be prepared just in case."

Tabitha had tried for a month to get Leonard to tell Wade how seriously ill Annie was but he just could not bring himself to put it into words.

Wade glared at Leonard. "What are you saying? Does that mean she might die?"

"She's mighty frail, son, mi-i-ghty frail." Leonard slowly shook his head.

"That can't happen, Pa. That just can't happen." He stood with the hammer in his right hand. He turned pale and sat down on the roof. Tumult hastily rose inside him. Now he was the one who felt like throwing up.

Joshua squatted beside Wade. "You be's white as a sheet. Don't you go 'n fall off'n this house top."

"Why don't you go to the house and be with Annie for awhile. Don't let on to her that I told you. Ain't no use'n upsettin' her." Leonard was well aware of his lack of skill in relaying such a heart-wrenching message to his son. He knew of no way to console him other than to urge him to go be with Annie.

Wade's legs shook as he descended the ladder, and mounted his horse. Leonard and Josh watched as he gave rein to the horse and coached him into a full gallop.

"I sho' hope nuthin' happens ta that baby. I sho do."

"It's not only the baby that's in danger. It's Annie as well."

"Uh, uh, uh. I sho' hates that. S'pose we need t' do lotta prayin'."

PRAYER CHANGES THINGS.

10

March 1881

Annie bit into the wet cloth her Mother pressed against her mouth. The pains had become harder and closer together and it seemed the arrival of the baby was imminent. Mrs. Hodges stroked her cheeks and held a wet cloth to her forehead. Mrs. Parker, the local Mid-wife puttered around the room.

Annie glanced anxiously toward the closed door that led into the hall. "Where's Wade?"

"He's across the hall. Do you want me to get him?"

"Please, Mama."

A chill had descended across the south during the night spreading a heavy frost over the land. Hopefully it would be the last of the season since it was time to plant corn. Wade stood rigidly in front of the fireplace in the parlor across the hall from the bedroom. He stared into the dying embers, too engrossed in his thoughts and prayers to add more wood to the fire.

"Wade," his mother-in-law called softly from a crack in the door. "Ann wants to see you."

He hurried toward the door. "How is she?"

"She seems to be progressing normally but with this being the first baby she might take a long time."

Wade slipped quietly through the door and sat on the bed beside Annie. He kissed her lightly on the cheek and forced a smile when she opened her eyes.

"How you feeling, hon?"

"Hurting."

"Your lips look dry. Want some water?"

He took a glass of water from the bedside table and tilted it to her lips. Annie took a sip then wet her parched lips with the cool water on her tongue.

Annie moaned and held her hands to her protruding belly. She rocked from side to side. Tears ran down the side of her face and into her hair. Her moans turned to a scream.

"She's having another birth pain." Mrs. Hodge explained.

"Do something for her!" Wade shouted.

Mrs. Parker smiled as she patted Wade on the arm. "It supposed to happen this way. Now that was a good one," she cooed. "Very good. Now the next time you have a pain like that push, push hard."

"When will it be over?" Annie moaned. Her face was covered with perspiration.

"Soon, real soon," her Mama assured her. "Just push it on out, push ha-a-rd."

"You really need to leave," Mrs. Parker told Wade as she took him by the arm and guided him toward the door.

He looked back at Annie and reluctantly closed the door behind him.

The afternoon slowly turned into night. Leonard joined Wade in the vigil in front of the fireplace. Wade prayed. He grimaced when he heard Annie scream.

"Son, that's just normal."

Hours passed. Annie's screams became more frequent.

"She's mighty weak, Pa. I hope it will soon be over."

"Sounds like it won't be much longer."

Wade stood by the bedroom door with his ear to a crack in the door. He heard the voices of the women assisting with the labor. There was a soft cry - the unmistakable cry of a newborn. He opened the door and rushed in to see the mid-wife wrapping a screaming baby in a blanket. Annie's eyes were open wide as she stared at the baby. She turned and smiled at Wade. Her voice was weak.

Annie reached for his hand. "It's a girl."

He pressed her hand to his lips. "That's great. You did good."

"Now, Wade, you don't need to be in here. This is no place for a man. You go on across the hall and we'll come git ye soon's we get them all cleaned up." Mrs. Hodge's authoritative voice shooed him back out the door.

Hours later Wade sat on the bed beside Annie and the baby stroking and kissing them.

It was two days before Annie gained enough strength to think about what to name the new baby. The baby was snuggled in her arms, her heart shaped lips pulled on her breast and her tiny fingers curled around Wade's finger.

"What do you think, Annie?" Wade whispered softly, "What do you want to name her?"

The crackling fire from the fireplace was reflected in Annie's eyes as she looked from the baby to Wade.

"What do you think of Mattie Parilee?"

"Mattie's a good name, but where'd you get the name Parilee?"

"I made it up. What do you think?"

"I don't really like it. Why not Mattie Lee?"

"Okay, we'll name her Mattie Lee but I just might call her Parilee."

Wade laughed as he smoothed the baby's black hair. "That's fine with me. How about you Parilee?" He smiled at the baby's chubby face.

******

The sun beamed down warmly on the wild spring flowers. A brisk late March breeze stirred the new leaves sprouting on the trees beside the road as Wade and Annie made their way to their new home. The horse pulling the wagon was oblivious to the precious cargo he pulled behind him.

The new baby was wrapped in a soft blanket with little flowers embroidered in each corner and an edging of pink crocheted around it. Annie had made all the baby clothes that winter sitting in front of the fire while Wade helped build the house, butcher hogs and cut firewood.

All of the rooms in the house were not yet finished. The kitchen stove was in place with plenty of wood for cooking. A bed and two rocking chairs were arranged in the large room where the fireplace was located. It would serve as the master bedroom and the sitting room until the time a "parlor" was made out of the bedroom across the hall. It would always be referred to as "the front room". Wade built a table and some benches to go in the kitchen. Both mothers had shared their cookware and dishes, which were not very many. But, then, two people do not require many dishes.

Wade had carried all their meager belongings to the house and put them in place so Annie would not have to do it when she came home.

The big house sat on a hill a mile southeast of the little settlement of Philadelphia, Mississippi, it's front porch facing the setting sun. The tall pillars under the porch held it a good four feet off the ground to compensate for the slope of the yard. The hallway down the middle was open to the front porch as well as the back porch.

Wade had no idea the porch he was walking across carrying his tiny Mattie, would one day hide her while she listened to his conversation with her suitor.

The good Lord knew what he was doing by keeping knowledge of the future from his creation.

11

Joshua raced up the trail across the pasture to Wade's house and rapped on the kitchen door. "Wade, Wade! Open up! I got a girl!"

Wade pushed his chair back from the breakfast table and rushed to the door. "Did you say a girl?" He punched his friend on the arm playfully.

"Dat's what I said. A girl!" He took a boxer's stance and punched the air in front of Wade's face. Wade playfully punched back at him.

"What did you name her?" Annie called from the kitchen.

"Naomi, jist like the brave woman in the Bible. That's what we done. Naomi Posey! Now what you think of that Mistuh Wade? You ain't the only one who's got a big ole girl!"

Children are a heritage from the LORD, and the fruit of the womb is his reward. (The Bible -Ps. 127:3)

******

Mattie's first memory was of a little baby, a very little baby with a red face, kicking its feet, crying and lying on the bed.

"Make her hush, Ma, make her hush!" Mattie begged.

"All babies cry some time, Mattie. She'll stop as soon as I change her diaper and feed her."

Mattie stood beside the rocking chair and watched as her new baby sister took her place in Ma's lap.

"You're the big sister now, Mattie. You'll have to help me take care of the new baby."

"Can I hold her?"

"Sure. You sit right over there in that chair and as soon as she gets through nursing I'll let you hold her." Annie closed her eyes and rested her head against the back of the chair. She was weary, from what - she did not know. She was happy for the new baby, yet, she was somewhat sad. Tears came easily and she was impatient with little two-year-old Mattie. Why *does she make me so angry? She's just a baby herself and, yet, she knows better than to do some of things she does. So headstrong! Guess I need to nip that in the bud while I can. I need to get her in line while she's little.*

Annie put the baby in Mattie's arms and hovered over the two as Mattie wriggled under the weight of the sleeping baby. It did not take Mattie long to tire of sitting still so Annie took Pearl and laid her in the middle of the bed. She put Mattie on the bed across the room and tucked her in for her afternoon nap.

******

"Ma, Ma," Mattie called as she slid off the bed beside the baby and ran into the kitchen. "Sister Pearl said ma-ma."

"That's nice", Annie answered, concentrating on the dumplings she was rolling out on the table. She was trying very hard to keep busy so she would not give in to the unpredictable sadness and feeling of impending doom that had, again, come over her. After three months Mattie had adjusted to having a new baby in the the house.

"She really did, come see. Please, Ma, please." Mattie patted Annie persistently.

Suddenly there was a thud from the bedroom. It sounded like a door slammed or a chair falling over on the floor.

"What was that?" Mattie asked. Of course Annie didn't have to wonder what it was, for immediately little Pearl started screaming.

46

"What have you done?" Annie screamed at Mattie as she ran to the front room. "You left her too close to the edge! You killed your baby sister!"

Annie ran to the room, scooped the baby up and tried to soothe her. Her face was flushed and her temples pounded with every pulse beat. She laid the screaming baby on the bed, took off all her clothes then examined every part of her body. She moved her arms and legs to see if they were broken. She felt of her head and there was indeed a small knot on the back of it. Pearl was crying. Annie was crying. Mattie was crying.

"You're a bad girl, Parilee! A bad, bad girl."

"I didn't. Ma, I didn't move her, really I didn't. She musta moved by herself." Big tears ran down Mattie's cheeks. She pulled on Annie's skirt pleading with her to believe her. Annie soothed the baby and tried to calm her. She sat down in a rocking chair and put the baby's mouth to her breast. "Is she gonna die, Ma? I didn't mean to kill her."

"You've been bad, Mattie. I'm gonna whoop ye when I put the baby down." She was strangely calm but she knew what she had to do. Mattie had to be punished.

"No, Ma, please don't."

Mattie ran out of the room and crawled under the table in the kitchen. A shiver ran through her as her eyes fastened on the dreaded pantry door. She put her hands over her mouth to muffle the sobs. "Ma won't never find me here," she whispered. Mattie heard the rocker stop and Annie's footsteps when she walked over to the bed to put Pearl down.

"You're gonna be all right, Pearlie. We'll see about making you a crib so you won't fall off the bed no more." Annie's chillingly monotone voice reverberated through the house. "You're a sweet baby, mama's baby," she droned on and on. Mattie was so happy to hear that Pearl was not dead. *Now maybe Ma will forget about punishing me.* "I didn't make Pearl fall," she whispered.

Annie stalked through the kitchen and out the back door. Mattie pulled her knees up to her chin and wrapped her dress and arms tightly around them. She closed her eyes tightly and sat very still. "She can't find me," she whispered.

The back door opened, then closed. Mattie squeezed her eyes tightly and put her hands over her ears. *If I can't see Ma then she can't see me.*

"Mattie, come out from under the table." The voice was not soft and it did not sound loving. Mattie saw a switch in Annie's hand and knew she was going to be punished.

"No, Ma, no Ma," Mattie screamed as she pressed her little body tightly against the wall. Annie crawled under the table, clutched Mattie's hand and backed from under the table pulling Mattie with her.

The sting of the switch repeatedly on her back and legs was nothing compared to the look in her Mother's eyes. She screamed and "danced" to try to avoid the switch.

"Don't you ever do that again. Do you hear me?" Annie screamed as the switch repeatedly struck Mattie's legs and back. "Don't you ever hurt your baby sister again. Stop that crying! Stop it, I said. I'm gonna lock you in the pantry until you stop crying and learn not to hurt your baby sister." She put her hands under Mattie's arms and set her down hard on the dark pantry floor.

The heavy wooden door to the pantry slammed and Mattie heard Annie hook the latch on the outside. It was so dark Mattie could see nothing around her. The odor was stifling with the musty smell of cornmeal and flour. The normally pleasant smell of spices, along with dried onions and potatoes, some rotting in the bottom of the barrel made it hard to breath. She could not stop crying. But she must if she was to get out of the pantry.

"Ma there's mice in here, lemme out, lemme out," she screamed and stomped her little feet. She beat on the door with her fist and screamed as loud as she could, "Ma open the door, Ma, Ma!" She managed to stop crying so she could listen for footsteps but big sobs came from her throat when she tried to listen. She wiped her eyes and nose on the back of her hand. She put her ear to the door to listen. "Ma, Ma!" But she could hear nothing, no footsteps, nothing. She lay on the floor to try to see through the crack under the door. She listened and then heard the rocking chair. Creak, creak, creak, back and forth.

"That's a sweet baby. You're gonna be just fine. Rock a bye baby in the treetop…" she sang. Words came out of her mouth but there was no tune, just the key of C throughout the little song.

"Ma, ma, kin ye hear me? Open the door! Please Ma, open the door. Ma, Ma!" She screamed with fright when she heard a rustling on a shelf behind her.

Louisa straightened up from the scrub board in the washtub and cocked her turbanned head to one side to listen. *Thought I heered Mattie callin' her ma.* It was not unusual to hear Annie's voice as well as Mattie's coming from their house but this sounded a little different. She slung her hands to get some of the water off and peeked in the window to be sure Naomi and her baby sister were still asleep.

The trail across the pasture to the Posey house was well worn from Louisa and Annie's frequent trips. Now Louisa rushed up the trail. She stopped midway to listen. She stopped at the edge of the back porch and heard Annie singing. From the words to the song she surmised she was rocking the baby. Louisa could hear Mattie's muffled sobs but could not tell exactly where she was. *Guess, she ain't wantin' to take her nap.* Louisa shrugged and rushed back down the trail to tend her washing and check on Naomi and Ruth.

"Spect I better be mindin' my own biz'ness. Uh huh, sho' 'nuff."

Where does one draw the line between minding your own business and protecting the innocent?

12

"Na-o-mi!" Mattie called from the shade of the oak tree in the back yard. "Can you come play? Na-o-mi!"

The trail winding across the pasture to the little sharecropper house began at the oak tree in the back yard where Mattie and Pearl waited for Naomi and Ruth. Louisa had a good view from her front porch so the four little girls all under five were allowed to play under the tree.

Louisa came out the front door holding Samuel, her six-month-old on her hip.

"They's comin'!" she yelled across the pasture. Behind her the two little girls ran through the door clutching their corn shuck dolls. Pigtails protruded from their little round black heads in a dozen places as they raced toward their playmates in their bare feet.

"Ya'll play sweet!" Little two-year-old Ruth was trying to keep up with her four-year-old sister.

The girls made little trails in the sand and built houses out of sand and sticks. Make believe animals and wagons were fashioned from twigs. Naomi and Mattie were practically inseparable. The disagreements were frequent and the fusses and fights inevitable. Pearl and Mattie's fights were easily squelched by the threat of "the pantry".

******

Mattie sat up in bed and listened, then nudged Pearl in the darkness.

"I heard a kitty. Listen."

Pearl blinked her eyes and sat up beside Mattie. "I don't hear nothin'." She lay back down on the pillow and pulled the covers around her. Mattie could see a light under the door and could hear her Papa and her grandpa talking on the front porch. The smell of the smoke from Wade's pipe was unmistakable. She opened the door slightly and heard women talking excitedly in the room across the hall.

"It's a mighty fine little girl," she heard her grandma say. Mattie's curiosity got the best of her and she went to the door of the room, opened it, and peeked in.

"Ma," she whispered.

She saw her grandma and Mrs. Parker leaning over Annie. She slipped through the narrow crack of the door.

"Are you sick?" Mattie asked as she inched closer to the bed where Annie lay in tousled sheets.

"Get her outta here," Grandma Hodge yelled. "Wade, come get Mattie. She's got no business in here. This is no place for younguns".

Wade rushed through the front door, picked her up and carried her back to bed.

"What is it Pa, what's the matter with ma?"

"Ma is just fine sweetie. You have a new baby sister. You go to sleep now," he cooed as he tucked the covers around her.

"Did you hear that sister Pearl?" But Pearl did not hear. She had gone back to sleep.

I heard she had awful hard labor," Thelma Glass said to Mrs. Hodge as she helped with the dishes.

"She did. Lotta bleedin' as well. I do hope she doesn't have any more babies. The next one might just..." she could not bare to finish the sentence.

"You just have to leave that in the hands of the Lord Almighty. Ain't much you can do about it except hope and pray she has an easier time with the next one. What they gonna name her?"

51

"I believe they've decided on Louella."

Wade took the jesting good-naturedly in the churchyard the next Sunday. The men gathered around him to offer congratulations and rib him for having all girls.

"Hear ye gotcha another girl. Can't ye git a boy?" George laughed as he slapped Wade on the back.

"The next one'll be a boy, you just wait."

"Yeah, yeah."

"We're mighty proud of this girl, thankful she was born healthy." Wade said, proudly.

"You'll have to hire on another hand to help ye if ye don't never have no boys."

Wade had a response for every jibe. "Girls can be taught to handle a mule as well as a boy, you know."

"I've already got me a boy," George bragged. "Amos is a big boy now. He's gonna be a strapping boy to go ahead of my two little girls."

"I hear it was touch and go for Annie." George said sympathetically. "How's she doing?"

"Better. I think she'll be fine if she stays off her feet for a few days."

******

Annie had four-year-old Mattie doing all sorts of chores.

"Mattie, go get me a diaper."

"Mattie, run outside and get some stove wood."

Mattie, go take these table scraps to the dogs."

"Mattie, run to the corn crib and get some corn and shell it for the chickens."

"Mattie, set the table, supper is about ready."

"Mattie, clear the table."

"Mattie, come dry the dishes."

"Mattie, the baby is frettin', go get her and rock her."

"Mattie, sweep around the fireplace. Be careful and don't catch the broom on fire.

"Mattie, go get the eggs outta the hen nests."

"Mattie, run over to aunt Delvine's and see if she has some vanilla flavoring."

"Mattie, run down to Louisa's and borrow a cup of sugar."

"Mattie, today is Saturday, we have to sweep the

"Mattie, the clabbered milk is ready to churn."

Annie would spread a clean towel across Mattie's lap to keep the milk from splattering on her dress. Of all her numerous chores Mattie hated this one most.

"I'll be glad when Pearl can do something. It's "Mattie this and Mattie that," Mattie said sullenly.

"Watch your mouth young lady! Pearl's time's comin'."

"Well, I'll be glad. She gets to play and I have to do all the work." She poked her lips out in a pout.

"That's just part of being the oldest." Annie tried to reassure her. "You'll be all grown up an' she'll still be a little girl."

Mattie smiled. "I'll be all growed up like you?"

"That's right. All growed up like Ma."

Seems like it ain't no time from the time a child is steppin' on your toes 'till he's steppin' on your heart.

13

September 1885

Wade and Joshua stood at the edge of the cotton patch looking at the fluffy, white bolls sprinkled across the field. Their overalls hung loosely over their naked torso in an attempt to stay cool in the summer heat. Perspiration trickled down the sides of their faces and down their spines. Joshua was barefooted which was usual for him during warm weather. Wade had heard him mimic his own father with regard to wearing shoes. 'Toes are meant to be free, not all squished up in cowhide. They wants to wiggle in the dirt and feels the hot sun and the cool breeze. Naw suh, the onliest time they wants to be all bound up is to keep Jack Frost off'n 'em.'

"What da'ye think Josh? Think it'll be ready to pick by Monday morning?"

"I sho' b'lieve it will. One mo' day o' this hot sunshine an' them bolls'll be jist right fer pickin'."

"Look at the big fluffy hunks a gold, Josh. I do believe we'll make more 'n a bale to the acre." He looked at his buddy and grinned.

"I sho' b'lieve you be's right. Our young'uns gonna all get new shoes 'fo the first big frost. Yep, new shoes for them little ole wiggly toes. Can't have Jack Frost nibblin' on them little toes." He laughed and rested his hands inside the bib of his overalls.

"Land, rich bottom land to add to this hundert acres, that's what I'm a buyin'." Wade grinned and jammed his hands deep in his pockets. He stiffened his back then rocked back and forth on his feet.

Joshua looked puzzled. "What land is that?"

"That fifty acres down by the creek. I'm gonna see if I can talk Jimbo outta it. If he'll sell we can clear it and make two bales an acre next year."

"The Posey's is sho' comin' up in this world." Joshua laughed and turned to go home. "We better go rest these ole backs 'fo Monday mornin'."

There are two things a farmer should never do. One is count the chickens before they hatch. The other is to spend the cotton money while the cotton is still in the field.

******

The sun was hot by the time it topped the pine trees behind the Posey house. Wade had already been to the barn and hitched the mules to the wagon and driven it to the middle of the cotton patch. Tall, sturdy wood frames towered above the buckboard and a sturdy tree branch protruded out the back corner. The scales attached to the branch beckoned for the first sack of cotton of the season to be weighed before being dumped into the wagon.

Annie hurriedly washed the breakfast dishes and dressed the baby. She filled the wooden water bucket with fresh, water and put the leftover biscuits in an empty syrup bucket for snacks. "Come on young'uns, time to go to the field. Mattie you take the biscuits and Sister Pearl can take the diapers."

Pearl and Mattie trailed along behind Annie clutching their rag dolls. Louella peeked over Annie's shoulder and laughed at the antics of her two sisters.

"Here, hold sister Louella while I spread the quilt under the wagon for ya'll to play on." She put the baby in the middle of the quilt and placed the water bucket and biscuits out of her reach. "I'll be pickin' right close to the wagon so I can watch ya'll. Call me if the baby wiggles off the quilt.

Louisa arrived with her three little ones. "Look like it gonna be purty crowded under this wagon, don't it?"

"They'll manage just fine. Just so the older ones don't trample the babies," Annie replied. She handed Louisa a cotton sack and put the strap of her own over her head.

There was almost a blanket of white extending to the edge of the swamp where the trees towered beyond the seemingly endless rows of cotton. The cotton puffed out around the prickly, dried burs and concealed their sharp tips. Before the day was over there would be snagged, bleeding cuticles and fingertips, to say nothing of aching backs and bruised knees.

Wade and Joshua picked at the far end of the field leaving the area around the wagon for Annie and Louisa. They snatched the "Mississippi Gold" as fast as their hands could move and stuffed it in the homemade cotton sacks. There was no predicting how many weeks they would be picking cotton. By the time they picked over every row in the field, the first rows would be white again with the late bolls that had opened. Then the process would start over again. If there were no rain, the cotton would be easy to pick.

This scene was replayed over every cotton field in Neshoba County. The farmers had prayed for rain during the summer when the sun-parched cotton rows were thirsty for moisture to mature the cotton stalks. Now they prayed the rain would "hold off" until the cotton was picked.

Nothing interrupted cotton picking. Well, almost nothing. Not school. Not church. Not square dances. Any socializing had to wait until after harvest. If someone were critically ill or died, of course that was different, but then only the immediate family would take off for not more than enough time for the funeral.

In the event of a serious illness the neighbors gathered around the sick bed in the evenings. If there was a death they would pick cotton all day, then sit up at night for the wake. Then everyone would go to the funeral. But there was no time for prolonged grieving if the death was at harvest time. It was back to work as usual.

In cotton fields all over Neshoba County heads and shoulders were bent beneath the weight of the cotton sacks. Occasional conversation could be heard when two people happened to be picking near each other. Occasionally one of them would stand to straighten his back or loosen the strap on his shoulder. To lessen the strain on their backs they crawled on their knees as they picked. When their knees were bruised and swollen they would have to stand again. Only a few dared sit on his sack for a few minutes to rest.

The water bucket was under the wagon and when they went to "weigh up" they drank heartily. The Negroes brought their own water kegs, or buckets of water and the whites brought theirs. It was an accepted fact that they did not drink out of the same dipper.

"It seems like slow pickin' with jist the four of us," Wade commented to Joshua on the third day of picking.

"It sho do. In some ways it be's mainly me 'n you. By the time them two gals of our'n tends to the chilluns and cooks dinner they don't get hardly two hundert pounds a day."

"Think we ought'a hire some pickers?"

"If'n you can find 'em. Mos' ever'body's busy pickin' their own." Joshua's hands fairly flew from boll to boll. He couldn't resist reaching over on Wade's row to pick some of the choicest bolls.

Wade usually picked three hundred pounds a day but it seemed Joshua easily beat him by a hundred pounds. Wade seemed puzzled that he had not picked as much as Josh since he kept his two rows up with him. Joshua would grin and keep his secret to himself.

Joshua reached across to pick some fluffy bolls off Wade's row. *Guess I'd better keep him up wi' me so's he won't have to stand up to talk to me.*

Wade stood straight and looked across the white field. "I think I'll run down to the gin early in the morning and see if I can find some pickers."

"That might be the thing ta do."

The trip to the gin proved fruitful with Wade bringing back three strapping teenage boys who were anxious to make some money before picking their own cotton. Now there were seven pickers and the cotton wagon was filling up fast.

"Weigh up time!" Wade yelled.

Shouts of jubilation sounded over the cotton patch. The tired bodies slung the full sacks over their shoulder and trudged toward the wagon. They all rushed to the wagon and stood around the water buckets for a drink. The cotton sacks were put on the scales, weighed, then thrown up over the tall frames of the wagon and emptied by the teenage boys.

"You young'uns git up there and pack that cotton down," Wade yelled.

Four little girls clambered over the sides of the rails to pack the cotton. They lay down in the cotton, stomped and fell in the soft, warm fibers of "gold". They picked up arms of it and threw it.

Annie and Louisa had left to cook lunch for all the "cotton pickers" taking the two younger children with them. Wade looked up at the sun and determined that it was almost directly overhead. Most of the sacks had been emptied and the little girls were having fun packing the cotton when the dinner bell clanged.

The giant dinner bell could be heard most anywhere on the Posey property. Any time the workers in the fields needed to be summoned for any reason Annie rang the dinner bell. If it rang at a time other than mealtime, it usually meant that something was wrong or that Wade needed to come to the house for some reason. Now, the bell rang loud and clear so everyone knew lunch was ready. There was no doubt that it would be good. There were still fresh vegetables in the garden and plenty of chickens on the yard so they were almost sure there would be chicken and dumplings, fresh corn bread and plenty of vegetables.

The children scrambled over the side of the wagon rails and ran to the house. All the "cotton pickers" gathered around the well where Joshua drew buckets of cool, fresh water for everyone to drink. Joshua filled the watering troughs so everyone could wash up for lunch. The children dabbled their hands in the water for a few seconds and then ran to the kitchen. The men reveled in splashing water on their heads and faces as well as their arms.

The smell of food wafted through the open back door and out the kitchen windows. An improvised table and benches were set up on the back porch for the Negroes. The rest of them sat at the table, which had been moved out of the kitchen into the hall because of the heat.

The tables were laden with good hot food. All heads bowed as Wade thanked God for their bountiful blessings.

Annie remained standing to help the plates of the children and pass the food around as well as re-fill the bowls when they were empty.

Louisa was doing the same on the back porch.

"Where's Ruthie?" Louisa asked no one in particular.

Well, I don't rightly know," Joshua answered as he looked around the table.

"Miz Annie, is Ruthie in there?"

"No she's not."

Louisa went to the end of the porch and called, "Ruthie, Ruthie, come eat."

Ruthie did not answer.

Louisa went down the steps and walked out into the back yard. "Ruthie, Ruthie."

"Josh, did you see Ruthie when you wuz commin' in from the field?"

"Sho' don't recall that I did. I was just supposin' she wuz wi' the rest of the youngun's. Naomi, go look for yo' sista."

Naomi swung her legs over the bench and started down the steps. "Mattie, come hep me look."

Mattie put her spoon down and went with her. They looked under the house, behind the smoke house, under the trees and even went to the outhouse to look for her.

"Ruthie, Ruthie!"

"Ma, I can't find her nowhere."

Abe, one of the teenage boys spoke up, "Maybe she went back home for something. You want me to run down there and look around? Save me some peach cobbler," he yelled as he sprang off the side of the porch and galloped across the pasture.

Since Ruthie was nowhere around it was presumed that she had, indeed, gone home so every one continued their meal.

"She ain't down there," Abe said when he returned.

"Where could she be?" Louisa asked becoming more concerned.

Annie put the pot of dumplings back on the stove and rushed out to the porch. "Well, we gotta' find her, come on."

Wade started toward the barn, then he thought of the well.

The well was dug by hand, so it was about four feet in diameter. Wooden timbers had been built up the side of it and the seams spread with tar to keep the water from seeping out. The wood timbers extended four feet above the ground. A roller was attached to a frame built over the well with a rope threaded through it. A wooden bucket dangled from the end of the rope. A cover had been made to put over the well when water was not being drawn. This kept any debris, animals and children from falling in. More often than not the top was inadvertently left open between chores.

Wade ran to the open well. He leaned over it and peered inside inside. The others flocked to the well, fear written on their faces.

"Ruthie, Ruthie! Ya'll be quiet so I can hear if she answers me!" Wade yelled at the excited group.

Louisa was seized with panick. She leaned over the well and screamed. "Ruthie, answer me! Ruthie!"

Joshua grabbed her by the shoulders, pried her hands away from the well timbers, and pulled her back from the well.

"Lawd, Lawd, don't let my baby be down there!"

The water in the bottom of the well was still and clear as Wade looked down in the well. He stood still for a minute or so to let his eyes adjust to the darkness. He moved from side to side so he would not cast a shadow and to let the sun reflect to the bottom of the well. He saw the bottom and the white sand that had been added for a filter. There was not a ripple, nor any sign of Ruth. He put the cover on the well.

"Now, listen, ya'll just listen!" His voice was one of authority. "Calm down. We will never do anything if we are all in a panic. Louisa, stop that screaming! You're upsettin' all the younguns'! Now, listen to me and lets make a plan. Annie, you take Lou and ya'll go in the house, look under every bed, under and behind everything. Climb up in the attic. She is probably curled up asleep somewhere. Whoever finds her, come ring the dinner bell. If you don't find her come back to the well and wait. Don't let us have to come looking for you." He added emphatically. "Joshua, you go to the barn and do a thorough search. Two of you boys go back down to Joshua's place and search everywhere, look at every possible place."

He nodded to the other teenage boy and instructed him to go down to the creek to search. "Look under all the bushes and brush heaps along the trail as you go. I'm going back to the cotton patch."

They all went in their designated direction calling, "Ruthie! Ruthie!"

"You three girls come over here, I need to talk to you." Wade said firmly as he motioned with his hands to Mattie, Pearl and Naomi.

"Now girls, I want you to think. Where did you last see Ruthie?"

"Mr. Posey, I sho' don't rightly know," Naomi offered.

"Did she wash-up with you at the well?"

"Pa, I don't remember. I just can't think," Mattie said as she twisted a twig of hair around her finger nervously.

"Pearl, stop crying, now. Let's think. Where did you see her last?"

"Pa she was helping us pack down the cotton. That's the last time I seen her," Mattie whined, near tears.

"The wagon!" Wade said hoarsely and ran across the yard with the three girls running behind him. He started talking to himself trying to be reassured that this is where he would find her. "Maybe she couldn't get down and when everybody left she curled up and went to sleep. I just know that's where she is." He almost smiled as he was now convinced that was where he would find her. Nevertheless, he ran as fast as he could through the tall cotton stalks knocking fluffy bolls of cotton to the ground. The three girls ran behind him, only the tops of their heads showed through the tall stalks.

"Ruthie, Ruthie," her name echoed repeatedly over the fields and pastures.

Wade knew what could happen if a little body got covered with cotton or a little face was pushed down in the compact fibers. Air could not circulate and a little mouth could not breath. He had heard of it happening once over in Kemper County. Some little boys had been playing in the cotton house where several bales of cotton had been unloaded, waiting to be taken to the gin. The boys had decided to make a tunnel. They tunneled deep under the cotton, packing around the tunnel so it would be firm. They crawled deep under the cotton and then the tunnel caved in. It was hours before they were found.

When Wade reached the wagon he looked under it and tumbled the cotton sacks and quilt as he searched under them. He grabbed the frames of the wagon and shook it. "Ruthie, are you up there? Ruthie wake up," he screamed as he climbed up and over the rails. He fell on his knees and dug with his hands.

He had been the one who had told the others to stay calm and not panic. He felt as though his chest was going to burst. He breathed in short gasps.

"God, don't let her be here," he prayed.

His hands felt something round, hard. What was it? His heart pounded faster. He could feel the tiny braids of hair as he pulled it up with one hand, using the other to lift the limp little body from beneath the soft, warm fibers. He pulled her closely to his chest then quickly laid her down. He slapped her face and blew in her nostrils.

"Wake up, Ruthie, please wake up!" Her eyes were open. Dark, black eyes, but they could not see. Her mouth was open showing little white teeth, but it could not speak.

He picked her up and shook her. Her arms and legs flopped limply. He put his face to her nose but felt no breath.

"Ruthie!" he screamed and pulled her against his chest. He rocked back and forth, clutching the still child. He turned his face to the sky and screamed. "Why? God, why? She is so precious."

"Pa, Pa, you found her." Mattie said as she peeked over the edge of the rails. "Pa, why are you crying?"

Gut wrenching sobs came from Wade's throat.

From the front porch of the house Annie and Louisa, heard Wade's screams. They raced toward the wagon.

"Wade, have you found her?" Annie yelled loudly with her hands cupped to the sides of her mouth.

"Oh, Lawd, Miz Annie he be's cryin'. Oh Lawdy, Lawdy take care of my baby. Let her be all right," Louisa screamed as she ran toward the field.

Louisa saw her little girl in Wade's arms before she reached the wagon. Wade's sobs were muffled as he buried his face in Ruthie's hair. Louisa quickly climbed over the rails and pulled the child from him. She shook her and screamed her name. "Ruthie! Ruthie!"

"It ain't no use Lou, she's gone."

Louisa held the stilled three-year-old against her and collapsed in the cotton. Annie put her arms around her and tried to console her.

Before the rest of the search party gathered at the well they heard the screams from the cotton patch and ran to the wagon.

Joshua climbed up the rails and over the side and pulled Ruth from Louisa. He held her up and shook her. "Breath, baby, breath."

"It ain't no use, Josh, she's gone," Wade yelled, as he gripped him by the shoulders.

Louisa held Ruthie tightly. Joshua clutched them both in his strong arms. Annie put her arms around Louisa. Wade's large hands gripped Joshua's shoulders. They sat in the cotton, rocking, moaning, and crying. All the rest of the crying faces lined the rails of the wagon as they watched.

Joshua cradled the child in his arms and carried her to the house. He put her down gently on Annie's bed and straightened her dirty little dress around her. Her bare feet stuck out below the faded cotton dress and her arms lay limply by her side. Louisa and Joshua sat on the side of the bed and stroked her face and hair. They moaned and wept loudly.

"One of you boys go saddle up my mare and go tell Josuha's folks to come over here. Another one of you take the old mule and ride over to George's place and tell them to let the rest of the relatives know."

Wade and Annie sat beside Joshua and Louisa on the bed until their relatives arrived. Mattie, Pearl and Naomi stayed in the other bedroom not knowing exactly what to make of all the carrying on. They took care of the little ones, kept them quiet and rocked them until they went to sleep.

Pearl and Naomi cried and Mattie tried to console them. "You know she's in heaven don't you? All children go to heaven when they die. That's what Ma tole me."

Joshua gathered Louisa, Naomi and Samuel around the lifeless body to tell her goodbye. They stroked her hair and kissed her. Louisa clutched the little girl to her chest then reluctantly released her to Joshua who handed her to Annie. "Miz Annie, would you bathe her and get her ready for burial?"

"I'll make her a nice little coffin." Wade offered.

Joshua led his little family slowly across the pasture to their house in the pine thicket.

Ellen Williamson

The wake lasted a week at the home of Joshua and Louisa. The funeral was held at the Negro church three miles away, then the little pine casket was safely tucked away in the Slave Cemetery.

The Lord giveth and the Lord taketh away.

14

Wade heard the sound of rolling thunder echo through the tall pine trees that stood between his farm and Philadelphia. He raised his head only momentarily from between the cotton rows and quickly glanced at the dark ominous thunderclouds emerging from the west above the tree line. He heaved his heavily packed cotton sack toward him and adjusted his shoulder strap.

"We're sure gonna get wet!" he yelled to Annie who trailed behind him between the tall stalks of cotton.

"Why don't you jist git to pickin' and stop lookin' around?" she yelled back at him without raising her head. She knew he, too, was picking furiously trying desperately to save every fiber possible. Her hands darted from one fluffy bowl of cotton to the next, snatched them frantically and stuffed them into her sack. She fell to her knees in the furrow between the rows and picked the cotton from the bottoms of the heavily laden stalks around her. She pulled her skirt from under her knees and crawled, inches at a time to the next stalk, then to the next. When her knees hurt so badly she could no longer kneel on them, she again stood and picked in a stooped position.

The two of them picked alone. Joshua and Louisa were leaving the funeral about now with their two remaining children protectively tucked on the wagon seat beside them.

Annie heard Wade up ahead of her singing. His voice was low but the words were unmistakable and eerie.

"Swing low sweet chariot,
Comin' for to carry me home.
Swing low sweet chariot,
Comin' for to carry me home.
I looked over Jordan and what did I see?
Comin' for to carry me home.
A band of angels comin' after me.
Comin' for to carry me home."

The thunder became louder. The wind blew harder. Annie's bonnet blew off her head but the strings under her chin held it securely. Wade stuffed his hat into his cotton sack. A sharp streak of lightening zigzagged across the sky followed by a loud crack of thunder. Annie's entire body shook from the suddenness of it. She glanced toward the house where she knew the children sat huddled under a quilt, frightened by the storm. "It's getting closer! Do you think we might ought to go in?" she yelled to Wade.

"Just a few more bolls!" he yelled back to her. He snatched the fluffier of the bolls and left the smaller ones on the stalk. A few drops of rain fell on his head, neck and shoulders. The rest of his back was protected by the cotton sack. Annie pulled her bonnet over her head in one swift motion, never losing her momentum. The tips of her fingers formed a pinching motion as they snatched the cotton from the sharp burs and shoved it into the opening of the sack beneath her shoulders. Her fingers bled from the gouges of the sharp tips of the burs.

The rain fell in sheets, soaking Wade and Annie's heads and backs. Still they picked. "The cotton in our sacks is getting' wet! Let's go in!" Wade yelled. He picked up the heavy sack and slung it across his shoulder. Annie tugged at hers, unable to get it off the ground and onto her back. Wade picked up the end of her sack and heaved it in position on her back. With one hand he held his heavy sack firmly on his back – with the other he lifted the end of Annie's, to make her load lighter. Slowly, they trudged down the muddy cotton rows to the house.

For two days the gale-force wind whistled through the trees, around the corners of the house, and through the cotton patch and beat the cotton stalks with a vengeance. Water penetrated everything under the shadow of the thick clouds from which it fell. It soaked the cotton bolls and weighed them down until they fell piece by precious piece into the mud beneath the towering stalks. The rain fell heavily all night and for the next two days, then changed to a slow, soaking rain, which lasted for three more days. It pounded the fallen cotton into the ground until only bits of white could be seen protruding from the red mud of the long, winding rows.

Wade stood on his front porch and watched as his precious "gold" cankered. "Two bales, two measly bales are all we got picked. Thirty or forty more gone, pounded into the ground," he muttered.

The rain had mercy on nothing. The animals found shelter in the barn or huddled under the low hanging tree branches in the pasture. The chickens and dogs took refuge under the house.

Annie tried to busy herself with housework, cooking and keeping the children entertained. At least once a day she would put on her coat, cover her head and make her way across the wet, soggy grass of the pasture to offer condolence to Louisa. Wade could only pace across the front porch watching as the drenching rain and wind devoured his profit.

"If it stops raining and we get a couple of days of hot sun we can still salvage some of the cotton," Wade said as he watched Annie stir a pot of something on the stove. He tried in vain to reassure her. He could tell by the sadness in her eyes that she was concerned, that she knew how dire the situation was. *I hope she doesn't lapse into one of her dark moods over this,* he thought. He was all too familiar with her dark moods, her foreboding, her keen sense of impending disaster.

"Wade, we just have to trust the good Lord," Annie said, not feeling very trusting. She knew they would have little left after they saved enough money for cottonseed and fertilizer for the next year. Her attempts to keep Wade from knowing she was worried were apparently not working. She fought her feelings of dread and the veil of darkness, which descended on her. Her impatience with the children was rapidly getting difficult to control. With Wade in the house most of the day her threats of "the pantry" had to be only implied. She knew he disapproved of her drastic physical punishment of the children but it seemed that was the only way to keep them under control. Her hand gripped the handle of the spoon much too tightly.

"Looks like it's gonna clear up back in the west." Wade spoke hopefully. "I expect we'll have a cool spell after this, it being late September."

The rain finally stopped as the clouds thinned and separated letting the blue sky be seen from the water soaked world of Neshoba County. The sun came from behind the thinning clouds and steam rose from the ground casting a veil of moisture as far as the eye could see.

After two days of warm sunshine Wade, Annie, Joshua and Louisa hunkered over the cotton stalks. Their hands flew from stalk to stalk tugging the few limp, tattered, mildewed fragments of cotton left hanging in the burs. They reached down in the dirt and picked up pieces of cotton, which had been beaten by the relentless wind and pelting rain. They shook the gritty pieces of cotton to remove some of the dirt then stuffed it in their sacks.

"This is some bad cotton!" Joshua moaned as he stood up straight and rubbed his back.

"Yep, we'll only get 'bout half as much for it at the market." "Wade, I sho' hate that. If it hadn't a been fer our troubles we would'a got most of it outta the field fo the gale hit."

"Now don't you talk like that. Wasn't nothing nobody could do about that and it shore wasn't your fault. It's bad enough you lost your baby girl. I don't wanta hear no more about it."

Joshua said nothing. He just picked faster so he could be ahead of Wade and give in to the sobs that were choking him. Wade's own grief was renewed by the sound of his racking sobs.

Annie and Louisa faltered behind and talked of the past two weeks with an occasional heart-wrenching sob from Louisa. Annie tried in vain to console her.

"My baby, my sweet little baby girl. I miss her so bad," Louisa sobbed softly. Tears coursed down her cheeks and reflected in the sunlight like diamonds against her black skin. She wiped her eyes and nose on her sleeve.

"We all do, but she is in a much better place now. She is in heaven, singing with the angels. Jesus is holding her in his arms and telling her to look down at her sweet mama," Annie said, trying desperately to find something positive to say while her own heart ached for Louisa.

"Do you knows that for sho', Miz Annie?" She straighted up and looked at Annie then bent back over the cotton stalks.

"Why of course. When little bitty children die God takes all of them to heaven. Didn't your preacher tell you that?" Annie stood up and looked at Louisa who kept her head low and continued to rhythmically move her hands.

"I sho hope that's right, I sho hope so."

They picked cotton in silence while Louisa sobbed and pondered what Annie said. Louisa stood up and massaged her neck. She moved her head from side to side to relieve the pain. "Miz Annie, can you read 'n write?"

"Yes I can. Why do you ask?" Annie wondered why Louisa's attitude changed so suddenly but was glad she was off the subject of little Ruthie.

"I wish I could read 'n write. Are you gonna send Mattie to school?"

"We plan to, soon as it starts. Don't know yet when that will be."

"I wish my Naomi could go to school. I don't want my chillun to grow up as ignert as me and Josh-a-way. Do you think there'll ever be a school for us niggers?"

"I doubt it. You know most folk think coloreds don't need to go to school."

"I wish my Naomi could learn to read and write. Do you think Mattie could show her what she learns at school?"

"I betcha she would really like that. I'll tell Wade to buy a tablet for Naomi when he buys one for Mattie."

Annie wanted Naomi to learn to read and she did not mind Mattie teaching her, yet she thought it best no one knew about it. "Louisa, lets keep this a secret between us, okay? You know how people are about Negroes learning to read and write. They already think we are too buddy, buddy with ya'll."

Annie began to scheme and ponder about the possibility of a school for the Negro children. *How could I get that to happen? Who could I talk to? Who could I write? Where could it be located? Who would teach them? Was there any Negroes that had finished high school that would come set up a school? Who would pay for it? How much would it cost?* "I think I'll ask Mrs. Hampton," Annie said aloud.

"Are you talking to me, Miz Annie," Louise called from several feet up the cotton rows.

"No, no, I'm just thinkin' out loud".

With Liberty and justice for all.
In post civil war Mississippi???

Ellen Williamson

Annie shifted her position on the hard church pew as the Baptist preacher pounded his fist on the pulpit and shouted the need of repentance. She was used to the harangues of the preachers and was usually prepared to endure it but today, for some unknown reason, she was unusually restless. Louella was asleep in her arms. Mattie and Pearl squirmed and wiggled on the pew beside her.

"I'm hungry", Mattie mouthed to Annie, who nodded her head in agreement, as she touched her pursed lips with her forefinger. Must be about one o'clock, she thought.

The air outside was extremely warm and humid. The recent rains thoroughly soaked the earth, every rotten log and the very core of every tree. The hot sun pulled the moisture to the earth's surface as the steam penetrated the pores of skin and the nostrils. All the windows of the church were open. The men pushed up the sleeves of their white, dress shirts. Many of them removed their pert, black bow ties. The mothers fanned their babies and their own faces, which were made hotter by the high collars on their dresses and blouses. Large hats laden with flowers and bows perched on top of every lady's head.

Babies were asleep on pallets at their Mothers' feet between the pews. The smaller children played on the pallet beside them. There were teacakes and jars of water to keep the younger children from becoming famished during the long service.

The preacher leaned over the pulpit, cupped his hands around his mouth and lowered his voice to a barely audible pitch. "Only faith in our Lord and Savior, Jesus Christ will get you to the promised land," he whispered. "NOT BAPTISM OR THE GOOD DEEDS YOU DO!" he suddenly screamed as his fist hit the pulpit. Mattie flinched. Delvine Posey's sleeping baby awoke and started to cry. The smaller children put their hands over their ears. They were used to this sort of preaching but still the sudden loud shout startled them.

This was the Baptist preacher's day to preach – next Sunday would be the Methodist's. The doctrines on which they differed were pounded into the heads of the people every Sunday. Their basic message was the same but each was adamant that his interpretation of the scripture was the correct one.

"The bible teaches that immersion is the correct way to baptize!" the Baptist preacher proclaimed. Loud Amen's were heard from the

Baptist men. Some of the Methodists shook their heads in disagreement.

When it was his day to preach, the Methodist preacher would shout, "Sprinkling is just as good as immersion." The Methodist elders shouted "Amen!" Then it was the Baptist's turn to shake their heads in disagreement.

"You can only miss hell by the power of the blood of Jesus Christ! Come to him now!" both Baptist and Methodist preachers exhorted. "Amen!" all the men said in unison. Each looked at his neighbor and nodded his head. On this they all agreed.

"Once you are saved there is no way you can be lost and go to hell! Once saved, always saved!" the Baptist preacher proclaimed adamantly.

"You have to repent and be re-saved after every sin, or you'll go straight to hell!" the Methodist preacher countered.

Both the Methodists and the Baptists of Philadelphia attended both services. They managed to keep their opinions to themselves when on the churchyard, but when they met in town or in their homes, each defended his belief with fervor.

Today, Annie glanced over her shoulder at Mrs. Hampton who was to be Mattie's schoolteacher. I want to be sure to catch her before she leaves, she thought. This would be a good time to ask her about schools for the Negroes.

15

The rays of sunshine filtered in Mattie's window and awakened her. She remembered it was the first day of school and she leaped from the bed. Annie dressed her in one of her best dresses with a long ribbon tied around her waist. She braided her coal black hair in two long braids. She was a startlingly beautiful child with deep-set bright blue eyes.

"Bye Ma," Mattie said excitedly as Annie kissed her cheek.

She clutched her new tablet and pencil in one hand and her lunch pail in the other. She ran out to the barn where her father lifted her up in the saddle, then put his foot in the stirrup and swung up behind her.

"Pa, are you coming after me when school is over?"

"No, I'll be in the field gathering corn but you know the way home, you've walked it plenty of times. It's not very far.

Wade clicked his cheek and nudged the horse with his heels. The horse's strong legs quickly lengthened into a gallop. Mattie felt the cool morning breeze in her face.

"Pa, when will I get my own pony."

"Maybe next summer?"

"Can I have my own saddle?"

"Uh huh."

"Will I know how to read and write when I come home tonight?" she questioned as she tilted her head and looked up in his face.

Wade chuckled, "No Mattie, It will be several weeks before you learn to read or write." He kissed the top of her head.

"Can I show Pearl and Louella how to draw the letters?"

"Uh huh."

"Naomi too?"

"Uh huh." He was so used to hearing the constant questions he just habitually made "Uh huh" his trite answer.

"Then can I read the Bible to you?"

"Uh huh."

Wade was not listening to her chatter. He was staring across the barren cotton patch thinking of the many bales of cotton he had lost due to the gale. He could see only tiny little bits of cotton hanging from bolls scattered over the field. The unsalvageable cotton that had fallen on the ground peeked tauntingly from beneath sand and rocks where the rain had pelted it. The hard work he had put into raising the cotton was to little avail. His plan to buy an additional fifty acres would have to wait, as would other things he had planned to buy. He did manage to buy new shoes for his and Joshua's children and save enough for fertilizer and seed for the next year. Hopefully he would not have to spend that money on some unexpected illness.

"Next year, maybe we'll have a little better luck," he spoke under his breath.

"Huh, Pa, can I?"

"Can you what?"

"Can I read the Bible?"

"Of course, if you're careful turning the pages. That's why you learn to read, so you can read the Bible," He smiled at her upturned face.

"Pa, can Santa Clause bring me a story book for Christmas?"

"Uh huh."

Thy word is a lamp to my feet and a light to my path.

(The Bible)

16

"Do you know what I heered my pappy tell my mammy when he come in from my grandpappy's house last night?" Naomi's eyelids were glared so wide the whites encircled the entire ebony corneae. She sat back on her heels and glanced toward the door to be sure no one could hear.

The two of them sat on the floor in front of the fireplace writing the alphabet.

Mattie sat up to face her. "What? Was it somethin' bad?"

Naomi glanced toward the door again to be sure Annie could not hear her from the kitchen. She lowered her voice and leaned over to Mattie. "What's a panther?"

"I don't know. I think it's an animal that lives in the forest in Alabama or some other far off country. Now tell me what your Pa tole you," she said impatiently.

"He didn't tell me. I heered him tellin' Mammy. I laid real still so's they'd thank I's sleepin'. I heered him say, he says, 'I ain't wantin' the chilluns to hear 'cause they'd be skeered.' That be's 'sactly what he says."

"Skeered 'a what?" Mattie leaned closer to Naomi. By now her eyes were also big with wonder. "Is it 'posed to be a secret?"

"I thank it is. I sho do. You gotta' promise not to tell."

Mattie crossed her heart with her forefinger. "I promise."

Naomi continued, "He said to Mammy, he says, 'You need to watch the kids when they's playin' outside for the next few days, I thank there's a panther on the loose.' Then my mammy says, 'A PANTHER!' real loud like it was a big surprise. Then my Pappy said, 'Sh-h-h, don't wake the younguns'. I laid real still like, so they wouldn't know I wuz listening."

Mattie pushed back the books and papers that were between them and inched closer to Naomi. "What else did he say?" Her glaring blue eyes stared intently into Naomi's.

"He was sorta whisperin', you know, kinda loud like, not 'sactly a whisper, but I could still hear him. He says, 'Yo pappy wuz down in the Pearl River swamp huntin' yestiddy when he heered sumpin'. Said it sounded like it was a fur piece off at first then it started gettin' closter and closter. It sounded like a woman screamin', then like the roarin' of a lion'. He said it was plum eerie.' Whatever eerie is."

"What was it?" Mattie's face was within inches of Naomi's.

"It was a panther, come all the way from Alabama."

"All the way acrost the ocean?"

"Yep. They can swim, you know." Naomi knew she had Mattie's attention. She delighted in telling Mattie some thrilling tale or folklore she heard from her many relatives. Now she was thrilled to embellish the story somewhat, even though she, too, was plenty frightened.

"Did he shoot 'im?" Mattie asked hopefully.

"Naw, he run! He run as fast as he could back to where his hoss wuz tied. He jumped on that ole gray hoss and rode as fast as he could back to his house. Then I heered pappy say, he says, 'Yo pappy could still hear that big, black cat with sharp teeth and long claws screamin' back in them woods. It sounded jist like a woman screamin', gettin' closter and closter'."

Naomi shivered as she looked toward the frosty window.

Mattie jumped from her sitting position and ran in the kitchen, Naomi close behind her. They hovered behind the kitchen stove under the protective eyes of Annie who was busy cooking supper.

"I think I hear Louisa calling you." Annie told Naomi.

"Can Mattie walk me half way?"

"No, I don't want to," Mattie objected quickly.

"Of course she can. Ya'll put on your coat."

"Ma, I don't want to," Mattie whined.

"Don't be silly. You always walk her home. Go get your coats."

"Our coats are in the front room by the fireplace," Mattie whispered to Naomi.

"You go git 'em." Naomi nudged Mattie.

"No, you do it."

"You girls go get your coats and stop arguing," Annie scolded them. The girls clung to each other.

The kitchen door rattled with a loud bang. Mattie and Naomi screamed and hid their faces in their knees, which were pulled up to their chins.

Annie laughed. "What's the matter with you two?"

"I come to git Naomi," Joshua called from outside the door. Naomi and Mattie looked at each other, relieved that it was not the panther.

"Come on in Josh. She's right here. She was about to get her coat when you knocked."

Naomi tugged Mattie toward the front room to get her coat. Mattie reluctantly went with her.

Mattie was too afraid to go to bed and sat wrapped in a quilt in a chair beside the fireplace until she fell asleep. She never knew when her father picked her up and carried her to bed. In the morning she awoke when her father lifted her from her bed and carried her to the other room to dress beside the fire.

"Time for school, Princess." He whispered as he stood her in front of the fire.

"I don't want to go to school today," she whined. She shuddered when she thought of walking down the road through the heavily wooded area.

"I'll take you today. It's too cold for you to walk. Go on and get dressed." He patted her on the head and left the room.

******

Mrs. Hampton tapped on her desk with the tip of her paddle and waited for the children to stop talking. Using her motherly voice, she instructed the children. "It's three o'clock and time to go home. It's cold outside so put on your mittens, caps and scarves. Remember to button you coats."

Ida and her brother Amos were George and Delvine Posey's children, Mattie's double first cousins. Her father, George was Wade's brother and her mother, Delvine was Annie's sister. Ida and Amos were only eleven months apart so they started first grade at the same time.

Mattie and Ida did as Mrs. Hampton instructed and raced for the door, yelling, "Bye, Mrs. Hampton, see you tomorrow." The wind hit their little faces and they pulled their hand knitted toboggans down to their eyes and down on the back of their necks. They covered their nose with a mittened hand. Their lunch buckets hung from their arms by the bail and the other hand clutched their tablet. They ran down the trail, which snaked across the pasture. The overcast sky hid the sun.

Mattie dreaded to cross the wooded area because of the panther story. "Ida will you'n Amos walk part of the way with me."

"Naw, Ma told us to not be dallyin' around after school."

"She won't know. Amos, will you?"

"You better not, I'll tell on you." Ida said as she ran up the road that turned to go home. Amos followed.

Mattie watched them for a few moments then began to run. She ran as fast as her little legs could go.

There was not another house between the fork in the road and Mattie's house. Towering pines on each side of the road blocked the sunlight. It was a welcome shade in the summer but in the winter it shaded the road making that stretch of the road the last to dry out after a rain and the last to thaw when there was ice. Today ice spewed up from the ground in the wet ditches along the side of the road.

Mattie ran down the middle of the road. She unbuttoned her coat so she could run faster. Her heart pounded and her eyes darted from one side of the road to the other, peering through the dense underbrush in search of "the panther." The cold air coursed through her nostrils down her throat and into her lungs.

From behind her, Mattie heard the fast moving hoof beats of a horse. She glanced over her shoulder and moved from the center of the road. She only hoped the horse had a rider and was not running wild.

The horse slowed to a trot, then to a walk. "Whoa, Whoa." The rider pulled back on the reigns and the horse stopped beside Mattie.

"Wanta ride the rest a the way?" He reached for her uplifted hands and hoisted her to the back of the horse.

The horse had no saddle on it, just a blanket over his back and a bridle over his head. There was a rope tied to each side of the bit in the horse's mouth. Mattie grasped the horse's mane tightly.

******

Annie took the lid off the pot of beans hanging from the rod over the fire in the fireplace and stirred them. The potatoes buried in the ashes were soft to her touch. She walked to the window facing the road and stared down the road and through the bare limbs of the oak trees. Her eyes searched every open space for the sign of the red cap she had knitted for Mattie. She saw nothing but the limbs of the pine trees swaying in the cold wind. *I need to go meet Mattie,* she thought, then glanced at Pearl snuggled under a quilt on the bed. The two smaller children could not be left in the room with an open fire. If Pearl were well she could dress them warmly and take them with her. Pearl 's head still felt hot with fever.

A sense of impending doom engulfed Annie since Wade told her about the panther. A terrible foreboding swept over her as she wondered where Wade had gone in such a hurry. She tried to dismiss it since a tragedy seldom happened when this darkness descended on her. But, then, sometimes something bad did happen, she reminded herself. Most of the time the sense of impending doom lasted only a few days but then there were weeks of extreme exhaustion when she could barely get out of bed in the mornings. She could not sleep at night and paced the floor going to the children's beds to check on them. When she eventually slept, she could hardly get awake. Now she sighed deeply as she resignedly accepted the fact that deep sorrow was again descending on her.

Wade had been working in the barn right after lunch when he came to the back door and yelled that he would be back in a little while, not bothering to say where he was going. That was not unusual, but Annie knew how he lost track of time when he got together with some of the men.

Talk of the roving panther struck fear in the farmers. From time to time a panther or some other wild animal wandered from the dense swamp of the Pearl River to prey on the cattle. Stories spread of how little children had been attacked, some carried off to never be seen again. This time, there had not been a sighting of the feared animal but it was rumored that its distinctive cry was definitely heard near the edge of the swamp. If the presence of this rogue animal was confirmed, the men would form a posse and sweep through the swamp until he was found and killed.

"It's probably just a rumor. You know how skittish some of these ignorant people are around here," Wade had told Annie, trying to reassure her. Nevertheless, he had agreed to take Mattie to school in the mornings and go get her in the afternoons until the rumor was either confirmed or lost its intensity.

Annie felt helpless as fear for Mattie's safety engulfed her. She put a shawl around her shoulders and walked out on the front porch.

"Oh Lord, please protect Mattie."

She listened. She could hear nothing but the wind whistling around the corner of the house as it whipped her skirt around her knees.

Blessed is the man who makes the LORD his trust. (The Bible)

17

Mattie wriggled her way into a comfortable position on the horse blanket. The horse was warm and felt good to her cold legs. He unbuttoned his big overcoat and pulled her close to him, then wrapped the coat in front of her and buttoned it.

"Hold on tight," he warned as he snapped the reins and nudged the horse in the ribs with his heels.

The horse started to run. Mattie could not feel the cold wind against her face since it was buried deep inside his coat.

"Why are we going so fast, Pa?" Mattie yelled loudly, tilting her head up so he could hear her. She felt the stiff bristles of his chin whiskers as he bent his head closer. "Pa, why are we going so fast? Where you been?"

"I've been to the store."

"Did Mr. Myers have any candy in the store?"

"Uh huh."

"Did you get us some?"

"Uh huh."

Mattie yelled again, "Pa what's a panther?"

"Why do you ask?"

Mattie gave him a furtive glance. "I just wondered, that's all."

"A panther is a big, black cat. Did someone tell you something about a panther?" Wade had hoped to spare his children from the rumor. No need for them to live in fear.

Mattie was silent, careful to keep her promise to Naomi.

"You don't have to be afraid of a panther. Your Papa is going to take care of you."

"I was scared back there in the woods."

"No need for you to be scared."

Wade slowed the horse to a walk. He had been afraid as well. Not for himself, but for Mattie. When he had suddenly realized it was past time for school to be over, he left the group of men sitting around the stove in the store and raced to catch her.

The gossip about the panther was growing and becoming more believable with each telling. The men at the store said they were not taking any chances. They were going to corral all the cattle they could in the barnyard and put the calves in the stalls. Wade was not one to believe all the tales he heard but he could not take a chance on this one. He had lost most of his cotton crop and he could not afford to lose some of his cattle to a panther.

******

The next morning was bitter cold. The wind had died down somewhat and a slow drizzle of rain during the night had left icicles hanging from the eaves of the house. The rain stopped and the sun dared to send pink and orange striations across the cold blue sky.

Wade was up by sun-up sharpening knives and gathering barrels and buckets around a large pot of water in the back yard. He built a big fire under the pot to get the water to the boiling point. The weather was just right to butcher the two hogs he had castrated and isolated in a pen. He had fed them corn for two weeks in an attempt to get them fat so there would be plenty of lard to use for cooking.

George arrived with another iron pot in his wagon. "Good morning, Annie. Delvine will be over to help you as soon as she gets the kids off to school."

"You not gonna' let them walk to school are you? You know with the panther scare…"

"Shoot no!" he interrupted. "Delvine's gonna' take 'em in the buggy. What about Mattie Parilee?"

"I think I'll just keep her home. We don't have time to take her and besides, I need her to watch Louella and Pearl."

The sun was shining, but not bright enough to melt the icicles hanging from the eaves of the house or the thick ice in the watering troughs. The weather was cold enough that the meat would not spoil while it was being butchered on the long tables improvised for that purpose.

Several of the neighbors gathered to help with the arduous task of lifting the three hundred pound animals. Homer Young and Jasper Crenshaw came to help Joshua, George, Wade and Leonard.

Wade went inside for his revolver. The men followed him to the hog pen where a horse waited to drag the two animals to the back yard.

Wade straddled the fence, walked up to one of the unsuspecting animals and put the revolver between his eyes. BAM! The animal fell on his side but his protruding belly kept him from remaining in that position. He rolled to his back. His feet jerked in convulsive spasms. Blood ran from the center of his head, into his eyes, down his nose and into his gasping mouth.

BAM! One more shot to put him out of his misery. Then two more shots. BAM! BAM! The second hog now lay quivering in the frozen mud of the hog pen. The men descended on the animals wielding long, sharp knives, which they used to slice through the carotid arteries. Blood spurted from the arteries to the ground and on the boots of the men standing in its trajectory. Long streams of blood flowed over the stinking, icy manure-filled mud, and under the fence to eventually mingle in the soil with the numerous other previously slaughtered animals. The smell of the fresh, warm blood wafted across the pasture into the dense trees to the north.

Wade dug a slanted hole in the yard near the boiling pots of water and slid an empty barrel into it. He placed it at an angle so the dead animal could be slid down into the boiling water, which had been dipped from the pots. The men grasped the front legs of the hog and turned him so the hot water could scald the hair off the other side. They pulled him from the barrel then took their sharp knives and scraped off his hair. The animal lay in the cold wind - a huge, white, hairless mass of flesh; Food for the Posey family for the rest of the winter.

Homer and Jasper put hooks in the ligaments of the back feet then attached them to a rope, which threaded through a winch on a large tree limb. Joshua turned the winch until the hog hung head down, his nose touching the ground. Wade ran his finger along the tip of his knife then he carefully slit the hog's abdomen from his crotch to his diaphragm. Entrails tumbled into a washtub. Wade tied a string around the bottom of the esophagus then cut it just above the string. He cut out the heart, liver, spleen, kidneys and lungs then put them in a bucket to be washed and cooked for lunch. Jasper and Homer carried the tub full of fat covered guts to the table.

Louisa, Annie and Delvine carefully ran the course of the entrails. They sliced fat from them and put it in a bucket to make into lard. When the tips of their knives pierced one of the dung filled entrails Annie simply tied that portion off with a string and rinsed away the foul smelling excrement. After Annie removed the fat, she cut the end of the entrails then squeezed the contents into a bucket. She held the end up while Delvine flooded the flexible pipe-like vessels with water. When all the waste was washed from the entrails the three women cut them into sections and washed them repeatedly. Louisa took them to the kitchen to cook them.

"Let's carry this tub of hog dung to the edge of the woods to empty it. We don't need the smell so close to the house," Annie told her sister, Delvine.

They lifted the tub and carried it down the long path leading to the clump of trees near the barn. The stillness of the ice-covered trees cast a pall over the dense shadows of the underbrush. Annie felt eyes watching her, waiting for her to come closer. She stopped abruptly. "I think we'll just dump it here." Her eyes searched the branches of the trees and the brush.

"I think this is far enough," Delvine replied. "It will be devoured by some wild animal before it starts to stink."

Annie shivered. The two of them retreated hastily up the path toward the house.

******

85

The sun cast long shadows across the barnyard as Wade finished his chores. The temperature plummeted as the sun withdrew its warmth from the frigid air surrounding the Posey farm. He could feel an ache in every muscle of his body from the strenuous work of the day. The hogs had been heavy, the butchering of the meat long and tedious. The smell of the fresh meat hung heavy in the cold air. Some of the meat had been ground into sausage, made into patties and cooked in a large pot in the yard. Annie, Delvine and Louisa put the patties into jars to preserve them. Hams and bacon slabs were hung in the smokehouse. A bed of slow-burning hickory limbs were placed on the dirt floor to season and preserve the meat.

Wade looked back at the barn where he had put the cows and horses in stables, then latched the doors securely to protect them from the panther, if indeed, there was a panther. The sun was behind the trees now. Darkness quickly invaded his surroundings and concealed the path to the house. A shiver ran through him in spite of the layers of clothes. He pulled his coat collar up to meet the rim of the back of his hat, which was pulled down on his head as far as possible. He set his pail of milk on the ground then closed the gate behind him and fastened it securely.

From the unpenetrating darkness in the trees behind the barn, Wade heard a low growl emitting from the bowels of a large animal. Fear petrified him. For a long moment he could not move. *The panther*, he thought. *He smells the fresh meat. Walk slowly, don't run! I can't out run him. Can't let him know I'm scared. Leave the milk.*

Wade walked backward, slowly down the invisible path toward the lights in the kitchen window. His eyes searched the darkness but saw nothing. The sweet fragrance of the smoking hickory wood floated from the smokehouse. *Where are the dogs? They're my only protection...can't whistle loudly...will startle the panther.* He took a few more steps and glanced over his shoulder. He clicked his tongue against his cheek hoping the dogs would hear. Then he whistled very low. The dogs raced toward him, wagging their tails. He turned to face the house and began to walk faster. As the dogs got nearer to him, their ears perked up into points, their tails stiffened, then they raised their hackles. They looked toward the barn and growled. A sharp shrieking sound came from the barn. The four barking dogs bounded toward it then stopped abruptly when they saw their adversary. Wade ran to the house and burst through the back door. Annie stood peering through the window. The girls clung to her skirt. They had heard the unmistakable scream of the panther.

"It's the panther ain't it, Wade?"

Wade had no time to answer. He sprinted across the hall to the bedroom and loaded his shotgun.

"Annie put out the light!" He opened the kitchen door and peered into the darkness.

"Don't go out there! Are you crazy?!" Annie yelled in a loud whisper. She lowered the wick on the lamp then blew into the chimney. Darkness enveloped the room. The girls began to cry. Wade closed the door and went to the window.

The dogs huddled under the kitchen floor, their fierce barking mixed with the angry screams of the panther as he approached the house. The dogs bravely and protectively ventured to the edge of the house then, as one, they attacked the huge cat.

Wade positioned his gun in the open window and waited for a clear shot. The dogs retreated to their sanctuary under the house. The angry panther bound after them. Deafening sounds of the cat's screams and dogs' snarls came through the cracks in the kitchen floor. The floor shook as the animals' angry, fighting bodies bumped against it. The four large, frightened, hunting dogs attacked the huge ebony animal from all sides, snarling, biting. The cat fought back, his long sharp claws and deadly fangs tore through the tough, hairy skin of the dogs. His deafening screams and snarls mingled with the dogs' barks and growls.

Wade's eyes adjusted to the darkness in the yard. He waited. "He has to come out eventually. When he does he's mine!"

Annie put the girls in chairs against the wall. "Do not move!" Mattie protectively pulled her sisters to her.

The bumping against the floor stopped. "The dogs got 'im cornered against this back wall!" Annie yelled, her words barely audible over the sounds of five angry animals.

"The dogs have backed off. They got 'im surrounded," Wade yelled.

Annie reached for the heavy kettle of boiling water on the stove then eased to the spot just above the panther. She could hear his hideous snarls and screams only inches beneath her feet. She held the spout of the kettle against the cracks in the floor and emptied the boiling water on the back of the raging cat.

Howls of pain emitted from the throat of the panther. He leaped through the barrier of dogs into the yard. Wade was startled by the suddenness of his emergence. The blast from his gun missed its screaming, speeding target.

A sharp flash of light, accompanied by the unmistakable sound of a shotgun, pierced the night. It was followed by a second one from behind the well.

"I got 'im! I shore got 'im!" Joshua yelled toward the open window. Wade lowered his gun and ran out the back door. He could see Joshua crouching, slowly advancing toward the moaning, writhing, menacing creature, as he wallowed in his own blood. Four feet extended outward from the convulsing body. Another flash of light and a deafening blast.

"One more for good measure!" Joshua yelled victoriously.

"Where'd you come from?" Wade asked as he approached Joshua, who now stood over the dying animal.

"I heered all the confound commotion, so's I come to ye rescue." He turned and grinned at Wade.

Wade ran his trembling fingers through his hair and then gripped Joshua's arm in an attempt to steady his weak knees. "Thanks, buddy."

18

Annie lay in bed with her feet propped high on pillows. Her face was white - her hands and feet cold. There was a pan of water on a table beside the bed with a cloth in it.

Pearl and Louella played on a quilt in front of the fireplace. Mattie ran up the steps and across the porch, then into the bedroom. She pushed the door open to the front room letting in a blast of cold air, then noticed Annie in the bed.

"You sick, Ma?"

"A little bit. Give me a hug." She extended her hand weakly to Mattie.

Mattie tiptoed to reach Annie's face. She put her arms around her and put her cheek against Annie's burning cheek. Annie brushed Mattie's hair back with her icy cold hands.

Mattie's brow furrowed with concern. "What's the matter?"

"I'm just a little bit sick, honey. Go in the kitchen and get you a teacake. Pa will pour you some milk when he gets inside."

Wade took an arm full of firewood and kindling to the bedroom across the hall and made a fire in the fireplace. He came back in the front room to check on Annie and the girls. "Are you any better.

"No I ain't. Is Delvine coming?"

"She'll be here directly. Do you think I need to ride over and get Dr. Powell?"

"It's a long way to Burnside and back and it would take too long for him to get here. Wait and see what Delvine thinks."

"I put a fire in the room across the hall so the girls can go over there and play. They don't need to be in here with all this going on."

"When Delvine gets here, go see if Lou can come up and watch the girls."

Wade opened the door to the cold hallway then closed it firmly.

Wade heard Delvine's horse and buggy and went out to meet her. He took the bundle of supplies she handed him then helped her from the buggy. Wade took the horse by the bridle and led him to the barn. He tied the horse under the lean-to leaving it hitched to the buggy and went back inside.

Delvine sat on the side of Annie's bed talking in a whisper so the girls could not hear. Wade went to get Louisa.

Louisa stood beside the bed and laid a cool hand on Annie's forehead. "You sho' bad sick ain't'cha Miz Annie?"

Annie nodded.

"Is they anything I could do fer ye?"

"The kids...take..." Her voice trailed off.

"You don't worry none 'bout them chil'uns. You hear me? I's gonna take care of 'em."

"I know."

"I'll git in the kitchen and cook up a big batch 'a soup fer ever'body, then bathe the chil'uns and put 'em in da bed. Josh is doing all Mistuh Wade's chores."

Delvine tugged Wade toward the hearth. "I think you need to go get Abby Parker. If we don't do something Annie's gonna lose this baby."

"If it's okay I'll take your rig."

Delvine nodded in agreement then walked to Annie's bed. "I think we need to get the mid-wife. Is that what you want?"

"Might be best."

"I can get her quicker than I can the doctor." Wade put on his coat.

"You go on Mistuh Wade. Don't you worry 'bout nothin'. Josh-a-way'll take care of yo' outside cho'es. I'll hep Miz Delvine and take care of the chillun." Louisa reassured him.

"Hurry," Annie said softly.

"He will," Delvine tried to reassure her. She took the wet cloth from Annie's head and put it in the pan of water beside the bed then squeezed it out and put it back on her head. "Abby can handle this better than I can. I've done all I know to do."

"Uh huh, she know her biz'ness awright." Louisa nodded in agreement. "She been mid-wifen a long time. She deliv'd mo' babies than Doc Powell. She say she don't claim to be no doctor but she can deliver a baby good's he can, pr'vidin there ain't no compl'cations."

"She usually takes care of the mothers long before delivery time, bossing us around, telling us what to do and what not to do." Delvine laughed.

"She have her own way 'a doin' thangs, that's fer sho'."

******

Abby Parker was a very large woman in her fifties, weighing two hundred to two-hundred-fifty pounds. Her gray hair was slicked back tightly on the top of her head in a big bun which exaggerated her pug nose which was nestled between her plump cheeks. Her brown eyes were big and expressive. If she was happy, sad, concerned, caring, stern, sympathetic, yes, and even angry, she expressed it with her eyes. There was never any doubt about what she meant when she spoke. Her long skirt hiked up in the back as her massive hips extended out further than her abdomen.

Wade let her out at the front steps of his house, then took the horse and buggy to the barn. She let herself in the front door without knocking and announced her arrival with a soft, "May I come in"?

Louisa opened the bedroom door, "In there", she said, pointing to the room across the hall.

Abby found Delvine pulling thick pads soaked with blood from underneath Annie. She shook her head and whispered to Delvine, "That don't look too good."

"Now, honey, you don't worry about a thing. I'm gonna take good care of you," Mrs. Parker cooed reassuringly as she patted Annie's hand.

Annie moaned softly.

Louisa had a fire in the kitchen stove and had plenty of hot water for cleaning up. She moved all six children to the kitchen and spread out the quilt on the floor. The older ones were instructed to care for the smaller ones.

Mattie eased up beside Louisa and tilted her head back to look up at her. "Lou, is Ma gonna die?"

Louisa dropped to her knees in front of Mattie. She pulled her close to her heavy breasts and hugged her tightly with her massive arms. Mattie clung tenaciously to her. "Now you don't go talkin' like that, honey chile. That ain't no way ta think. You gotta think 'bout your Ma gettin' well."

Mattie pulled away from Louisa's tight hug. "You know what you tole me one time when I was little? Do you member sactly what you said?" She clutched her rag doll to her as she looked trustingly in Louisa's black eyes.

"Now which time was that? I don't 'sactly recall. Can you gi' me a hint?"

"You member one time when you found me in the pantry asleep and you promised to always be around to help me if I need you."

"I sho do remember that time, swee' pea." She again pulled Mattie to her. "How can I ever forget that?"

Thoughts of that day flooded Louisa's memory. *I can still see Annie sauntering acrost the pasture with Louella in her arms and Pearl trailin' 'long behind. When I axed her where Mattie wuz she didn't answer. She wuz jist in a trance-like, that she wuz. I decided I'd better go up to the house to see if'n I could find Mattie. She wuz jist a little bitty tyke.*

"'Twas like it was yestiddy." She glanced down at Mattie clutching her dirty little rag doll then kneeled down and pulled her snuggly against her bosom.

I couldn't fin' her nowhere then I heerd sobs comin' from that locked pantry. I unlatched that do' and picked her up and carried her out to the po'ch. Her little legs wuz bleedin' from the stripes uv that ole leather strap. I jist carried her home wid me. Didn't make no diffe'nce wid me where her Ma liked it or not.

"Tell me that again, Lou, say it again," Mattie pleaded as she patted Louisa's cheek to get her attention.

Louisa got up from her knees. "Come over here and set on my lap, les jist talk this over. Now tell me which part you wants me to tell you ag'in." She lifted Mattie up to her lap.

"About the part that you love me, just like you was my own Ma and you'd never tell me a lie."

"Now I remember. Like I said then, I love you jist like you wuz my own young'un. I'll always be here to take care uv you. You can tell me anything you want to and I'll never tell a living soul."

"Now tell me the part about Ma being sick."

"Sometimes yo Ma gets real sick in her mind and she don't act 'sactly the same to'ard you as she do when she all well 'n ever'thang. So if'n she ever gets real sick and acts kinda strange like, you jist come runnin' down that trail acrost the pasture to Lou. I'll take good care uv ye."

"If Ma dies can I come live with you?"

"Now, you listen to me! We ain't gonna talk about yo Ma dyin'."

"You promised me! You promised." Tears flooded down Mattie's cheeks. Louisa took her thumb and wiped her wet cheeks.

"Okay, okay. I promise you if'n yo Ma dies you can come live with me if'n yo Pa'll let ye. But she ain't gonna die!"

Louisa knew the instant she said it, she should not have. *Annie's mighty low. Mi-i-ighty low.*

Louisa took her apron and dried Mattie's face then tilted her chin so she could look directly into her eyes. "You look at me square in the eyes, little girl." Mattie's unblinking eyes stared into Louisa's. "I ain't God so I can't tell you if'n yo Ma's gonna die or not. I shouldn'ta oughter said she ain't gonna die, cause I don't know. One thang I do know, Almighty God up in hebin is gonna do the right thing." Louisa rolled her eyes up and looked at the ceiling as she pointed her finger straight up. "Now you an' me, we can't do but one thing about it 'cept pray. I promise you again, I'll be here to hep you no matter what God decides. Now you jist go back to your playthings and say a prayer for yo Ma."

Mattie obediently got off Louisa's lap and joined the other kids on the quilt. Louisa smiled when she heard Mattie tell the other children to bow their heads and pray.

Louisa proceeded to cook supper. She made cornbread and opened a jar of tomatoes, for a pot of soup. Her knife cut too deeply into the potatoes and onions as she peeled them, taking big chunks out that should have gone in the soup. Maybe it was because she had her eyes closed most of time, praying for Annie. Her eyes burned and tears escaped her eyelids. She was glad she could blame it on the onions. She put the knife on the table, walked into the dark pantry and closed the door. Relief from holding back the tears came as she leaned against the door and buried her face in her crumpled apron.

Darkness seemed to envelop the kitchen in such a short time. When Louisa opened the door of the pantry she could see flickers of the flames in the firebox of the stove - Flames that went unnoticed in daylight. The children still sat on the quilt talking baby talk to their dolls. The darkness had crept in the room so gradually they were not aware of it. Louisa opened the firebox of the stove and shoved in two more sticks of wood then pulled a straw out of the sagebrush broom standing in the corner. The flames from the stove ignited the straw immediately. She went to the table, took the globe off the oil lamp and stuck the burning straw to the wick. The darkness of the room was gone, except for the long shadows that were cast when Louisa walked by the lamp.

Wade sat in a chair in front of the fire across the hall from the front room. His elbows were on his knees and his chin in his hands. His eyes sparkled with the water that filled them. Occasionally a drop trickled down his cheek. He wiped his cheeks oon his shirt sleeve.

Joshua finished Wade's chores, then did his own. He came back to the house and sat beside Wade. Neither said a word. He reached over occasionally and patted Wade on the back, the shoulder or the knee. He poked at the fire then added more wood. Words were not needed as the two kept their vigil. Together they had endured bad times. No need to speak of "what ifs" or "just in case". No need to speak vain words of encouragement - they just might come out wrong when they went from the brain to the tip of the tongue. There were no words that could express the same meaning as a strong hand on the shoulder, a pat on the back or a grip on the knee. When a man throws corn to a neighbor's cow in times of his troubles or pours slop to his hogs or puts his hands around the teats of his neighbor's cow to pull nourishment for his children, there's just not a lot else to be said.

"Wade, can you eat a bowl of hot soup with some cornbread and milk?" Louisa asked as she walked softly into the room.

"Don't believe I'm quite up to it right now. Thank ye' though. Josh, you go get you something."

The fire from the fireplace brightened the room except for the little bits of darkness still hiding in the corners and under the edge of the beds.

"Do you want me to light the lamp? Might cheer you up a bit?"

"The fire gives off enough light," Wade said without looking toward her.

After supper Louisa took a pan of warm water and washed all the children then put them in the bed. Three in one bed. Three in the other.

"No talking. They wants peace and quite," she whispered and nodded toward Wade and Joshua who were still sitting silently beside the fire.

Joshua and Wade kept their vigil in front of the fire while the ladies puttered around their patient in the room across the hall. The ladies kept Wade apprised of Annie's condition. He wanted to be by her side but it was not proper for a man to be in the birthing room. Louisa went in to help Mrs. Parker and Delvine. She took bloody pads to the back yard, put them in a washtub and drew buckets of water and poured it over them.

Mrs. Parker opened the door to the room where Wade and Joshua were sitting and tiptoed to the hearth. Joshua immediately got up from his chair and offered it to her. She pulled it closer to Wade so he could hear her.

He took his handkerchief and wiped his eyes and nose. "How is she?" he asked anxiously.

"She lost the baby," Abby said sadly.

"I figured as much."

"It was just a tiny thing, couldn't even tell what it was. Probably weighed about a pound. Something was wrong with it from the beginning, else it would've weighed more, considerin' she was almost four months. I'll take it home with me and dispose of it so you won't have to worry with it. Annie lost a lot of blood and I packed her with clean rags. If the bleeding stops she might do fine. If it don't..." She shook her head slowly. "You can go in now."

The rest of the night Wade sat beside Annie's bed, stroked her hand and talked softly to her. She could barely speak above a whisper. Mrs. Parker had not told her the seriousness of her condition, but she knew.

"I lost the baby," her almost inaudible voice said to Wade more than once during the night.

The three women sat by the fire at the foot of the bed and talked in whispers.

Louisa held the firepoker most of the night occasionally poking the fire and watching the sparks fly up the chimney. When the fire burned down she went to the porch and brought in more wood and put on the hot coals.

The clock struck two. Wade folded his arms on the bed, laid his head on them and slept.

Mrs. Parker got up from her chair every few minutes, went to the bed, raised the covers and felt to see if there was any blood.

By four O'clock Mrs. Parker's chair had stopped rocking and her chin rested on her chest. Her eyes were closed and she made a soft snoring sound. Delvine was much too anxious to sleep so she sat and rocked back and forth. Louisa sat by the fire and gazed into it. Her eyes would close for long periods of time so Delvine never knew whether she was sleeping or awake. Occasionally Delvine would hear her say, "Uh, uh, uh, Lawd hep."

Delvine closed her eyes momentarily. She was soon asleep.

The rooster jumped up to the barnyard fence and announced the approaching sunrise, moments before the sun tipped the tops of the trees. The sky turned a brilliant pink. There were only soft white clouds in the sky and the wind was still. Wade awakened with a start. Realizing where he was and the situation, he stood up, leaned over Annie and put his ear to her nose to see if she was breathing.

All the ladies stirred at the same time. Louisa awoke and began poking the fire. Mrs. Parker put her hands on the arms of the rocking chair, pushed up and hurriedly made her way to the bed. Delvine anxiously followed.

Mattie's eyes opened slowly and saw that it was daylight. Remembering that it was a school day, she threw back the covers and her stocking feet touched the cold wood floor. She felt the cold air coming between the cracks of the floor and colder air when she opened the door to the hall. She anticipated the warmth of her mother's room as she put her hand on the knob of the door. When she opened the door, she saw four people leaning over Annie's bed shaking her and frantically calling her name.

"Annie, wake up! Annie, Annie!"

"Annie can you hear me?"

Mrs. Parker slapped Annie on the cheeks, one side, then the other. "Git me a wet rag," she ordered authoritatively to no one in particular. Delvine rushed around the bed to the pan of water on the table. She quickly squeezed out the cloth then handed it to Mrs. Parker. A stream of water made a trail across the floor and on the bed. Mrs. Parker washed Annie's face and neck while she continued to slap her cheeks and call her name.

Mattie heard the panic in all the voices and sensed the possibility of impending tragedy. "Pa, how's Ma?" She tugged at the tail of his shirt, "Pa, Pa, what's wrong? Is Ma dead?" When he did not answer, she pushed past him, sprang up on the bed and shook Annie. "Ma! Ma!"

Annie opened her eyes slowly at the sound of Mattie's voice. Parilee?" Her voice was hoarse and soft. Sighs of relief were audible.

"Thank you God." Issued from each one hovering over the bed.

Mrs. Parker raised the covers to see if there was any blood. Delvine peered over her shoulder. Louisa stood at the foot of the bed massaging Annie's feet.

Parilee." Annie whispered. Mattie snuggled down on her shoulder then pressed her cheek against Annie's.

She raised her head to peer into Annie's face. "You feelin' better Ma?"

"Uh-huh. Go to school."

Okay, Ma." Mattie slid off the bed and ran to the fireplace. "Pa, what am I gonna wear today?"

"I'll get your clothes he said," then turned to go to the other room, leaving Abby and Delvine to take care of Annie.

Louisa started for the kitchen. "You can come in the kitchen to dress while I cook breakfast,"

"Bring my clothes in the kitchen, Pa," she yelled to him as she ran down the cold hall to the kitchen.

Annie's recuperation was slow. Mrs. Parker removed the packing the third day and just as she had hoped, it had put pressure on the bleeding points giving the blood time to clot and stop the bleeding.

There had been so much blood loss that it took a long time for Annie to gain strength. Every neighbor in the community brought food to the family and always a special food for Annie, "To build up your blood."

******

At the first sign of spring, Wade hustled around the farm and prepared for spring planting. There was so much to do and Annie still was not well enough to help.

An intense, unexplainable sadness gripped her, sapping every ounce of strength in her. In the mornings she would lie in bed as long as possible then, with great effort make her way to the kitchen to make breakfast and get Mattie off to school. She would lie across the bed most of the day not sleeping, not thinking - simply staring at the ceiling or out the window. Pearl and Louella would play in front of the fire and outside if the weather was warm. Annie had no enthusiasm about the house or the garden, which she needed to prepare for planting. She had never been lazy and felt guilty doing nothing. She did not wash clothes until she absolutely had to and had not really cleaned house since her miscarriage.

"What's the matter, are you sick, do you hurt anywhere, are you still grieving, what is it?" Delvine had prodded on a recent visit.

"I don't know what's wrong. I don't sleep at night and I can't eat."

"You're just not the same. You gotta get hold of yourself. These younguns need you to take care of them and it's time to plant the garden."

Annie knew this was true and she would - tomorrow.

"You're being too harsh with the children. You need to have more patience, after all they're still little."

Tears came to Annie's eyes. Her voice quivered. I know, but sometimes...sometimes, I get so nervous I...I...I," she stammered.

She knew Delvine was right but her thinking just was not clear. Little things were magnified and she would get agitated at the slightest provocation. It seemed she cried constantly.

Few people knew of her condition – Wade and Delvine made sure of that. They knew she would be labeled lazy, or worse crazy and lots of things in between. There was just no tolerance for them. They had no use for the lazy and ostracized the crazy, so Annie, for the most part, kept her symptoms to herself. There was certainly no medication for it. At times she seemed happy, almost giddy and was able to take care of her family and do the necessary chores. Then without warning, it was as though darkness enveloped her and took away all her energy and her motivation to do anything but sleep, sit and stare. She had no interest in anything and often stated that she had no reason to live. During these times Wade had to cook and do the family wash or get Louisa or one of Annie's sisters to help.

"You need to snap out of it," Wade told her. She wanted to and would have if she had known how.

If she voiced her opinion about her feelings of despair her mother or sisters would say, "You need to look around you and count your blessings," or "Annie don't be so lazy, it's not like you!"

Mattie was given more responsibilities and an increasing number of chores. She did them to the best of her ability and soon learned not to complain, literally fearing her mother's reaction. She was often punished severely without the slightest provocation. Pearl was expected to help her and they shared their feelings of fear. They each had their turns of being locked in the pantry and knew the fear of the darkness and the feelings of the switch to their legs or the leather strap to their backs. They had been warned not to tell Wade or the punishment would be worse.

The good times were welcomed by the whole family. When Mattie and Pearl came from school they tiptoed across the front porch and stopped to listen to see if they could hear Annie in the kitchen or humming while she did her chores. A tumult of love for her and fear of her boiled inside them.

19

Three years had passed since Annie's miscarriage. The family had learned to cope with Annie's frequent, drastic mood swings.

Mattie and Pearl came home from school and stopped to listen at the door to determine Annie's mood. They heard a baby crying and Mrs. Parker's soothing voice talking to Annie and the baby. They peeked through the window where they saw Annie in the bed and Mrs. Parker busily puttering around the room. Their father was sat on the side of the bed. It didn't take them long to realize there was another baby in the family. Annie held the baby lovingly to her breast. She was smiling and obviously happy. She looked up at her two little girls as they climbed up on the bed beside her to peer at the little bundle of pink flesh.

"Meet your new baby sister," Wade proudly announced. "Her name is Alma."

******

Springtime brought with it elation and a renewed hope. Annie's depression seemed to vanish and the warm, spring air refreshed everyone. The happiness of the new baby had somewhat diminished her episodes of depression. When she seemed to be getting sad or melancholic Wade stopped what he was doing, put Mattie in charge of the younger children, then he and Annie took a ride in the buggy.

Wade was began to get some insight into Annie's illness. It was not that he knew anything about it except from what he had learned from experience. He only knew what worked with her and what did not. His father suggested she was just feeling sorry for herself – whatever that meant. He realized that was not the case and that she wanted to feel better and didn't know how. Neither did Wade, but he soon learned that reassurance of his love, relieving her of some of her household chores and just getting her away from the daily grind helped her tremendously. There were times he felt he did not have time to leave the fields or the sawmill but knew that if he did not she would gradually descend into an unfathomable depth of despair.

Mattie and Pearl were old enough to adequately care for the younger children so they were often left in charge of them while Wade took Annie on one of their little jaunts around the countryside. The trips were invigorating to both of them. If the children begged to go with them, Wade had the foresight to forbid it, then promised to take them on a picnic or somewhere special. The picnic often would be no more than packing their regular lunch, walking down in the pasture beside the creek and spreading the lunch on a quilt. After a couple of hours they were all ready to go home but they felt they had been on an adventure. Wade encouraged Annie to go visit the neighbors. She could either take the children or she could leave them and he would watch them. With his tender care she would gradually get better after one of her episodes of depression and would be able to function in her usual manner.

As her depression lifted, Annie became increasingly concerned about Louisa's children not getting to go to school. She visited Goldie Hampton and learned that laws had been passed to start a school for the Negro children. It remained to be seen whether the white people would allow it to happen.

******

Wade was delighted to hear Annie humming as she cooked supper. "Did you have a nice visit with Mrs. Hampton?" He pulled her close and patted her.

"Wade!" Annie said as she turned quickly to look around the room. "One of the young'uns might see you."

"The young'uns are all outside." He nuzzled the back of her neck.

"Stop it!" Annie said sharply, but the brief "hug" of her head against his said, "don't stop".

"Put the spoon down," Wade suggested as he turned her toward him. She obediently dropped the spoon and responded to his affection.

"Hm-m-m, nice."

Annie returned to her task. "Silly."

Wade splashed water on his face from the pan on the washstand. "I seen George in town this mornin'. Said they're going to have a dance this Saturday. You wanna go?"

"Of course. We don't ever miss a square dance do we?"

Wade made sure the family went to everything possible, even if he was exhausted after a hard day's work. He knew Annie liked these things, and even when he was not in the mood he would feign excitement and thus create anticipation about some up-coming event. This took a lot of effort on his part but he knew this kept Annie from relapsing into one of her dark moods.

******

Mattie ran her hand over her breasts and stared critically at her figure in the mirror. "Pull it tighter," she told Pearl who stood behind her pinning a cloth binding around her breasts.

"You can't hide 'em much longer, They're blossoming out like a rose in the summer sun." Pearl giggled at her poetic metaphor, pulled the strip of cloth tightly and pinned it in the back.

"Maybe not, but I don't want nobody to see 'em 'till I'm fourteen."

"When will mine start growing?"

"When you're thirteen, I suppose, just like me."

"Has Ma noticed 'em yet."

"No! I'm scared for her to know they're starting to grow. There ain't no telling what she'll do."

"What can she do? You can't help it. It just comes natural like, doesn't it?"

102

"Yes, but I'm not ready for them to be seen."

"There, that's as tight as I can get it. Put on your blouse and see how it looks."

Mattie buttoned her blouse and examined her torso in the mirror. "I hope Leon will be at the dance tonight,"

"Is he gonna be your beau?"

"Maybe, after tonight. Cousin Amos is putting in a good word for me."

"Better not let Ma see ya'll sparkin'. She'll raise cain."

"She'll be too busy gossiping with all the women to notice. You'd better get dressed. Pa'll be hollering that it's time to go."

Pearl stripped to the waist and stared at her plump figure in the mirror. She was shorter than Mattie and somewhat heavier, but attractive in her own way. Her rosy cheeks emphasized her pug nose and blue eyes, which gave her a little girlish look. Her hair was dark brown but not black like Mattie's.

"Humph! Mine's not even beginning to show."

Mattie tilted her chin and turned to leave the room. "I suppose I am a little bit more mature than you."

Pearl threw her wadded up blouse at her as she left the room. "There, Miss High and Mighty."

It is impossible to hide the transition from childhood to womanhood.

******

Delvine's kitchen table was laden with numerous delicacies. There was a big bowl of apple cider on the table, which had to be watched closely since there was always someone with some home brew to "add to the flavor".

Several of the men brought their fiddles, banjos, mandolins and guitars. The youth danced for several rounds then the adults had their turn.

The night was hot and sticky but no one seemed to mind. Perspiration dripped from the faces of the young people gathered out under the oak tree to cool off after dancing. They heard the fiddle music emanating from the open windows and heard the caller. "Swing your partner, do-ci-do, circle left! … Circle right! … Swing your partner … La-dies back … Gents in the center … Swing your partner! … Prom-e-nade!" The stamping of feet and the shrill laughter of the ladies made a joyful sound in the night air. A full moon illuminated the yard.

Leon Sinclair had moved to Philadelphia during the summer so he was the center of attention. He was small for his age of fourteen with carrot colored hair, blue eyes and a sprinkle of freckles across his nose. He was bursting with personality. He and Amos Posey became instant friends. Leon brought firecrackers left over from the Fourth of July celebration, which he was anxious to share. The boys gathered twigs and firewood and put them in a pile to make a fire. The young people gathered around the fire and ignited the firecrackers. Four frightened cats ran from under the house to the refuge of the barn.

Amos and Leon looked at each other mischievously then chased the cats to the barn.

"Here kitty, kitty!"

"Where'd they go?" Amos asked, not expecting an answer.

"There they are in that pile of hay."

The cats trembled as they attempted to burrow into the hay. Amos and Leon reached in and pulled two of them out and carried them back to the bon fire.

"Look a here what we got! Ida's kitty cat!" Amos said as he stroked the trembling cat.

"What are you gonna do with my kittens?"

"Nothing, just have a little fun."

"How do you like firecrackers?" Leon said as he stroked the cat's head.

Leon reached in his pocket and took out a string of firecrackers. "Clarence, tie this to his tail."

Clarence grinned then tied them securely to the cat's tail. Billy Jamison stepped up to help. Zeke Henshaw looked on with interest. All the young people gathered around to participate in the fun.

"What will they do?" Ida whined.

"Who knows? I've never seen it done before."

John Thomas Posey took a flaming twig from the fire and lighted the firecrackers. Amos and Leon wasted no time putting the cats on the ground. The firecrackers began to pop and the cats ran to their favorite hide-a-way in the barn, and burrowed up in the hay.

George called to the young people from the front porch. "It's your time to dance!"

They all had started for the house when George noticed a light coming from the barn. He stared in disbelief, then the reality hit him.

"The barn's on fire!" he screamed.

The young people turned in horror. Leon whispered to Ted, "The cats!"

"The hay!"

Everyone ran from the house. One of the boys ran and opened the barn gate to let out all the animals. Chickens, pigs, cows, horses ran from the barn in a panic.

George went to the well, took a bucket and dipped it in the watering trough and ran toward the barn. Delvine went in the house to find more buckets. Wade drew water from the well and poured it in the trough. The burning barn illuminated the night sky.

"Bucket brigade! Relay!" Someone shouted.

A human chain formed and the buckets of water were passed from hand to hand and poured on the fire. It was soon evident that the fire in the dry hay could not be extinguished. The dry wood on the barn soon ignited and became an inferno. The men poured water on the grass around the barn to keep the fire from spreading to the woods. They all stood helplessly as the winter's supply of hay burned and the barn was reduced to ashes.

Big sobs emitted from Delvine's throat and George stood with his hands stuck deep into his pockets. "How in the hell did this happen?"

"It's a mighty big loss but don't worry we'll all help build it back," one of the men assured him.

"We'll all share our hay with you. Try not to worry."

The pale and silent young people huddled in a group. Leon was on the fringe, wanting to leave but didn't dare for fear it would show his guilt.

"We're in bad trouble," John Thomas whispered to his brother, Amos.

Amos saw the tears in Leon's eyes and the look of fear on his face. Leon turned to one side and wiped his face on the sleeve of his shirt.

"I never thought about the darn cats running back in the barn."

"Me neither. But we should have known they would."

"I guess we just didn't think at all. What we gonna tell your pa?"

"I guess we just haf'ta tell the truth."

The rest of the young people gathered around the boys and watched as the roof of the barn caved in.

"Ya'll gonna git the whupping of your lives," Pearl warned.

"I'm glad it's you and not me," Ida chided.

"Truth be known, it was all of us," Mattie reminded them. "We all thought it was funny and nobody tried to stop it. We were all egging it on, wanting to see what the cats would do."

"That's right, we were all part of it," Clarence added. "If one gets in trouble we all will."

John Thomas turned and stared at the huddle of men. "But what're we gonna tell Pa?"

"If nobody tells who done it, he won't know."

"It's not like we intended to do it."

It was agreed that no one would tell. They huddled closer together and shivered with fear when Leon's father started toward the group. A hush fell over them.

"Leon, did you have anything to do with this?" He spoke sternly, squinting his eyes at his son.

Leon did not answer immediately. His arms gripped his chest in a tight squeeze.

"Boy, I'm a talking to you! Did you light a firecracker in the barn?"

"No sir, he sure didn't." Amos volunteered. "None of us did."

The rest of the group spoke at once and eagerly came to Leon's defense. They denied that Leon or anyone else had gone into the barn with firecrackers.

Wade and George then walked toward the kids to confront them, determined to learn what happened. The other fathers followed.

All the young people vowed, declared, crossed their hearts and hoped to die that no one took a firecracker to the barn.

"That's right, we sure didn't. We knew better'n to take firecrackers around the hay. If anybody had done that I think we would have known it." They all talked at once.

"Well, maybe a spark flew from the bonfire to the barn," Wade speculated.

"Probably so. That's the only thing I can think of." Leon's father agreed.

The men turned their backs on the kids and stared at the inferno that was once the barn. The kids huddled together, shaking, teeth chattering in spite of the heat from the fire. None dared speak. They all wondered what happened to the cats and hoped they did not turn up later with a string dangling off the ends of their tails.

The men left the group and reported their findings to the others. Nevertheless, the kids knew on the way home they would be questioned further by their parents. They all agreed to play dumb, volunteer no information and unless they were asked specifically if someone tied firecrackers to a cat's tail, they would deny everything.

They, indeed, were questioned at length but none of the parents asked, specifically, "Did someone tie lighted firecrackers to a cat's tail?"

Ask me no questions and I'll tell you no lies.

******

The barn was essentially the focal point of any farm and the loss of it demanded immediate action. It was often the first thing to be noticed when approaching a family farm since it stood taller than the house and was in an accessible spot from all the pasture land. The barn, fences and gates were kept in good repair at all times to contain the animals, and store the hay and corn. The stables had to be kept dry for the animals, so the roof was kept in good condition. The upkeep of the barn sometimes took priority over the upkeep of the house. It was, indeed larger than the house and the centerpiece of the farm.

George Posey wasted no time in starting to rebuild the barn. It had to be finished before the fall gales began and the winter set in, as well as before the cotton was ready for harvest. His neighbors assured him they would all help. The first week after the "barn burning" George and his boys cleaned all the burned debris from the site.

The second week thirty men and boys descended on George's forest with crosscut saws, bow saws, axes, wagons, oxen, mules and horses. George went through the trees and marked the ones to be cut, then the men paired off in twos with a crosscut saw. The sound of the saws back and forth could be heard for a mile. The smell of the fresh sawn wood permeated the forest. The falling towering pines echoed through the forest as they crashed to the ground taking smaller trees with them. The virgin timber was strong, and some of it grew to be one hundred feet tall. After the tree hit the ground several men attacked it with a vengeance, taking off the limbs, leaving nothing but a very long tapered, naked tree trunk. All boys who were large enough pulled the end of a saw. The others piled the tree limbs in a heap to be burned or cut up for stove wood.

Horses and mules were harnessed to a log then pulled it to the edge of the woods to the waiting wagons. Men tugged and guided the logs on the wagons.

The men had to be strong and tough. The hot summer weather made pausing for water and a rest in the shade a frequent necessity. The densely wooded area blocked any breeze, if there was a breeze, which was rare.

The ladies of the community brought food to help Delvine serve the workers. A table was put under the trees beside the house and the food was spread on it. At noon Delvine went to the backyard and rang the dinner bell loud and long so the workers could know that it was time for lunch. The men unhitched the animals and took them back to the barn for water and a rest. The ravenous men devoured the food then lay down on the grass to rest before going back to the woods.

It was necessary for the freshly cut lumber to dry for a couple of weeks before building the barn. Then the men again descended on George' barnyard for another day of work. They built the sides of the barn on the ground then raised them and nailed them to the posts that had been secured deeply into the ground. The major part of the barn was built in two days. George and his boys could do the final touches such as stable doors, troughs and gates after the cotton was picked.

Leon, Amos and Ted worked harder than most of the other boys. They were the first to arrive and the last to leave.

"I'm mighty proud of those hard working boys." Their fathers exclaimed.

Sometimes guilt brings out the best in a man.

20

Summer 1885

The warm sun and the spring breezes prompted the equestrians to take their saddles from the shelves and polish them with beef grease and tallow. They washed their horses and ponies and brushed them until their coats glistened. The boys prided themselves on having the fastest or the strongest horse.

The girls were equally as competitive with their highly groomed horses. Sometimes they braided their tails adding a pretty ribbon. The manes were trimmed and brushed until they glistened. Each girl attempted to train her horse to be the most graceful as well as the fastest. They polished their sidesaddles to a high gloss. It was not considered lady-like to sit astride a horse and was almost an impossibility with their long, flowing skirts and numerous petticoats. Their riding boots were of the latest fashion, laced to mid-calf with heavy stockings underneath. Their cotton bloomers with lace and ruffles came down over their knees to the top of their stockings, just in case the wind should catch their petticoats and possibly show their legs.

The horses were trained and put through their paces in preparation for the August horse show. There were races for the men and boys with various riding contests and races for the women and girls as well.

On warm Saturday and Sunday afternoons the teenagers gathered to ride and show-off their steeds and riding abilities. Pearl and Mattie had their own horses, which doubled as plow horses during the week but with their weekend grooming, they were presentable as fine, gentle riding horses.

Mattie gently pulled the curry comb down Prince's side and looked at her father out of the corner of her eye. "Pa, may I ride Prince in the races at the county fair this year?"

"What makes you think he could win the race? You've never raced him before." Wade was sitting in the door of the corncrib shucking and shelling corn to carry to the gristmill.

"But he can run Pa, I mean real-l-ly run. When I take him out in the open where he has plenty of space he can go fast!"

"I guess I haven't seen him when you're riding him on the road. How do you get him to go so fast?" Wade was doubtful the horse could run as fast as Mattie thought.

"I talk to 'im," she answered as she gently brushed the recently trimmed mane. "I give him treats too."

"Talk to 'im? What do you say?" Wade asked, amused at his high-spirited, somewhat tomboyish, teenage daughter.

"I just say sweet things to him, you know, like, 'come on boy, let's go, atta boy, you're doin' good.' You know, things like that." Mattie dipped a cloth in a bucket of water and washed around the eyes of the horse.

"What kind of treats do you give him?" Wade prodded. He was surprised that she had thought of rewarding her horse.

"Sugar from the molasses can. You know, when the molasses goes to sugar around the edge of the can? I just scrape it off. See." She reached in the pocket of her skirt and pulled out a lump of molasses sugar and held it up for him to see.

Wade laughed. "Where did you learn to bribe a horse?"

"From Lou. Besides, it's not a bribe - it's a reward. She told me that people and horses are about the same. They will both be more apt to cooperate with you if you talk nice to them and reward them."

"Sounds like Lou knows what she's talking about."

"Well, can I?" She stood resolutely facing her father.

Wade turned a dried ear of corn in his hands and pulled the brown silks from between the kernels. He did not answer immediately.

"Please, I know Prince could win, I just know it."

"It takes a lot of training to get a horse ready for a race and besides Prince is a work horse. We have to plow him every day of the week. He needs to rest."

"I've already been training him. When we go riding every Sunday I train him."

"You shouldn't be running him on Sunday. He has to work hard on Monday."

Mattie felt disappointment rising inside her, yet she didn't give up easily. "It's two months 'til the race. We won't be plowing him very much in July. The crops will all be laid-by and I can train him then."

"I guess that's right." Wade said thoughtfully. "You'll need somebody to show you how to ride. You don't just get on a horse and ride in a race the same way you do when you're riding for pleasure."

"I know how to ride." She replied emphatically.

Wade rolled his eyes. "You know how to ride? Do you think you know how to ride a race horse?" He asked sarcastically.

"Yes I do! I've been watching the riders every year at the race and I've been practicing." She stood facing him with her hands on her hips. "Can I do it?"

"You're determined ain't you?"

She bobbed her head up and down vigorously and waited for him to give his permission.

"We-e-e-ll, I guess it wouldn't hurt you to enter the race. You're not gonna be too disappointed if you lose are you?"

"I'm not gonna lose! You'll see. I AM NOT going to lose."

Mattie trained Prince regularly. She would prod him into an even gallop then lie forward on his neck with her face near his ear talking softly to him and patting him. He would run faster and faster to please her. When he finished she rewarded him with a hard crystal of sugar. Mattie worked with him any time he had not been pulling a plow or a wagon. She would take him around the bend in the road where no one could see her, then straddle him, and dig her heels in his ribs to keep from falling off. They would fly, the wind in their hair. She knew she had the fastest horse of any of the girls and she was anxious to prove it.

******

The first week of August the entire community gathered at the County Fair to watch the contests and the races. Eyes searched the skies for any hint of rain. As badly as rain was needed most everyone hoped it would hold off until after the events of the day. There were prizes for all the winners and, as usual, when all the community came together there was plenty of food.

Mattie rode Prince the short distance to the racetrack. She knew what she would have to do to win. *I'll pick just the right time, then I'll do it. I know Prince is the fastest horse here. All I have to do is prove it.*

Her new homemade riding skirt was long and flowing. She had put three yards of fabric in it so it would spread down both sides of the horse. *I'll take the outside racing lane and when I get to the back side of the track I'll do it and nobody will ever know.*

Wade went with her to the beginning of the track. He held her steady in an effort to help her on the horse - as if she needed any help. "You can do it! I know you can. Just ride like you do at home when nobody's looking." He patted her knee.

"I'll do it just for you Pa. I can ride as good as any boy you may have had."

"Yes you can." Wade reassured her.

At Mattie's request Wade asked for an outside lane and Mattie had Prince ready to go. She stroked his neck, massaged his ears and talked to him in a low, soothing voice, almost a whisper. Prince smelled the molasses sugar on her hand and heard her soothing voice. He knew this meant more sugar.

When the gun sounded Molly Henshaw and her horse took the lead with Ida Posey in second place. Mattie pushed Prince as hard as she could and attempted to talk loud enough for him to hear her above all the cheering. The sidesaddle kept her from getting close to his ear. Prince was not gaining the lead. Mattie felt discouragement rising in her. She knew what she must do.

When she reached the back of the track, she slipped her left leg across the horse being careful to keep her billowing skirt over her foot. She pressed her breasts on Prince's freshly shampooed mane and whispered in his ear. "Come on boy, run. You can do it. That's a good boy." She stroked his throat with her right hand as she clung to his mane with the other. She clung to his sides with her heels pressed tightly against his ribs. "Come on Prince, baby, you can do it," she droned.

Prince stretched his legs and she felt as if he took wings. He easily passed Ida and her red mare and then Molly and her pinto. Prince ran through the finish line with more than a full body length ahead of Molly. The flag fell. The crowd cheered. Mattie tucked her left leg under her riding skirt and pulled it over the side of the saddle with the other. "Number six, Mattie Posey the winner by a full horse length!" she heard the judge yell to the crowd.

Wade ran to the track and took the reins from Mattie. "You did it baby girl, you did it! Go claim your prize."

She slipped Prince a piece of sugar then hurried toward the judges' platform to claim first prize - a silver studded horse's bridle.

"Skuse me, skuse me jist a minute! I need to have a word with the judges." The voice was deep and loud, that of a man. He pushed his way through the crowd. Mattie turned to see Ed Henshaw rush up the steps of the platform. The judges huddled close to him and they spoke in hushed voices.

"Are you sure?" Mattie heard one of the judges ask him. "'Course I am! If you don't believe me ask Bud over there. He seen it too." He pointed with his head toward Bud Smith who was peering over the heads of the crowd trying to push his way through.

The judges called Bud to come to the stand. The judges huddled around Ed and Bud.

Bud's head bobbed up and down. "I hate to say it but it's the truth," Mattie heard Bud tell the judges. Her palms started to perspire and her heart pounded from the fear of being caught in her deception.

Wade was used to Bud Smith and Ed Henshaw objecting to everything. No matter whether it was a decision in a horse race, whether to paint the church, what day to start school or anything on which the two of them did not have the final word, they objected. So when he noticed the two of them huddled with the judges he knew there was an objection to the decision of the horse race. Ordinarily Wade shrugged off their contrariness but today it involved his daughter. *Don't know what they could object to on this one. Mattie was clearly the winner.* He handed Prince's reigns to George and pushed through the crowd to defend her.

The judges called Mattie. "Mattie, these two gentleman said you were straddling the horse part of the way around the track. Is it true?"

Mattie looked at Wade who had climbed up in the judges' stand along with the other men. She looked at all the questioning eyes of the judges and the accusing eyes of Ed Henshaw and Bud Smith then she looked back at Wade.

"Did you, Mattie Parilee?" Wade asked her simply. She knew she could not lie with all these eyes looking at her. The crowd was hushed.

"Yes, Pa, but…but I won didn't I? I told you Prince could do it!"

"I'm sorry, Mattie. You know the rules of the ladies' competition. It must be side-saddle," one of the judges said sympathetically.

Mattie shrugged. "I know," she responded casually, "but I knew Prince was the fastest. I just had to prove it, rules or no rules," she said defiantly and whirled around. She walked calmly down the steps, her head held high. She waved to the hushed crowd.

She left the judges stand feeling more triumphant than defeated. She had to go give Prince some more sugar.

Victory is not always in winning first prize.

21

"Girls, get up, first day of school." Wade called as he knocked loudly on the bedroom door, then opened it wide, leaving it open.

Mattie anticipated the first day of school. *I'm fourteen now, soon be fifteen. Wonder if Leon will like me in this dress.* She turned and looked at her profile in the mirror then smoothed her blouse that was pulled tightly across her now voluptuous breasts.

Pearl giggled.

"What you snickering about?" Mattie snapped.

"You can't strap 'em down no more, can you?"

"I'm old enough now for them to show, and show 'em I will!"

"You bet you will! You can't hide them now." Pearl laughed heartily.

Mattie could not help but smile despite the fact that Pearl's comment angered her.

"You're just jealous. You wish yours blossomed like mine." Mattie shot back.

"It won't be long, you wait and see." Pearl stuck her tongue out at Mattie and left the room.

Mattie stood in the window and brushed her long black hair as the breeze played in it. I think I'll leave my hair down. I'm too old for pigtails. Leon will like that. She turned a full circle in front of the mirror.

The smell of hot biscuits, milk gravy and scrambled eggs flooded through the open door. She hurried to the kitchen and sat on the bench beside Pearl.

Annie stopped in her tracks and stared at Mattie. "My, my, you look sort of… well…sort of grown-up today."

"I'll have you know I'll soon be fifteen, remember?" She said in a rather flippant tone.

"You may be fifteen but that's not too old for me to bring you down a notch or two - remember?" Annie emphasized, "remember" as she looked at Mattie sternly. "When you get through eating put that stringy hair in braids."

"But Ma I'm too old to…"

"Eat and hush!"

"Annie, can I have a word with you in the kitchen?" Wade said as he pushed back his chair and walked toward the kitchen door. He turned and winked at Mattie.

Mattie and Pearl listened hard to hear the whispered conversation being held in the kitchen but all they could hear were a few agitated words from Annie.

"You better watch your mouth or you might spend the day in the pantry," Pearl whispered to Mattie.

"Yes, and you'd better watch yours before I stuff more biscuit in it." Anger darted from Mattie's eyes.

"Ma'll probably make you put on a loose blouse, too. You been hiding them all summer, now all of a sudden you're letting them poke out."

"Well it ain't none a your business so you'd best keep your mouth shut, flat-iron chest!" She glared at her sister.

"Ma, Pearl and Mattie's fixin' to fight!" Alma yelled.

Both Mattie and Pearl glared at her.

Wade and Annie came back to the table and sat down.

"Me and your Ma had a little talk about your hair," Wade said, addressing Mattie. "Tell her, Annie."

Annie reluctantly began, "Me and your Pa agreed, you're too old to be wearing your hair in pigtails. We also agreed that we WILL NOT stand for a smart mouth." She paused and raised one eyebrow as she glared at Mattie. "You may wear your hair down today but I suggest you take some hairpins just in case you decide to put it up. It can get awful hot hanging down on your back this time of year."

"Yes ma-am," Mattie said meekly.

Annie reached for the butter. "Pass the butter, please." She took her fork and opened a biscuit, then stuck her fork in a rounded mound of soft butter and brought a generous helping back to her biscuit. She closed the biscuit then patted it firmly on top. She held her hand firmly on the biscuit and looked at the three girls lined up on the bench against the wall. "Ya'll all look mighty pretty today."

Mattie shoved her elbow in Pearl 's side.

"Stop pokin' me!"

"Ma, I wanna go to school too." Alma whined.

"You're not quite big enough. Just you wait 'til next year, then you can go."

"Are you gonna take us to school in the buggy today, Pa?" Pearl asked as she stuffed her mouth full of jellied biscuit.

"Naw, I gotta pull corn. It won't hurt you to walk. As a matter of fact it'll do you good… and don't talk with your mouth full," he added sternly, pointing his fork at Pearl.

"It's really not that far," Mattie offered.

Louella leaned over and whispered to Alma, "You better eat everything on your plate or Ma'll make you eat it before you have any supper tonight."

"I know, I 'member last night," Louella whispered as she sopped her syrup with a piece of biscuit.

"That's so you won't take too much on your plate and waste food," Wade whispered back to them.

The three girls finished their breakfast and hurried down the road toward the schoolhouse. They were anxious to join their cousins at the fork in the road.

Annie stood in the doorway with her arms folded across her chest watching the girls walk down the driveway while Wade pulled on his boots. "You know, them's three purty little girls," Annie beamed.

"Yep, and this un here makes four," Wade said as he ruffled Alma's hair. "We need to get us a boy, don't we?" He spoke half teasing and half serious.

"How you know the next one won't be another girl?" She smiled shyly.

"Naw, the next one will be a fine little boy," he joked as he kissed her on the cheek, patted her on the behind then bounced down the front steps.

Annie watched him as he hurried toward the barn, pulling his hat down on his forehead to keep the early morning sun out of his eyes. He seemed to always be in a hurry. There was always something to do. Corn to pull for the next few weeks, the sugar cane to strip and carry to the cane mill, cotton to pick, and sweet potatoes to be dug. Thanksgiving would arrive before he had all the harvesting completed.

"Wade, you're a mighty fine husband," Annie muttered to herself as she turned and started toward the kitchen.

"What'd you say, Ma?" Alma asked.

"Just talking to myself, honey. Lets go wash breakfast dishes."

Count your many blessings, name them one by one.

******

Mattie held her back straight and her head high as she ascended the steps of the schoolhouse. She could feel the breeze toying with the hair hanging around her shoulders. Strands of it blew across her face. Her hand daintily smoothed it in place. She felt the eyes of the boys staring at her, staring at the transformation from a girl to a young woman. Ida and Georgia, likewise had undergone quite a change. Amos, as usual, tagged along behind his three cousins.

Amos winked at Leon and the other boys who stood with their mouths open as they stared at his sister and two cousins. A new boy stood on the fringe of the group of boys.

The first day of school was exciting. The boys tried to impress the girls with their antics and the girls pretended to ignore the boys. This year there were many new students since several families had moved to the area with the coming of the railroad. There were the Morton's and Haney's who had bought the old plantation at Tucker. In addition to farming they planned to start a newspaper in town. Between them they had seventeen children with twelve of them in school. There were now far too many pupils to confine them all to one room.

Mrs. Hampton stood in the doorway and greeted all the children. They were glad to see her, and she them. The new teacher Liza Coombs welcomed the younger children and showed them to their places in her room. Mrs. Hampton had been designated to teach the fifth through eighth grades.

The school consisted of two rooms now. An extra one had been added to accommodate the exploding number of students. The rooms were somewhat crowded but plans were made to add an additional room next year. The room was filled with benches and tables. A few desks had been bought for some of the young children. The older ones still had to share long tables and benches.

Mrs. Hampton tapped on the desk with a ruler and spoke softly, "Children, children, it's time to take your seats." No one seemed to hear her so it was necessary to speak louder. "Be seated, please!"

"Now let me show you how the class is to be divided. The younger will sit on these two rows," she instructed and pointed with her ruler as she walked to one side of the room. "Come on children if you are in the fifth grade take your seat on this row."

The children scampered to find a seat. She organized the other pupils and except for an occasional giggle from one of the girls, they all sat silently. Thirty sets of big eyes filled with anticipation stared at her. *Will I survive this year?* She thought. Thirty students, four grades. She felt overwhelmed by the enormous task.

"We have some new students this year." She smiled and tried hard to relax. "They just moved to this area this summer and I am going to introduce them at this time. Please stand as I call your name. Lloyd Morton, Mary Rose Morton, Charles Morton, Annie Sue Haney, T. J. Haney, and Frank Haney. When you go out at recess I want all of you to introduce yourselves to these new students and make them feel welcome. Now lets all stand and say the Pledge of Allegiance and the Lord's Prayer."

They all stood but all eyes were not on the flag. Georgia nudged Mattie and whispered out the corner of her mouth, "The new boy is looking at you."

"I know. He's good looking, ain't he?"

"Better'n Leon?"

"Uh huh! With liberty and justice for all."

The eighth grade was not very large since some of the boys had dropped out of school for one reason or another. They were needed to help with the farm work so their parents did not insist they stay in school. Some were not very diligent with their lessons and were frequently held back a grade. By the time they reached eighth grade they were much more mature than the others and felt they did not fit in so they refused to go to school.

Zeke Henshaw was an exception this school year. Having failed the third and fifth grades he was now much more mature than the rest of the boys. He would not have gone back to school this year except for the fact that he had a crush on Mattie and wanted to be near her as much as possible. Zeke was always at Mattie's elbow during the social functions vying for her attention. Mattie considered him rather obnoxious but since he had been around since she could remember, she considered him a friend rather than a beau.

Zeke's ideas about Mattie were different, however. Since he had no competition - until now - he felt secure in his imagined status with her.

Mattie was always too busy to think of having a beau. Besides none of the boys appealed to her in that way. They were all – well – just there. Somehow over the summer her thinking about such matters changed. Leon was the first new boy near her age to move into the community so she, as well as all the girls, had a crush on him. Leon was too busy having fun to notice. Being a late bloomer he still had his mind on mischievous "child's play", like tying firecrackers on cats' tails.

Mattie had been dead set on getting his attention and winning him from the other girls, that is until she met Frank. Now things had changed. Her entire focus, interest, and aspirations had changed completely.

Ten girls and seven boys sat on benches at two long tables. Mary Rose Morton and Frank Haney, and Leon were the new ones in the eighth grade. Of course, Leon was not new to most of them since they all went to church together. Mrs. Hampton was busy with the fifth graders and left the older children to entertain themselves until she finished.

"What's your name?" Mary Rose mouthed to Georgia who sat across from her trying not to stare at the two new students.

"I'm Georgia Glass, these are my cousins Ida and Mattie Posey," she whispered. "We're all cousins. Marshall Glass is my brother." She pointed to Marshall then to Amos. "Amos is Ida's brother."

Mary Rose arched her eyebrows causing her forehead to wrinkle. "Is everybody kinfolk?"

Georgia laughed. "Just about. Leon, sitting up there with the blue shirt on is no kin to any of us. Neither is Zeke Henshaw. He's the one throwing spitballs at Mattie. He's always had a crush on her but she has never liked him."

"He acts like he's crazy about her."

Mattie glanced at Frank Haney periodically and then looked quickly away as he turned toward her. *I'm glad I wore my hair down.*

When Mrs. Hampton dismissed for recess all the eighth graders huddled together to satisfy their curiosity about the newcomers.

"Where did you live before you came here?"

"How old are you?"

"Do you like to square dance?"

"How many brothers and sisters do you have?"

They soon learned that Mary Rose Morton and Frank Haney had lived in Jackson, gone to the same school and church and their mothers were sisters, which made them first cousins. Their fathers had both worked for the newspaper in Jackson.

Amos' eyes were fastened on Mary Rose. "What made ya'll want to come over here from the big city?"

Mary Rose looked at Frank and indicated she wanted him to explain.

"Number one," Frank began, "Our fathers plan to start a newspaper, but we need to farm until it starts making enough for us to make a living.

Billy Jamison had wondered why they had bought a farm if they were going to publish a weekly paper. "So that's why ya'll bought the Killebrew plantation together."

"Right. Another reason," Frank continued, "was that our parents plan to start a church here. They're sort of - missionaries."

"We already got a church," Ida spoke up. She couldn't imagine needing another one.

"Yeah, it's big enough for everybody," Amos added.

"But, it's not like our church." Frank explained.

"What kinda' church is yours?" Mattie asked.

"Catholic."

"What's a Catholic Church?" Mattie was curious. She had never heard of a Catholic Church, nor had any of the others.

Mary Rose shrugged. "It's just a church, is all I know." She had never been in any church other than a Catholic. She was not allowed to go to any other. The priest said it was a sin for a Catholic to go to another church so she had never even considered going inside one. Why it was a sin she could not imagine, but if the priest said it – that settled it.

Mary Rose was a very petite girl, far less developed than the other girls. She had creamy white skin, hazel eyes and blond hair, which she still wore in pigtails. Her features were delicate and her fingers and hands were small. Her dresses were hand sewn by her mother and were still in the little girl styles. She was somewhat younger than the other girls in the eighth grade having advanced rapidly in her schoolwork with the urging and assistance of her parents.

"All us Posey's are Methodist," Ida volunteered.

"I'm Baptist," Georgia stated proudly.

Mattie informed them, "We Methodist and Baptist all sort of go together to the same church. The Methodist preacher comes once or twice a month, depending on the weather, and so does the Baptist. We all go to hear both preachers. Pa says the Baptist are wrong about lots of things like baptism and being able to sin all you want and still go to heaven."

"We don't believe that!" Georgia said indignantly.

"You do too," Mattie argued back.

"You need to listen more closely to the Baptist preacher instead of talking while he preaches," Georgia shot back at Mattie, gazing at her through narrowed eyes.

"Have any of you ever been to a catholic church?" Frank asked.

"Never heard of one, much less been to one," Zeke Henshaw answered sarcastically.

"Our priest will be here in a few weeks so when we get the church started you can come." He was speaking to all of them but his eyes were glued on Mattie. Mattie could not hold his gaze. She blushed and looked at her feet. When she ventured a glance at Frank she offered a faint smile then resumed interest in her feet.

Frank was tall with blond, wavy hair and dark brown eyes. He was somewhat skinny Mattie thought. He walked with his shoulders back and his head held high exhibiting an air of self-confidence, which also showed in his manner of speaking as well as in his demeanor. He was obviously a couple of years older than most of the boys in the eighth grade, except Zeke. The unasked question about his age circulated through the inquisitive minds surrounding him. Mary Rose hastened to answer.

"Frank's been sick a lot, had to miss lots of school when he was younger."

All questioning eyes turned toward Frank.

"Weak lungs," Rosemary added. It took no other explanation.

Mattie suddenly lost interest in Leon. It was a good thing, too, especially since he and Mary Rose were obviously locked into some kind of fascination for each other. It looked as though Amos would need to direct his amour to someone else.

Zeke had noticed the amazing transformation in Mattie over the summer months and fanned the flame in him that had refused to be extinguished. Aware of the "sparks" flying between Frank and Mattie, "the green eyed monster" made his appearance. *I'll put an end to that,* he thought. *I'll nip it in the bud once and for all.* He narrowed his eyes and stared without blinking at Mattie then at Frank. His lips were drawn into a tight straight line. He stepped away from the circle and waited for his chance.

Mrs. Hampton came to the front door and rang the bell.

The younger children streamed out the door of the school ready to play. The older children went back inside.

It's a good thing recess is over. I was fixin' to clobber him. Zeke thought. He may have been thinking but he may as well have said it aloud as far as Amos was concerned. It was as if Amos could read his mind.

"What you fummin' about?" Amos asked as they made their way to the table against the wall.

"It ain't nothin'.

"Yep, it's something, all right. I saw the way you were lookin' at Frank."

"Did you see the way he was lookin' at Mattie? He ain't got no right to come in here and take my girl."

"Since when is she YOUR girl? You have got no claim on her."

"We'll see about that on the way home today." He sat down hard on the bench, his long legs sprawled across the floor at the end of the table. His lips were drawn tight in a pout and his face resembled a dark thundercloud.

"Better pull them lips in and pay attention to the teacher," Amos advised him. Zeke scowled at Amos. If looks could kill!

Before school was over at three o'clock Amos knew he needed to do something to intervene in the inevitable altercation between Zeke and Frank. Frank would be no match for Zeke in a fistfight. Zeke was older, bigger, and stronger and had developed biceps the size of a softball. Frank was a city boy and had not done enough work to develop muscles. Besides he was not even aware that he was about to have to defend himself. Amos would have to intervene. But how?

Amos nudged Billy Jamison under the table with his foot. When he looked at him, Amos cut his eyes toward Zeke. He mouthed the words, "mad, wants to fight."

Billy looked a little confused and whispered, "Fight who?"

Amos cut his eyes toward Frank then jerked his head in that direction.

"Why?"

Amos then jerked his head toward Mattie.

"Oh-h-h-h." Billy said indicating he got the message. Billy then nudged Marshall and whispered. "Stick with me 'n Amos after school. Tell Clarence."

Lawton nodded. He knew trouble was brewing somewhere. The four of them stuck together like glue. Right or wrong they were always on the same side. Of course feisty little Leon would be right at Amos' heels.

Amos knew that neither he nor any of the boys were a match for Zeke. *He could whup either of us with one hand tied behind his back but with all of us together…*

When Mrs. Hampton dismissed the class Zeke headed for the door. Amos, Marshall, Billy and Lawton were right behind him. Leon didn't know what the rush was but he hurried to catch up with them. Frank lingered over his books then sauntered toward the door, staying as near Mattie as possible.

"What are you so all fired up about?" Amos asked Zeke who stood at the edge of the schoolyard with his feet spread apart and his arms folded across his chest.

"It ain't nothin' to ye. You jist go on about your biz'ness."

"I gotta' feelin' it is my biz'ness, especially if it involves my sisters or my cousins."

"It don't involve nobody but me 'n that city dude."

"Frank ain't done nothing to you! You're just mad 'cause he caught Mattie's eye." Amos was not being very successful at diffusing the bomb ticking in Zeke's brain.

"When I get through with 'im he ain't gonna ketch nobody's eye." He leaned to look over Amos's shoulder at the door of the schoolhouse. The giggling girls were bouncing down the steps with Mattie and Frank behind them.

"Now Zeke, you listen to me!" Amos said forcefully. "Ain't no good can come from fighting Frank. Mattie's gonna' be the one to choose who she takes a liken' to."

If Zeke heard Amos at all it didn't show in his facial expression. He stepped around Amos to meet his supposed enemy. Amos, Billy, Marshall and Leon flanked his sides, ready to subdue him any way possible.

"Hey, city boy!" Zeke called to Frank. The entire group of girls stopped at once and turned toward Zeke. It was obvious to them that he was angry and they knew Zeke well enough to know he would not stop with words. He was hot-headed and always ready to fight. The girls parted as he pushed through them to face Frank.

"Are you talking to me?" Frank asked. A big smile showed a mouth full of white teeth. He detected anger in Zeke's voice but ignored it. "I don't believe I was introduced to you. My name's

Frank." His outstretched hand reached out to the level of Zeke's puffed out chest.

Zeke stared at the hand obviously unsure how to respond to kindness in return for anger. He shuffled his feet and stuck his tightened fist in the pocket of his overalls. Frank dropped his hand to his side and shrugged, still smiling. The girls snickered.

"Guess he doesn't want to be friends," Frank said to no one in particular, then casually walked past him.

"Where you goin' Frankie boy? Are you too skeered to fight me?" Zeke asked with a sneer.

Frank stopped abruptly then turned slowly to face him. He took a step forward and very calmly looked Zeke in the eyes. "If you must know, I am going home and, no, I am not afraid to fight for any just cause but you don't seem to me to be a just cause. I don't have any reason to fight you." He turned to walk away.

"You mean you don't think Mattie's a just cause?" Zeke yelled after him.

Frank turned and looked back at Zeke then at Mattie.

Mattie's face was ashen. Tears filled her eyes. Clutching her books tightly with both hands she stepped to the front of the group of girls. She started to speak, to defend Frank from the school bully, but thought better of it when Amos shook his head. *Guess Frank doesn't need a girl's coattail to hide behind.*

Frank ignored Zeke's fire-darting stare and looked at Mattie instead. "I most certainly do consider Mattie a just cause and if it were necessary I would go to battle for her any day." He then turned to look at Zeke. "But tell me, Zeke, why do I need to fight for Mattie?"

"'Cause she's my girl, that's why." He stuck out his chest, pulled his fists from his pockets and took a step toward Frank.

Mattie could hold her tongue no longer. Now she was angry and like a little bantam rooster she jumped between them. "I ain't your girl, never have been!" She said angrily her nose within inches of Zeke's. "I never have liked you...you...you big bully!"

Amos grabbed her by the arm and snatched her to one side.

Frank raised one eyebrow and stared in the eyes of Zeke. "Looks like you don't have anything to fight about, Zekie boy."

127

The girls laughed and the boys guffhawed. "Zekie boy," one of them twittered. Zeke turned red.

The boys walked past Zeke to where Frank was standing. "Let's go home, Frankie boy," Leon giggled as they all turned their back on Zeke and started down the trail. The giggling group of girls followed them leaving a humiliated Zeke standing in the schoolyard.

By the time Mattie arrived home her anger at Zeke had subsided and her repulsion for him had increased. She admired Frank for his diplomacy and the gentlemanly way he handled the encounter. She could hardly wait for the next day of school so she could see Frank again but she dreaded to see what else Zeke was going to try.

Zeke did not usually let humiliation and anger stop him from revenge but after a few days of seething he decided to stay away from school and give-up on his pursuit of Mattie's affection.

"We got a lotta new kids in our school," Pearl said at the supper table. Her cheek was packed with food.

"Don't talk with your mouth full." Wade admonished. "What are their names?" Wade asked as he lifted a glass of milk to his lips.

Making an effort to swallow Pearl answered, "Don't remember. Do you remember their names, Mattie?"

"The ones in my class are Mary Rose Morton and Frank Haney," Mattie answered. "They're cousins. They bought the Killebrew plantation down at Tucker. At least that's what they told us at recess."

"I met Mr. Morton and Mr. Haney at the feed store a few weeks ago," Wade remembered. "Names are Joe and…" he tilted his head upward and closed one eye as he tried to remember the other name. "Something from the Bible, I believe, can't remember right off what the other was. Plan to start a newspaper here as soon as they can get the money. Seem to be nice folk."

"I hear they have lots of young'uns just like the rest of us," Annie added. "We need to go visit them before the weather gets too cold."

Mattie was pleased to hear that. *Maybe they'll take me along.*

"Do your lessons before you go to bed, girls. I want to see some good marks this year," Wade told them as he pushed his chair back from the table and went out on the porch to chew tobacco and spit off the edge of the porch.

"Mattie, you and Pearl clear the table so you can spread out your books and get up your lessons," Annie told them, as she scraped the tiny bits of food from the plates into a bowl of gravy.

"Ma, when do you think we can fix up the parlor?" Mattie asked, as she carried a stack of plates to the cabinet.

"I told you, when you start courting," Annie reminded her, wondering what made her mention it at this time. She lifted the iron kettle from the stove and poured steaming water over the dishes in the dishpan.

"Do you think we could go on and do it so when a beau comes calling it'll be ready? Most of the girls my age are already courtin', some are even married." Mattie was hoping that would convince Annie.

"You have plenty of time. Do you have a beau in mind?" Annie asked inquisitively.Pearl cleared her throat to get Mattie's attention then grinned broadly. Mattie frowned at her and made a "shushing" motion with her lips.

"No, but you can't ever tell when one will come along," Mattie said matter-of-factly. "I heard Pa say we had a good cotton crop and the sawmill was getting busier all the time. Do you think we might have enough money to fix it up by Christmas. I could have a square dance for all the eighth graders and some of the older kids who want to come."

"I'll talk to your pa, now go get your lessons," Annie said as she shooed the two of them toward the table.

"I saw that new boy making eyes at you in school today," Pearl whispered.

"You didn't do nothing of the sort!" Mattie said emphatically. She kept her head down over her book.

"I sure did! Every time I looked up he was looking at you. He's handsome!"

He's got the biggest brownest eyes I have ever seen on a white boy," Mattie exclaimed. She forgot that she was attempting to deny to Pearl that she was infatuated with him.

"So you did notice him. Do ye think he'll be your beau?"

"Maybe so, if I can get my hooks in him before Ida or Georgia," she answered seriously.

"You better hurry. If you gonna go fishing for him I'll get Pa's fishing pole for you," Pearl giggled.

"I got my own fishing pole." Mattie threw her shoulders back.

They started giggling. Annie yelled from the kitchen, "You girls better pay attention to your school work!"

It takes more'n a Ma's rebuke to keep teenage girls' attention on schoolwork and off boys.

22

Frank attempted to keep his mind on his reading assignment. THE ANCIENT MARINER was not as interesting as Mattie. He looked from his book to the opposite side of the table to try to catch her eye. When she looked up he winked at her and her cheeks turned pink. A touch of a smile showed around her eyes but she was able to suppress it from spreading to her lips. Frank smiled and went back to reading. He scribbled a note on a small piece of paper and slid it under her book.

Mattie slipped the note from under the book and held it in her lap so she could read it undetected. In very small print he had written, "Will you see if I can recite my poem during recess?"

Mattie looked up, nodded and again blushed when he winked. She slipped the note in her literature book then continued the class assignment.

When Zeke did not arrive in time for school Amos expected him to show up for recess. Amos knew Zeke was not one to let the humiliation of the previous day go without retaliation. At recess he and Leon walked around the schoolhouse to see if he was lurking in the edge of the woods.

Leon smirked. "I suppose Zekie boy decided that even a fight wouldn't win Mattie."

"Suppose so. I hope we don't see any more of him."

Most of the class lounged around the steps of the school. Frank managed to wedge between Mattie and Mary Rose to sit on the steps.

Frank nervously ran his fingers through his blond, wavy hair. "What poem did you decide to recite?"

"I haven't decided on anything yet." Mattie answered, trying hard to use proper English. "What are you going to recite?"

"You can bet it will be something by Tennyson," Mary Rose offered. "He lo-o-oves Tennyson."

Frank turned his head sharply. "I sure do. I've read everything by him I can get my hands on."

Mattie glanced in his direction. "Maybe you can suggest something for me"

"I have a few ideas but first I need to know what kind of poetry you like. Do you like Tennyson?"

Mattie shrugged. I don't know as I've read anything written by him.

"Here's what I've decided to recite. See how you like it." He handed Mattie a sheet of paper. "This is one of Tennyson's poems. He's still living, you know, even though he is very old. See if I can quote it?"

"Sure." She took the paper from him. Mary Rose leaned to look on with Mattie.

When Mattie looked up from the paper, her face was inches from Frank's. She quickly looked back at the paper. "Okay, go ahead."

"Come not when I am"…he began.

"Stop, stop." Mattie held her hand out in front of her, the palm facing Frank. "Mrs. Hampton said we have to stand then state the name of the poem and the author before we recite it."

"Yeah," Leon chided, "Stand up and recite to us."

Mary Rose gave Leon a slight push. "Don't tease him. Let him practice."

"Go ahead, Frank," Ida encouraged. "We want to hear it."

"I was just teasing. I would really like to hear it." Leon said earnestly.

"Okay, I will." He stood rigidly in front of the steps, with his hands hanging stiffly at his side trying to hide his embarrassment with humor. He stiffened his neck, and held his chin slightly tucked in. "How's this?"

Everyone laughed.

Mary Rose touched him lightly on the arm. "Relax!"

Frank spread his feet, let his arms go limp and let his head roll lazily in a circle. "All right, here goes. Come Not When I Am Dead, by Alfred Lord Tennyson.

Come not, when I am dead,
To drop thy foolish tears upon my grave,
To trample round my fallen head,
And vex the unhappy dust thou wouldst not save.
There let the wind sweep and the plover cry;
But thou, go by.
Child, if it were thine error or thy crime
I care no longer, being all unblest;
Wed whom thou wilt, but I am sick of Time,
And I desire to rest.
Pass on, weak heart, and leave me where I lie;
Go by, go by."

Frank then put his hand across his abdomen and bowed low. The girls applauded.

"That is so sad!" Mattie said, rather dramatically.

Noticing Mattie's seriousness, Frank laughed to lighten the moment. "It's just a poem, for crying out loud! Now lets find one for you." He sat back down on the steps. Mattie put his poem inside her literature book then handed the book to him. He thumbed through the book and scanned some of the poems. None seemed to be to his liking.

"My mother has a book of Tennyson's poetry. Would you like for me to bring one for you to learn?" he asked, putting both elbows on his knees and locking his fingers.

"Sure. Do you have one in mind?" she asked hopefully as she looked at him in the eyes for the first time at such close proximity.

"I like, <u>CROSSING THE BAR</u>. We had to recite it in the seventh grade. Do you want me to write it down for you?" His eyes held her gaze for a few seconds.

"Do you still know it?" Her blue eyes looked at him admiringly. She was amazed that he could recite more than one poem. "Say it for us."

He hesitated, a little embarrassed at the thought of performing again. He glanced around to see if anyone else was listening. Mary Rose and Leon were bantering with some of the others. Georgia and Ida joined in their antics leaving Mattie and Frank sitting on the steps. Frank spoke softly. His face was expressive and his hands were in constant motion as if he needed them to make the meaning of the poem clear. He raised his eyebrows then lowered them, looked briefly in Mattie's eyes, then across the field, then back at her as he recited the poem from memory.

"Sunset and evening star,
And one clear call for me!
And may there be no moaning of the bar,
When I put out to sea,
But such a tide as moving seems asleep,
Too full for sound and foam,
When that which drew from out the boundless deep
Turns again home.
Twilight and evening bell,
And after that the dark!
And may there be no sadness of farewell,
When I embark;
For tho' from out our bourne of Time and Place
The flood may bear me far,
I hope to see my Pilot face to face
When I have crost the bar."

A chill ran over Mattie while he was reciting the poem; almost a feeling of impending doom. *Death, dying.* She trembled.

When Frank finished, Mattie's eyes were moist. "I didn't mean to make you cry. I'm sorry," he said sympathetically.

"It's just so beautiful. You say it so well. Besides I'm not crying," she said defensively as she blinked her eyes repeatedly to clear them.

"You will do a well reciting it in front of the class, wait and see. It's easy to learn." He turned his head and coughed, then left the steps when he continued coughing.

Mary Rose noticed him and said to Mattie, "Asthma. He's missed lots of school because of it. He's prone to pneumonia."

The rest of the group nodded their understanding and resumed their conversation attempting to ignore Frank's efforts to recover.

Mattie doubted the poem would be easy to learn but she was determined to learn it because Frank had suggested it.

Frank soon learned that writing poetry to Mattie was a good way to express his growing fondness for her without making it seem too personal.

She cherished each poem and note he gave her and kept them in a box in a secret place, away from prying eyes at home.

It did not take many weeks for Mattie to realize she was in love with Frank. It was evident to all the other teenagers. The girls knew instinctively that Frank was "hands off".

Every day after school, Frank walked Mattie to the crossroads. They walked slowly and she insisted that Pearl and Louella walk ahead of them. They knew it was not proper to be touching in public but when no one was looking, they walked close together and let their fingers entwine. He would squeeze her hand briefly then let it go. How he longed to hold it for a longer period of time and how he would love to kiss her on the cheek but that was certainly not permitted. He would get his chance though, someday.

23

Mr. and Mrs. Morton decided to host the annual Thanksgiving dance. Their house was large and they felt it would accommodate the people if they moved some of the furniture from the living room and dining room.

Wade snapped the reins against the horse's back. "Giddyup!"

"This is a good time to get to spend some time with the Haneys and Mortons," Annie said as Wade guided the buckboard out of the yard.

His eyes searched the darkening clouds for the possibility of snow, or worse rain, which would immediately turn to sleet. "We've been so busy with getting the crops in we've had no time for visiting. Since they don't go to our church, there's not much time for getting acquainted," Wade replied. "It'll give us men some time to find out more about their business. George told me they're still waiting for money to start the paper."

"Wonder why they don't come to our church?" Annie pondered aloud.

Mattie wanted to speak up and tell them they were Catholic but she still was not quite sure what a Catholic was so she thought it best not to say anything. It could be something a lot different from the Methodist.

Mattie leaned over and whispered to Pearl. "Pearl, you ain't said anything to Ma or Pa about Frank being sweet on me have you?"

"No, you told me not to. I promised I wouldn't tell if you wouldn't tell about me and Bobby."

"Just remember, it's our secret. Maybe Louella won't tell," Mattie added hopefully.

"If she does, we'll just say she's lying," Pearl was confident the two of them could convince their parents. It had worked before.

"I suppose we'd better remember the 'Thou shalt nots'. We don't need to be lying if we can help it," Mattie replied feeling somewhat guilty about the prospect of telling a lie.

The Poseys arrived at the Morton house along with other wagons. Mules and horses were tied to the hitching post flank to flank.

The Morton house was a large, two-story house that had survived the war but was in need of paint. There was a large magnolia tree in the front yard. Large oak trees lined the driveway. Mr. Morton stood on the porch and welcomed his guests. He shook hands with the men and bowed to the women. He was a small man with delicate features, which belied his strong, masculine voice.

Fireplaces in two large rooms of the house made the rooms toasty warm. All the furniture had been removed from the rooms and chairs and benches had been placed around the perimeter.

It was obvious the Morton's had nice furniture from what could be seen crammed in the other rooms of the house. There were heavy brocaded curtains on the windows and paintings on every wall. Each mantle above the fireplace held a clock and expensive bric-a-brac sat on hand embroidered scarves and crocheted doilies. The women looked around the rooms and oo-ed and ah-ed over how nice everything looked.

"You have done a good job of fixing up the place." Each lady exclaimed. Esther Morton thanked them graciously and proudly took them on a tour of the rest of the house.

The men stood around in the hall and on the porch gossiping and smoking, occasionally going to the edge of the porch to spit. Joe Morton and Paul Haney answered their numerous questions with dignity and caution. They considered many of the men's questions nosey but still answered them, although somewhat vaguely. They considered their plans and financial matters personal and were careful to reveal nothing that could be a source of gossip.

The neighbors' questions about their church affiliation were met with the simple comment that they were Catholic and would hold services in their homes until a priest could arrive to conduct the proper services and initiate a building program.

The men, still perplexed, scratched their heads and answered with "Is that so?" "I see." "You don't say?" or some other such comment since they knew nothing about the Catholic religion.

George tuned up his fiddle and began playing, "She'll be Commin' 'Round the Mountain". After several sets with the adults growing tired, George decided to play a waltz. He began with Brahm's Waltz, which Mary Rose had hummed for him. After playing through it once he thought it best to explain to the crowd about the change in music and the waltz.

"Frank and Mary Rose are gonna show ya'll how to waltz." He said as he stood up. "Now just pay attention and you'll see exactly how it is done." He resumed his playing.

Frank and Mary Rose started the waltz while the rest watched, amazed. Their parents joined them on the floor, then their brothers and sisters.

When the first waltz was over George silenced the crowd. "Well what ya'll thank? It ain't no more a sin than square dancin' is it?" Most of the adults nodded in agreement. "Now all who want to learn to waltz just choose a partner from these that know how and let them teach you." The violin, again screeched out the melody of the Brahm's Waltz.

Frank was quick to reach for Mattie's hand although he had already taught her to waltz on Sunday at Amos and Ida's house. He was not interested in teaching anyone else since he wanted to spend the entire time dancing with her. The floor was crowded as more people joined the dancers on the floor.

Frank and Mattie had eyes for no one else. No one noticed that they did not change partners all night. He got his chance to pull her close to him after he looked around and made sure all the adults were occupied elsewhere. She allowed him to hold her briefly then pulled away as they resumed the dance.

Frank's heart pounded and his face flushed as he watched Mattie glide across the floor next to him. *Such beauty! Tall, slender, graceful, bright blue eyes set in creamy white skin! That hair! It's black as a crow with little wisps falling around her face.* He pulled her close to him again and squeezed her tightly.

Mattie looked around to see if anyone was watching. She felt her cheeks turn pink, then smiled.

When time came for snacks they all gathered around the table to give thanks. All except the younger children dutifully bowed their heads. When the prayer was finished the Morton's and Haney's made the sign of the cross. No one noticed except the children who were peeking. The parents would soon hear about it from them.

The sun dropped low in the west long before Mattie and Frank were ready. The men put on their coats and hats to go out and bring the horses and wagons to the front for the ladies and children. The evening chores still had to be done before dark.

Mattie looked back through the door at Frank as she started down the steps. He winked and she mouthed, "bye."

I'm going to do it! I'll ask Mister Posey if I can come calling, he thought as he went inside and began helping his aunt and uncle put the furniture back in place.

Mattie and Pearl huddled together under a quilt, exhausted but not so much so that it kept them from sharing the excitement of the afternoon. They pulled the quilt over their heads to shield the cold wind from their faces and so they could whisper and not be heard by the others.

"Mattie, I just love to waltz. Did you see me and Bobby dancin'? He's so-o-o handsome!"

"Frank twirled me around and pulled me close to him. It felt so good. I love him so much!" Mattie sighed.

Pearl giggled. "Yeah, and it shows."

"Do you think Ma and Pa noticed?" Mattie asked anxiously. "Naw, they were too busy gossiping."

"I can't wait 'till we have another dance."

"Do you think Ma and Pa will let Frank come courtin' you?"

"I hope so, I sure hope so." Mattie closed her eyes and re-lived every minute of the afternoon.

Ellen Williamson

Wade and Annie discussed the afternoon and exclaimed about the lovely things that were in the house.

"Did you find out anything about their religion?" Annie questioned Wade.

"They're Catholic, what ever that is. I'm gonna ask the preacher about it the next time he comes. He'll know."

Birds of a feather flock together and they're all the same religion.

24

The dark clouds of winter descended on Philadelphia, Mississippi, and brought rain followed by cold, icy wind. Families hovered around their fireplaces and went outside only when necessary.

The weather permitted only a few days of school between Thanksgiving and Christmas. Frank and Mattie had a very difficult time keeping their minds on their schoolwork.

Frank took Mattie's books and the two walked down the trail to the road.

"When can I ask your papa if I can come calling on you at your house?"

"I'm scared, Frank. Ma had always said she wanted me to marry one of the Henshaw boys and if she finds out I love you she'll".... She paused in mid-sentence.

"She'll what?" he asked curiously, stopping to wait for an answer. "She'll what, Mattie?" He stopped and looked at her, insisting on an answer.

Mattie stopped walking and turned to face him. Her face was pale. She was too embarrassed to make eye contact. "Ma'll be upset that I'm interested in an...outsider. She'll probably whip me and lock me in the pantry," she said hesitantly. She laughed, as though she was joking about the "pantry part" but that was, indeed, her fear.

Frank laughed, taking it as a joke. "What has she got against me? Am I not as good as the Henshaw boys?"

"Sure you are. She just doesn't know you, that's all." Mattie pulled her coat tightly around her and tightened her knitted scarf under her chin.

"How am I going to see you over the Christmas holidays? We won't know if they will permit it until we ask. I'll ask him today." His eyes narrowed and his lips closed tightly.

"No Frank, I'm too afraid of Ma. Please don't," Mattie pleaded.

"Okay, I won't but tell me how can I see you over the Christmas holidays?"

"Maybe I could sneak off somewhere to see you."

"And just how are you going to do that? And where would we go? Besides I don't like sneaking around."

"I've been thinking about it already. I often spend the night with cousins Ida or Georgia, maybe we could meet over there. You could come over there with their beaus and we could all sit in their parlor."

Frank was wary and skeptical. "How long will we have to sneak around?"

"I don't know, I just don't know! You don't know how afraid I am of Ma." Mattie's voice quivered. She held her mittened hand over her nose and mouth.

"You're really afraid!" Frank suddenly felt protective of her. "I feel so helpless. I want to protect you from any hurt. But...but...how?"

******

"I brought you a Christmas present," Frank whispered shyly at recess.

"You did? What is it?" She looked at him quizzically.

He reached in his coat and took out a package wrapped in plain brown paper. "I didn't want to wrap it in Christmas paper because..."

"Oh, how nice!" Mattie interrupted him as she clutched it to her bosom. "Can I open it now?" She asked as she glanced around the schoolyard to see if anyone was watching.

"If you want to. Nobody's looking."

Mattie untied the cotton string, then removed the paper. A soft, glistening, red velvet box emerged from the rough, brown paper. She clutched it to her breasts and stroked the soft side of it. She closed her eyes momentarily, then opened them to look into Frank's grinning face. "It is beautiful! Thank you so much!" Her arms ached to hug him tightly. His hands were plunged deep into his pants pockets and his arms stiffened as he shrugged an "Oh, shucks, it ain't nothing" type of shrug.

Inside the box were two folded sheets of tablet paper. She started unfolding them.

Frank glanced furtively around the schoolyard. "Don't read them now. Wait 'till you get home."

She put the box inside her coat, shivered from the cold and they hurried back to the classroom.

Mattie hid the box under her coat until she got home. She went to her room and put the box under her bed. *I'll read my note when they're asleep.*

She hurried to finish the supper dishes and helped Louella and Alma get ready for bed. She put more wood on the fire in their bedroom so it would burn long enough to read Frank's letter. She went to bed and pulled the covers up under her chin. Pearl climbed into bed nestled her cold feet against Mattie's and was soon asleep.

Mattie lay very still until she knew Pearl was asleep, then eased out of bed. She pulled the covers up around Pearl, then retrieved the box from under the bed. *I'll have to find a better place to hide it tomorrow.* She reached for her heavy red, crocheted shawl on the back of a chair and pulled it around her. She sat cross-legged in front of the fireplace and anxiously opened the box. She unfolded the paper and began to read.

My Dear Mattie,

When I moved here I never dreamed I would meet someone I could love with all my heart. You have made life here worth leaving all my friends back in Jackson. I never thought I would be ready to marry anyone at the age of seventeen but I want desperately to marry you.

As I have told you before, my parents have planned for me to go back to Jackson to go to high school. This is what I want as well. I need to graduate so I will be able to carry on the work in my father's newspaper. This is my last year in this school, as it is yours, and then I will have to leave. We will go back to school after Christmas and can be together there for four short months.

I want desperately to come calling on you in your home during those summer months. Since I can see you at school until then, I can wait about coming to your house. Please consider asking your parents if I can come calling on you?

You cannot know the love I have for you and the longing to be with you. I can be patient knowing that you feel the same about me but please don't make me wait too long.

I have written a poem for you. This is not by Alfred Lord Tennyson, by the way. I wrote it, myself, especially for you. I love you. Frank

She opened the next page and read the poem.

You're the fairest of fair, my dearly beloved
with hair of perfect hue.
The mem'ry of your fragrance haunts me
In the night when I think of you.
The longing for you will linger still,
even when I'm far away,
For I'm assured that you will wait
'til we're together for aye.

She read it again and again then folded the letter, held it to her breast and smiled into the yellow flames licking the logs. She curled up on the hearth and went to sleep. When she awoke the fire had burned out and she was shivering. She put the letter and poem back in the box and slid it under her bed, then snuggled under the covers against Pearl.

The Christmas holidays were cold and rainy. Mattie wanted to walk over to Cousin Ida's house and spend the night but the rain and sleet prevented it. She did not know how she could get in touch with Frank but hopefully she and Ida could figure something out. Her heart ached with longing. She read the letter repeatedly, refolding it and putting it back in the box. She retrieved all the other notes and poems

Frank had written her and put them in the box. ·She vowed to find a better place to hide it before she started back to school.

The night before school was to start again it began to rain – a cold, freezing rain, followed by blinding, snow. When Mattie awoke there was a blanket of white as far as the eye could see. The pine trees were bent toward the ground under the heavy weight of the snow. Some of the limbs had snapped off and lay on the ground around the trees. Icicles dangled off the eaves of the house – long pointed pieces of ice glistening in the morning light.

She pulled her shawl around her and rushed into the kitchen where she knew she would find a hot fire in the stove and her ma cooking breakfast.

"Where's Pa?" Mattie asked anxiously.

"He's at the barn," Annie answered as she rolled the last biscuit in her hand then placed it in a black iron skillet and slid it into the hot oven.

"Is he gonna drive us to school in the wagon?" Mattie asked hopefully.

"Heavens no! You know there won't be any school today. It's too cold,"

Mattie's shoulders sagged. "I just wondered." *I'll bet Frank will be there,* she thought as she left the room. *He'll think I may have made it through the snow.* She went back to bed and pulled the covers around her.

The snow stayed on the ground all week, only starting to melt on Saturday. The sun came out and its warm rays began to melt the snow.

"I wonder if the preacher will be here tomorrow?" Annie asked Wade during breakfast.

"I imagine so. It's some warmer today and I think we can make it to the church if there is no more snow."

******

Reverend Whitley was a short, fat man, bald and clean-shaven. His cheeks, normally rosy, were red from the cold wind. A wool cap with earflaps was pulled tightly over his ears. He rode his horse to the

145

Posey's front porch and tied him to the porch railing. Wade heard him as he gingerly ascended the steps and went to the door to meet him.

"Howdy Reverend. Come on in outta the cold." He gripped the preachers' extended hand.

"Put another plate on the table. The preacher can stay for supper," Wade called to Annie.

Mattie helped Annie finish cooking then went to the front room to call the rest to supper.

Half way through supper Wade broached the subject of the Catholics.

"Preacher, what can you tell me about the Catholics? Two families have moved here and are going to start a church." Wade stared at the plump little man over a fork piled high with potatoes.

Reverend Whitley took his eyes off his plate and stopped chewing long enough to look at Wade briefly. He nodded, put his fork down and finished chewing. He took his napkin and wiped the corners of his mouth then propped his forearms on the edge of the table. His serious gaze into her father's eyes alerted Mattie to the ominous reply that was to follow.

"I can tell you a lot, Brother Posey, a who-o-le lot." His eyes circled the table as he looked at Annie and each of the children to be sure they were all listening. "I seen Brother George in town last week and he was tellin' me about them. That's one reason I came over to talk to you today." He crumbled cornbread in some turnip green pot likker he had left in his plate. "I want to warn all of my congregation about them. They ain't nothin' like us Methodist." He cut his eyes to look at Wade, then to Annie, then back at his plate. "They teach things that are a lot different than what we believe. I hear they have some young people about the ages of some of yours." His piercing eyes looked directly at Mattie, then at Pearl who were listening closely. Mattie looked back at her plate. "It is my fear that they will try to recruit our young folks into their church and corrupt them. Why else would they be here?" He spoke in a very concerned yet condemning manner.

Mattie listened intently. She had discussed the Catholic religion briefly with Frank from time to time but he did not express any kind of belief that seemed harmful to her. He did make the sign of the cross at times, which she did not understand and according to him, neither did he. "It's just something we do after we pray," he had said.

Reverend Whitley talked on and on about the dangers of the Catholic Church. Mattie listened apprehensively. She pushed her food around her plate unable to eat for the big lump in her throat. She knew she must eat it or Annie would make her eat it for breakfast the next morning. How could her beloved Frank be involved in something so evil? Who was she to believe, Frank or Reverend Whitley? She started to tremble and left the table taking her plate with her. She went to the fireplace in the front room and sat on the floor with her arms wrapped around her knees, which were pulled up to her chin. She stared into the crackling fire and cried. She just wanted to be away from the condemning, accusatory, inflammatory words of Reverend Whitley.

Annie, Wade and the preacher left the table and went to sit by the fireplace to further discuss the evils of the Catholic Church. "Go help with the dishes," Annie ordered. Mattie obeyed without objecting.

"Why are you crying?" Louella asked sympathetically. "What's the matter?"

Mattie lashed out at her. "Nothing. It ain't nothing to you." She wiped her nose on her sleeve and plunged her hands deep into the hot, soapy water.

"Well you don't have to be so snappy."

"Just clear the table and hand me the dishes," Mattie barked.

"Just ignore her, Lou," Pearl said.

They finished the dishes without further conversation.

Wade invited the preacher to spend the night. They had an extra bed, which he had used several times before.

Ordinarily when Reverend Whitley was there to spend the night the entire family sat around the fireplace and listened intently as he expounded the scriptures and the doctrines of the Methodist Church. His criticism of the Baptists made staunch Methodists out of the Posey's. Baptist was the only other religion in the area so, of course, it took the brunt of his admonitions. Preachers of the two denominations often held debates on points of differences.

******

147

The small group of people huddled around the pot-bellied stove in the middle of the church until the room was warm enough to sit closer to the pulpit. Mattie anticipated the subject of the sermon but could find no reason to stay at home.

Reverend Whitley read a passage of scripture from the Bible then started his tirade about the Catholics. Mattie wondered why he bothered to read the scripture since it had nothing to do with his subject. He proceeded to warn the congregation about the evils of the Catholic Church. He admonished the parents to make sure their children did not get involved with a Catholic.

"We have to be cordial to these families. They are part of our community and we must all act in a Christian manner but be wary of their teachings and their indoctrination of our youth. And, to you young people, just remember, birds of a feather flock together and a catholic is not your kind of bird." He pounded his fist on the pulpit, then paused and looked each young person directly in the eye. On and on he preached for an hour and a half on the evils of the Catholic Church.

By the time the last Amen was said Mattie was weeping. Georgia and Ida tried to shield her from the inquisitive eyes of the ones around her. The ride home was not a pleasant one.

"What are you crying about?" Annie asked when she heard Mattie sniffing.

"I ain't crying." She lied. "Just got a cold."

"Well, cover up good and get out of this wind," Annie instructed. "Wade, what did you think of the sermon?" Annie asked as she turned to face the front of the wagon.

"If any of our kids ever try courtin' one of them catholics, I'll beat the hell out of em," Wade declared.

"We'll just have to nip it in the bud, is all I can say." Annie replied, a determined set to her jaw.

Mattie burrowed between the quilts to stifle her sobs.

25

Mattie was more than glad to get back in school after the holidays. The sun peeked through the limbs of the naked oak tree in the back yard. The ice was melting fast making the road to the school nothing but slush. Wade hitched Prince to the buggy and the three girls climbed into it for the ride to school.

The pupils kept their coats on and huddled around the wood stove in the classroom. They were all talking at once.

Frank searched Mattie's face intently. "You look like you've been crying. What's the matter?" He spoke in a low voice, which was almost inaudible over the laughter and talking of the other pupils.

"It was just awful, just awful. Our preacher preached about Catholics yesterday."

Frank laughed. "Oh is that all? Did he say we were demons?"

"Almost. He warned about being indoctrinated and told all the parents to never let their children get romantically involved with a catholic."

"Oh Mattie, don't take it so seriously. It is just because they don't understand what we believe about Jesus. It will pass. Everything does."

"But you don't understand. It gets worse. Pa said on the way home he would beat the hell out of one of his kids if they started courting a Catholic."

"That's terrible! I can't believe it. Would he really do that?"

"He sure would! Or worse, Ma would. She would probably lock me in the pantry for the rest of my life!" Her voice was shrill and louder than she intended.

Frank was appalled. "You know she wouldn't do that! Not lock you in the pantry!"

"She would, too. She's done it plenty of times." Her eyebrows almost disappeared under the strands of hair on her forehead. Her eyes were blared so the whites could be seen surrounding the bright blue pupils.

"I can't believe that! We'll just have to be careful not to get caught until school is out."

Frank's thoughts were in a blur. *How can I convince Mr. Posey to let me call on Mattie? How can I stand not seeing her on the weekend? What will I do when school is over in the spring and I can't see her every day? Will they really lock Mattie in the pantry? What will happen when I go off to high school? I need to talk to Pa about this but he won't like it if I court a girl who is not a catholic.* Frank knew Mattie would have to convert to Catholicism if he ever planned to marry her. Before now, he did not foresee a problem and thought there would be plenty of time after they made plans to marry. He saw no reason she would not convert if she loved him enough.

Mattie, too, was disturbed by the possibility of not being able to have Frank court her in the traditional and socially proper manner. Now, what was she to do?

Neither of them learned much at school that day.

******

"Mattie, Mattie." Pearl nudged Mattie under the cover. "Does Ma look like she's in the family way?"

"I noticed that today for the first time. Do you think she is?"

"It looks like it to me. I wonder how far along she is."

"I have no idea. I wish she would tell us."

"You know she's not going to do that! We'll just have to wait and see."

******

150

"Mattie, get up and come in the kitchen." Wade whispered as he gently shook her awake.

"Is something wrong?" Mattie asked, pulling her shawl around her as she followed Wade into the cold kitchen. He began to make a fire in the stove.

"It's your Ma's time so you need to stay home today and help out." He paused as if waiting for Mattie to ask what he meant by "Ma's time". Mattie said nothing. "I have to ride over and get Mrs. Parker. The other girls can go on to school. I'll be back in a little while. Stay with your Ma and take care of her."

Mattie followed him to Annie's bedside listening to his instructions. "Tell Pearl to take Alma down to Lou's before she goes to school. Put some water on the stove to heat so we will have plenty of warm water," he told her as he went out the door. He left hurriedly in the buggy.

"Ma, are you all right?"

"Yes, I'm fine, just hurting. Tell Pearl to help the little ones get dressed." She grimaced in pain.

Mattie gave Pearl a note to give to Frank. "Don't you lose it and don't read it," Mattie instructed her sternly. Pearl shoved it deep in her coat pocket.

Mattie watched Annie writhe in pain. She pulled wet pads from under her and replaced them with dry ones. She washed her face with wet cloths. After two hours she heard the buggy drive into the yard and watched as Mrs. Parker climbed from the buggy with her satchel. She burst through the door and went straight to Annie's bedside.

"Looks like your water's done broke," Mrs. Parker said after lifting the covers and examining Annie carefully. "It won't be too much longer. Mattie you can go on into the kitchen and keep a fire going in the stove so there will be plenty of warm water to wash up." She made a shooing motion to Mattie with her hands.

Mattie heard Annie's moans and low screams as she huddled in the kitchen. She had never heard anyone give birth. Mrs. Parker called for pans of water, clean cloths and other necessary things but would not let Mattie stay in the room to help. "This is no place for chillun. You just do my fetchin."

Mattie did not feel like a child and resented being treated like one. At sixteen she felt she should be in the room to help.

Wade paced the floor in the hall. When the baby cried Wade was relieved that Annie was no longer in pain.

Mattie went to the door and put her ear against it. Wade could stay out no longer so he went inside.

"It's a big ole boy!" Mattie heard Mrs. Parker exclaim. "You got your boy, Wade, and a mighty fine one he is!"

The baby cried loudly. Mattie was so excited she could hardly stay outside the door and was relieved when Mrs. Parker called her in to take out some wet sheets.

"We got a boy!" Annie told her when she came in the room.

Wade held the screaming baby wrapped in a blanket in front of the fire. "Tom. Tom Posey. Right, Annie?"

Annie nodded and smiled. "Tom it is."

Mattie stayed home from school for a few days to help Annie with the baby and the household chores. Every day she sent a note to Frank and he sent one in return. She secretly tucked them away in her treasured red velvet box.

Annie seemed to be well physically but she languished in bed or sat motionless in front of the fire. If she had any interest in household chores it did not show. She was content to sit by the fire and rock the baby. That was fine with little Tommy, as a matter of fact, he was very discontent to be elsewhere and he let it be known.

Mattie and Pearl cooked supper every evening when they came home from school. It soon became evident to Wade that Annie was not her normal self. Try as he might, he was not able to get her out of her pensive moods. She merely sat in front of the fire holding little Tommy and staring into the glowing embers.

Wade watched her intently, thinking every day she would be better - would start eating or talking. After four weeks of her near catatonic state Wade decided Annie needed more help than he could give her. It seemed to him she had had enough time to recuperate from giving birth but he thought it best to consult with Mrs. Parker.

26

Mattie was awakened on Saturday morning to the smell of sausage and gravy and the sun filtering around the edges of the heavy quilts which had been hung over the windows to keep out the cold wind. She nudged Pearl.

"Do you smell that? Ma must be feeling better." For the past few weeks the two of them were the ones making breakfast.

Pearl pulled the covers over her head. "It's Saturday so maybe we can stay in bed a little longer,"

Mattie was relieved to think of her Mother back to her normal self. She was awake now. Her habit of getting up early kept her from going back to sleep. She put her stockened feet on the cold floor and pulled her shawl around her. "Ma, Ma," she called softly as she opened the door to the kitchen.

"She's still in bed," Wade answered as he pulled a pan of large, wrinkled biscuits from the oven.

"Oh, I was hoping…Why'd you cook breakfast?"

"So you and Pearl can get a early start on the washing. None's been done in three weeks to amount to anything 'cause of the weather."

"Yeah, and it'll probably take all day," Mattie added with dread.

"At least the sun's shining, even if it's still cold out. Go tell the girls breakfast is ready. I'll see if I can wake Annie."

153

Mattie watched him wearily make his way into the front bedroom. The spring had gone out of his step and the joy of having a son was diminished by Annie's lack of enthusiasm. Mattie heard Tommie cooing as she passed the door. She waked the girls then took Tommy from beside Annie and carried him to the kitchen. She hugged him tightly. "You're wetter'n a drowneded rat." After changing his diaper she cradled him in the crook of her arm as she put food on the table.

Pearl and Mattie drew water from the well and filled the two black wash pots with water. They built a fire around the pots and when the water was hot they dipped enough out to warm the water in the washtubs. Mattie put the dirty clothes into the tub and rubbed them with lye soap. After wringing the water from each garment she dropped them into the pot of boiling, soapy water. "Wonder where Pa went," she said to Pearl, not really expecting her to know.

"He didn't say. He muttered something about getting help for Ma." Pearl took the battling stick and pushed the clothes down into the boiling water. "Looks like Ma should be well enough to help us." Steam rose from the pot into the cold, damp air as she punched the clothes deeper into the water.

"It seems that way. I suppose she's not over having the baby just yet." Mattie pushed the burning sticks of wood further under the pot then added more dried limbs.

"Do ye think she's having another one of her crazy spells?" Pearl asked sullenly.

Mattie whirled to face her. "Don't you dare call her crazy!" she yelled. "She's just got the after baby blues, that's all. Don't you NEVER call her crazy again!" Anger spewed from Mattie's countenance.

Pearl took a step toward Mattie and pointed her finger at her. "Don't you go yelling at me! She seems crazy to me."

"If you go around saying she's crazy there ain't a woman in this county who'll have anything to do with her. We'll all be shunned like we got the plague."

"I ain't said it to nobody but you, for crying out loud!" She turned back to the tub of clothes on the wash bench.

"Then don't say it to me! If word gets around that she's crazy, that will be the Posey legacy as long as a Posey lives! Now, grab hold of that side of the tub and lets take it to the pot so we can get the clothes out."

Pearl lifted the side of the tub and helped carry it to the pot. She then took the battling stick and lifted the steaming clothes, a few at a time from the hot water, holding them over the pot until some of the water drained from them. "How long's she gonna be like this, any way?"

"Who knows? It looks to me like we might as well get used to doing all the work." Resentment showed in her voice in spite of her efforts to squelch it. She added more pre-washed clothes to the pot of boiling water.

The two of them carried the hot tub of clothes to the wash bench and covered them with fresh, clean water from the well. Mattie took them, one garment at a time and rubbed lye soap on the dirtiest part then scrubbed them hard across the ridges of the washboard.

"It ain't fair we have to do all the work." Pearl rinsed the clean clothes in a tub of cold water then twisted them in a wringing motion before taking them to the clothesline.

"No, and it's not fair we have to do the work of a man either. I'm not particularly fond of plowing a mule but I have to cause Pa's got nobody else to help 'im."

Mattie rubbed the knees of a pair of work pants on the washboard. She had long ago resigned to accept hard work as a way of life.

Pearl slung a wet towel into the tub. "I'll be good and glad when I can marry Bobby and get away from all this."

Mattie scoffed. "What makes you think you'll get away from it? You'll just be working at another wash pot, scrubbing another man's clothes and wiping the snotty noses of your own younguns." Mattie's sarcasm was evident.

"Humph!" Pearl grunted. "At least I'll be doing it for the man I love," she said as she lifted a heavy bucket of wet clothes and headed for the clothesline.

******

"Come on in!" Abby Parker yelled to Wade when he stepped up on the porch. "I'm in here by the fire."

Wade removed his hat and opened the door to a warm, cozy room. A quilting frame hung from the ceiling by ropes with a quilt stitched to strips of wood attached to the length of the quilt. Abby sat in a straight-back chair pulled up to the edge of the quilt. One hand pushed a needle in and out of the brightly colored squares. She held the other one underneath the quilt to guide her needle. Straight little rows of stitching traversed the cotton packed quilt top and lining. She smiled and motioned Wade to sit in the chair by the hearth.

"Have a seat. The old man run to town, ought to be back in a little while. How's that big ole boy doing?"

Wade stood facing the fire and held his hands near the flames to warm them. "He's fine, growing like a weed. You want me to stoke up the fire and put on another stick of wood?"

"I'd appreciate that. I've been thinking every minute I'd get up and put on another stick but I kept waiting until after the next stitch." She laughed.

Wade chuckled. "Putting it off 'til after the next stitch, then the next, then the next, huh?"

"Is Annie and the rest of the young'uns doin' all right?"

"Everybody's fine except Annie. She can't seem to get going ever since Tommy was born, suppose it's the after-birth

blues again. I thought you might come check her out and tell me what you think. I hate to insist she get up and do something if she's not well."

"I'll be glad to. Do you want me to come today or will it wait until Monday?"

"Monday's fine. One day won't make any difference."

******

Annie didn't bother to turn her head or answer when Mrs. Parker knocked on the door on Monday. She continued to rock slowly, back and forth, her eyes fixed on the flames licking the logs.

Abby pulled off her coat and headscarf. "Annie, how you feelin'?" She pulled a ladder back chair up near the fireplace, facing Annie.

Annie turned her unblinking eyes toward Abby and slowly shook her head. Her face showed extreme sadness. Her thumb gently rubbed

156

the back of the baby's hand as he curled his little fingers around her forefinger. She rhythmically rocked back and forth.

Mrs. Parker noticed that Annie had tears in her eyes.

"Are you still passing blood?"

"No."

"Is the baby getting enough milk?"

"I guess so."

"If he twernt you'd know it."

"Are your teats sore?"

Annie shook her head.

"Then you ain't got no infection in 'em."

"Here, give 'im to me. Let me hold 'im." She took the baby from Annie, then pulled back the soft blanket and examined him carefully. She pulled off his diaper and checked his navel and genitals. "Looks like the cord has dropped off and healing up real good. Well endowed too," she chuckled. "Is he having good bowel movements?"

"Yeah."

"Are you getting' up and moving around? Doing the cooking?" she quizzed Annie, knowing she was not. Her eyes narrowed suspiciously.

"Sometimes I just don't feel like it." Tears started spilling down Annie's cheeks.

"Now, honey, you just go on and cry." Mrs. Parker spoke soothingly, "You got a bad case of the after baby blues."

"I brought my baby into a bad world! Something bad's gonna happen to 'im, I can feel it."

"Nonsense, you stop thinking that," Abby admonished. He's going to be fine. Just look at him, smiling and kicking, just raring to get down on that floor and start crawling around."

She wrapped the blanket snuggly around the baby and laid him in his cradle at the foot of the bed. She pulled her chair up to Annie's so she could look her directly in the face. She spread her knees apart, propped her elbows on them, leaned forward within inches of Annie's face then took both her hands in her chubby ones.

"Now, you listen to me," she began, "I seen a lot of women with the after baby blues, I had it myself once, so I understand how you feel. It's ha-r-r-d, real hard. Some women get over it in a few weeks but sometime, why sometime, I seen women pine away for the rest of their lives."

Annie cried harder. The thought of enduring this sadness for the rest of her life was unbearable. Sobs wrenched from her throat and her shoulders shook. She pulled her hands from Mrs. Parker's and took one of the diapers hanging on the side of the cradle and wiped her eyes and cheeks.

"Now you just gotta get a holt a yourself. You gotta put that youngun down, and make yourself do things. Yore man and younguns need you. When you hear that rooster crow first thing in the morning, you throw them covers back, swang them legs over the edge of the bed and hit the floor. You go in that kitchen and start rattling them pots and pans," she ordered authoritatively. "Don't let this thing get the best of ye."

Little Tommie started to cry. "You see, you done got him spoilt already," she chuckled.

Annie got up from her chair and picked up the baby, cuddled him to her then sat and started rocking. He stopped crying.

Mrs. Parker sat with Annie for an hour and tried to cheer her. Annie did stop crying and was feeling much better.

Mrs. Parker rose from her chair and patted Annie on the arm. "Now you snap out of it, and get in there and see to them girls. I'll let myself out." She waddled out the front door pulling her coat around her and tying her scarf snuggly under her chin. Annie pried herself from the chair and went to the kitchen leaving Tommy in the crib, whining for attention.

Wade met Abby at her buggy. "Just a bad case of after baby blues." She told him. "Just give her lots a tender lovin' care. It'd probably do her good to encourage her to get back to her regular chores."

It seemed no one Wade consulted knew anything about depression. Oh, they knew about it, many experienced it, but, of course, it was not called depression. It was called the after baby blues if it was soon after the birth of a baby. At other times it was usually considered laziness. Annie had experienced it after her miscarriage and was able to overcome it with time and by the help of Wade's love, caring, and understanding. He had been willing to put forth the effort and take the time to give her the attention she needed. Now she was experiencing it again. There were all sorts of home remedies and many of them helped in the less severe cases. In the more severe cases, as Mrs. Parker had said, "Women pined away for the rest of their lives". In many cases their lives ended all too soon. Some from neglect of their health and some from suicide. Some were labeled crazy or lazy. Some became reclusive. "She just feels sorry for herself, a bad case of self-pity," some would say. The words self-pity and crazy only showed their ignorance of the illness. To "snap out of it" was impossible.

Annie tried to do as Mrs. Parker advised. She forced herself to get up in the mornings but did only the necessary chores. She cared for the baby and often went back to bed after the girls went to school. She would cover her head or simply stare at the ceiling. Sleep would overtake her at times but for the most part, she slept little. She became increasingly cross and impatient with the children, punishing them harshly for the least infraction.

Wade knew what he needed to do. He encouraged her to get up in the morning, went to the kitchen with her and helped her start breakfast. Before going to the sawmill or the field, he helped her get started on breakfast dishes. He spent time alone with her and initiated things that she had previously enjoyed. He also gave the girls extra attention in an effort to make up for Annie's illness.

Little Tommy never lacked for care or attention from Annie. He was the center of attention at all times and brought joy to the whole family. Annie clung to him, smothered him with attention and shielded him from anything she perceived as harmful. She robotically went about her chores with her face showing no emotion.

"I've brought my baby into a bad world," Wade heard her say softly as she rocked him and held him to her breast. *It will take some doing to get her over this but I'll do my best,* he promised himself.

******

The spring rains drenched Mississippi on this Monday morning when time came to get up for school. Wade opened Mattie's bedroom door and shook her. "Get up, girls. Your Ma's not feeling so good and ya'll need to help cook breakfast." He reached over Mattie and patted

Pearl on the forehead. "Get up, time for school." He then turned to the other bed and shook Louella. "Wake up sunshine, time for school."

"Come on, girls, rise and shine," he said over his shoulder as he left the room.

Mattie went to the window to see if it was still raining. The clouds were beginning to thin in the west and the warm sun peeked out and cast long shadows of the tall pine trees at the edge of the pasture. Sunday night had brought one of the frequent early April thunderstorms with lightning, thunder and a deluge of water. If thunderstorms still threatened, there would be no school. She was relieved to see the bits of blue sky peeking through the thinning thunderclouds. She really wanted to go to school if possible. She longed to see Frank. He was always at school if there was any way. Sometimes he rode his horse and at other times he drove the rest of his siblings in the buggy. His parents put a lot of value on education and were determined their children not miss a day of school.

Mattie made her way to the kitchen in her nightgown and put Annie's apron over it. She made biscuits while Pearl fried salt pork and set the table. Louella curled up on the bench at the table and went back to sleep.

By the time biscuits were done Wade had returned with the milking pail brimming with milk, the foam still spilled over the edge. He strained the milk through a clean cloth into a stone pitcher to remove any debris.

"I think the thunder and lighting is over but I'll hitch the horses to the buckboard and drive ya'll to school. The creek is prob'ly running over the road down at the creek." He poured the four of them a glass of the warm milk then went to the bedroom to see if Annie could eat.

"I'll eat later," Annie's muffled voice said from under the pillow.

Mattie went in to tell Annie they were leaving. Little Tommie was kicking both feet, cooing. He reached for Mattie when she got to the side of the bed. She picked the urine soaked baby up and kissed both his cheeks. "Ma, what's the matter? You sick?"

Annie moved the pillow and sat up on the side of the bed. "I'll be all right in a little while. You go on to school."

Mattie changed Tommy's diaper and put him back in the bed, then covered him with the sheet, which he promptly kicked off. Mattie tickled him under his chin. "Bye, bye."

Pearl and Louella came in and played with Tommie then told their Ma goodbye. Alma was still asleep in the other room."

"Bye girls. I want you to be good, okay?" Annie said tenderly. "You know your Ma loves you, don't ye?" Her tone had a ring of finality to it. She hugged the three of them tightly. They rushed to the front yard where Wade was waiting with the wagon.

Mattie paused at the top of the steps then turned and went back to Annie's bed. It was not Annie's way to hug them so tightly and to express her love for them. She was not very demonstrative at any time and usually kept her feelings to herself, especially when she was as withdrawn as she had been lately. Mattie sat beside her on the bed. "Are you gonna be okay here by yourself?" Annie only nodded. Mattie reluctantly left the room.

Wade returned from the school with an extremely muddy wagon and horse. He drove to the well and drew up water to wash them before the mud dried. He took his time putting the buggy and horse in the barn then fed the animals and did other chores around the barn. *I can't work in the fields today, they're nothing but mud.* Water covered the freshly tilled rows in some places and the rain had washed gullies across the fields. The creek was flooding its banks and was quite deep in places, especially down at the swimming hole at the foot of the hill.

When Wade opened the kitchen door he expected to see Annie in the kitchen feeding Alma and Tommie. The kitchen was just as the girls had left it. The table wiped clean, the dishes stacked neatly in a pan to be washed when they returned from school.

"Annie!" Wade called softly as he walked down the wide, open hallway to the bedroom. He pushed open the door to their bedroom. She was not in the bed - neither was Tommy. "Annie," he called again. *She must be in the other bedroom getting Alma dressed.* Alma was curled up in a little ball, her golden curls spread out over the pillow. He pulled the quilt over her, closed the door then went to look for Annie. He looked in every room, calling her name. No answer. Why, of course, she is at the outhouse, he thought as he went out the back door calling her name louder.

Annie was not in the outhouse. He hurried to the smokehouse, then to the barn. He stood in the barnyard, cupped his hands on either sides of his mouth, "Annie, Annie." He yelled, in one direction, then in another. He stopped to listen for an answer. He heard nothing.

Louisa heard him calling and walked out on the porch. She held a baby to her naked breast. Wade hurried down the path to her house. "Louisa, is Annie down there?" he called.

"No she ain't. You mean ye can't find 'er?"

Joshua heard the yelling and appeared in the doorway of his barn. "Is something wrong?"

"I can't find Annie and the baby. You know how she's been lately. His voice sounded frantic even though he was trying not to panic.

"Where's Alma?" Louisa asked.

"She's still asleep. If she wakes up she won't know what to think with everybody gone."

"Let me get on some shoes and I'll go stay with her while you and Josh-a-way go looking for Annie." She stuck her feet in a pair of Joshua's old high top brogans, which were laced only half way. She handed the baby to Naomi. "You watch the little 'uns whil'st I'm gone." She jumped from the porch and ran up the hill.

Wade and Joshua pushed through wet grass and waist-high weeds looking for footprints. They were soon wet to their knees.

Louisa searched the Posey house for Annie then awakened Alma and dressed her.

As Wade neared the creek he saw Annie standing near the swimming hole. She was bare footed, still in her nightgown, which was soaked with water to her hips. She was standing perfectly still staring down into the swirling water. She cradled Tommy in her arms as he nursed contentedly.

Wade was relieved to find her but also very frightened to think what was going through her mind. He had heard horror stories about women who had the after baby blues and many of them raced through his head as he stopped, afraid he would startle her if he spoke suddenly or touched her. He remembered hearing about a woman in Leake County who had the after baby blues and had walked out in the river carrying the baby with her. A fisherman was able to pull her out of the water but he could not find the baby. Two weeks later its little body washed up on the bank of the river in the pasture of one of the neighbors. The woman was said to be crazy and was committed to the asylum at Whitfield. Wade never heard whether she was ever able to return home.

Annie did not move. As he got closer to her he heard her singing very softly to the baby.

Rock a bye baby in the treetop.

When the wind blows the cradle will rock.

Sleep my sweet baby, sleep

In the warm waters, swirling so deep.

She pulled Tommie from her breast and kissed him on the cheek. Wade approached her from behind, spoke her name softly then gently pulled them to him in a bear hug. He turned her away from the muddy water, which lapped the sides of the bank. He took the baby then held Annie's hand and led her slowly up the hill. She did not resist but obediently followed him andd continued to hum. She showed no indication that she heard Wade's soothing, reassuring words. His questions about why she went to the creek or how she was feeling went unanswered.

Joshua saw them and ran through the woods to tell Louisa they had found her. Louisa was in the kitchen making Alma's breakfast.

"Is she all right?"

"She's alive but she shore do look mighty strange t' me."

"Maybe I'll just take Alma and Tommy home with me while Mister Wade gets her settled in."

"That'd probably be the best. You'll have to bring him home to nurse."

"Naw, I got plenty of milk for two. He won't never know the difference."

******

Wade knew he needed help but did not dare ask help from the neighbors. Most of them were afraid of a person they assumed crazy and would not come near, besides, he wanted to keep her condition a secret, if possible.

"When the young'uns come home I'll send one of 'em to get Delvine," he said to Annie as he changed her wet gown and put her back in bed to get warm. *I'll let her sleep for awhile, then see if I can get her to eat. Maybe I'll kill a chicken and make her some chicken soup.* He sat down on the side of the bed and watched her as her unseeing eyes stared at the knotholes and the striations in the unpainted lumber of the ceiling.

Delvine arrived the next morning before the girls left for school. "Mornin', how do?" She inquired of her brother-in- law.

"Fair t' middlin."

"Is Ann doing any better?"

"No. Same as yesterday. I'm hoping you can get her to eat something. Maybe she could eat some chicken soup."

When he put Delvine's horse in the barn he took an ear of corn back to the yard. He shelled it on the ground around his feet. "Here chick, chick," he clucked. When they flocked to his feet he picked up one and grasped it with both hands. He took it's head in one hand then swung it in a circle until he felt the neck snap. He threw the flapping chicken on the ground and built a fire under the wash pot. When the water boiled, he dunked the chicken in it and waited for the feathers to loosen, then plucked them all out. After gutting the chicken, he washed it and put it in a pot of water on the stove to cook.

Delvine spoon-fed Annie some warm milk and chicken soup. She wouldn't chew so she could not give her anything more nourishing. Her trance-like stare concerned Delvine.

"If you can stay with Annie again tomorrow, I think I'll ride over to see the doctor and ask him if he knows what we can do for her."

"Of course I'll come stay."

"Do you want me to keep one of the girls home from school to help you?"

"Naw, I can handle it. Alma's no trouble and neither is the baby."

******

When Delvine arrived shortly after sun up Wade had Prince saddled and was ready to go. The girls were eating breakfast and Tommie was kicking and playing beside Annie. Delvine picked him up.

"You're soakin' wet, you little booger. Good morning, Annie," she said spryly as she pulled the sheet from her head.

Annie squinted her eyes in the bright sunlight. She moaned slightly and turned to her side then pulled the sheet back over her, which Delvine promptly removed.

"No more of that, big sister. You're gonna get up, get dressed and help me with these younguns today. You just swing those feet to the floor and hop to it!"

She took Annie by the arm and pulled her up from the pillow. Annie did not resist. "Now you just set there on the bed and get awake while I change this big boy's diaper."

With Delvine's urging Annie ate some breakfast but did not volunteer any conversation. She held the baby and let him nurse while Delvine fed Alma.

"Alma, you go give your Ma a big good morning hug," Delvine ordered her. Alma hugged Annie tightly but Annie did not hug back. Her arms were limp and her face was void of any expression.

"Don't you drop that baby - hold onto him tight," Delvine commanded. "Keep them little naked toes covered up."

A knock on the back door interrupted Delvine's instructions to her sister. "Come in", she called.

Louisa opened the door and stepped inside. She had one baby riding on her hip. Two others clung to her skirt and stared at Delvine. One of them had her thumb in her mouth.

"Come in Louisa," Delvine said cheerfully.

"I come to check on Miz Annie?"

"You're getting better, ain't you, Annie? You gotta plant your garden next week, you have to get better." Delvine laughed and patted Annie on the arm.

"Miss Annie is there anything I can do fer ye?" Louisa peered into Annie's face.

Annie looked at her blankly.

"Tell me, is there anything I can do?" Louisa insisted.

Annie's expressionless eyes gazed past Louisa.

Delvine shook her head slowly conveying hopelessness and sadness.

"Uh, uh, uh. Lawd hep," Louisa said under her breath and shook her head slowly. "Anything I can do to hep you, Miss Delvine?"

"I can't think of anything right now. Wade's gone to talk to the doctor. Maybe he'll have a suggestion."

Louisa bent over Annie and looked in her face. "I'm gonna go back to the house and when Miz Delvine has to go home you send one of the younguns down to the house to get me." She looked up at Delvine and smiled. "You send Alma to fetch me when you has to leave."

It was late when Wade came home from the doctor. Delvine was anxious to hear what the doctor had to say, as were Mattie and Pearl.

"Pearl, take the younguns to the front room so I can tell Mattie and Delvine what the doctor told me."

Pearl reluctantly but obediently shooed all the children out of the kitchen.

"The doctor said just what Mrs. Parker did – that it's just a case of the after baby blues. He called it depression."

"What did he say to do for her? Did he send her any medicine? How long will it take her to get well?" Mattie fired the questions at him faster than he could answer.

"I told him about the spell she had when she had the miscarriage and the things I did to get her out of it. He said for me to do the same things now. He told me definitely to not leave her alone at any time and to watch her closely when she was holding the baby."

"Why did he say that, Pa?" Mattie's blue eyes searched Wade's.

"He says that sometimes when women get like Annie, they'll hurt the little one, not because they don't love 'em but because they love 'em so much they think they're better off than…" his voice trailed.

"Better off than what, Pa?" Mattie suddenly felt afraid.

"Well, you know…" He didn't finish his sentence and Mattie didn't insist because she was afraid of the answer.

"Ain't there no medicine for her?" Delvine asked, hopefully.

"Yes. He gave me something called… called…" He pulled a small white cloth bag with a purse-string tie out of his shirt pocket and handed it to Mattie to read the label.

"St. John's Wort. Will this cure her?"

"The doctor said that sometimes it helps in mild cases. He said to give it without fail like he wrote on the note inside the bag. Said he'd be coming over this way in two or three weeks to check on her and would bring some more."

"Am I going to have to stay out of school to take care of her while you plant the crops?"

166

"You don't have to do that," Delvine spoke up quickly. "You don't need to miss any school right here along the last. You sure want to graduate.

Wade looked thankfully at his sister-in-law. "I shore appreciate that. Looks like I just got to get some seed in the ground."

"To say nothing of the garden. I'll get some help from one of the neighbors with mine if I get in a tight. We don't need to tell the neighbors what's wrong with Annie. Just say she's not feeling so good. You know how some of 'em are."

Wade and Mattie agreed.

"I can cook supper when I get home from school," Mattie volunteered.

"Between us all I think we got it licked, don't ya'll?" Wade said as he got up from the kitchen table and started to the bedroom to check on Annie.

"...In sickness and in health, 'till death do us part."

27

Wade took the time from his farm labors to spend time with Annie. He made it a point every day to take her for a ride in the buggy and talk to her about the children and plans for the future. He insisted that the children talk to her and tell her what happened in school.

"If you can't think of something to say, make up something. Read to her."

Some days when the weather permitted, he took a quilt to the field where he was working and spread it under the trees at the end of the rows. Annie sat and watched Alma play in the sand, Wade plow and little Tommy crawl around on the quilt. She began to relate to the baby then to Alma. Wade kept a jar of water and snacks beside them.

Wade gave her the St. John's Wort religiously, just as the doctor prescribed. Annie began to smile and contribute to conversation. Wade was encouraged. "She'll be back to herself in no time," He muttered to Prince's rear end as he watched the fresh soil turn over behind the plow. He kept a close eye on her and the children but he did not have to fear that she would not take good care of them. She protected them like a mother hen.

"She's a little bit too protective of those two children," Delvine suggested. "She's going to spoil them rotten."

"I know." Wade was somewhat pensive. "Guess it's better than what almost happened down at the swimming hole."

******

The lavender blooms of redbud trees and white dogwood blossoms sprang to life among the sprouting new leaves of the hardwoods. The towering evergreen pines stood majestically throughout the forest, vying for space with the oaks, hickory, sweetgum and other hardwoods. Grass turned green and tiny little wild flowers bloomed across the pastures. Birds cavorted and built nests. Men were in the fields with their team of oxen, struggling to hold up the handles of the heavy plows breaking up the soil that had been packed hard by the winter rains. Soon they would have it ready to plant cotton.

Even though there were times Annie still isolated herself, she attempted to take her place as head of the house. She busied herself with housework and cooking, most of the time balancing Tommy on one hip.

Frank felt giddy with love for Mattie. The warm weather allowed him to again walk close to her and clasp her soft hands when no one was looking. They made plans to meet somewhere when they could sneak away from home, and were very creative in finding places to meet. She spent more nights with her cousins and they and their beaus helped her and Frank with their rendezvous plans.

The spring also brought out the equestrians and each Sunday afternoon was anticipated by Mattie and Frank. This was a time they could see each other without lying and sneaking around. Pearl and Mattie saddled their horses and rode to their designated meeting place. Frank and Bobby were there, waiting for them.

Today Mattie and Frank and other young people were letting the horses walk lazily along the heavily wooded road. The couples were well spaced for privacy and for a mile or so there were horses and young riders.

"School will be out in a few weeks," Frank reminded Mattie.

"I know and I hate to see it end."

"I've been talking to Papa about going to school in Jackson this summer instead of waiting until the fall."

169

Mattie was startled at his announcement. "No!" She responded, loudly. "I don't want you to go until the fall. I can't stand these Sunday afternoons without you."

"We had a letter from my uncle who owns the newspaper in Jackson. He said I could work for him and go to school at the same time. Papa said he thinks I can handle school and work if I set my mind to it."

"But I would never see you," Mattie objected.

"Maybe you could go with me." He waited for her response.

Mattie's brow furrowed. "How is that possible?"

"Well, we could get married. With what I make at the paper we could rent a room."

Mattie almost fell off her horse. "You know Pa and Ma would never let me do that!"

"We could ask them. If they won't let you, we could elope. Just ride off on Prince one day and keep riding. We could get on board the train and be in Jackson before they ever missed you."

Apprehension made Mattie's heart flutter. "You mean I would never see all my family again?"

"Sure you would. After a few weeks, they would welcome you back with open arms. I guarantee it."

"Let's wait 'till school is out to ask them, okay?" Mattie suggested.

"I agree with that."

"Frank," Mattie said softly. "You know something?" She hesitated long enough for him to wonder what she was going to say.

"Well, know what?"

"You've never officially asked me to marry you." She tucked her chin and looked at him from under her eyebrows wondering what his reply would be.

Frank abruptly pulled back on the reins and stopped the horse.

"Sure I have. Don't you remember? It was…" He closed one eye and looked up in the sky with the other.

"See, you can't remember can you?"

"Well. I guess I haven't, just in my dreams. But we've talked about it."

"That's not the same.

He swung one leg over his horse and landed in the middle of the road with a thud. He reached for Mattie's hand and pulled her down from her sidesaddle. He held both her hands in his and knelt down on one knee. Mattie giggled and he grinned showing his big, white teeth. His brown eyes laughed though it was evident he was serious.

"Mattie," he began, "I love you with all my heart. Will you marry me?" His brown eyes became serious and looked from one of her blue eyes to the other. She knew he was not joking. It was a very seriously romantic moment.

She pulled her hands from his and pulled his face up to hers. "Yes, oh yes." She pressed her lips against his.

"Hey, What's going on up there?" A male voice yelled from one of the two horses coming around the bend behind them. A girl laughed loudly.

Frank waved his hand. "You'll find out soon enough," He yelled back. He helped Mattie back on her horse.

******

Sunday morning arrived bright and sunny. The weather was warm and the air was filled with springtime anticipation. The fragrance of freshly plowed earth wafted through the air - earth that was waiting until after the last frost to be planted with cotton.

"Guess we'll be having services at church tonight," Wade called to Annie from the back door as he stepped out in the fresh spring breeze.

"Probably so."

This meant a busy Sunday. Go to church, back home for lunch, the girls out for their afternoon horseback ride then back to church. Annie busied herself with cooking.

"Annie," Wade said thoughtfully. "We really need to do something about fixing up a parlor for the girls. Mattie's old enough to start courting and she hasn't had the first beau to call on her. Think about it. Most of the girls her age are talking about marriage. Even Pearl has a beau. I seen that Colette boy makin' eyes at her."

Wade shrugged. "They're just kids."

"I told Mattie way last year sometime we'd fix up the front room into a parlor when a beau wants to come callin'."

171

"What would you like to buy to put in the parlor?" Wade could tell by the expression on her face that she was pleased with the idea of buying new furniture. Her eyes sparkled with hope and anticipation.

"I got no idea. There's not much choice here in Philadelphia."

"Next week Mr. Cook is bringing some logs to the sawmill to be cut. He's building his oldest boy a house. That'll bring in a pretty good chunk of money."

"Enough to buy brand new furniture?" Annie asked hopefully.

"If not we can put a little with it. Why don't we take the girls into town next Saturday and see what he's got to offer?"

Annie's eyes twinkled ever so slightly.

Wade immediately knew that this would be just what it would take to give Annie hope. Something to look forward to - to plan - enjoy.

Annie's eyes brightened. "Do you mean we can get a real sofa, maybe a gold or red brocade? What about two chairs to match and a table with them French lookin' legs?

"Maybe so. We'll have to look at his catalog and see how much they cost."

"What about a flowered rug and a lamp with a shade and…"

"Hold it. Hold it." Wade held his hands up in front of him. "We'll see. No promises. We'll see on Saturday. Yep, this is just what we all need. Fixin' up the parlor'll do wonders for everybody." Wade laughed and patted Annie on her behind. She giggled and put her arms around his waist.

The girls were as excited as Annie about buying new furniture. They were permitted to go with Annie and Wade to the mercantile store in Philadelphia to order what they wanted. They looked through a catalog and pored over it until they decided exactly what to buy.

The furniture came by train the next Saturday and Wade took the buckboard to the depot to pick it up. He stacked the furniture in the front room, still in crates.

"Tomorrow's Sunday and rearranging the furniture will have to wait until next week. This would be the last week of school so after that there would be plenty of time to rearrange the entire house.

The new furniture would have to stay in the crates for a few days until there was time to clean the room and put it in place.

Thursday Annie decided to start moving things from the parlor to the smaller bedrooms. Mattie and Pearl would share a room and Louella and Alma another one. She could get most of it done by the time the girls came home from school then they could put the furniture in place after supper.

After school the three girls raced up the road to the house. As Mattie started up the steps to the porch she stopped short. Annie was standing in the doorway with one hand on her hip and in the other hand she held Mattie's red, velvet box.

"Just what is this, young lady?" Annie demanded.

Mattie felt the blood drain from her face. She walked on up the steps and reached for the box. Annie snatched it out of her reach and held it behind her back.

"Who do you think you are, sneaking around with that Catholic boy!?"

"You didn't read my letters did you?" Mattie's lips quivered as she stood shaking before her raging Mother.

"I shore did. Ever' lasting one of 'em and I'm gonna burn the whole bunch."

"No! No! Ma please," Mattie begged pitifully.

"What are you, a little bitch? Sneaking 'round to see that heathen?"

"But I love him, Ma, and he loves me too," she sobbed.

"Love, my foot. You don't know what love is. I'll teach you to sneak around. I'm gonna beat you to a pulp. You get in here, right now."

She grabbed Mattie's arm and pulled her toward the kitchen.

Mattie wrenched from her grasp, snatched the box from her hand then ran as fast as she could toward the barn.

"You come back here, right this minute, Mattie Parilee or you'll be sorry," Annie screamed angrily.

"I'll get you when you do come in," Annie screamed after her.

Mattie scampered up the ladder to the hayloft. She sat on the hay and hugged her treasured box of letters and poetry and allowed her tears to flow uncontrollably. When she heard someone climbing up the ladder into the loft, she hid the box under the hay.

"Ma sent me to tell you that you'd better come to the house," Pearl called to her from the top of the ladder.

"I'm not coming in," Mattie said between sobs.

Pearl sat down beside her. "What you gonna' do? You can't stay out here all night. You have to come eat supper."

"I'm not hungry."

"I'll sneak you some supper out after dark. What can I tell Ma?"

"Tell her I'm not ever coming back inside."

"You can't stay up here forever. What you gonna do?"

"I don't know yet. I'll think of something. You better go back inside. She'll be mad at you too."

Pearl backed down the ladder but stopped on the second rung. "You'd better hide that box where Ma can't find it or it'll be gone by tomorrow."

"She won't find it where I'm gonna put it. Besides she's too scared of heights to climb up here."

Mattie looked around the loft until she found a safe place for the box. She took off one of her petticoats, wrapped the box securely in it then tucked it deep in the hay. She sat very still when she heard Wade come into the barn from the field, feed Prince then go to the house. She peeked out a crack in the loft and saw Annie meet him out by the well. Mattie heard her accusatory voice clearly. Wade turned and walked back to the barn. He stopped at the gate.

"Mattie, get down from there and come to the house right this minute! Do you hear me? I mean it, you have to get your just dues and I better not have to come out here again to get you. Do ye hear me?"

"Yes Pa," she answered, barely audibly.

He turned and walked back to the house.

Mattie dried her eyes on her skirt, sat there a few minutes, then slowly backed down the ladder. She went to the stable and patted Prince, buried her face in his dusty mane for solace, then walked slowly toward the house. Darkness cast deep shadows around the house and barn.

Mattie walked past the well then past the smokehouse. Annie stepped out of the shadows in front of her. She held the leather razor strap in one hand and reached out and grabbed Mattie's arm by the other. She dragged her through the door of the smokehouse and closed the door. The fingers of her left hand dug into Mattie's arm so tightly Mattie could not pull free. Annie raised her right arm above her head and the strap fell across Mattie's back. Mattie screamed. Another hit her on the shoulder, another on the cheek.

"No Ma, no, it hurts, please stop."

"I'll teach you to get involved with them Cath'lics!" Annie screamed as she swung the leather strap repeatedly. "Promise me you won't do it again. PROMISE ME!"

"I won't, I won't, I promise!"

"Swear to me Mattie, swear to me!" she screamed in gasps as she repeatedly swung the strap across Mattie's back.

"I swear, I swear."

Mattie pulled from her grasp and huddled in a corner by the meat box, which emitted the strong odor of the salt pork. Annie swung the strap again and again, striking Mattie on the head, back and arms, stopping only when she was exhausted. She opened the door to the smokehouse, then closed it and pulled the chain through a hole in the door. Mattie heard the heavy metal lock snap.

"Ma, Ma!" Mattie screamed.

Pearl heard Mattie screaming but was too afraid to intervene. Wade showed no indication of hearing anything. He was content to let Annie punish Mattie for her rebellion – punishment, which he felt she deserved. He sat silently, and ate his supper. No one spoke a word.

Annie came back through the kitchen door, walked to her bedroom, picked up Tommy, sat down in a rocking chair and started rocking. She hummed softly.

Mattie shook the door hard. "Ma! Ma!" Her back, arms and legs were stinging painfully. She put her hand to her face and felt blood running from the whelp on her cheek. She cried until there were no more tears. She sobbed for a long time then sat quietly with her arms hugging her knees.

She could hardly bare the stench of the rotting potatoes and onions. The salted meat in the box and the smoked meat hanging from the rafters emitted a horrible odor. She moved to sit by the door. Rats and mice rattled the empty molasses cans in the corner. The door was fastened by a chain looped through the door and held together by a padlock. Mattie shook the door, again with all her strength. "Ma, Ma!" she screamed as she pounded on the door with both hands. "Ma! Ma!"

"Maybe Pearl will come let me out," she said aloud. But Pearl had gone to bed and had the covers pulled down tightly over her head. She was too afraid of Annie to try to help.

Slivers of moonlight cast streaks of light on the floor through the cracks of the smokehouse. It was a welcome sight to Mattie. At least some of the darkness had to flee in its presence.

Exhausted, the open wounds over her body stinging, she sat huddled in fear. After what seemed hours she heard Buster barking, then a low whine. Footsteps approached the smokehouse. She sat still and listened. *Maybe Pa is coming to let me out. If its Pearl I hope Ma didn't hear her leave the house. Ma will beat her if she tries to help me. It's somebody Buster knows,* she determined from his low whine.

The footsteps stopped by the door and the chain rattled on the door. "Mattie, you in there?"

"Naomi! Thank God you came to help me. See if you can get the chain off the door?"

"I sho' can't. It's locked up tight."

"I'm thirsty. I wish you could get me some water."

"Let me see what I can do. I'll be back in a few minutes," Naomi whispered through the door.

"Don't let Pa or Ma catch you!"

Mattie heard Naomi's bare feet running down the path to her house. She was back in a few minutes tapping on the back of the smokehouse.

"I'm back here," She whispered softly.

"What are you doing?"

"I went 'n got my pappy's hammer. There's a loose board back here and I'm gonna pull it off to get you out." Buster wagged his tail and nudged her as she pulled the nails out of the boards. At the slightest noise she would stop for a long while and listen.

Mattie crawled cautiously to the back corner of the smokehouse where Naomi was pulling on the board. Mattie pushed from the inside and the board pulled loose letting in the moonlight. "I can't get through that, we'll have to take off another board." She pushed on another board while Naomi pulled out the nails with the hammer. With the second board off Mattie squeezed her slender body through the hole in the wall.

"You shore do look a mess!" Naomi said as she shook her head slowly from side to side. "Does that hurt?" she asked pointing to Mattie's cheek. "Come on down to my house and we'll get you cleaned up."

"I can't go down there. What if Ma comes out and finds me gone? If she finds out ya'll are hiding me your whole family will be in trouble."

"If she comes down there lookin' fer ye. You can run in the woods an' hide. I won't tell a soul. Ain't you hongry?"

"More thirsty than hungry."

They pushed the boards back in placeas tightly as they could and made their way down the path.

"How did you know I was in there?"

"Law me, honey, You woke the dead with that screamin'. I heerd you all the way down to the house. I run up here to see jist what was goin' on. I heard yo Ma beatin' ye and I hid behind the house. I run back home and tole my mammy. She said it'd be up to me to hep ye 'cause if'n she did she'd be in a heap a trouble. You know, with me bein' a youngun, an all, they won't say much to me. Come on lets go in the kitchen door. Pa is sleepin' like a log. He won't never know we're in there."

Louisa paced back and forth on the back porch. "Mattie, is you all right?" She held the door open. A dim light came from the oil lamp sitting on the kitchen table.

Naomi and Louisa helped Mattie take off her dress, which was soaked with blood.

"Oh Lawdy mercy, my chile, what has yo Ma done to you this time? This is the worstest beatin' I ever seen. Oh you po' chile." Louisa moaned, shaking her head slowly. "Let me wash you off. Naomi get her a drank of water."

Naomi filled the goard dipper with water, which was in a wood bucket of water. Mattie drank thirstily, then handed the dipper back to Naomi to put it back in the bucket.

"I don't know what in God's big worl' 's happen't t' Miz Annie," Louisa droned. "I think she done jist 'bout los' her min'. I been thinkin' she a whole lot better but now I jist don't know. You po' pitiful chile, uh, uh, uh. What wuz the beatin' 'bout this time?"

"Ma found the letters from Frank…"

177

"You mean the ones from the little Cath'lic boy?" Louisa interrupted.

Mattie nodded, then suddenly arched her back. "Ouch."

"This antiseptic sho gon burn a bit. If'n you cain't stan' it you tell me." She dabbed a little on one of the open, bleeding stripes. "Say she fount yo love letters, huh? What was in 'em?"

"Nothing bad, you know that. I showed you most of them. A lot of it was poems. She was mad because I sneaked off to meet Frank."

"I tole you long time ago that deceivin' 'll ketch up with ye. You know the old sayin', 'O-o-oh what a tangled web we weaves when first we practices to deceive'."

"How else was I going to see him?"

"I know, I know, sweet baby. You jist fell in love with the wrong fella, tha's all I got t' say." Louisa patted her shoulder.

"Mama, you know a girl ain't got no control 'bout who she falls in love wid."

"What 'cha have to do is be careful who ye 'sociate wid. Jist don't go 'sociate'n wid de wrong kinda people."

"Mama!" Naomi chided. "Are you sayin' Frank was the wrong kinda' people?"

Mattie turned to look at Louisa, wondering exactly what she meant.

"No, I ain't sayin' that atall. Far's I know twernt nothin' wrong with Frank 'cept he's Cath'lic. If'n Mattie had a knowed from the beginnin' he wuz Cath'lic and that her Ma wuz gonna object she could'a jist kep' 'er distance. That's all in the worl' I's sayin'."

"I'm glad I fell in love with him," Mattie said, a touch of defiance in her voice. "I'd do it all over again in spite of the beating and every other unpleasant thing that's happened. As far as I'm concerned there is no other boy in the world for me. I'll never love anybody but him." She jutted her chin forward and squinted her eyes. "I promise you one thing, I'm gonna be with him one way or another." Her jaw was set in determination.

Louisa stopped dabbing at the bleeding cuts on her back and walked around in front of her. She took Mattie's chin in her hand and tilted her face so she could look her in the eyes.

"The Good Book says 'don't say I's gonna do sech and sech tomor', say if it's the Good Lawd's will, I's gonna do sech and sech tomor'. Now you don't go an' let yo stubbornness git you in mo' trouble." She let go of Mattie's chin and returned to her task of dabbing antiseptic on her raw back.

"What about Isaac, is he the right kinda fella fer me?" Naomi couldn't help ask her Mama. *Now might be a good time to tell her we're thinkin' about marrin'.*

"If'n he twern't I wouldn't 'a put up wid him hangin' round ye all these monts. I tell you one thing, that's 'sactly why ye pappy run that boy 'a Roscoe's off'n da' place."

"Pa run 'im off!? I thought he jist didn't show up like he promised? Ain't no wonder he looked so confused when I slighted 'im at church."

"Uh-oh, look like I done run off at my mouth one time too many." Louisa glanced at her daughter. She was glad Naomi was smiling. "Runnin' 'im off wuz the best way a gettin' shed uv 'im. Guess if Isaac be's the right one you's glad we run ole Roscoe's boy off."

"I guess so." Naomi shrugged. "What you gonna say if'n Isaac axs me t' marry 'im?"

"Yo pappy ain't gonna let you marry no man 'til you got a good place to live and he gots somewheres t' work. You ain't movin' in here wid a pile 'a younguns. Yo man'll have to stan' on his own two feet. No spongin' off'en rel'tives."

Naomi looked at Mattie and shrugged. She thought it best to change the subject. "Think you could eat sumpin'? Mama had some milk and bread lef' from supper."

"I couldn't swallow a bite."

After Louisa washed all the cuts and bruises, she rubbed salve on them, which soothed the burning from the antiseptic. She helped Mattie back into the torn dress. "I'd give ye some clean clothes but your Ma'd know I'd hept' ye. I sho' hope she don't fin' out." She shook her head.

"She'll never know. I'm just glad you got me outta there. Rats were running everywhere. Thank you." She put both arms around Louisa and squeezed her. "What would I ever do without you?"

"Well, you sho welcome but you know you's gotta go get back in that smoke house 'an wait fer mo'nin', don't 'cha? Naomi can go and set with ye. When she hears the chain comin' off the do' she can sneak out the hole in the wall and run home. You ain't gonna tell is you?"

"I swear on a stack a Bibles," Mattie promised.

Louisa thrust a quilt in Mattie's arms. "Take this for ya'll to cuddle up in."

The night seemed like it would never end. The two girls sat huddled on the quilt beside the hole in the smokehouse and talked. They watched as the moon slowly followed its trajectory across the night sky. It had been sometime since they took time to share their secrets. Mattie felt badly that she had neglected her dear friend.

"Are you still reading, like I taught you?" Mattie asked.

"I sho' am. I've teached' the little uns to write their letters and do some addin' and s'tractin'. Ever one uv us can read an' write a little bit, just from you teachin' me. It's jus' like my mammy always say, 'If'n somebody does you a favor and you can't return it to them jus' pass it on ta somebody else'. That's 'sactly what I been doin', passin' it on to my brothers and sisters. Pa said he 'spects one of us'll be a teacher one day 'an come back to Philydephi and teach other colored chillun' to read 'n write."

"That would be great wouldn't it? I heard Pa tellin' Ma a colored school's gonna open in the next few years."

"Ye don't say? I ain't heered my pappy say nothin' 'bout it." She lowered her voice and a little regret crept into her next words. "It'll be too late for me though, won't it? I'll be too old to go to school with the little young'uns. Besides that, Isaac's already axed me to marry him,"

"He has?" Mattie was surprised. "Why haven't you told me before now?"

"When could I 'a tole ye? You been so busy wid sneakin' 'ron wid Frank I ain't had no chance!"

"Are you gonna do it?"

"Yep! Soon's somebody'll take him on as a sharecropper and give us somewhere's ta live. You heered what my mammy say."

"I'm really happy for you." She instinctively reached over and hugged her. "If you love him you better marry him while you can."

They talked until the eastern sky turned into hues of pink and purple.

"You better go home, before Ma comes out and catches you out here."

"You're right. Give me the quilt. Are you sure you gonna be alright?"

"I don't know. I'm scared, Naomi. I'm really scared."

"Call me 'fo she beats ye to death. She could kill ye, ye know? I'll hep ye even if it do get me in trouble. Now crawl back in there and let me shove da boa'ds in place."

Mattie crawled back through the hole and Naomi pushed the planks back in place. "Don't nail them, it'll make too much noise. I'll put them in place later."

"Okay," Naomi whispered loudly through the wall. "I'm gone now."

Mattie moved closer to the door and waited. When she heard the key opening the lock outside the smokehouse door she moved back in the corner against the loose boards just in case Annie was bringing the leather strap again.

"Mattie!" Pearl called as the door eased open. "Mattie, Ma said you can come out now."

Mattie emerged from her dark corner. Her hair was stringing down her back and in her face, which was dirty from wiping her tears with her dirty hands. Her cheek was swollen and her eye was almost swollen closed from the lick on her cheek.

"I wanted to come help you," Pearl said sympathetically, "but I was scared of Ma."

"She would have beat you, too. It's best you didn't."

Mattie and Pearl went in through the kitchen where Annie was washing the dishes. Wade had already gone to the field to plow and the girls were ready for school. Mattie gave wide berth to Annie and refused to look at her.

"Do you think you've learnt your lesson?" Annie sneered, her eyes snapping fire.

"Yes, Ma." Mattie felt fear and something akin to hate inside her as she went to the bedroom and locked the door. A glance in the mirror warranted a closer look. She examined her swollen eye and winched as she gingerly touched the large whelp on her cheek. She pulled off her dirty, tattered clothes and eased under the sheet, flinching as the rough fertilizer sack sheets rubbed the raw places on her body. Exhausted from crying and the pain of her body, she lay still and was soon asleep.

28

"Where's Mattie?" Frank asked Pearl when they met at the crossroads the next morning.

"Mattie's sick..." Pearl hesitated. "Well, not really sick...she's..."

"She's what?"

"Ma found the letters you wrote her and..."

"Oh no! What did she say about them?"

"Plenty, but mostly she beat Mattie and locked her in the smokehouse. She threatened to burn the red box and the letters."

"I'm going over to see about her right now," he said as he turned to go back down the road.

"No, please don't!" Pearl pleaded. "Believe me it will just make it worse on her. Ma might beat her again, and believe me she can't take another beating like last night."

"Then I'll go tonight," he said resolutely as he stalked off toward the schoolhouse. When he got to the classroom he asked Mrs. Hampton if he could leave for the day.

"Sure, since this is the last day we won't be doing anything but getting our report cards and saying goodbye."

Frank did not feel like talking to anyone, much less saying goodbye.

Mrs. Haney was surprised to see her son back home so soon.

"Mama, you just won't believe what has happened to Mattie," Frank's lips trembled.

"Frank, you are shaking all over sit down and try to calm yourself."

He sat down at the kitchen table and drank the glass of water she handed him. Then he told her about Mattie being beaten for seeing him.

"Did Pearl say she was all right?"

"She didn't know. She said Mattie went inside and went straight to bed. I want to go over and see about her."

"You can't do that. When your papa gets home we'll talk to him about it."

"I can't wait until tonight. Where is he?"

"He has gone into town and will be back in a little while. Poor, poor Mattie. I hope she's going to be all right. She doesn't deserve to be beaten."

"She certainly does not," Frank said, then laid his head on his folded arms on the table and cried.

"I'm sure you are hurting, Frank but we'll do something as soon as your papa gets home."

"Her Ma was going to burn the velvet box and the letters and poems I wrote her. Mattie loves those poems," Frank sobbed.

Mrs. Haney sat beside him, stroked his hair and patted him on the back assuring him that it would all turn out right.

Puppy love, she thought, *it can hurt as much as the real thing.* It didn't occur to her that it might be more than puppy love.

When Mr. Haney came home Frank related the entire event to him.

"You know we shouldn't interfere in their family affairs."

"But it's because of me. The least I can do is go see if I can make things right," Frank pleaded.

"You're right, Son. Give Mr. Posey time to come in from the fields and I'll go with you."

Frank went to his room and wrote Mattie a letter. *Maybe I can sneak it to her if I don't get a chance to talk to her alone.*

"Papa, I'm going to ask Mr. and Mrs. Posey if I can marry Mattie," Frank told his father as they rode their horses over to the Posey's house.

Mr. Haney was shocked that he was thinking of marriage but thought it best that he not object at the moment. He wanted Frank to get his education and, besides, Mattie was not Catholic. He decided to wait until after tonight to voice his objections. "I don't think they will give their consent. Not after what happened last night."

"If they don't, we'll just find a way," Frank added firmly. I will NOT let her stay there and be beaten again."

Mr. Haney wanted to object but felt it best to wait. He decided not to ask questions since he knew Frank was not thinking straight. *Just give it a little time. It will pass,* Mr. Haney reasoned. *His pain will lessen with time and when he goes off to school he'll find another girl.*

******

The Posey's were eating supper when they heard the clicking of the horses' hooves coming up the driveway. The dogs ran from under the house and barked loudly at the strangers. Wade pushed his chair back to go to the porch and greet the visitors. Louella and Alma scrambled from the bench and started to follow him.

"Get back up there! You'll know who it is soon enough," Annie scolded them.

"Howdy!" Wade called, as he peered into the darkness, not sure who he was greeting. "Come on in!"

"Thank you kindly, Mr. Posey. My son and I would like to talk with you. Do you know my son Frank?" he asked, pointing to Frank with a nod of his head.

Frank extended his right hand and Mr. Posey reluctantly grasped it.

"Good to see you, sir," Frank spoke, nodding politely.

When she heard Frank's voice Mattie left the table and hurriedly went to the front porch. Annie started to reprimand her but by the time she opened her mouth to do so Mattie was already at the front door.

Mattie nodded to Mr. Haney and glanced at Frank without moving her head.

185

"Come on in." Wade hesitated then led the way to the front room where several chairs sat around the cold fireplace.

Frank gasped when he saw Mattie's swollen face and the gash across her cheek. Her eyes were red and swollen.

"Annie!" Wade called.

Annie appeared in the doorway, her fists pressed tightly in her apron pockets.

Frank and his father rose from their chairs and nodded to her. "Good evening, ma'am," They greeted her in unison. She did not respond. She just stood in the doorway and glared at them. Suspicion and hostility boiled inside her and showed in her squinted blue eyes, the set of her jaw and the thin tight line of her lips.

"Come on in and set down," Wade ordered her. She reluctantly sat on the edge of a straight chair in the corner, folded her arms to her chest and glared at the two visitors through narrowed eyes.

Mr. Haney cleared his throat and hesitated briefly not knowing exactly how to start. He knew it was not his business how they disciplined their child so he could not broach that subject. Wade and Annie waited, staring at him expectantly. Mattie squirmed in her chair and studied her trembling hands, which were clenched in her lap.

"I brought my son over here to see Mattie. You see…"

"Mr. Posey," Frank interrupted, "I want to ask you if I can marry Mattie."

He blurted it out while he had the nerve, not waiting to soften the issue or lead up to it gently. Mattie's head jerked up to look at him then at her parents, anxious to see their reactions. Annie moved to a half standing position then quickly sat back in the chair when Wade spoke up.

Wade chuckled nervously, a smirk on his face. "Why son, you ain't never even come courtin' her. How could you expect to marry her?" He spoke condescendingly directly to Frank ignoring the pleading eyes of Mr. Haney who was trying to convey the need for understanding.

"Sir, I…I…" Frank stuttered.

Wade interrupted. "Mattie, did you know this boy was gonna come ask for your hand in marriage?"

"No, sir, but…"

"But what? You know exactly how we feel about you marrin' a cath'lic."

"If that is the only objection," Mr. Haney interjected, "we can talk about the difference in our beliefs and we may be closer than you realize."

"Our preacher has done warned us about lettin' our young'uns get involved with the likes of you. Me 'n Annie's done talked about it and there ain't no way one of our younguns is gonna marry a cath'lic." Wade's jaw was set and his eyes squinted as he stared at Mr. Haney.

"Please, Pa, please. I love him and I want to marry him." Mattie was willing to beg, grovel if necessary to get him to concede.

"I love her and I'll be good to her. I have a job waiting for me in Jackson…"

"There ain't no use talkin' about it no more," Wade said, rising from his chair. "We done made up our minds. Now I think it best you both leave." He picked up Mr. Haney's hat and thrust it at him.

Mr. Haney started to speak but Wade stopped him. "Just don't say nothin' else, sir. I don't want to have no words with ye."

"Mr. Posey, please…" Frank began.

Wade glared at Frank. "That goes for you too, boy!"

"Pa, just listen to us, please," Mattie pleaded. Annie glared at her so she knew better than to say anything more.

Mattie walked out with the two of them. In the darkness of the porch Frank slipped a note to her, then defeatedly walked down the steps and out to his horse. He turned to look back at Mattie but she had disappeared in the shadows cast by the oil lamp from the bedroom.

Mattie went to her room and fell across the bed and cried.

Wade opened the door. "If you know what's good for you, young lady, that's the last we'll hear about that," he said harshly, then slammed the door.

Mattie clutched the note in her hand, then got into bed with her clothes on. She would have to wait until daylight to read it. She slept little.

At sunrise, Wade opened the bedroom door. "Breakfast is ready girls. We have to start hoeing cotton today."

The girls threw back the sheet and immediately started putting on their work clothes. They hurried to the breakfast table. Mattie took a small amount of scrambled eggs and biscuit on her plate and forced it down her restricted throat. She said nothing. Annie and Wade mercifully said nothing to her.

Mattie took her plate to the kitchen and put it in the hot pan of water on the side of the stove then went outside and picked up her hoe. She walked fast to get to the field before the others.

It was only after she was alone in the field that Mattie dared to read the note from Frank. She propped her hoe against a tree at the end of the cotton rows and sat down on the grass.

Dear Mattie,

I am writing this for you if your Papa says we can't get married. I do hope he says, yes, but just in case he doesn't, please think about the following plan. I am going to Jackson on the train Sunday after next and would like for you to go with me, like we talked about a few weeks ago. We will get married when we get to Jackson. You can leave me a letter under the rock by the side of the bridge that crosses the creek below your house. Let me know where we can meet to make plans. I will go look for the letter early Sunday morning right after sun-up.

Remember, I love you.

Frank

Mattie read the letter twice more then started hoeing. She was smiling and humming a tune as she made her plans. "Scared or not. I'm gonna do it," she said out loud. "I'll do it come hell or high water."

The three girls had made a good showing when Wade arrived in the field with the horse and plow. "I just finished plowing the back field." He called to them. "Come on to the house, I spect lunch is 'bout ready."

The food smelled good wafting from the open windows and door of the kitchen. There is nothing like vigorous hoeing to make girls hungry. Mattie had eaten very little in two days and she was famished. Her new plans made her appetite return. She ate voraciously then asked to be excused. "I think I'll rest awhile before we go back to the field." She went into her bedroom and quietly locked the door behind her. She took her tablet and pencil and wrote a letter to Frank.

Dear Frank,

I can see you Sunday afternoon at the crossroads to make plans to elope the next Sunday. That is if Ma will let Pearl and me ride our horses at that time.

I love you.

Mattie

She quickly tore the page off the pad and stuffed it in her bosom. *While we're hoeing this afternoon I'll sneak off to the creek and hide the letter.*

She lay across the bed for a few minutes then got up. "I'm going back to the field, she yelled as she went out the front door. When she got to the field she left her hoe and ran across the field to the road and down to the bridge. She put the note under the rock.

She was busy hoeing when Pearl and Louella followed Wade to the field. He had a hoe across his shoulder and was whistling.

"We're gonna hoe a couple of hours then we're gonna quit and go arrange the new furniture in the parlor," Wade announced.

"Big deal!" Mattie muttered. "It won't be doing me any good. I won't be doing any courting in there."

"You sour puss!" Pearl spat at her. "You could be happy for us."

"I just hope you don't plan on courting a catholic."

29

Sunday morning Mattie could not sleep knowing Frank was retrieving her note from under the rock at the creek. *If I could just slip off down there and see him,* she thought to herself. But she knew her father would be out early doing the morning chores and would see her from the barn when she returned. She tried to go back to sleep but just could not. She lay awake making her plans to elope.

I'll put on layers of clothes, all I can get under my riding skirt. I'll get my red box from the barn, then get on Prince and ride to the train depot. I'll have to leave him tied at the train station but he'll be okay. Everyone around knows who he belongs to.

By the time Pa misses me we'll be on the train, probably somewhere near Brandon on the way to Jackson just chugging along on our "weddin' train". She smiled in the darkness.

After she finished washing the dishes on Sunday afternoon Mattie folded her apron and went to her bedroom to change into her riding clothes. "Ma, I'm taking Prince for a ride," she yelled as she closed her bedroom door.

"Only if Pearl goes with you."

"You better get ready in a hurry if you're going with me," Mattie ordered Pearl as she slipped her riding boots on and started lacing them.

"I'll be ready by the time you are."

Mattie ran to the barnyard and whistled for Prince. He came from the pasture in a gallop. Mattie extended her hand and gave him a lump of molasses sugar then hastily saddled him. By the time Pearl reached the barn Mattie was in the saddle ready to ride. Mattie clicked her tongue and snapped the reins. Prince galloped from the barnyard and across the yard.

She did not slow the horse until she reached the crossroads. Frank was not there. She slid from her saddle then loosely tied Prince to a tree branch. Pearl saw Mattie pacing, anxiously looking for Frank when she came around the bend in the road.

"You didn't bother to wait for me. What am I supposed to do while you have your rendezvous with Frank?"

"Suit yourself. Just don't get back home before I do."

"I think I'll ride over to Georgia's house. Come by there when you get ready to go home." She snapped the reins and nudged her horse with her heels. He galloped toward the bend in the road. "Don't be late, we got church tonight," she yelled over her shoulder as her horse disappeared behind the branches hanging over the road.

Mattie heard the hoof beats of Frank's horse long before she could see him from the crossroads. He brought his horse to a halt, swung one foot across the saddle and strode over to her with a big grin. His arms pulled her close to him in a tight hug and he even dared to kiss her lightly on the lips. *After all, she'll soon be my wife.* Mattie did not respond to his kiss. In her mind kissing was tantamount to fornication. Frank could not help but smile. His smile quickly turned to a look of concern.

"You just don't know how I have worried about you," he told her as he gently touched the disappearing gash on her cheek. "Are the other places about well?"

She pulled up her sleeve and showed him the bruises. "Pearl told me the ones on my back are worse. They've just about stopped hurting."

"I'm so sorry I was the cause of this." He touched her swollen cheek gently. "I wouldn't have had this happen to you for the whole world."

"It's not your fault. Ma has always been this way. She's always been strict and has given me lots of whippings but never anything like this."

"Well don't you worry, I'll never let anything like this happen to you again." He spoke soothingly as he brushed wisps of hair from her face.

"Let's go sit by the creek."

Mattie untied Prince and the two of them walked hand in hand through the woods.

"I'll get the train tickets sometime next week and we'll take the train that leaves at four o'clock on Sunday afternoon."

"I can't let Ma and Pa see me leave with my clothes so I think I will put on a dress under my riding skirt. I need to have a change."

"Do you think you can hide a bundle of clothes in the woods and pick them up Sunday afternoon?"

"I'll try but it won't be easy. I'd sure hate to get caught."

"If you can't you can just wash one dress while you are wearing the other." They both laughed.

"Do Mr. and Mrs. Haney know about our plans?"

"No and it's best they don't. They need to be able to say they knew nothing about it after it happens. Besides, Papa says it's just puppy love. I started to talk to him about it but they've always been determined that all us kids marry a catholic."

The sun filtered through the leaves of the trees and a gentle breeze ruffled the leaves overhead. Their feet sank into the heavy layers of dried leaves, which covered the floor of the forest. Frank loosely tied the reigns of the horses to a small sapling, then searched until he found a clean, dry place to sit under a hickory nut tree. They leaned back against the trunk of the tree. Frank picked up one of the hickory nuts and threw it to the middle of the slow moving creek water.

"Will we have any trouble getting a marriage license in Jackson? You know, with us being so young...an all."

Frank threw another nut in the water. "I haven't thought about that. Do you think we look eighteen? We may have to fib about our age. Are you bothered by that?"

"No, I don't reckon. I don't want to have to come back to Philadelphia not married. I can imagine all the gossip."

192

"We'll cross that bridge when we get to it. The main thing now is to get out of Neshoba County without getting caught."

She was somewhat apprehensive, yet excited. She had never been any further from Philadelphia than Meridian and then only a few times when she would go with her father to get supplies. Her insides quivered. The thought of eloping excited her, yet she feared the consequences if they were caught.

When the shadows seemed to be getting longer they led their horses back to the road. Frank helped Mattie on Prince then held both her hands in his. "You're not afraid are you? You do want to go away with me don't you?"

Mattie nodded. The love she felt for him far exceeded the fear that reared its ugly head. She smiled and touched the blond curls that framed his face. "Will I see you before then?"

"Leave me a note every day then if either of us can figure out a way we'll go from there."

When Mattie and Pearl arrived home the rest of the family were dressed for church and ready to eat supper.

******

The sun sank behind the trees that lined depot hill just as the Posey buckboard joined the others at the Methodist church in Philadelphia. The church was a few blocks south of Main Street with the cemetery behind it. White tombstones stood like soldiers at attention and cast long shadows as the last glimmer of sun glistened on their marble tops.

Wade tied his team to the hitching post then joined the group of men who stood in a circle discussing the usual topics of weather and crops. The girls followed Annie inside the church.

Amos was busy lighting the lamps, which were perched on shelves around the perimeter of the church and on the pulpit. He pretended that he just could not seem to get the lamp to light that was over the pews in the back where all the young people sat. He called attention to it by sighing loudly and making a big display of disgust that "something was wrong with the wick". He gave up and took his place on the end of the pew. "Guess we don't need much light back here."

The girls giggled. The boys grinned.

When the organ started playing and the congregation stood for the opening song Amos made his way down the pew and wedged himself between Mattie and Georgia. He cupped his hands around his mouth and put them to Mattie's ear.

"Frank's waiting for you in the cemetery," he whispered.

Mattie pulled her head away to turn and look at him. A question formed on her face with her eyebrow. "Now?" she mouthed.

Amos nodded. "Wait till they bow their heads to pray."

Mattie eased past Amos and Georgia so she would be on the end of the pew.

"Brother Cedric, lead us in prayer," Reverend Whitley said loudly.

Mattie looked around to be sure no one was watching then tiptoed out the open door. She stood in the shadow of the church and gazed across the blackness of the cemetery. A chill ran through her. She shuddered. The moon was not shining and there were few stars to light the sky. She eased toward the cemetery and hoped no one looked out the window of the church to see her. Annie and Wade sat on the opposite side of the church but Mattie could see them still standing with their heads dutifully bowed.

Mattie stepped behind an enormous Woodmen of the World monument and stood still. Her eyes scanned the cemetery and wondered where Frank could be.

Frank raised from his squatting position behind one of the stones and waved his arms. "Psst, psst"

Mattie heard him, then saw his waving arms. She started in his direction but stepped in a sinkhole on one of the graves. She grabbed at the headstone and pulled herself up. Stories of ghosts and the walking dead flooded her mind. She groped from headstone to headstone, feeling her way in the direction of the waving arms.

"Over here", Frank whispered loudly as he walked to meet her.

"You crazy fool," she said aloud. "I almost sunk into hell getting here."

Frank laughed. "You aren't afraid of grave yards are you? We're the only live ones out here."

"Yes, I AM afraid of graveyards!" she replied emphatically.

"The dead can't hurt you. It's the live folk you have to look out for." He laughed.

"Don't be laughing at me, I can't help it if I'm afraid."

Frank cupped his hands around his mouth and made weird sounds like a ghost then suddenly jumped toward her. "Boo!"

Mattie screamed. Frank clasped his hands over her mouth and stared toward the church to see if anyone heard her.

Strains of There is a Fountain wafted from the church. He moved his hand then slipped his arms around her waist.

"Why'd you come here? Has there been a change in plans?" Her face was only inches from his. She could feel his breath against her cheek.

"No, I just wanted to see you again. I saw Amos after I left you today and he told me if I wanted to see you he would help me." He shrugged. He could feel the warmth of her body as he daringly and slowly pulled her closer to him. His arms tightened around her waist.

"I'm glad." The words were barely audible as she felt his cheek press against hers. Her arms tightened about his shoulders as she rested her head on his chest. They stood motionless, silent then started to move slowly as though they were moving to a waltz. They did not dare move their feet for fear of stepping in a grave. They had no idea how long they stood in one spot swaying to some tune inside their heads. As long as they could hear the exuberant voices joining in songs inside the church or the booming voice of the preacher they felt safe in their secret rendezvous

"One more week, just one more week," Frank said as his hand moved slowly up her back then down again. He felt passion flood his entire body but dared not let Mattie know. Mattie wanted to moan at the pain when his hand touched the still raw bruises on her back. The ecstasy she felt at his touch was far more wonderful than the pain was unbearable. Frank dared not venture more than the light touching and the closeness of Mattie. He respected her purity and her determination to stay that way until their wedding night.

Reverend Whitley's booming voice bellowed through the open windows drowning out any sounds of crickets, frogs or other sounds of the night.

Mattie pulled away. "Look! A shooting star!"

"That's a good sign; don't you think? One more week. I can't wait."

"I'd better go back inside." She let her arms slide from around him and he reluctantly pulled away from her soft body.

Frank grasped her hand. "Follow me." They made their way slowly through the stark monuments. They stopped behind the Woodmen of the World monument near the edge of the cemetery to say goodbye.

A figure appeared in the doorway of the church.

"Pa!" Mattie gasped. Her knees went weak.

"What'll we do if he comes out here?" Frank whispered.

"You sneak off and hide. I'll tell him I'm sick." In the midst of all the confusion, Mattie could almost hear Louisa's words: "Oh what a tangled web we weave when first we practice to deceive."

The figure advanced toward them. "Mattie, Mattie." A low voice, almost a whisper rang through the tombstones.

"Amos!" the two of them said almost simultaneously.

"Mattie, you'd better come back inside."

"Next Sunday!" Frank whispered; then he was gone.

Mattie exhaled in a sigh of relief. "I'm right here," she whispered as she stepped from behind the simulated tree trunk monument. Frank was nowhere in sight. The two of them walked back to the church then quietly took their places when all heads were bowed during the closing prayer.

30

Mattie's happiness could not be concealed the rest of the week. It was manifest by humming, playing with little Tommy and bustling around to complete her chores.

"What's going on with Mattie?" Wade asked Annie after hearing her singing while hanging out the clothes.

"I don't see any difference in her."

Of course, Annie was in her own little world most of the time, oblivious to what was going on around her. She did manage to methodically do her normal chores with a lot of help from the girls.

"Well, something's going on, I tell you that," Wade declared. "She would bear watching if you ask me." He sloshed water from the well bucket into the watering trough.

******

"What are you planning?" Pearl whispered as she and Mattie washed breakfast dishes.

"Planning? What makes you think I'm planning something?" Mattie grinned.

"I just know you are. I sure hope you don't get caught. Are you and Frank gonna elope? C'mon you can tell me."

"If I don't tell you, Ma can't beat it out of you."

"It's so exciting," Pearl giggled. "I sure hope they won't stop me from marrying Bobby when the time comes."

"They probably won't since he's a Methodist." Mattie's sarcasm was evident.

"He's coming to court me in our new parlor next Sunday afternoon, if Pa don't run him off."

Mattie whirled to face her. "No, not next Sunday! You need to go riding with me so Pa won't get suspicious."

"So you're planning it for next Sunday!"

"Pearl, please. I need your help."

"I'll talk to Bobby at church Sunday, maybe we can work something out."

"Mattie! Pearl! Time t' get going." Wade called from the back yard.

"I'll tell you more when we get to the field."

Pearl opened the kitchen door and saw Wade leading their two horses across the back yard. The bridles were in place and the trace chains were looped and attached to the mules' collars. Wade led them in the direction of the cotton field where the plows were left the day before.

"I hate plowing those dang stubborn ole mules," Pearl said as she sloshed the dishwater out the back door.

"It doesn't matter whether we hate it or not, we still gotta do it." Mattie wiped the tabletop with a quick swish of the dishcloth sending crumbs scattering across the kitchen floor. "Ma says that's the price we pay for being born girls instead of boys."

"I still hate it but not as bad as I hate pulling on a hoe handle."

"You'll get that pleasure next week after we finish plowing that cotton field today." Mattie paused with one hand on her hip grinning at Pearl's back. "You notice I said, 'YOU will get that pleasure'."

"You mean WE, don't you?" Pearl said sarcastically.

"No, I mean, YOU. I'll be far away from here this time next week, just jogging along on the weddin' train." She did a little jiggle with her upper body and couldn't help let a smirk mar her face.

"Well don't rub it in!"

"Mattie, Pearl! Get yourselves out here!" Wade yelled from the edge of the yard.

"We're coming." Pearl yelled loudly and took her work bonnet off a nail on the back porch.

"Louella, it's your time to sweep the kitchen," Mattie called loudly from the back porch as she tied her bonnet under her chin and followed Pearl down the path to the field.

******

Mattie could hardly sit still during church the next Sunday. She was so restless she could not sit still another minute so she went outside to the outhouse. She noticed Wade watching her out the window and chuckled to herself yet hoped he would not be suspicious for the rest of the day. On Saturday she had carried a bundle of clothes to the woods along with her red velvet box and buried them under a pile of leaves and brush. All she had to do now was to put another dress over this one, put her riding skirt over it, saddle Prince and ride.

When the dishes were all finished she made a big deal of going to the bedroom to take a nap. "After my nap I'm going riding. You going with me?" she asked Pearl loud enough so her parents could hear.

"Sure am. This time you better not run off and leave me," she winked at Mattie.

Mattie carefully layered her clothes so the ones underneath would not show then tied a lace scarf around her bouffant hair and hurried to the barn. Her face was flushed with anticipation. She felt her heart would pound out of her chest. Perspiration moistened her forehead. "I hope Pa's asleep settin' all reared back in that rocking chair," she muttered to Pearl as they saddled their horses.

"Wouldn't count on it. Fact be known, he's got one eye cut around toward the barn watching every move we make."

"You are going to try to keep him occupied when you get back to the house aren't you?"

"I'll try, but you know how hard it is to keep up with Pa when he saunters across the fields looking at the crops."

Mattie's hands shook as she fastened the straps to the saddle. "Please try. I'll re-pay you for this some day."

199

"I'll do my best but I'm not promising anything."

"I hope Ma and Pa don't find out you were part of it."

"They better not! I'm not hankerin' for a beating like you got."

"If Bobby will be convincing I believe it will work. You did tell him not to tell anybody, didn't you?"

"He won't tell, I know he won't. He seemed excited to be able to help, especially after I told him about how Ma beat you."

Mattie reached through the gate to lift the latch and swung it open wide enough for her and Prince to get through. Pearl followed them riding Socks then fastened the gate behind her. Mattie pulled herself up on the sidesaddle and adjusted the heavy weight of garments that fell from her waistline to her feet.

"Can't hardly breath with all these clothes around my waist," she muttered.

A half dozen white leghorn hens scattered as the two horses trotted gingerly across the yard.

"Pearl, run the dogs back. I'm shaking so hard I can't hardly talk."

Pearl yelled at the dogs to go back to the house.

"Where you girls gonna be if I come looking for you?" Wade called from his perch on the porch behind the wisteria vine.

Mattie looked at Pearl helplessly, unable to make a sound.

"Over at Ida's or Georgia's, as usual," Pearl yelled over her shoulder, sounding a whole lot calmer than she felt.

"Don't be racing the horses. They have to work tomorrow," Wade called to them without changing his position.

******

Bobby arrived at the Posey house at three o'clock as planned. His heart skipped a beat and he felt a lump in his throat when he saw Wade sitting on the front porch. *What I won't do to help out a couple 'a lovers! This ain't exactly what I anticipated for the first time I come callin' on Pearl.* "Evenin' Mister Posey." The words came out a lot sooner than they should have. *I shoulda waited 'til I got to the edge of the yard before I spoke.* His sleek tan horse pranced impatiently when Bobby pulled back on the reins to stop him before he trampled in the bed of zinnias bordering the yard.

Mr. Posey's feet dropped hard from the railing to the floor of the porch. Bobby jumped, startled at the sudden thud. Wade leaned forward and peered at the horse and rider. The sun was blinding to his recently sleeping eyes. "Howdy, light down!"

Bobby wrapped the reins around the saddle horn then swung one leg back over the hip of the horse. For a split second he balanced with one foot in the stirrup then landed easily on the ground. His long stride made it to the front steps in only a few paces. He made the steps two at a time and extended his hand to his curious host. "Eve'nin Mr. Posey. Hot day ain't it." Wade grasped his hand firmly, then pulled back a sticky palm. Without thinking, he wiped it on the leg of his overalls.

"Yep, looks like summer's done made it to Neshoba County." Wade cocked his head to one side and looked at him curiously. "You're Bobby, ain't you? Burdell Collette's boy?"

"Yes sir. I didn't think of introducing myself, thought you knew me."

"I reckon I do, didn't expect you here, that's all."

"Well...I was out riding and thought I'd stop by." He plunged his hands deep in his pockets and grasped the lining of his pockets to absorb the perspiration.

Wade stared at him sensing his embarrassment. He remembered his early days of courting and decided not to make him squirm. "Out riding, huh. Guess you're looking for my two riders."

"Yes sir, I..." This was harder than he thought it was going to be. "Just thought we could...uh...all ride together, like we all do...sometimes."

"The two gals said they's gonna ride over to their cousins for awhile. You might catch them over at Brother George's."

"I believe I'll ride over that way." He backed down the steps not taking his eyes off his object of fear. He missed the bottom step but recovered quickly. He nodded briskly. "Even'in." He turned and walked as calmly back to his waiting horse as his racing heart would let him.

******

201

When Mr. and Mrs. Haney arrived at the depot with Frank and his trunk of clothes Mattie was nowhere in sight. Frank's eyes scanned the surroundings hoping to catch a glimpse of Prince, maybe tied to a hitching post or to a tree in back. He was anxious for his parents to leave before she arrived. How he was going to get them to, he did not know. He had not planned that part. *Guess she'll have to jump on the train just before it pulls out, then they can't stop her.* He wiped his sweating palms on the leg of his pants then adjusted his ascot. His white shirt, coat and vest were too hot for this weather but any traveling man was expected to dress properly when traveling. A new black derby hat completed his attire.

"Think I'll go inside for a minute," he said hoarsly as he started across the creaking board platform. He pushed the door open and scanned the room. Mattie was nowhere in sight.

"Good afternoon. May I do something for you?" The pudgy man behind the counter asked. As a matter of fact that is what every one in Philadelphia called him. Pudgy. Pudgy Dodson.

Frank walked to the counter and nervously looked over his shoulder toward the door and then to the platform. His father was unloading his trunk and helping his two baby sisters out of the buggy.

"Yes sir. I need a ticket to Jackson…please."

Pudgy grinned. "Son, your Pa got your ticket last week. What you need with another one?"

Frank stared at him without changing his expression and without batting an eye. He needed another ticket and he refused to explain why. *Nosy busybody!* Frank thought.

Pudgy fidgeted and shifted from one foot to the other. "A ticket?" He hitched his pants up over his belly leaving the belt buckle lying almost horizontally on the ledge under his sagging breasts.

"Yes sir, a ticket. One ticket to Jackson." *Did I stutter?* Frank thought, but knew better than to utter the words. His upbringing did not permit him to be sassy with adults, even a nosy one. *You need to mind your own business.*

"One way?"

"One way."

Pudgy reached in the drawer and laid a bright orange ticket on the counter. "That'll be eight bits."

Frank put his fist on the counter and spread his fingers to release a silver dollar from his wet clutches. In the same motion he picked up the ticket and walked to the front door.

"Have a good trip!" The puzzled chubby man called after him. Frank nodded then let the door slam behind him.

Wade was still sitting on the porch when Pearl and Bobby came around the bend that led to the house. "Do you think your Pa suspects anything?"

Pearl shrugged. "Hope not. Do you think he did when you were here earlier?" "

"Couldn't tell. I was so nervous I couldn't talk."

"Just let me handle it. I'm used to lying for Mattie."

Little puffs of dust flew from beneath the horses' hooves as they pranced up the driveway. Bobby and Pearl tied the two horses to the hitching post at the end of the porch and took their time walking up the steps.

"Where's your sister?" Wade gazed at them out of the corner of his eyes, not bothering to turn his head to face them.

"Still over at Georgia's when I left."

"Why'd she not come back with ye?" He pulled his stocking feet from the rail and slipped them into his still laced and tied dress shoes in front of the rocker.

Pearl pulled two chairs to the front of the porch. She took her time about answering. "Dunno." She tried to sound casual but realized that was not a sufficient explanation to satisfy her inquisitive father.

"Me 'n Bobby wanted to come back early to ask you…" She stopped in mid-sentence and looked at Bobby who stared at her, anxious to hear the rest of the sentence. "Go ahead Bobby, ask him."

Bobby was speechless. He faced her, shrugged, and spread his hands toward her, palms up, as if to say 'help me, here'. He mouthed, "What?" He hoped Mr. Posey did not understand what he said.

"You know about…" She nodded her head and batted her eyes as if to say 'go on, you know what we talked about'.

But they had not talked about anything. She had said she was going to do all the talking and now she stood facing him, expecting him to give Mr. Posey an explanation. *How can she do this to me?* He felt the blood drain from his face. His lips tightened.

Wade stood in front of his chair facing them, amused at his daughter's speechless, self-conscious beau. He covered his grin by allowing his fingers to toy with his mustache.

"You know…" Pearl nudged Bobby with her elbow then leaned closer to him and whispered, …you know, about courtin' me."

"M…M…Mister Posey, Pearl and me, wondered…" he looked helplessly at the object of his affection.

"He wants to know if he can come courtin' me," Pearl blurted out.

Wade could not bear to see them stew in their predicament any longer. "I shore 'preciate you coming and asking me like a man. I'd be mighty proud for you to come courtin' my Pearlie."

He grasped Bobby's shoulder with his rough calloused hand then patted him on the back firmly. "I'll go water the horses." He briskly descended the steps and was able to suppress laughter until he walked around the corner of the house.

Bobby sank down in the closest chair and audibly released the pressure that had built up in his chest. The blood came back up his neck and to his cheeks turning them a bright red.

Pearl plopped down in the chair beside him. "Now that wasn't so bad, was it?"

31

Mrs. Haney perched on the corner of Frank's trunk and watched Kate and Theresa race across the squeaking boards of the depot platform.

"Stop running, you'll trip on the loose boards!" She smiled at Frank as he came out the door.

He stood beside her, wondering how he was going to get rid of them before Mattie arrived. He walked to the end of the platform and stared up Depot Hill to see if he could see any sign of her. *Only fifteen minutes until time for the train. Where is she? How am I going to get my parents to leave?*

Kate started screaming from the other end of the platform. Mrs. Haney left her perch on the end of the trunk and hurried toward her. "I told you not to run! See, now you have fallen and skinned your knees." She picked her up from the dust-covered floor and brushed the front of her dress with her hands. Kate held her hands out for her Mother to see the scratches on her palm. Mrs. Haney took a white handkerchief from her pocket and dabbed at the specks of blood on the tiny hands of the two-year- old. She put her pursed lips near the hands and attempted to blow the sting away. "Now, now. Is that better? Let Mother kiss the hurt away."

She kissed the uplifted palms and the little girl dropped her hands and turned to run across the boards to her sister. Her mother quickly grabbed her hand and made her walk beside her.

"Mother, why don't you take the babies home? It is so hot out here and they haven't had their afternoon nap." Frank tried to put it in the form of a suggestion but it sounded more like pleading.

"Frankie, I want to see you off." Her eyes searched her son's for understanding.

"Mother, I'll do nothing but step from this platform to the steps of the train then ride off. You can say bye now."

"But, Baby…"

"Mother, I am NOT a baby." It came out more harshly than he intended. He would not hurt his Mother's feelings for anything.

"Frankie," his father interrupted. "Your Mother just wants to say goodbye."

As if by a pre-arranged signal, the two little girls started crying. "Mo-ther, Kate pushed me."

"She pushed me first." They pulled on their mother's skirt then lifted their arms for her to take them.

"Come to Daddy." Mr. Haney said as he reached for three year old, Theresa. She pulled away from him.

"I want Mother to hold me like she's holding Kate."

Mrs. Haney looked helplessly from Frank to his father then sat down on the trunk and pulled both little girls on her lap. They screamed loudly, vying for her undivided attention.

Frank sat beside her and put his arm around her shoulder. "Mother, please. I'll be fine."

Both girls reached for him. He spread his hands helplessly. "Mother," he said simply as he took both girls in his arms.

"I suppose it would be better to take them home. Are you sure you don't mind if we leave you? What if the train doesn't come? What if…"

"Honey!" Her husband reprimanded tenderly. "He's a big boy. He'll be fine."

"Well okay," she said reluctantly and took Kate from Frank.

Mr. Haney took Theresa and put her in the buggy. Frank set Kate beside her and kissed them both. His mother stood facing him, the lace of her little white hankie escaping her grip as she dabbed her eyes. She kissed Frank on both cheeks. Frank hugged her then helped her into the buggy.

After hugging his son, Mr. Haney took his place on the seat beside his wife. "Goodbye son. Remember all the things I taught you."

"I love you!" they all called back to him as the docile pony pulled the buggy toward the corner.

"I love you!" he yelled back and reached to pull the little girls' kisses out of the air and press them to his lips. He watched as the now well-worn buggy made it's way up depot hill.

A dust devil played in the dusty street across from the depot. His eyes searched the hill for Prince and Mattie. They were nowhere in sight. In the distance he heard the low, long whistle as the train chugged toward Philadelphia from Burnside.

Pearl giggled as Bobby replayed their conversation with her father. "You said, 'Bobby, you tell him,' and I had no idea what to say. I just stood there, waiting for you to tell me what to say. I was scared plumb to death I would say the wrong thing."

Pearl giggled aloud. "You turned white as a sheet," she managed to say through her laughter. "I thought you were going to faint."

"You blurted it out. 'Bobby wants to come courtin', I thought I'd die right there in front of your Pa."

"But you didn't die, and everything turned out fine." She dabbed the tears from her eyes with her fingertips.

Their laughter suddenly stopped when Wade came from the back of the house riding Socks.

"What if he's going looking for Mattie?" Pearl was the one at a loss for words, a plan or one of her lies that would keep him at home.

"You'd better think of something to stop him!"

"Pa!" Pearl yelled loudly. She had no idea what she was going to say. She stood helplessly on the top step.

"Woah." Wade pulled back slightly on the reins. He turned to face the house as he waited for her to say something. "Well, what do you want?" He looked toward the house expectantly.

Pearl ran down the steps to the edge of the yard. "Aren't you gonna come sit 'n talk with Bobby?"

"Bobby didn't come to set 'n talk with me." He laughed. "You're the one he wants to talk to."

"But this is his first time here and you need to be cordial to him."

"Go tell your Ma to come talk to him. She's in the back yard with the little 'uns. She might even give him a bowl of that peach cobbler she had left over from lunch."

"But Pa!"

Wade clucked his tongue and snapped the reins. "Giddy-up."

Pearl stood helplessly as she watched Socks trot down the road and around the bend, toward Philadelphia.

Mr. Haney turned south off Main Street toward Tucker. The wheels of the buggy and the rapid pounding of the horse's hooves made a whirl of dust behind them as he urged the horse into a full trot. Mrs. Haney fanned the dust from her face with a little folding fan.

Mr. Haney turned to look on the back seat at the two little girls. They were sleeping head to head on the narrow back seat. Their arms dangled limply over the edge. "It didn't take long for the babies to go to sleep."

His wife did not answer him right away. Her thoughts were on her eldest son whom she had left standing forlornly on the platform of the depot. He hadn't seemed himself for the last few days. Not since he came home from school and told her about Mattie's beating - a beating by her parents. *Maybe her father did not have anything to do with the beating but, apparently he had done nothing to intervene - nothing to defend his daughter.*

She stared off in the direction of the Posey cotton field where the rows were laid out symmetrically, straight as an arrow. They were equal widths beside the road then appeared to taper off in the distance to meet in a point. At the very top of each row was a little trail of green sprouts extending the length of the rows. There was not a sprig of grass in sight as far as she could tell. She wondered if their own cotton patch was as clean and pristine. As hard as her husband and the older children had worked for the past few weeks she was sure it must be. Most of her experience in the cotton fields was limited to what was nearest the house where she could watch the children and take care of the house. Her garden and vegetable patches pretty well kept her busy while the others took care of the cotton patch. *The Posey's must be hard working folk.*

208

"A penny for your thoughts, Mrs. Haney." Mr. Haney said as he bumped his wife's arm with his elbow. "Are you inspecting Mr. Posey's cotton field?"

She turned her head toward him and smiled. "No, not really. I suppose I was admiring the long clean rows but I was mostly thinking of Frankie and how he's changed since…since you and he went over to the Posey's that night."

"Love can do strange things to a boy. He's been different all right."

"Back there at the depot…He just wasn't the same, somehow. Things would have been different if the Posey's were Catholic."

"Or if the Haney's were Methodist." His forehead wrinkled in furrows as he raised his eyebrows at her.

"I didn't think of it that way."

Mr. Haney was all too familiar with the predicament of Mattie and Frank. He empathized with them, having lived it. He had been the one who was not Catholic, falling in love with a Catholic girl. The only difference had been that his parents had no religious affiliation and had no objection to him marrying a Catholic so he simply joined the Catholic Church and thus they were permitted to marry. He often wondered what would have happened if he had refused to become Catholic. *Would her parents have threatened to disown her if she married a non-Catholic? Would she have agreed to marry me? What will we do if Frank insists on marrying Mattie?* He would never know the answer to these questions. His son had left by now. Mattie would be too far away for their love to flourish. There would be other girls. Beautiful girls. Educated girls.

His son's pain would last for a little while, then as the summer gave way to fall and fall to winter he would hardly remember Mattie at all. By Spring he would be writing home about some girl he wanted to spend the rest of his life with. He slipped his right arm on the back of the seat then let his hand rest on his wife's right shoulder. She slid closer to him as he gripped her shoulders in a hug.

******

Frank walked out to the tracks and looked to the north down the tracks as far as he could see. He felt the tracks tremble and he heard the chug, chug, chug as it gradually became louder. He turned to gaze again up Depot Hill. Nothing. No black horse. Nothing. *Where is she? What if she backed out? Worse yet, what if her Mother learned of our plan and locked her in the smokehouse? Maybe I should go check on her. How can I leave if she doesn't show up?*

The unmistakable sound of pounding horses hooves came from the back of the Depot. Frank turned to see Prince coming around the south side of the building. "Mattie!" He called as he ran toward her. "Where have you been?"

Mattie handed him her bundle of clothes. She felt shaky and perspiration poured from her red face.

"I had to take the long way around. Too many Sunday afternoon riders on the main road." She looked for a place to tie Prince and decided the best place would be in plain view so he was sure to be noticed.

"I was getting..." The shrill whistle of the approaching train drowned out the rest of Frank's sentence. He tied Prince securely beside the watering trough.

The panting horse drank in big gulps. Mattie stroked his neck and when he raised his head from the watering trough, she put her face against the white blaze on his forehead. "Goodbye, boy."

Frank tugged her toward the platform.

Billows of smoke rose above the trees around the bend and another shrill blast from the whistle pierced the air. The loose boards on the platform trembled as Frank tilted his trunk on its edge and grasped the handle, ready to pull it up the steps of the train. His stomach churned.

Mattie clutched her little bundle protectively. She felt little trickles of perspiration coursing down her back and legs. Her chest and abdomen were constricted by her tension making it difficult to breathe.

The tops of the trees were obliterated by black smoke as they stood and watched the train emerge from around the bend. The smokestack belched out enormous puffs of black smoke sending flecks of soot falling on Mattie and Frank and the platform around them.

The massive engines screeched past the depot, the huge steel drives churned slowly, reversed a half turn and came to a halt a hundred yards beyond where they stood. The bell clanged loudly announcing the arrival of the passenger car. The conductor leaned out the door and held on with one hand as he waved a greeting at the two lone passengers standing on the platform.

Frank tugged his trunk and Mattie's meager little bundle toward the open door. He was ready to step aboard when the conductor stopped him.

"Just a minute, son. It's not time to get on board yet. Let these folk off first."

The two of them stepped back to let a woman with a little boy pass. A man wearing a dark brown suit emerged and hastily made his way toward the outhouse in back of the station. The conductor walked back inside the railroad car. Frank followed him.

"May we get on now and find a seat?"

"What's your hurry? There are plenty of seats. Just hold ye hosses." He looked at Frank sternly. His heavy, black eyebrows met in the middle forming a straight line above his eyes and the bridge of his nose.

Frank's brown eyes pleaded. "We just need to sit down and re…"

"Oh all right. Go ahead, get aboard." He rolled his eyes toward the ceiling.

Frank walked briskly to where Mattie had collapsed on the edge of the trunk. "He said we could go ahead and get on. Come on." He hoisted the trunk through the door then lifted it over the backs of the seats and set it on the back seat of the railcar. It did not occur to him to check it in the baggage car. Mattie followed him down the aisle.

Mattie clutched her little bundle tightly as she looked through the windows nervously. She was perspiring profusely and her face was red. The temperature outside was ninety-five degrees and she had on three sets of clothes. She removed her bonnet and wiped her brow with her lace handkerchief.

She fanned frantically with her handkerchief. "Can you open the window?"

He opened the window and a slight breeze filtered through.

Frank bit his fingernails as he stared through the windows of the depot. "I wish they would hurry."

"Me too. I'm all shaky inside."

The lady with the little boy appeared in the doorway of the depot and started toward the train. Frank could see the conductor through the open windows of the depot leaning on the counter talking with Pudgy. They laughed and looked out toward the passenger car. After about ten minutes the male passenger came through the door followed by the conductor. When the man was seated the conductor stepped up on the step of the train and clung to the handrail. He leaned out the door and yelled, "All aboard!" as if there were any other passengers. He closed the door and the train started to move very slowly.

Mattie buried her face in her bundle of clothes and cried with relief. Frank put his arm around her, put his face in her hair and whispered softly in an attempt to console her.

They failed to notice that the train did not continue to pick up speed. If they heard the slow grind of the brakes that brought the train to a stop, they were unaware of it. They were lost in the release of their pent up emotions.

******

Pearl and Bobby listened for the low rumble of the train to approach from the north. Their chatter stopped as they listened intently for it to rumble through Burnside and approach Philadelphia from the north. They watched over the trees as the sky to the north turned a pale gray, then back to blue as the smoke from the train dispersed. Their eyes followed the trail of smoke as the train approached north Philadelphia. The blackness over the tops of the trees grew blacker as the origin of the smoke came closer. They listened as the shrieking whistle pierced the air. The clock on the mantle in the front room chimed four times.

"Wonder if Mattie made it in time?" Pearl whispered to make sure Annie did not hear.

"Dunno."

They were anxious to see the sudden puffs of smoke and the shrill whistle as the train started its journey toward Deemer, Neshoba, Union then to Newton. There the lovers would transfer to another train going west to Forest, Morton, Brandon and Jackson.

"I sure hope she made it. I dread thinking what's going to happen to her if she didn't and Ma and Pa find out she tried to elope."

"I hate to think of what will happen to you if they learn you helped her." Bobby turned to face Pearl just in time to see her close her eyes tightly and her mouth grimace at the thought.

As the crow flies it was little more than a mile from the Posey front porch to the depot. The sound of the train was becoming a familiar sound as it traveled through the center of Neshoba County to exit into Newton County on the South or to Winston County on the North.

For years the anticipation of the railroad caused a great deal of excitement as plans were made for its trajectory through the countryside. The surveyors left bright orange stakes across cotton fields, pastures, swamps and in some cases, across front yards. Top prices were paid to the landowners for the right-of-way.

As usual, there were objections to progress. The farmers claimed the noise would make the hens stop laying eggs, the cows stop giving milk and their sleep would be disturbed. There were other, real as well as imagined, reasons for their objections. Of course, most of the objections came from the people who were not getting a share of the money being paid for the right-of-way.

Now, after a year of seeing, hearing, and smelling the train most of the people had become dependent on the necessities as well as the luxuries it brought to Neshoba County. They not only enjoyed the benefits it brought in, saving trips to Meridian, but they now could set their clocks by its arrival. The train whistle announced the time to all who could hear its whistle or the rumble of the earth as it lumbered down the tracks.

"Hello Bobby." The sound of Annie's voice startled them both as she opened the door and stepped out on the porch. "Would you two like some lemonade?"

Bobby stood up and greeted her with a nod.

"That would be good, wouldn't it Bobby?" Pearl said as she indicated with her eyes for him to sit back down. He eased down on the edge of the chair.

The lemons and ice were some of the luxuries brought in by the train.

"That would be nice," he answered shyly. "Thanks." He took the cold glass from her.

The two resumed their vigil, their eyes glued to the top of the trees.

At precisely a quarter after four they heard the train whistle and saw two puffs of black smoke rise above the trees. The smoke slowly moved toward the south, leaving its trail behind.

"I suppose they're gone," Pearl said softly.

"Guess so."

32

Frank was suddenly aware that the door of the car was opening. He heard the conductor talking loudly to someone on the outside. Raising his head just above the back of the seat, he looked to the front. Mattie still had her face buried in the little bundle on her lap. He felt the blood drain from his face as his eyes met the cold, harsh eyes of Wade Posey. His grip tightened around Mattie's shoulders as he spoke her name. "Mattie." He shook her. "Mattie!"

Mattie raised her head just as Wade took her by the arm and jerked her from Frank's grip. She stumbled down the aisle behind him, clinging tightly to her little bundle. When she reached the door she looked back. Frank was following them.

Wade pulled her out the door and spoke sharply to the conductor. The conductor hurriedly closed the door and motioned to the engineer just as Frank attempted to push past him to get off the train.

"You going with us, son?" It sounded more like an order than a question. His body was pressed firmly against the closed doors.

Frank did not answer. He just stared out the window watching Wade pull Mattie toward the depot.

"I think you would be a whole lot safer staying on this train," the conductor said somberly.

The train moved slowly, increasing in speed. The conductor did not budge from his position. Frank leaned out the window and watched as Mattie became smaller in the distance, then disappeared as the train went behind a line of trees.

Frank sank down on the front seat. He felt weak and sick. Sick from a mixture of indescribable emotions.

Pudgy stood in the doorway of the depot watching. The news of this little scene would soon spread over the community. Pudgy would see to that.

******

Pearl and Bobby were still sitting in the rockers on the porch when they heard the horses' hooves clapping on the hard dirt sod of the road. Mr. Posey's horse was leading the way keeping his pace to a walk because of the heat. Prince followed him with Mattie sitting straight in the saddle

"Oh no!" Pearl exclaimed as she quickly covered her open mouth with the palm of her hand. She sank back in her chair.

Bobby gasped. "They didn't make it!"

"Bobby, you'd better go home. I'm going inside like I know nothing about what's going on."

Bobby hurried down the steps. "See ye later." He hurried to the hitching post and mounted his horse.

Pearl walked inside and let the door slam behind her.

"Is that you, Pearl?" Annie called from the kitchen.

"Yes'm."

"Has Bobby left?"

"Yes'm." She went into her and Mattie's bedroom and closed the door.

Bobby nodded at Wade when they met in the driveway. "Eve'nin, Mr. Posey."

"Eve'nin, Bob."

Bobby looked at Mattie but her sweaty face, red eyes and tightened lips told him it was best to say nothing.

Mr. Posey stopped his horse at the end of the path leading to the house and waited for Mattie to get along side him. He reached for Prince's bridle. "I'll take care of the horses. You go on inside." He spoke sternly.

Mattie slid from the saddle dragging her bundle with her. She stomped up the steps defiantly. "This ain't the end of it. You'll see," she said loudly enough for Pearl to hear through the open window in the bedroom but Wade had gone around the house to the watering trough and did not hear her.

Mattie slammed the bedroom door behind her and locked it. She slung her bundle on the bed and started removing her clothes, which were soaked with perspiration.

"If they want to beat me, they'll have to break the door down first."

Pearl started helping Mattie undress. "What happened?"

"He caught us."

Mattie's face was red and her hair was wet. She took the pens out of her hair and it fell down on her shoulders. It was a relief to get out of the shoes and stockings as well as all the skirts and petticoats.

"I'll spread these clothes on the chairs to dry," Pearl volunteered. "Was Pa mad? Did he hit you? What did he say?" she asked in fast succession.

"Yes, he was mad! He jerked me off the train but never said a word. NOT A WORD! He dragged me off that train, got on his horse and rode off. He just left me standing there."

"I guess it's coming later, Huh?"

"I ain't takin' another beating! I promise you that! Some way or other I WILL make it to Jackson before this summer is over." Her puffy eyes narrowed to a squint. She took her writing tablet from the dressing table and fanned her face. She sprawled across the bed to try to cool off.

Annie had returned to the back yard to watch the younger children play in the shade, oblivious of all the happenings of the afternoon.

******

Frank sat in the back of the train fuming. He even allowed himself to cry since no one was near him to see. His emotions were mixed. Anger, fear, worry, sadness, loneliness, apprehension. *What is Mattie going through right now?* His coat, hat, ascot and vest lay in a heap on the seat beside him. He took out his book of prayers to search for one suitable for his situation and tried to concentrate on praying but it was difficult for him to keep his thoughts on God. His anger at Mr. Posey kept rising up inside him. He prayed silently for Mattie's safety then crossed himself. He leaned his head back against the seat in exhaustion.

The train huffed into the depot in Newton where all passengers going west would have to transfer. Frank lugged his trunk off the train and sat on it staring at his feet. People milled around him but he barely noticed. *I think I'll simply take the next train back to Philadelphia and claim what's mine. I refuse to leave Mattie there to be beaten and worked like a slave.*

The conductor watched the grief and sadness of the young man he had held hostage on the train. He reminded him of his own son. No explanation was needed for him to understand the circumstances behind the scene in Philadelphia. It was obvious that two young lovers were eloping over the objections of the girl's father. At the time he felt he was doing the right thing, blocking their departure. *They looked so young, maybe fifteen or so. On second thought, the boy is older than that, maybe seventeen. I was just about his age when I married my sweetheart. That was thirty years ago. Didn't get to be with her long. The Lord took her and left me with a baby to raise. Life is short and young'uns have to marry young so's to have enough time to satisfy the passions raging inside 'em. Maybe I should not have allowed the girl's father to get on the train. If I had kept that door closed there would be two happy kids settin on that trunk.*

"May I sit down beside you there?"

Frank was unaware he was being watched and did not notice when the uniformed conductor approached him. He nodded and slid over to make room for the scrawny little man.

"Hey son, whatcha contemplatin'?"

"Nothing."

"Nothing? I know better'n that. Name's Kemp." He extended his right hand in a friendly gesture.

Frank stared at it, reluctant to grasp the hand of the man that kept him from following Mattie. "Mine's Haney." He extended his limp, wet hand.

"Sorry about keeping you on the train back there."

"You should have let me off." He shot a darting glance at the old man then looked back at his feet. "I'd be by her side right now, instead of here waiting for a train to take me further away from her."

"You might not be by her side. You might be lying in a ditch somewhere beat to a pulp by her angry father."

Frank straightened up and for the first time looked in the face of his "captor". "I never thought of that but then it is better me than her."

"Yep, I might have done you a big favor keeping you on the train. What are you considering now?"

"I'm considering catching the next train out of here back to Philadelphia." His answer was a sharp one and had the ring of determination.

"What're you going to do when you get there?" He knew it was none of his business but a little advice from the experienced to the inexperienced could do no harm.

"I'll find Mattie and take her away so fast and so far Old Man Posey will NEVER find us." Vehemence mixed with hurt showed in his eyes and in every word and gesture.

"Do you think her father will let her out of his site long enough for you to get near her? He'll probably sit up at night listening for your steps outside her window. If you continue your trip to Jackson, what will you do when you get there? Got a job waiting for you?"

Frank nodded. "A job and school."

"Would you like some advice from an old man with lots of experience?"

Why don't you just leave me alone and mind your own business! went through Frank's mind but he did not voice it. He thought better of it, having been taught to respect his elders.

"Might as well like it. I got a feeling you're going to give it to me whether I want it or not." He refused to look at his advisor.

"That's right I am. That is if you sit here long enough to listen to it."

"I'm listening. Go ahead."

"I got a feeling you're hurting mighty bad inside right now and I want to say how sorry I am about that." He paused briefly and looked at Frank's unresponsive face. Frank rolled his eyes upward.

"You need to put some space between you and your problems back in Philadelphia. If you go back now it'll be like rubbing salt in an open wound to that old man. He's not going to let you see your girl and if you show up there it'll only get her in more trouble with her pappy.

I knew a boy once who ended up dead by persisting on running away with a man's daughter. The old man shot him as he climbed up to her window. The law didn't do anything about it either. The old man claimed he was breaking and entering. If you ask me, and you didn't, mind you, but its my opinion that if you go on to Jackson, start school and work at the job you got waiting for you, things'll go a whole lot smoother when you return home. Give things time to heal."

He paused and waited for Frank to say something, anything - just stop looking at his feet. He looked at his watch. "Time for me to board the train." He stood up. "The train to Jackson should arrive shortly after this one pulls out. Good luck." He again offered his hand.

Frank stood up and grasped it firmly. His eyes softened and the hint of a smile spread the corners of his mouth. "Mister, I know you mean well and you may be right. I guess I need to think on it for a little while."

"You got about fifteen minutes."

One doesn't have to learn the hard way. He can listen to someone who has been there.

******

Pearl pulled the sheet off Mattie's head and shook her nude body. It was obvious to Pearl she was not asleep and she could understand why. How could she possibly sleep after today's ordeal? The anger, anxiety, disappointment and longing for Frank would probably prevent her from sleeping for some time.

"You'd better quit playing possum and get ready for church. Ma'll be calling us to supper pretty soon."

"I'm not playing possum. I'm asleep, if anyone asks, and I'm not going to church either."

"You know Pa's not gonna let you stay home from church!"

Mattie sat up in bed. "Do you think for one minute I am going to church looking like this? Look at my swollen eyes and face. I'm red as a beet from getting so hot today with all those clothes on. I'm so mad it wouldn't do me any good anyway - got too much hate for Pa inside me." She flopped back down on the bed and turned her naked back to Pearl. The stripes from the beating in the smokehouse were still evident. Pus oozed from the edges of one of them. Pearl shook her head and pulled the sheet up over Mattie's head.

"Okay then, you're asleep. I tried to wake you and couldn't." She pulled the door to behind her. Mattie got up, turned the wooden latch on the door facing and returned to bed.

Wade felt weary as he returned from the barn with the pail of milk. His steps were slow and his eyes focused on the well-worn trail directly in front of the next foot that was to touch the ground. Milk sloshed over the sides of the pail and the latest litter of kittens licked at it hungrily. It seemed they never got enough of the rich, warm, frothy delicacy. They had rapidly lapped their share from the hand hewn wooden bowl in the barn then followed the sweet fragrance expectantly.

A Pa's gotta do a lotta unpleasant things to keep his young'uns on the right track. It wasn't anger that made me jerk her off that train. I hated to do it, but I had to for her own good." He reasoned. *Cath'lics! Guess there ain't no need in telling Ann 'bout today. It'll throw her into one of her fits.*

The sun was sinking over the top of the trees as he opened the kitchen door. Annie was taking the tablecloth off the leftovers from lunch. He set the pail of milk on the table and went to the washstand then dipped a dipper of water from the bucket into the pan to wash his hands.

"Do you mind driving the wagon to church tonight?"

"Are you not going?"

"Naw, I don't feel so good."

"Guess so. Girls, supper's ready!" She called loudly. She reached down and picked up Tommy who was tugging at her skirt. Three of the girls ran to the table and took their usual places on the bench. "Where's Mattie?" Annie asked.

"Asleep. Couldn't wake her," Pearl volunteered.

"Mattie Parilee, you'd better get yourself out of that bed this very minute and get to this table! Do you hear me?" Annie screamed as she walked toward the bedroom.

"Let her sleep!" Wade called after her.

"What do you mean, 'let her sleep'? We need to leave for church in a few minutes."

"I said to let - her - sleep!" The words were sharp and short. Words of authority. "It won't hurt her to miss one time."

"Let her miss one time and pretty soon she'll want to miss another, then another. Then you'll have a little heathen on your hands, Wade Posey!" She pushed her plate out of Tommy's reach.

"Let's say the blessing."

******

It was well after midnight when the train reached Jackson. The heat of the engine and the smell of burning coal filled the night air as Frank stood on the platform waiting for his trunk to be taken off the baggage car. A dense fog hovered over the tracks and Gallatin Street. He looked around to see if his uncle had possibly come to meet him but he had not. *He really didn't know which train I would be on.* A dozen people stood around him waiting for their luggage.

The baggage handler unloaded his trunk and slid it across the boards toward him. Frank retrieved it and carried it inside and approached the young man at the counter. He was only a little older than himself with brown hair and light colored eyes. The sleeves of his shirt were rolled above his elbow and his bow tie was somewhat askew.

"Is there somewhere I can leave my trunk until morning? I can't very well carry it up Capitol Street."

"Sure thing! I'll be glad to hold it in the baggage room. You got far to go?"

"No, just a little way down President Street."

"Are you new in town?" He busied himself with papers scattered over the counter.

"No, not really. I lived here all my life until I moved away last summer."

"Then you know your way around. Are you back to stay?"

Frank hesitated before answering. "Probably. I'm starting to high school next week."

"Is that right? I go to school there. I'll graduate the twelfth grade next summer. Good to have you." His hand shot across the counter and Frank grasped it readily. "I'm Stephen Croswell."

"Frank Haney. Maybe we'll run into each other." Frank dropped his hand to his side and turned to walk toward the door. "I'll be back tomorrow."

"See you then."

Frank walked out into the moonlit night, down the steps and onto the tracks. The earth trembled under his feet. The quivering ground announced an approaching train a mile or so away. The haunting sound of its still distant whistle echoed through the night air.

The sky was clear. A million stars and a near-full moon illuminated Capitol Street. The stark form of the State Capitol Building was silhouetted against the eastern sky at the far end of the street. The familiar form gave Frank the feeling that he was back home. He had walked the familiar street almost every day since he was old enough to walk to the newspaper office. The Capitol Building had loomed over him every day as he neared President Street where he turned north to go home. *I'll be making this same trek starting next week, I suppose.*

Many lonely, forsaken chimneys still pointed upward over the city. Chimneys, which remained after the Yankees marched up from Port Gipson and Vicksburg and set fire to all the nicer homes in the city. So many blackened chimneys had been left pointing toward the sky that someone referred to it as Chimneyville. Many people still called it that.

Frank's grandfather's house had been confiscated by the Union Army for their use and the family had more or less been held hostage to serve the soldiers while they were there. As a return favor the Yankees had not burned their house. Frank's family had lived there, along with his uncle's family after the war until they moved to Philadelphia. He was going back to the same house now to stay with his aunt and uncle.

Frank took his time as he trudged up the hill of Capitol Street and let his eyes take in all the familiar places. He had been homesick for some time after he moved away, that is until he met Mattie. Time had passed quickly after that. He felt hollow inside at the thought of living here again without her. He had such big plans for them. There was plenty of room in the big house for the two of them until they could get a place of their own. Now, his plans had changed. *Or rather revised. I'll send her train ticket to her and she might even be here in a few days.* He smiled at the thought. His steps quickened.

There was no need to tell Uncle Thomas and Aunt Priscilla about his failed elopement, he decided. *I'll send Mattie her train ticket and maybe she can slip away soon.* "I'll start to school, study hard, work every minute Uncle Thomas will let me, and save my money," he said aloud to the North Star. Where there is a will there's a way!" He began running toward his uncle's house, which was dark but he knew the front door would not be locked.

******

Wade felt he had made a wise decision not to bother Annie about the details of the Sunday afternoon happenings since it had all been taken care of and she did not need the added stress. Besides, he didn't think Mattie needed any further punishment. He knew she was hurt and angry and it was just best to say no more about it. To attempt to console her would only bring more tears and anger. He would just keep a close eye on her for the next few weeks. Frank was gone now and she would not be tempted to slip away again. They would all go about their life as usual. Mattie would just have to deal with the disappointment.

But life for Mattie would never again be the same.

"Get up girls! Time to go to the cotton patch!" Wade yelled as he knocked loudly on their bedroom door Monday morning. He learned long ago not to open the door unexpectedly.

The girls threw the sheet back, crawled out of bed and put on their work clothes, then went to the kitchen. Pearl sat down at the table to eat but Mattie stalked out the back door. "Are you gonna eat breakfast?" Annie called after her.

"I'm not hungry," Mattie yelled back as she picked up her hoe, threw it across her shoulder and strode off to the cotton patch. Her old calico dress was one she had outgrown and struck her well above the ankles. It had long sleeves to protect her arms from the hot sun, as was the purpose of her work bonnet, which she had tied snuggly under her chin. It was important to keep the sun off so she could maintain creamy, white skin. She wore an old pair of shoes that barely hung on her feet. Half the sole was torn off but they would protect her feet from some of the sticks and briars on the way to the field. She would pull them off when she started hoeing so she could feel the fresh, cool soil between her toes.

Pearl slipped two hot buttered biscuits in her skirt pocket and walked out the back door then made her way to the field.

"Brought you some biscuits."

"Thanks, I'm starving. I didn't eat supper last night and not much dinner after church yesterday."

"Now tell me what happened at the train station," Pearl prodded anxiously as she started hoeing the grass from around the cotton.

Mattie told her every detail. "It's strange to me that Pa hasn't said anything to me about it. I expected him to fuss at me all the way home then hold me while Ma beat me."

"It's probably coming later on today." Pearl said.

Mattie stopped and stood rigidly as she stared at Pearl. "I'm not taking another beating! Do you hear me? I AM NOT TAKING ANOTHER BEATING!"

"Maybe he'll let it ride. Probably figures you've had enough punishment."

"I wish he'd go on and have his say." Mattie banged her hoe hard against the soft dirt sending grass and tiny stalks of cotton flying into the middle of the row.

"You're cutting down too much of the cotton!" Pearl yelled at her.

"I don't care if I cut it all down!" She was angry, hurt and disappointed and she vented by pounding her hoe into the soft soil.

******

Thomas Haney awakened at the sound of the dogs announcing the arrival of an unfamiliar person in the neighborhood or possibly another dog invading their territory. He wondered if it could be Frank. The grandfather clock in the hall chimed twice. The unmistakable sound of steps on the porch then a sharp rap on the door brought his feet to the floor. He pulled on his pants and padded barefoot toward the top of the stairs. The knob of the front door turned and Frank stepped over the threshold.

"Uncle Thomas! It's me, Frank," he called into the dark foyer.

Thomas appeared at the top of the stair. "Hey buddy, come on in. Let me light a lamp." He met Frank at the foot of the stairs and put his arms around his shoulders. He pulled him to him. "My, I had to reach up higher to hug you than I did when you left!

"Sorry to come in so late but I didn't have much of a choice. How is Aunt Priscilla?"

"I'm fine. Come here and let me see you." She advanced toward him with her short, plump arms spread apart. "Let's get some lights on so we can see."

The room suddenly brightened as Thomas struck a match and touched it to an oil soaked wick on the lamp on the foyer table. She pulled back from Frank and held him at arm's length. "You've grown up on us, Frankie. You hungry?" She led the way to the kitchen without waiting for an answer.

The soft bed felt good to Frank. He stretched out full length and sighed deeply. Loneliness overwhelmed him. He replayed the day's events, starting from the time he left home. He looked back at the scene at the train station and ran the "If only's" through his mind. *If only we had tied Prince behind the depot, out of sight. If only I had been watching for Mr. Posey and convinced the conductor not to open the door. If only...If only...If only.* He reached for his rosary and said his prayers, then prayed for Mattie's safety. *Tomorrow I'll write to her and send her train ticket. I'll have to send it to Mary Rose and get her to take it to her. I'll tell Mattie how much I love her and then I'll say...*He was asleep before he could write the letter in his mind.

Frank awoke to the sound of children's voices in the yard across the street. It took him a minute to get oriented to his new surroundings. Then he realized where he was and wondered what the time was. He listened for the chimes of the clock. He could see the sun shining through his window and imagined that it was early in the day. He listened for the noise of his aunt in the kitchen cooking breakfast but heard nothing. He soon drifted off to sleep again.

A tap on his door awakened him the second time. "Are you going to sleep all day?" Thomas opened the door a crack then pushed it open wider when he saw Frank stretch his arms out over the sheets.

"Uncle Thomas!" He sat up in bed and blinked. "What time is it?"

"Twelve fifteen. I came home to lunch expecting to take you with me back to the paper but you're still snoozing." He sat on the side of the bed and punched at Frank's bicep. "I hope you slept well. You were one tired turkey when you finally got to bed."

"I did. I slept very well." He threw back the sheet and put his feet on the floor. "I'll be right down."

Frank could not believe the changes as he and his uncle made their way down Capitol Street. The daylight revealed a lot of building and restoration in downtown Jackson. Some of the chimneys had been torn down and in their places new houses were being built. Some of the small houses that had been hastily built after the Yankee occupation were being torn down and replaced with stately homes fit for the elite of Jackson. New businesses had sprung up along Capitol Street and there was talk of replacing the dusty street with bricks.

"I don't expect you to start to work today, but thought you might want to come look around and get acquainted with the new fella I hired after your Dad moved off."

"I guess it's pretty much the same as it was when Dad worked there, huh."

"Pretty much. I've made a few changes. Do you think you'll be able to keep up with your school work and work at the paper as well?"

"I'll give it my best shot. Mama has threatened my life if I don't get good marks in school."

Frank had to wait until after supper to write to Mattie. He wrote the letter to his Mama first, and then wrote to Mary Rose. He would have to depend on her to get his letters to Mattie.

He took his time with the letter to Mattie. Each word, each curve of his pen was made deliberately and carefully. All the emotions of the previous day, his sincere love and devotion to her and his hopes for the future filled page after page. He told her about his conversation with the conductor and the reason he decided to go on to

Jackson. He gave her instructions on where to go and what to do should she get a chance to use the train ticket and arrive in Jackson unexpectedly. When he finished he put the letter and ticket in the envelope with the letter to Mary Rose, confident she would, somehow, find a way to get it to Mattie.

******

Mattie, dutifully and sullenly made her way to the cotton fields every day. Her hands gripped the hoe handle much too tightly as she relived the events of the past Sunday. Blisters formed at every pressure point in her hands then burst, oozed clear pus then formed hard calluses. Nothing she tried eased the pain inside her. If she got lost in thought and moved slowly along the rows the sadness and regret seemed to overtake her. When anger, frustration and helplessness became overwhelming, she pounded the hoe into the hard soil with a thud sending little cotton plants, grass and dirt on her feet. *Where is Frank? What is he doing? Why didn't he come back for me? Maybe he did and he can't get to me for Pa. Did he make it to Jackson safely? Will I ever see him again? Will he write? Even if he does, how am I going to get the letter without Pa and Ma seeing it?* The questions gnawed at her mind as she worked, then at night until she cried herself to sleep.

"Thought there 'twernt no secrets 'tween us," Naomi chided when the two of them were out of hearing of the rest of the people in the field.

Mattie did not look up. "Don't suppose there is," she answered sullenly.

"Then when you gwin t' tell me what happent las' Sunday?"

Mattie jerked her head erect, her hoe in mid-air. "What do you know about last Sunday? I ain't said a word to nobody."

"Ye didn't hafta. That Mistah Pudgy down at the depot. He done took care a that."

"Why that..., I should have known he had his big nose up to the window watching everything. Who'd he tell?"

"Probly ever'body to my notion. My Pappy heered him tellin' 'bout it up at da gen'rl sto."

"What exactly did he say?"

"I don't rightly know. I heered my Pappy talkin' 'bout it to my Mammy. I knowed better'n t' axe questions. They don't like to spread dirt on folk. So tell me, what happent?"

"Not a whole lot. Me 'n Frank got on the train and Pa stopped the train and jerked me off."

Naomi put her hand over her mouth and gasped. "What ye Pa do next?"

"That's what so strange about the whole thing." He didn't say anything…"

"Not narry a word?"

"Not a word!"

"Did he beat cha?"

"Didn't lay a hand on me."

"Guess he lef' that up to ye ma, huh?"

"Ma hasn't mentioned it either."

"Then ye Pa didn't tell her 'bout it! If he hadda you'd be fried meat!"

"That's what I figure. For some reason he didn't bother to tell her."

"Woe to you when somebody else put their nose in it and mention it to 'er."

Mattie slammed her hoe hard on the ground in an upright position. She firmly held both hands on it and leaned against it. Her squinted, piercing eyes stared straight into Naomi's. She spoke softly and firmly. "I'm not takin' another beatin' from Ma." She gritted her teeth. "I tell you that right now! I ain't - takin' - another - beatin!" She added in staccato.

"Can't blame you for that. Uh, uh, uh. Sho wisht I could do somthin to hep ye."

"Bear ye one another's burdens…" (The Bible)

229

Frank, Wallace and Kenneth casually strode up the steps to the schoolhouse then down the hall to the classroom. They were greeted jovially by their elderly teacher who was just arriving. He fumbled in his pocket to find the key to the door.

"Good morning, boys!" He extended his plump right hand in a firm handshake. "My name is Ernest Barber. I'll be your teacher for the next few weeks."

Frank grasped his hand. "I'm Frank Haney, sir. Pleased to make your acquaintance."

"I'm Wallace Overby." He clutched Mr. Barber's hand and nodded politely.

"I know this young man. How are you Kenneth? Ready for another session of summer school?"

He shrugged, then smiled. "I suppose so, at least my father says I am."

Mr. Barber laughed. "Come on in and find a desk."

The boys avoided the front row seats and chose instead desks on the second row.

Mr. Barber plopped a well-worn leather satchel on his desk, which was piled with paper and books. He removed his hat and hung it on a peg beside the door. His white hair hung jaggedly over his collar. He glanced toward the boys.

"How about opening the windows? Its kind of warm in here."

He removed his coat revealing a buttoned up vest, which barely met over his protruding belly. A gold watch chain, draped from the bottom buttonhole to a pocket in the side of the vest. He took the watch out of his pocket and held it at arm's length.

"I set this watch with Big Ben in London thirty years ago," he proclaimed proudly. "It's been wound every day since - never been allowed to run down. When Big Ben strikes twelve noon over London, you can bet your bottom dollar, both hands of this watch will be straight up on twelve."

Frank and Wallace were impressed.

Kenneth looked at them and smiled, nodded and raised one eyebrow.

Frank gathered he had heard that before.

"I wonder where the rest of my pupils are." He walked to the door and looked down the hall.

Four girls rushed down the hall. They had obviously been running and were panting for breath. They took the desks in front of the boys.

"You made it just in the nick of time," Mr. Barber said as he again took his watch out and looked at it. "Another thirty seconds and I would have had to mark you as tardy." He smiled and looked at each of the girls. They giggled and squirmed in their seats.

Mr. Barber's expression turned serious. He addressed the entire class. "You can save yourselves a lot of anxiety in this class if you will make plans to arrive five minutes early. As a matter of fact, you will find that true for the rest of your lives. Simply plan to be five minutes early to wherever you have to be."

The girls glanced at each other. They proceeded to straighten their skirts over their knees and pat their hair in place.

Frank stared at the back of the fidgeting girl in front of him as she attempted to secure loose strands of hair to the top of her head. The unruly strands refused to stay in place. In frustration, she took all the pins from her hair and let it fall loosely down her shoulders and back. Yellow ringlets lay on Frank's desk and his fingers tingled at the thought of reaching out to touch them. He exchanged glances with the other boys. *This could prove to be very distracting if she sits there every day.*

Yield not to temptation.

******

Saturday afternoon all the cotton had been thinned and the grass cleared out of it. Mattie hitched the mule to the side harrow and made her way to the cornfield. She watched as the teeth of the harrow stirred the soil and uprooted tiny sprouts of grass. She stopped the mule to look back where she plowed. Satisfied with a job well done she clucked her tongue and the mule resumed his slow trudge toward the end of the row.

Mary Rose rode her horse to the edge of the field and waited for Mattie to reach the end of the row. Mattie slapped the side of the mule with the rope to get him to walk faster. "Giddy-up!" He jerked his head up but in his stubborn manner continued at the same pace.

"Hi! Where did you come from?" Mattie said loudly when she neared the end of the row.

Mary Rose got off the horse. "From the post office." She smiled mischievously.

Mattie's heart started to race. She guided the mule to a shade tree and loosely wrapped the reins around a tree limb. "You got a letter from Frank, didn't you?"

"Sure did! Look what was in my letter!" She tauntingly waved an envelope above her head.

Mattie smiled then playfully snatched it from her and sank down on the grass. Her hands shook as she tore it open. She took a deep, quick breath when a train ticket slid from between the pages.

"Look!" She handed the ticket to Mary Rose.

"Wow, that's terrific! Now you can go to him! Think it will be soon?"

Mattie looked up from the letter she held in her hand. Dejection was displayed in her every movement, every dart of her eyes, every turn of her mouth. She felt hopelessly trapped on her father's farm. "I don't see how I can ever slip away. Pa watches every move I make, and besides, if I try to get on the train that nosey Pudgy is sure to try to stop me."

"What business is it of his?"

"Pa has probably convinced him it would be in my best interest to keep me off the train." She unfolded the letter and started to read.

"Maybe you can figure out something."

"I wish I could but I'm scared of Ma." She glanced up briefly. "You can't imagine how mad she can get."

"I wish you could go and get away from her beatings. Frank loves you so much."

"I want to go but I am so afraid. I am going to see if I can find a way."

"I hope you can. Let me know if I can help you." She put her foot in the stirrup and pulled herself on her pony by the saddle horn.

Mattie looked up at her. "You've helped me already. I am so-o-o glad to get this letter." She stood up and walked over to the pony. "Thank you for bringing it to me."

"No trouble at all. I have to ride into town almost every day to get the mail or something from the store. Is there a place I can leave your letters so nobody will find them?"

"Under the rock by the bridge. I'll go look every day."

******

"Hi Frank! What did you do over the weekend?" Susanna asked as she stepped up her pace to climb the school steps beside him.

"Oh, hey Susanna. Worked."

"You can call me Susie. Everybody else does."

"Okay, Susie it is. What did you do?"

"Nothing exciting. Just sat around the house mostly. I wanted to go to the dance but nobody asked me," she hinted.

"I don't have much time for dances since I work after school and on weekends." Frank was glad they had reached the classroom. "Good morning, Mr. Barber."

Frank sat at his usual desk and Susie, as usual, sat in front of him. *At least her hair is pinned up today. I hope she keeps it that way.*

Susie turned around in her desk with her feet protruding in the aisle. Her skirt was pulled above her shoe top revealing her bare ankles, which swung back and forth from her crossed knees. Frank looked away. She crossed her arms on his desk and faced him, her porcelain face inches from his. Her violet eyes searched his. "Do you ever go to dances?"

"Not since I moved back here. I've been too busy with school and working."

"Where do you work?"

It seemed to Frank that she batted her eyes a little bit too often and periodically allowed her long, dark lashes to lay on her cheeks just a little too long. "I work down at the newspaper office."

"Do you write?"

"Oh no!" He chuckled. "I hope to some day but not now. I have been granted the wonderful privilege of sweeping up and cleaning the type." He grinned.

Her laughter rang through the classroom. "Maybe I'll stop by there one day. It's on my way from school." She turned in her seat to face Mr. Barker.

Frank stared at the back of her head and watched as her slender fingers pulled the pins from her hair. The blond curls fell on his hands. He did not move them immediately.

******

"Breakfast is ready!" Priscilla called from the bottom of the stairs.

"Coming," Frank said and then traipsed down the stairs and took his place at the table.

Priscilla's eyes searched Frank's face. "You studied until pretty late last night didn't you?"

Frank closed one eye and looked toward the ceiling as he tried to remember. "I think it was about two o'clock."

Priscilla held the platter of bacon in mid-air. "Honey, you have to get more rest. Thomas, look at the dark circles under his eyes."

"Oh, Aunt Priscilla!"

Thomas laughed. "Is she a little over-protective?"

"Over-protective, phooey! He goes to school until three in the afternoon, then works until eight, then he studies half the night."

"I'm fine!" Frank put down his fork and reached for his coffee. "I'm glad you're concerned but, believe me, I'm fine!"

Thomas looked up from his plate. "She's right. You need plenty of rest. Is the work getting to be too much for you? If it is…"

Frank interrupted. "No sir, it's not. I need to work all I can."

"Your school is more important than work. Are the lessons very difficult?"

"It's really not that hard, it's just that Mr. Barber gives us so much homework."

Priscilla narrowed her eyes at her husband. "Maybe you'd better cut back on his hours."

"No, please," Frank objected. "I can do it. I need to be saving money."

Priscilla touched his arm lightly with her fingertips and looked at him lovingly. "Frankie dear, money will do you no good if your health suffers. With your delicate lung condition, you need plenty of rest."

"I promise, I'll get to bed earlier. Please don't cut back on my hours," he pleaded with his uncle.

"We'll see how everything goes, okay?"

Frank rose from the table. "Thanks. Enjoyed my breakfast. Gotta go."

"Prissy, that's one hard working boy!"

"Seems to be. I wish he would eat more. He's beginning to look awfully thin."

******

The weeks passed very slowly for Mattie. She stayed busy with the work in the fields and garden. She helped pick and preserve the numerous fruits and vegetables. By the end of every week she was exhausted but Wade and Annie insisted she participate in all the social events. She attended the square dances, County Fair, horse races and riding competitions without an escort. Annie insisted she accompany them to every event and was more than a little irritated if she did not act her usual, jolly self.

Annie could not understand Mattie's pensive behavior, nor why she was not anxious to attend every event. Wade, on the other hand, said nothing. He understood but let Mattie know he was watching her every move.

Annie began to feel uneasy that she did not have a boyfriend. "Why don't you have a beau callin' on you, like the rest of the girls?"

"I'm not interested in any of these hicks around here," Mattie answered sharply.

"Hicks huh? Well, Miss high and mighty, just who are you interested in?"

Anger and resentment boiled inside Mattie. She glared at Annie through narrowed eyes. It took every bit of control she could muster to keep from lashing out at her.

"I suppose you're waiting for that cath'lic boy." She turned her back to leave the room. "Humph! I'm sure he's found him a high falutin city girl by now."

Mattie threw the book in her hand across the room then fell across the bed and cried.

Word had gotten around the community about Mattie and Frank's failed elopement. Women put their heads together, cut their eyes in

235

Mattie's direction and whispered. Mattie was somewhat embarrassed, but her defiance made her send darting glances in their direction.

None of the teenage boys attempted to flirt with her or make any overt advances to her. Zeke Henshaw only grinned and asked her where "Frankie boy" was. She didn't bother to answer since she was sure he already knew. He had his eyes, and hands, on Albie Sturges, which relieved Mattie a great deal. She sat out most of the dances unless her cousins Amos Posey or Lawton Glass asked her to dance.

It seemed the entire community was progressing speedily toward the end of summer, but for Mattie the time crept by.

Mattie encouraged Pearl and Bobby to see each other as much as possible. If they loved each other, she wanted them to be together and not suffer like she had in the past year. Louella was also a teenager and would soon have a boyfriend. Mattie determined to do what she could to help their romances.

Mattie lived for Frank's return in September.

******

Frank stood in the foyer and watched the long hand of the grandfather clock move slowly toward seven. Ordinarily by this time, he was out the door and well up the street on his way to school.

I guess I'll be tardy today. He dreaded the harsh reprimand of Mr. Barber, but he had to somehow avoid the temptation that seemed to be luring him every day. The long hand finally reached seven. Frank flinched when the sudden boing of the chime startled him. He opened the front door and looked up and down the street before he stepped out on the porch. No one was in sight.

Frank took the usual path to school where normally other pupils, including Susie, usually waited to join him. His eyes searched the street in front of him. Apparently, the others had already gone ahead. He quickened his pace until he was a block from the school then slowed it again when he saw Susie and her friends approach the school and ascend the steps. He stepped behind a tree and waited for them to disappear through the doorway then he made his way to the schoolhouse door.

Mr. Barber's room was the second on the right so Frank could easily hear the chatter through the open door. He waited in the hallway until he saw the door begin to close then stepped toward the door. Mr. Barber's head appeared around the facing.

"Oh there you are, Frank! I wondered where you were." He stepped back and held the door open.

"Good morning! Thank you, Sir." Frank nodded politely to his smiling teacher then put his books on the desk nearest the door. He avoided Susie's smiling eyes across the room as he slid behind the unfamiliar desk.

"Psst," hissed from Wallace Finley's teeth as he ducked behind Eliza's head. Frank glanced at him while he attempted to listen to Mr. Barber. "What's up? Why aren't you sitting behind Miss Doe Eyes?"

Frank riveted his attention on Mr. Barber until he turned his back to write on the chalkboard then he mouthed to Wallace, "It's your turn. I'll swap places with you."

"Deal."

The next morning Wallace took the desk behind Susie. When her hair spread over his desk he let his fingers caress it then turned and winked at Frank. Frank gave him thumbs up.

Wallace devoured every flutter of the long, dark eyelashes and the luring glances of the "doe" eyes. He even ventured to touch her on the hand or arm when he talked to her and little tugs on one of her curls let her know he was attracted to her.

******

As hard as Mattie tried she could not seem to add anything cheery to the letters she wrote Frank. If there were anything at all cheerful in her life she did not recognize it. The only bright spot she could see was when Frank returned from Jackson, then, and only then would she find any joy. The days and weeks passed slowly.

Sunday morning arrived with a slow drizzle falling, soaking deeply into the freshly plowed earth. Mattie was awakened early to the smell of frying fat back and hoecakes. She pushed the covers back and walked to the window. Seeing the rain, she went back to bed, closed her eyes and attempted to go back to sleep. The noise from the kitchen did not permit it. Wade knocked on the door and announced that breakfast was ready. Pearl got out of bed and dressed.

"You'd better get up and eat. We have to go to church today."

"I'm not going. I'm tired of working all week and I just want to rest, besides, I'm not hungry."

"You're not hungry a lot of the time lately. You'd better eat or Frank will come home to find a dried up little old lady waiting for him." Pearl thought the metaphor hilarious and laughed at her own comparison. "When is he supposed to get here, anyhow?"

"Two weeks from today, if nothing drastic happens.

"And then?"

"And then I'll be in the arms of my beloved," she answered, using a phrase from one of Frank's poems.

"In the arms of my beloved, my foot! You'd better wait 'til the wedding vows are said before you fall into anybody's arms."

"Wedding bells or no wedding bells I'm gonna hug him tighter 'n that wisteria vine hugs the post out there on the porch." It was Mattie's turn to laugh at her own metaphor. Pearl laughed as well.

Pearl left the room and closed the door behind her.

"Where's Mattie Parilee?" Annie inquired of her.

"Asleep. Said she was tired from all the hard work she's done this week. Besides, she's got the monthly miseries." Pearl lied. It seemed she lied a lot for Mattie but she was sure Mattie would do the same for her.

"She needs to get up and get ready for church," Wade said as he pulled out the chair at the head of the table and sat down.

"Are we going to church in the rain?" Alma asked. She was the only one who did not have a boyfriend waiting to sit by her at church.

Louella glared at Alma. "A little rain's not gonna hurt anybody! We can wrap up in quilts if it don't rain no harder than 'tis now,"

"You just want to get there to set by your fellar," Alma chided.

"No such thing. I want to hear Brother Whitley preach the word a God." Louella declared loudly. The entire family burst into laughter.

"Well, I do!"

"Sister Louella's got a fellar. Sister Louella's got a fellar," Alma chanted. Tommy joined in the sing-song.

"That's enough. Eat your breakfast." Wade's words had a ring of finality, which were heeded without question.

When he finished eating, Wade went to Mattie's room and opened the door. "Mattie, time to go to church."

Mattie did not answer him. He closed the door and walked back to the kitchen.

"Since it's raining, why don't we leave the baby with Mattie and let her stay home?"

Wade had watched Mattie closely all summer and she had shown no sign of running away. The summer would soon be over and as far as he knew, she had had no contact with Frank. He had asked around about "the Haney boy's" whereabouts and learned that he was in Jackson going to school. Pudgy reported to Wade that he had not arrived home on any of the trains. Wade felt safe leaving Mattie home alone today and reasoned that with her having to tend a toddler, she would not be going anywhere.

Annie opened the bedroom door and set Tommy in the middle of the bed with Mattie. "Since you ain't going to church you can tend ta him while we're gone." She closed the door then opened it again. "And you can have dinner ready when we get home." Her aggravation at Mattie's rebellion was quite evident but Wade had made the decision and she was in no mood to object. It would be a relief not to have to try to keep Tommy quiet during church.

Mattie rolled her eyes but said nothing. "Sure, I'm the slave around here," she muttered. "That's all right," she said aloud. "I'd rather be cooking than listening to preacher Whitley proclaiming the evils of the Catholic Church." Mattie pulled Tommy under the cover hoping he would go to sleep but he was ready to play. That suited Mattie just fine. He was the one joy in her life. She loved that little boy as well as if he were her own. She tickled him and kissed his belly. His laughter made her laugh.

"Do you want to go with me to the barn loft?"

******

Frank closed his Algebra book with a snap then stacked it on top of the rest of his books and hastily started to leave the classroom.

"Frank I need to have a word with you before you leave." Mr. Barber was busy stuffing papers in a leather pouch.

Frank stopped to wait until the other students walked past him toward the door then he walked over to the desk piled high with books, and papers. Frank stood in front of the desk of towering books and waited for Mr. Barber to begin. The old man put on his coat then took his hat off a nail behind the door.

"If you're going to the newspaper office I think I'll walk with you. Is that okay?"

"Certainly, be glad to have your company," Frank replied politely.

With his key in his hand, Mr. Barber held the door open for Frank. He pulled the door to and put the key in the lock.

Frank stepped out on the walk and gazed intently at the western sky. Like a curtain closing, a dark line of thunderclouds made a distinct, sharp line across the western horizon, obliterating all the blue sky in its path. The wind ruffled the leaves and the trees swayed in a somewhat unsettling manner. "Looks like we'll be getting some rain by night fall."

Mr. Barber pulled his hat more snuggly down toward his ears and paused long enough to examine the approaching storm. "I don't think it will wait until nightfall. The way those clouds are churning there will be more than rain." He quickened his steps. Frank's long stride kept up with him easily.

"Son," he glanced at Frank then in the direction of the approaching cloud. "What I wanted to tell you is that I'm mighty pleased with your class work."

Frank knew there was a "but" coming next.

"But, I'm a little concerned that you don't seem to socialize with the other young folk. You can't study and work all the time. You know what the old saying is – 'All work and no play makes Jack a dull boy'".

Frank looked at him blankly.

"Do you know what that means?"

"No sir, not exactly."

"It simply means that if you work all the time and never play you won't be very pleasant company."

"It's just that I don't have a lot of time for play with studying and working," Frank replied defensively.

"Don't you like any of these pretty girls?"

"No sir – uh – I mean yes sir, I do, it's just that – uh – I'm - sort of engaged to a girl back home."

"Oh, I see. That's well and good but you still need some recreation. What do you do when you're not in school?"

"The first thing I do is go to the newspaper office and help Uncle Thomas."

"And after that?"

"Well, I go home and eat supper then I study - you know the assignments you give us? That pretty well takes up most of my nights."

"And on the weekend?"

"I work on Saturday morning."

"What about Saturday night when all the other young people are at the dance?"

"I need that time to read." He hesitated then added, "and write."

"I have learned what your reading interests are but, may I ask what kind of writing you do?"

"I have to write letters home to my folk, and to my sweetheart."

"Is that all the writing you do?" He glanced at Frank. "What I'm asking is, do you do any other writing, like stories."

"Yes sir." Frank blushed and paused slightly. "I don't say anything to the guy's in class but I write…poetry."

"Poetry!" Mr. Barber exclaimed. "I knew it! I just knew you had a creative streak in you! I can tell by the way you write in class. I'll bet you write stories also."

Frank nodded. "Yes Sir."

"Does Thomas let you write anything for the paper?"

"Heavens no! I'm not that good."

"You will be. Of that one thing I am sure!" He glanced from Frank to the sky. "That storm is approaching rapidly. I think we'd best get a move on." He took his hat off and held it in his hand to keep the wind from claiming it. "Will you think of what I said about socializing more? Don't take life so seriously. Lighten up!"

"I'll try." Frank answered half-heartedly.

"I would hate to see you get burned out with school before the first year is over."

"I understand your concern and I'll try to do better."

"I'm just thinking about your own good. You understand that, don't you?"

"Yes sir, and I appreciate it."

"This is where we part. See you tomorrow." The old man said with a salute.

"Good evening, Sir."

Frank turned to go down Capitol Street.

"Oh, Frank!" The aging teacher called after him.

Frank turned around.

"I won't say anything about your writing poetry."

"Thank you." He felt somewhat relieved. It seemed that during most of his school years he had been teased by his friends for writing poetry. Now he mostly kept his writing a secret, except for sharing it with Mattie.

Lightening sent jagged streaks down through the increasingly darkening clouds, then disappeared behind the depot and the slow-moving rail cars lined up across Capitol Street. Loud claps of thunder followed. The wind carried the lonesome sound of the train's whistle across the city of Jackson as the line of cars crept slowly to the northeast toward Canton. The wind whipped the treetops sending leaves and small limbs tumbling to the ground. Frank raced toward the safety of the newspaper office.

"A storm's coming!" Frank called to Thomas who was hunched over the printer setting type. Frank pushed hard against the door to get it to close.

"I can hear it. What does it look like out there?"

"Terrible. Looks like a tornado cloud to me." Frank peered out the window. "The clouds are tumbling and churning."

"Is that right?" Thomas answered, absent-mindedly. He was obviously preoccupied with the task at hand. The fact that a storm was brewing did not bother Thomas. He had seen many before and was never one to run for the storm pit every time there was lightening. "Do you mind proofing the front page for me."

Frank was surprised that he asked him to proof read. "Me? You want me to proofread YOUR writing?"

"Uh-huh. You do know proper English and punctuating don't you?"

"Sure, but…"

"Then hop to it. I have confidence in you."

Frank spread the front page out on the counter and pulled the oil lamp closer to him. He shuddered slightly at the sound of snapping limbs and loose objects pounding the side of the building. Thomas seemed oblivious to the devastation going on outside.

"Uncle Thomas," Frank called loudly. "I really think we should take cover. Listen to the wind."

Thomas raised from his position over the press. "Really?" He walked to the windows, which lined the sidewalk and peered out at the threatening storm. "You're probably right. Put out that light. Don't need it to blow over and start a fire." He turned back to the window to watch the approaching storm. Little fingers seemed to protrude out of the clouds then recede.

Frank tilted the globe of the lamp and blew through the opening to extinguiish the flame. The room seemed terribly dark for the middle of the afternoon. Thomas was still peering out the window when the tree in front surged and bowed sharply toward him. He retreated toward the press. "Dive for cover!" he yelled to Frank just as limbs from the tree crashed through the windows. The two of them cowered under the edge of the heavy press. Frank felt drops of water splattering on the floor around him.

"The roof!" Thomas shouted over the sound of the roaring wind. When they looked at the ceiling it was filled with a large leaf-covered limb. The tree had blown on the roof and gouged a large hole just above the press. The two of them stood up and stared through the leaves and twigs at the clouds swirling above them. Rain poured in their faces and wet their hair and clothes. Water washed over the press sending little black, ink filled rivulets down the side.

A low roaring, whining sound advanced toward the east as the swirling clouds moved toward President Street. "A tornado! I hope Priscilla has the presence of mind to go to the storm pit," Thomas said as he looked helplessly at the wet printing press.

The wind abated somewhat, the bulk of it being in the center of the tornado. The rain poured through the hole in the roof and washed over the press. Ink darkened the water as it dripped off the sides of the press and made puddles on the floor.

Thomas stood over the press shaking his head unsure of what to do next. He reached for a raincoat hanging on a peg in the back of the room and spread it over the most delicate workings of the machinery.

Frank lifted reams of paper and shoved them under the counter to try to protect them from the destructive water that poured through the roof. The front page of the paper that was spread on the counter was lying under the side of the press soaked with water. He tossed his schoolbooks under the counter with the paper along with stacks of printed brochures that were ready for delivery.

Thomas threw his hands in the air then ran them through his rain soaked hair. "Forget it! Just forget it! There's not much we can do here. Come on, we need to go check on Priscilla." He pushed his way through the limbs protruding through the front windows and stepped over the windowsill. Glass crushed beneath his feet. Frank followed him out into the rain.

The street was filled with debris and broken limbs. House shingles, chairs, paper, pots and pans littered the street and sidewalks. Broken windows and doors lined one side of Capitol Street leaving the opposite side of the street unscathed. Then after a few blocks there was evidence that the twister had switched sides of the street as it danced its way through town.

Frank and Thomas raced past the Governor's mansion where trees were twisted and lay on the ground. Curtains blew through the broken windows on the west side of the large building. The large, round columns on the front of the mansion were still intact.

At the very east end of Capitol Street there was not a broken glass or downed tree. Apparently the twister had simply lifted and gone over the tops of the trees completely missing the magnificent Capitol building.

Frank and Thomas ran up the street then across lawns and gardens in an attempt to get home. The wind whipped their wet clothes and hammered the needlepoint raindrops in their faces. Some of the houses were completely flattened by the wind, others only had parts of them remaining. Other houses had no damage, only trees lying precariously close to vulnerable glass panels and delicate trellises.

"The house! I can see the top of the house!" Frank yelled at his uncle who was trailing behind him some thirty feet. Frank climbed over the trunk of a tree, which lay across his path then sprinted toward the house. The house, at first glimpse, seemed to be undamaged. His eyes scanned the large back yard and the pasture area for damage. The small barn was still standing. *Don't see the horse. Probably in the back of the pasture under the trees.*

Debris filled the yard and the half-acre pasture. Rocking chairs were turned on their sides on the front porch. One was lying in the yard under a broken limb from the pecan tree. The sound of his heavy foot hitting the porch only added to the numerous sounds of the wind and the voices of neighbors. Some screamed loudly as they looked on the devastation surrounding them. There were calls for family pets and neighbors mixed with the sounds of snapping limbs and more thunder. Sheets of rain pounded against everything under its domain.

"Aunt Priscilla?" Frank called as he pushed the front door open and entered the pristine foyer. Water dripped from him onto the polished oak floor. Thomas was close behind him.

"Priscilla!" Thomas called, then paused and listened for her to answer. The two of them ran through the dining room past the lace-covered table and into the kitchen. "Priscilla! Maybe she's in the storm pit." He made a dash for the back door. When he opened the door he was greeted with a tree limb that was pressed against the closed door.

The two frightened, water soaked men climbed over the branches of the tree and what remained of the back porch. They could see the door of the stormpit hanging by one hinge allowing rain to pour inside. Thomas wrenched the door to one side and climbed down the steps into the darkness. "Priscilla!" he called hopefully. As his eyes adjusted to the darkness he saw her huddled in a corner. She sobbed loudly, her face in her hands. He reached for her and pulled her to her feet. Her arms went around his waist and clung to him. He squeezed her trembling body against his.

"Are you all right?"

She nodded. "The house?"

"It's still standing."

Frank stood on the steps inside the storm pit looking at the back of the house. He could see nothing but limbs and leaves, debris and the crumbled roof of the back porch. "Aunt Prissy," he said tenderly. "When you look out you can't see much of the house just the oak tree against the back porch so don't get upset, okay?" He tried to prepare her for the devastation. He went to her and put his arm around her shaking shoulders. "The main part of the house is in good condition. Give me your hand."

She dropped her arms from around Thomas and reached for Frank's hand. He led her up the steps of the storm pit. At the site of the crumpled back porch she covered her mouth. "Oh no!" she screamed.

"It's not as bad as it looks." Thomas tried to reassure her. *I hope.* "Let's stay in here until the rain eases up." He pulled her away from the door and out of the rain.

They stood in the back of the storm pit and watched the deluge until it slowed to a drizzle and the wind lost some of its ferocity. In the west the setting sun sent streaks of pink and orange across the sky. The dark clouds advancing to the northeast picked up the reflection of the sun, which turned their edges an eerie purple glow.

"It's moving toward Philadelphia." Frank's words were not meant for anyone in particular, just an expression of apprehension and dread.

******

Wade stood on the front porch and watched the sun send eerie rays across the sky as it hovered over a bank of clouds in the west. *Looks like we might be gettin' a shower shortly*, he thought as he went down the steps to go into the back yard. A full moon was rising above the firmly rooted trees around the creek to the east. He jammed his fists to the full depth of his overall pockets and looked from the streaks of sun coming from the line of dark clouds in the west to the hazy, cream-colored moon in the east.

"Yo, Mistuh Wade! What you thank it gonna do?" Joshua yelled from his house across the narrow stretch of pasture. He stood on his porch along with Louisa and all the children. Louisa's elderly mama, Mammy Kaiser, leaned on a cane on the edge of the porch.

"I have no idee," Wade yelled back then straddled the fence and took the path to Joshua's house. The yelling got the attention of Annie and the girls and one by one they followed Wade down the path.

"I tell ye, there ain't no good can come outta a big white moon sech as that," Mammy Kaiser said as she pointed a scrawny finger toward the huge oblisk in the sky. "It be's a bad omen when the sun and the moon shines in the same sky. Give it a few mo' minutes and the moon'll be pulling a twister right outta them black clouds. If'n it turns a deep yellar and get circles 'roun' it, there ain't no keepin' trouble from comin'."

Lou's smallest children clung to her skirts. Joshua and Louisa took Mammy's prediction seriously. Joshua took one child in each arm and Louisa pulled the others close to her.

"Is she right, Pa?" Pearl asked. She hugged herself with both arms. Mattie and the three younger ones huddled together on the edge of the porch.

"Mammy ain't never wrong 'bout perdictin' the weather," Louisa offered. "If she say it gonna rain, you might as well head fer cover. If'n she say they's gonna be a twister you sho' better head fer the sto'm pit. Uh-huh, sho nuff."

All heads turned to Mammy Kaiser as she stepped off the porch to the steps. Wade grasped her arm to keep her steady. She was stooped and weak but she insisted on walking to the corner of the house so she could watch the moon. The oak walking stick trembled under her thin, wrinkled hand. She stared at the moon as it changed from a pale cream-colored obelisk to a pale yellow, then to a dull orange. A mist rose from the horizon and crept over the moon.

"HERE IT COME!" Mammy Kaiser screamed sending chills over the crowd standing around her. "KEEP YO EYES ON IT."

"Mammy, hush up! you scarin' the little 'uns," Louisa ordered.

"Don't aim t' skeer nobody but you watch that moon. If'n it gets white circles 'roun' it, they's gonna be trouble. One circle mean a ba-a-ad storm, two circles mean a death of somebody clost to ye."

Mattie sniggered and nudged Naomi. "How can it be the death of somebody close to everyone. The whole world is watching the same moon?"

"I don' know nuthin' 'bout that, but if'n Gran'mammy say it, you can betcha' britches it gonna happen."

Annie and Louisa watched Mammy as she watched the moon. The children stared at the moon waiting for something strange to happen. They expected an explosion or something to leap from it. Wade and Joshua turned their attention to the storm clouds. A brisk wind started blowing as dark, rolling clouds approached from the west.

"THERE IT IS! LOOK A YONDER, YA'LL!" Mammy screamed. The children jumped at the suddenness of her voice. Annie could not help but be startled as well.

"What, what is it?" Louisa screamed.

"It be's a circle, see it." Mammy pointed her trembling, skinny finger toward the moon and drew a circle in the air.

Indeed, a circle had formed around the moon. The haze over the horizon covered the moon and turned it to reddish-orange. The second circle emerged from the haze to circle the moon.

"There she is, jist like I tole ye'. There's gonna be a heap a trouble." She turned to walk back toward the steps.

Lightening zipped through the sky followed by a loud crack of thunder. The dark mass of clouds was almost above them. A second streak of lightening followed by another lit the late afternoon horizon. Mammy stood with her face tilted toward the dark cloud, then she looked at the moon again. "Lawd, Lawd, have mercy on us all. Amen an' amen."

"Think we might orter go ta' th' stom pit?" Joshua asked Wade.

"Might be a good idea. Probably just a rain storm, still I don't like the looks of that yellow haze mixed in with the clouds."

"Come on ev'er body we's goin' ta' the stom pit." Joshua waved his big arm in a motion for all to follow. All the children ran across the pasture.

"I cain't make it to no sto'm pit," Mammy said as she started toward the steps. "I'll stay right inside the house, and tough it out. If it be's my time ta go, I'll jist go."

Joshua took two strides toward her and with one swoop lifted her up in his arms like a baby and carried her toward the pit.

Louisa and Annie lifted the younger children and ran to the pit. The rain had already started pelting them.

Wade fought against the wind to close the heavy doors of the pit. The wind blew hard against them but Wade and Joshua pulled harder until the doors closed tightly. Wade reached for a heavy limb he had placed beside the door and wedged it in the slots he had built on the door for that purpose.

The little children started to cry and the older ones shivered in the darkness. The storm pit was an ideal place to store potatoes, onions and other root vegetables to keep them from freezing. Now the smell of rotten potatoes and onions was stifling. Mammy Kaiser sat perched on a wooden bench extending the depth of the pit. Louisa and Annie sat on the same bench holding their youngest on their laps. The rest stood crowded together in the nine by nine-foot pit dug into the side of the hill.

Westin, Josh and Louisa's oldest son was enjoying the tension. "This is where me an' brother Bo come to catch lizards and snakes," Westin announced. The girls gasped and shrieked. Westin giggled.

"There be's lots of em in here, too," Bo added, hoping to get another shriek from the girls.

"Somebody light the lantern!" Pearl yelled.

Wade took the lantern and the syrup can that held the matches off the peg beside the door. The light of the little kerosene lantern revealed the frightened faces of everyone in the little hole in the ground. Joshua started laughing.

"Ya'll sho' a funny lookin' sight! Black faces pale as white folk and white faces whiter'n cotton."

Wade grinned but nobody else saw anything funny. The wind and the rain battered the door. "Ever'body be quiet so we can hear the roar of a twister."

The intense silence and the eerie shadows cast by the lantern made the seconds seem like minutes and the minutes seem like hours. Three minutes of silence was about all Pearl could tolerate.

"Can we get out now? I think it sounds better outside."

"Shush! Let me listen a minute." Mammy Kaiser rose from the bench and with the help of her cane hobbled to the door. She put her ear to the crack in the door and listened for what seemed a long time. "There ain't no twister in that storm! It done pass us by."

"Then, can we get outta here?" Pearl persisted.

"Open the door a crack and see how hard it's raining," Annie suggested.

"If'n there ain't no lighten' in five minutes, it be's a definite sign the wurst a da stom's purty near gone by," Mammy Kaiser added. "Is it still thunderin?" She put her hand behind her ear to indicate she was trying to hear. Joshua always said she was so deaf she couldn't hear it thunder. This pretty well proved his point.

Wade opened the door. "Still raining." Then the rain slacked for a brief period.

"Rain or no rain, I'm getting out of this hole," Pearl said as she climbed up the steps and made a dash for the back door.

Mattie followed her. "Me too!"

"Don't leave me in here!" Naomi lurched for the open door.

249

"I need to watch the cloud," Wade commented as he and Joshua both ran out into the rain.

Wade and Joshua stood on the back porch and watched as the cloud boiled and rolled to the east.

Wade watched the eastern sky. "It's over Preston 'bout now."

"Yep, headin' fer DeKalb."

33

Mattie was weary from the drudgery of field-work, as were the rest of the Posey family. With every turn of the plow, every pull of the hoe and every tug on a pea vine, her thoughts were on Frank. She lived for the letters he wrote and longed for a way to leave on the next train. She was aware of being watched closely by her father. She was not so sure if her Mother was watching her. Probably so, she decided. If Wade had told Annie about the failed elopement, she had not mentioned it. Mattie felt sure if she knew she would have spit out venomous words and threats, but still, what if she knew and was just waiting for Mattie to make a slip. The thought of Annie's violent temper kept Mattie from making any definite move to leave. Then there was Pudgy, watching, waiting for Mattie to make an appearance at the depot. She could just picture the Sheriff coming after her and escorting her back to the waiting belt of her parents.

As the cotton and corn had been "laid by" no more hoeing or plowing was to be done. The cotton and corn were big enough to be left alone for the warm sun, rain and the Good Lord to produce an a good crop. The garden and the vegetable patches, however, were another matter. Vegetables were hanging from the vines ready to be picked.

First, it had been the green beans and green peas in the early spring, which were picked, shelled, cooked and put in hot jars and sealed for the winter. The hot summer sun had made it necessary to gather what remained of the cabbage, onions, turnip greens, carrots, and beets. These were canned and now sat neatly on the pantry shelves. It was now the middle of August and the vines were loaded with peas, lima beans, cucumbers, okra, squash, tomatoes, and numerous other vegetables. It took Annie and all the girls working every day to can the vegetables, make fig preserves, apple jelly, and jams.

In June the blackberry vines had been loaded with the plump, purple fruit. The entire Posey family advanced on the prickly vines that covered the creek bank and the swamp area. Jars were filled with the delicious berries for pies as well as jelly and jam. Nothing went to waste, not even the watermelon rinds, which were cut in chunks and made into preserves, then the unusable scraps fed to the hogs. There was no end to the numerous chores. When it was even intimated that enough had been canned to do until the next year Annie or Wade would put forth the question: "And if the ground doesn't produce next year because of drought or flood, what will we eat the next winter?"

So the family picked and shelled and canned and dried and pickled and stewed and jellied and sauced.

When the girls grumbled about never-ending chores Annie would always tell them: "It will taste mighty good this winter when its cold and there's nothing growing outside to eat."

When all the jars were filled with fresh vegetables and fruits, the remaining peas and beans were allowed to dry on the vine, then they were picked and shelled. Enough for seed for the next spring's planting were kept in a place safe from mice and weevils. The rest were put in the oven for a short while to kill any weevils then put in a sack and hung in the smoke house to be cooked during the long, cold winter days.

The sweet potatoes were dug and piled in the storm pit. Peanut vines wilted, signaling that it was time to pull up the plants and let the green plump nuts dry on the vine then be picked off and put into burlap bags. The bright green cotton bolls would soon start opening and have to be picked, then the sugar cane stripped, cut and carried to the syrup mill. After that the corn would have to be pulled and put in the corncrib.

Mattie worked determinedly. Conditioned by her years of working on the farm, there was never a question of whether or not to help. It was just something she did. Everybody worked. Everybody worked hard. Everybody worked consistently. Everybody worked until everything was done. Then everybody played – if they had any strength or stamina left.

Naomi could talk of nothing but her beau, and their plans to get married. "Just as soon as we can find someone who wants another hand on his place," she told Mattie while they were picking peas that had been planted among the corn stalks.

"Maybe Pa could use another hand," Mattie suggested.

"He ain't got no house for us to live in," Naomi replied. "My pappy said he won't consent 'til Isaac's got a good place fer me. Says that'll prove he be's responsible."

"If they could come to an agreement, then ya'll could build a house. It won't take a very big one for the two of you. Josh and Isaac could get it done in no time. Then Isaac's folk could help. Do you want me to ask him?"

"Naw, I need to mention it to Isaac an' see what he thinks."

"All Pa's girls will soon be married off, gone somewhere else to live. He's gonna need some extra help."

"Do you think there's a chance in God's good worl for that ta happen?"

"Maybe. It sure would be a comfort knowing you're snuggled into a little cabin here close to your Mama. Before you know it there will be nobody left here but them and Ma and Pa. Sure as shootin', Sister Pearl's gonna marry Bobby and Louella, as young as she is, has already got her eyes on that Gray boy."

"What about you?"

"I think you know what my plans are. As soon as Frank gets back from school this fall, one way or another, I'm marrying him."

"I sho do hope nuthin' interferes with yo' plans."

The clapping sound of horse hooves echoed through the corn stalks. Mattie dropped her sack and ran to the end of the rows to see who was approaching. She peered through the corn stalks not wanting to be detected unless it was Mary Rose. The sound of loud singing accompanied the beating of the hooves. *Mary Rose! She always tries to make me hear her if I have a letter.* Mattie ran to the edge of the road. "Did I get a letter?"

"You sure did. I left it under the rock down by the bridge."

"Did you mail my letter to Frank?"

"Yep, dropped it in the mailbox at the post office. He told me in his letter he'd be home in two weeks. Sounds a little bit homesick."

"Two weeks! I can't wait!" Mattie danced a little jig. I'm gonna run down to the creek to get my letter."

"I'll ride down and get it for you."

With that, she snapped the reins and nudged her pony with her heels. The pony loped off toward the creek.

Mattie waited for Mary Rose to return with the letter then ran back to the cornfield where Naomi was waiting. She sank down in the shade of the corn stalks and opened the envelope.

Dear Mattie,

Just two more weeks of school and I will be home. I can't wait! I plan to be home on the first day of September. There is no need for you to write me anymore after this week, as I will probably be back there before the letter gets here. I am tired of studying and working. I cannot wait to see you and make plans for a SUCCESSFUL elopement. Let Mary Rose know where I can meet you on September first.

I love you,
Frank

Mattie turned the page to read another poem Frank had written. She folded the pages and stuffed them in her shirtwaist where they would be safe until she could sneak off to the barn and put it safely away in her treasured, red velvet box.

******

Frank pulled the sheet under his chin, then over his head to try to get warm. He was exhausted from the hard labor at the newspaper office. He had a severe cold and congestion from getting wet the night of the tornado. At night he suffered chills and fever but managed to keep it from his aunt and uncle. *If I can only manage to keep well enough to stay in school until September first then I can go home and see Mattie.*

Eventually the shaking stopped and he could concentrate on saying his prayers. He thought of Mattie and for some reason the mystery of his subconscious mind made him return to the day on the schoolhouse steps when he quoted the Tennyson poem. With his eyes closed tightly in the darkness, he again saw the tears that had welled up in her bright blue eyes. He heard his own voice whisper his favorite poem as he re-lived that moment.

"Come not when I am dead
to drop thy foolish tears upon my grave,
To trample round my fallen head..."

He smiled at the thought of a grown boy quoting poetry aloud in the middle of the night and wondered what his friends would say if they knew.

Pass on weak heart, and leave me
    Where I lie.
Go by, go by...go by...go by...go by."

******

33

Naomi and Isaac sat on the edge of the porch, shielded from the hot August sun by the tall pine trees surrounding Joshua and Louisa's small house. Rooms had been added to both ends of the house as their family grew larger. Joshua was the proud, protective father of eight children now. It would have been nine if little Ruthie had not smothered in the cotton.

Isaac kicked at Naomi's foot as she let it swing limply over the edge of the porch. She giggled and attempted to out-maneuver him.

"I sho' do thank we'd be happy livin' here on Mistuh Wade's place. Do you really thank there's a chance he'd build us a house?" Isaac was ready to get married. He was seventeen and had decided Naomi was the one for him. He was putting in hard days of heavy work on Homer's place and was ready to get away from his slave-driving tactics.

"Mattie thanks he might if'n you let it be known what a good worker you be."

"I'm sho' a hard worker. An' I don't mind it a'tall if I's 'preciated. Mistuh Homer don't 'preciate nuthin'."

"I ain't never heered my pappy say Mistuh Wade wuz mean to him. They's frien's. Been frien's all their lives. Pappy say he don' never 'member a day in his life he ain't seen Wade Posey at some part 'a the day."

"Do ye thank ye pappy would put in a good word fer me?"

"Yonder he comes acrost the pasture. Wanna ax him?"

******

Joshua pondered how to approach Wade about building a house for Naomi and Isaac and letting them live on his farm. He was not sure whether Wade actually needed another hand. It seemed they had made it fine over the years and were able to increase the number of acres in cultivation after Mattie and Pearl were big enough to plow. Either of the two could do the work of a man. But it was like Naomi told him - it wouldn't be long until Wade's older girls would be gone, as well as herself and her two brothers just under her.

Joshua stood beside Louisa as she sifted flour in the biscuit tray. "It'd be kinda nice if Naomi and Isaac could live clost 'round us, don'cha thank?"

"Looks like they bound and determined to tie the knot. If they gonna do it anyway I'd ruther they'd be here than under Mistuh Homer's domination. Do ye thank Isaac would be a good worker? You knows well as I do Wade ain't gonna tol'rate no laz'ness." She looked up from the biscuit tray. Lard and flour oozed through her fingers as she massaged the mixture, merging them together and adding buttermilk to make biscuits.

"I thank I'll jist cash-aly mention it to 'im and see what he says."

"I wouldn't wait too long. Them two's courtin' hot 'n heavy." She inclined her head toward the two lovebirds strolling down the path toward the creek.

******

The cotton stalks reached to the waist of Wade and Joshua as they strolled casually across the field attempting to estimate how much cotton would be harvested per acre. The rains had come at the right times bathing the growing plants in moisture and soaking the nourishing soil. The dark green stalks were loaded with large green healthy bolls - twenty to thirty to a stalk in some places. They absorbed the hot August sun. Tiny cracks had begun to appear in the

257

bolls nearest the top of the stalks revealing the beautiful white fibers inside.

"Looks like we're gonna have a bumper crop this year." Wade was beaming, anticipating the revenue. "Thank God!" he added as an afterthought.

Joshua laughed. "You better be thankin' God. If it wadn't fer him we'd have no crop a'tall."

"You're right about that." Wade spit brown tobacco juice across the green stalks. It dripped off the leaves to the ground. "I figure it'll be about two weeks until time to start picking. What do you think?"

"If the sun stays this hot and the rain holds off it might be ready 'fore then. It's a good thang that twister didn't hit us. If it hadda all these stalks 'ud be flat on the ground."

Wade shook his head and again remembered where his blessings had come from. "Thank the good Lord." Wade added.

"You got a lot to thank the good Lord fer, Wade Posey - as well as myself. Where'd you be if'n yo pappy hadn't gave you this hundert acres? An' me where'd I be if'n me an you had'nt a growed up together? I'd prob'ly be stayin' on some Klu Kluxer's place. Uh, Uh, Uh." Joshua shook his head and ran his fingers through his thick, kinky hair.

Wade stopped, then turned to face Joshua. "I can remember as good as if it was yesterday - the day Pa said I could have the land. Do you remember?"

Joshua grinned and nodded his head in the affirmative. "Just where would we be now? Do you ever wonder where you'd be if'n yo pappy hadn't give you this land? You got all this hundert acres..." - Joshua waved his arms in a circle - "and the thirty-five acres along Ridge road..."

"To say nothing of another fifty I bought to the south of us," Wade interrupted.

He sounded somewhat boastful and this made Joshua shudder. Here he stood beside a rich man, at least rich as far as land was concerned. What was a man without land? Joshua had to work hard at not envying his friend. He had accepted long ago that colored men were not allowed to own land. Still he held on to his dream of owning some of it - If it were not but an acre, or even a half an acre. Just a little bit of solid earth beneath his feet that he could claim as his own that nobody, not the government, not a neighbor, not even the Ku Klux Klan could take away from him.

"Land. Acres and acres of land. What if'n you wuz like me and didn't have none. Not nary solid grain o' sand to call yo' own. What if'n all these here rich bolls o' cotton belonged to another man? What if'n all the work you'd done this year wuz fer nuthin? "jist fer absolutly nuthin'?"

"Guess I'd be in a pitiful shape, wouldn't I? Maybe I'm getting a little too proud." He stared at the rich brown soil beneath his feet.

"Where would you and me be if'n we hadn't had all these hard working gals?"

"Where would we be if they'd been boys?" Wade's forehead wrinkled in a question as he glanced at Joshua. Evidently he felt he would possess a great deal more.

Joshua shuddered again at the thought that maybe Wade was somewhat ungrateful for his healthy girls, wishing they'd been boys. He was afraid his friend had misplaced his priorities. *I'm a thinkin' he's gettin' jist a little too proudful.*

"They's purty soon gon' all be gone." Joshua paused to let Wade digest that little fact. He wondered if Wade had thought of that before now.

Wade stopped, stood very still and stared at Joshua's back.

"How you figure that?" Wade's voice was somewhat shrill. Joshua kept walking, refusing to look back.

"Did you hear me? How do you figure that?" Wade ran to catch up with him. Now he walked beside him and glared at his calm black face. Joshua refused to turn his head but stared toward the end of the rows where they all seemed to merge as one.

"Where you think they're gonna go?"

Joshua's answer was slow in coming. He weighed his words for the most effect. "You been so taken up in things that you ain't stopped to consider yo' chillun." He glanced at Wade but hurried to finish before he could interrupt him. "Now look at Mattie – she's already wantin' to git married. Jist cause you stopped her las' time don't mean you'll stop her the next 'un. If she don't marry that Cath'lic boy it'll be somebody else. I dare say by next crop time she won't be here to hep you."

Wade crammed his left hand deep into the pocket of his overalls and twisted the end of his moustache with his right. "But, I got..."

Joshua interrupted. "Now let me finish what I gots to say then I'll listen to ye." He raised his eyebrows and looked sternly at Wade. He was well aware there was no other white man he could speak to in this manner. But, then, Wade was not just another white man. He was his long-time friend. "Now you take your Pearl – she ain't fer behind. That Collette fella ain't hanker'n ta do no farmin'. You ax anybody! They come here from somewheres in the Carolinas and that's right where they's goin' soon's they can get the money. I heered the old man say that very thang down at the gen'rl sto'. He said he'd lots ruther work in the cotton mills than plow a mule. If'n Pearl marries his boy they'll be goin' with 'im."

Wade's head spun around, his eyes wide with question. "They ain't said anything about marrying."

"Nuthin' to you, maybe. Then there's my Naomi. Why she an' Issac's done axed me if'n I approve. My answer to them wuz 'soon's you have a job an' a house t' live in'. They's lookin', ain't found nuthin' jist yet. "That'd be three workers gone. Three hard workin' hands, gone."

Wade tucked his head and stared at the stalks of cotton that were smaller at the end of the rows where the trees had sapped most of the nutrients from the soil, leaving the little stalks to languish in the their shade.

"'Less we can fig're someway to keep 'em here." Joshua hoped this would be a leading statement – leading Wade to think on it. "Gotta go do the milkin'." Joshua strode off toward his house leaving Wade standing in the shade at the end of the cotton rows.

Wade's arms were stiff as he held his clenched fist in the bottom of his pockets. The straw hat tipped downward. His eyes examined the tiny rocks in the sand.

Annie was taking left over food from the pie safe when Wade walked through the kitchen door. He hung his hat on a nail beside the window.

"Supper'll be ready in a few minutes. I'm glad I have enough left from dinner. It's way too hot to heat up the kitchen."

Wade said nothing. He leaned over the wash pan and washed the perspiration off his face, then splashed water on his arms.

Annie handed him the flour sack towel to keep him from dripping water on the floor. "What's the cotton crop look like?"

"Real good. Might be the last good one we have."

Annie whirled to face him. "Why do you say that?"

"With all the gals getting all grown up they might not even be here next year to help us work."

Annie couldn't help but laugh. "Is that all? And just where do you think they'll be going?"

"Marrying off, no doubt."

"Not much chance of that. Mattie ain't even got a beau, and Pearl and Bobby ain't even mentioned marrying. She's too young anyhow."

"That's now. What about a few months from now?"

"We'll cross that bridge when we get to it." She walked out the back door to the well. Wade was right at her heels.

"Has Lou said anything to you about Naomi wanting to get married?"

"Yeah. Says they're courtin' hot 'n heavy. He's trying to find somebody that needs a hand. She unwrapped a rope from around the post of the well and slowly pulled it to her.

Wade shook his head. He reached for the wooden keg attached to the end of the rope and untied it. He handed the keg to Annie. She took the cap off it and held it to her nose. "Don't seem like the milk's soured." She hurried back to the kitchen.

Wade trailed along behind her. "Who's she courting?"

"One of Homer's coloreds. I think his name's Isaac."

Mattie was in the kitchen putting plates on the table. "What about Isaac?"

"Your Pa was just wondering who Naomi's courting."

"Oh." Mattie's mind clicked with an idea. "They don't have anywhere to live so they can't get married. You don't need another hand do you?" She looked at her father and waited for an answer.

"He probably won't work worth a damn. I sure don't need a lazy loafer lounging around the place."

"He might. Why don't you ask some of the hands he works with?"

Wade didn't answer but it was obvious he was thinking about it.

261

34

Frank buried his head in his pillow to keep his cough from waking the rest of the family. His father had come to help his brother repair the newspaper office. He was sleeping in the next room.

Paul Haney had not gone to bed until after midnight. For four days, he had worked with his brother, repairing the office and getting the weekly paper ready to print. Between the three of them the next edition was ready to go to a printer in Canton the next morning. The repairs on the office and the printing press were about half finished. In another week it would be, and Frank, his father and his uncle could return to Philadelphia.

Four more days of school, Frank thought. He pulled his hand from under the sheet and massaged his aching temples. *I think I have fever.* The clock in the foyer struck four o'clock.

Frank's cough had gotten worse over the weekend so Priscilla ordered him to bed where she slathered his chest in salve and put a hot cloth on it. The steam from the cloth permeated his nose and eased his cough somewhat. Priscilla had used every home remedy she knew on Frank so he would be able to start his final week of school on Monday.

Frank attempted to subdue his cough when he went down to breakfast on Monday morning. He could not afford for his father to know he was sick. The last four days of school were vital for him to pass his courses.

"Are you feeling any better?" Paul asked him, putting his hand on his fevered brow.

"Somewhat."

"Do you think you're able to go to school?" ˙

"I've got to go to school! I don't want to flunk out after all the work I've put in this summer."

"That's well and good, but you come home if you think you have a fever."

"Okay, Papa." The glass of cool water helped to quench his fevered thirst. He attempted to eat but could hardly swallow. He pushed his chair back. "Excuse me, please," he said politely. "Time to go to school." He hurried out the door.

"That boy doesn't eat enough to keep a cat alive! Look at that plate." Priscilla pointed at the plate of food.

"He's not feeling well. Besides he's homesick. He'll be fine once I get him home."

******

"Well," Wade drawled as he removed his hat and scratched his head with three fingers of the same hand. "I guess when I think about it, my girls'll be marrying off before too long and there ain't no telling where they'll end up, then I'll need some extra help around here. Is he a good worker?" Wade looked up at the bulky, black man standing before him.

"Isaac's a mighty good worker Mistuh Posey. That boy 'o mine's mighty strong, and honest as the day is long. He'd make you a mighty fine hand. Sho' would." Isaac's father looked pleadingly at Wade.

Elijah held his tattered hat in both hands in front of him. He held the reins of his mule between his fingers. There was a rim around his head where his hat had pressed his kinky hair to his head. Perspiration trickled from his graying hair past the tip of his eyebrow. He reached up and wiped it with the back of his hand. The mule snorted and pulled hard on the rope to reach a tempting clump of grass.

"I hates to see him have to settle down wi' some fella who'll treat 'im like a slave. You gots the repitation of treatin' colored folk in a decent way. I promise you he'll make you a mighty fine sharecropper. All I ax is you give 'im six mont's, then if'n he don't work out to suit ye, come an' tell me. I'll person'ly come over here and load him up and take 'im outta yo hair."

Wade watched the muscles ripple in Elijah's arm as he snatched the reins hard to pull the mule toward him.

"What's Homer think about him leaving his place?"

Homer didn't take it lightly when one of his neighbors hired a colored hand off his place. He felt he owned them and treated them in a way they felt an obligation to stay with him. His threats kept most people from attempting to recruit them. Wade Posey was not recruiting Isaac. He had come to him, and besides he would waste no words explaining to Homer the circumstances. Isaac was free to go where he wanted.

"To tell you the truf, Mistah Posey, he don't know he's thankin' bout leavin'. I don't thank I'm obliged to tell 'im since we ain't slaves no mo'. I's took 'bout all I can take off'n him. I axed him onct 'bout building one'a my boys a house so's he could stay and work there on the place. He said 'I ain't inter'rested in havin' no mo' nigger houses on my place. Let 'im live wif you'."

Elijah shuffled his feet nervously and looked down across the field. His dark eyes reflected an emotion Wade could not identify. Sadness? Dread? Worry? Fear? Anger? Determination?

"You know what my boy done?" He looked at Wade in the eyes for the first time.

"No, I..."

"He run off and went up No'th. Uh-huh, sho' did. Took his gal wif' 'im. They's doin' fine up there – gots a job an a house – two little young'uns." He beamed with pride then his expression turned somber. "I don't know if'n I'll ever get to see 'em agin."

"What did Homer say about that?"

Elijah was looking past Wade in the direction of the barn. "Wadn't nothing he could he say. He had the firs' chance."

"Will this get you in trouble with Homer? What will he say about it?"

"Between you 'n me..." He looked back at Wade "...he can say anythang he like – I'll jist take it and keep my mouf shet. I don't aim fer my younguns to work fer 'im, if'n I can hep it. He be's me-e-e-an.

264

It be's bad enuf we has to carry his las' name, but I s'pose that can't be hoped since my great-gran-pappy had to be called sumpin'."

Wade stared at the ground, deep in thought. He ran his hand over his scruffy beard. "I'll tell you what - if you 'n your boy will help Josh, ya'll can cut some timber and build them a house, you know, a place to live and raise some young'uns," he chuckled. "You send him to me. The two of us need to do some private talking and have an agreement. We need to shake hands on it."

"I shore 'preciate that Mistuah Posey, and I'm shore my Isaac'll be much obliged to ye. Josh-a-way tells me you're a mighty fine man ta work fer."

"You tell Isaac that I'll help him just as long as he'll work hard and be a man of his word."

"I sho' will Mistuh Posey. I sho' will. You can count on 'im. I gives ye my word on it. Uh-huh." He smiled and extended his hand to Wade. Wade grasped it and shook it vigorously.

Elijah threw one leg over the back of the mule. His smile seemed to spread from ear to ear showing a mouth full of jagged teeth. He tipped his hat at Wade then clucked his tongue at his mule. When the mule hesitated he kicked him hard in the flank. The mule reluctantly and lazily made his way toward the road. Elijah's long legs hung past the mule's belly, his feet only inches from the ground.

Wade walked to the back yard where Annie and the girls were finishing up the weekly laundry. "Annie, you and Mattie come with me."

"Where you going?" Annie dried her hands on her apron.

"You coming?" He called to Mattie.

Mattie wrung the water from a shirt and dropped it in the tub of rinse water. "What's this all about?"

"You'll see." Wade straddled the fence to cross the pasture that led to Joshua and Louisa's house.

Annie and Mattie walked through the turnstile and followed him down the trail.

Joshua was coming from the barn as they approached the house. He waved a greeting.

"Is Lou and the younguns in the house?" Wade yelled to Joshua.

"Sho' is. Go on in. I'll be there in a minute."

Wade stepped hard on the porch then tweaked the cheek of three small children that blocked the door.

Louisa came from the kitchen. "Well, Lawsy me! To what do we owe this honor? All three of you at one time! Have a seat. Naomi, get some more chairs."

Mattie reached and picked up the youngest child, then followed Naomi in the kitchen.

Naomi eyed Mattie curiously. "Is sumpin' wrong?"

Mattie shrugged, then whispered: "I don't know. Isaac's Pa just left the house."

Naomi gave her a puzzled look just as Joshua came through the back door. He nodded to Annie then sat astride the chair facing Wade and Annie. He looked from one to the other.

"Mighty proud to have all uv ye visit us at the same time." He grinned.

Wade looked toward the kitchen door. "Mattie, you'n Naomi come in here. I want you to hear this."

Louisa's face had gone somber. Her eyes searched Annie's for some explanation.

Annie turned her palms up and shrugged.

Wade looked at Joshua then reached out and touched his arm. "I've been thinking about what we talked about down in the cotton patch the other day."

Joshua nodded, knowingly.

Wade continued, "I'm a mighty blessed feller. I've been a successful farmer and landowner and..." Joshua nodded again, not daring to say anything. "...lots of my success I owe to you..." He looked at Joshua and then to Louisa. "...and to you too, Lou. I'm not leaving out your young'uns neither." He glanced at Naomi and the older children leaning against the door facing. "Ya'll been mighty fine workers and I want to say thank ye."

Annie squirmed in her chair. She had no idea what was coming next. She knew this tender side of Wade but she had never seen him reveal it to anyone but she and the children. She looked at Mattie who was staring at her father.

"Isaac's Pa came to see me a while ago." He watched as Naomi blanched pale and clutched the back of her mama's chair. "He wanted to ask about his boy sharecropping with me." He paused and waited for some sort of reaction from Joshua or Louisa.

Lou could only stare at him, not sure whether or not Wade was agreeable.

"What did you tell 'im?" Apparently Joshua was the only one with the ability to speak. Naomi had sunk to the floor beside her Mama's feet.

"I told him I'd try him out if he'd work hard and be a man of his word."

Naomi sighed audibly, then smiled. She looked up at Mattie who put both hands on her shoulders. She squeezed tightly then sat on the floor beside her.

Joshua wasn't smiling. Then he asked the question both Louisa and Naomi were anxious to ask. "Where would they live?"

"That's up to you 'n him. Do you think y'all can throw up a little shanty for the two of them? I'll furnish the logs and saw them."

Joshua started laughing. "You'd do that for one 'a my young'uns?" He pounded Wade on the back.

"Reckon I would, as much as for one of my own."

Louisa nudged Naomi with her foot. "Thank him," she whispered and nodded her head toward Wade.

"Mistuh Wade, I sho' do thank ye," Naomi blubbered.

"You're welcome." He couldn't understand why she had tears in her eyes.

Annie beamed at her husband. She could only smile at the happy family.

Wade stood up and pushed his chair from between him and the door. He wanted to be able to leave quickly after his next statement. Annie and Mattie stood to leave with him.

"One more thing." Wade steadied himself on the doorknob. He looked at Louisa then held his eyes firmly on Joshua's. "I'm having a deed drawn up for y'all to have this twenty-five acres around your house here." With that, he twisted the doorknob and walked out to the porch and down the steps. He didn't look back.

Joshua stood transfixed with his hand on the back of his chair and his mouth open. He looked at Annie for verification, then to Louisa then back at the open door. He could see the back of Wade as he hurried up the trail. He ran after him.

"Wade, Wade! Wait up!" He caught up with him and grasped his shoulder with one hand. "I wanna thank ye, man!"

"You go on back in the house. That can come later." Wade turned quickly toward the path home. Joshua thought Wade's chin quivered. He was not quite sure but decided it was best to do as Wade said. Words of gratitude and continued commitment could come later. *Besides, mine and Wade's communication don't need no words.*

Ties that bind are not always obvious.

35

September 1896

September first arrived with the hot fall sun bearing down on the cotton bolls, which responded in bursts of fluffy, white cotton. The fields of Neshoba County were dotted with stooped shoulders pulling long, white sacks bulging with the wonderful white fibers that would be the family's source of supplies for the next year.

Mattie made it a point to pick on the edge of the crowd nearest the edge of the woods. Her plans were to sneak down to the bridge as near noon as possible to meet Frank. Annie would leave the field early to prepare lunch and hopefully Wade would be too busy to notice she was missing. Pearl and Naomi would cover for her if they missed her. Frank was to have arrived home the day before and was to meet her down by the bridge.

Mattie watched the sun closely and kept an eye out through the tall timber searching the undergrowth for any signs of Frank. When the sun seemed to be at its Zenith she motioned to Naomi that she was leaving then crouched under the tall stalks of cotton to the edge of the field. When she was out of sight she ran the short distance to the bridge.

She saw Frank's horse tied to a tree. Her eyes scanned the creek bank for Frank. Then she saw him sitting on the bank with his knees pulled to his chest, his blond head rested on his folded arms around his knees. Mattie's heart pounded and she ran through thick grove of trees.

Before she reached him he heard her and stood to face her. His fevered face, from the corners of his eyes to the dimple in his chin, was a big smile. He ran toward her and picked her up and twirled her in a circle.

"It is so good to see you!" He exclaimed standing her on the ground and pulling back from her to look at her from head to toe.

Mattie blushed. "I'm not much to see in these old work clothes." She untied her bonnet to let the air cool her sweating head.

"You look good to me!" He pulled her to him again and kissed her on the lips. He knew it was a daring move since she might misinterpret it. Her response let him know quickly there was no misunderstanding. They clung to each other in an effort to quiet the longing inside. After a few minutes she pulled away from him.

"You look kinda' pale. Are you sick?" She questioned him putting her hand to his red cheeks.

"I still have this chest cold. It just seems to be hanging on. Can't seem to get rid of it." He turned his head and coughed.

"You feel like you have a fever. That is a terrible cough! Sounds deep. Does your mama know you're sick?"

"Yeah. She said when I get home she's going to put me to bed and put salve on my chest. I will probably sleep for a week. She will be poking all kinds of awful tasting medicine down me." He wrinkled his nose and made a gagging sound.

Mattie laughed. "It's good you're home so she can take care of you. How long 'till you have to go back?"

He put his forefinger under her chin and tilted it up toward him. "When I go back it will be WE."

Mattie was filled with apprehension. "We'll have to make better plans than last time."

"You don't know how much I hated to leave you standing beside that train," Frank said regretfully. He explained again, as he had in his letter about the conductor refusing to let him off the train and then about the advice he gave him at the station in Newton.

"I was so angry at Pa I couldn't see straight. He got on his horse and just rode off, never said a word to me about it. Still hasn't."

"It won't be that way next time. You'll see. We may have to ride to Neshoba to catch the train but this time we will make it.

The few minutes they had together were filled with passion and exhilaration in an attempt to satisfy the hunger and loneliness of the past few months.

Frank smoothed wisps of wet hair off Mattie's cheeks and forehead. "Can you meet me here again tomorrow?"

Mattie nodded. "I sure can! I'll be here, one way, or another. I'll see you then." She slipped her hands out of his and walked backward, blowing kisses to him.

He grinned and caught them in mid-air and pressed them to his lips.

The others had left the cotton patch for lunch when she returned. She threw her sack across her shoulder and trudged slowly across the field toward the wagon where the rest were weighing their cotton. She threw the heavy sack on the ground and sat on it. Pearl looked at her questioningly. Mattie winked.

The following day when Mattie arrived at the meeting place Frank was not there. She paced up and down the road, watching, listening for the sound of his horse. She looked under the rock to see if he had left her a note. There was none. She waited as long as she dared then went back to the field. She took her cotton sack to the wagon but no one was there. They had finished weighing in and had gone home for lunch.

"Where you been?" Annie asked when she came in. "Had to go to the woods," she replied nonchalantly.

"You better set down and eat so you'll have time to rest before you go back to the cotton patch," Annie instructed her, nodding to her place at the table.

Mattie sat down and looked at Pearl somberly. Pearl didn't have to ask whether Frank was there.

It was a long afternoon as Mattie attempted to keep her rows picked as fast as the others. She imagined all sorts of reasons why Frank was not at their meeting place. The thought that he was sick kept nagging at her. His family was busy in the fields so there would be no one to bring her a note. She knew that if there was any way possible he would get a message to her.

She, Pearl and Naomi tried to think of a way the three of them could contact him. They decided to wait until after noon the following day to see if he would be there at that time. He was not.

******

Frank felt the cool cloth rest on his forehead and his mama's hands brushing back his wet hair. The perspiration soaked sheets clung to his chest and legs. He had lost account of time, being awakened only by his spasms of coughing.

"Turn on your side," he heard his mother say softly. "I have to get these wet sheets off the bed." He managed to maneuver in the bed at her instructions then could smell the clean fresh sheets as she tucked them around him.

He heard a strange male voice but could not seem to focus his eyes on him. Cold fingers pried his eyelids open. First one, then the other.

"Now open your mouth, wide," the strange coarse voice instructed him.

Frank attempted to open his mouth but did not know how wide he was opening it. A cold metal object touched his chest and the voice told him to breath deeply. When he attempted, he had another spasm of coughing. The stranger, who by now, he had decided was a doctor, ordered him to turn to his side. The cold object moved over his back, under his shoulders and over his ribs.

Mrs. Haney tucked the sheet around him, then took the cloth from his head and replaced it with a colder one. Frank felt cold water on his lips and he thirstily licked them. He attempted to look around the room but the light hurt his eyes. He closed them tightly and thought of Mattie. *I have to meet her at the bridge,* he thought but did not have the strength to get up. He could hear voices at the foot of his bed. His mama's. His papa's. The doctor's. Then he drifted off to sleep again.

The doctor stepped away from the bed and walked to the fireplace. He shook his head slowly and spoke softly. "You have a mighty sick boy here. Looks like he has pneumonia."

The word pneumonia struck fear in them. People died from pneumonia.

"The only treatment I have is to keep him warm and apply poultices to help him cough up the phlegm."

Mrs. Haney looked at him pleadingly. "Is it bad, doctor?"

"It's double pneumonia. Looks to be in both lungs top and bottom. I don't want to scare you but barring a miracle – well, I'll just say it looks mighty grave."

Mr. Haney peered into the doctor's eyes. "Is there any other medicine or anything else we can do?"

"Not that I know of. Just keep on doing what you're doing. Make him drink plenty of fluids. Do you have any family off anywhere?"

Paul's heart skipped a beat. "Yes. Do I need to send them a telegram?"

The doctor nodded.

"Mama." Frank's voice was weak.

"What is it, sweetie? What can Mama do for you?"

"Mattie." He whispered.

"Do you want me to get Mattie for you? Is that what you said?"

Frank nodded slowly and opened his eyes ever so slightly.

Mr. Haney came to the bedside and put his hand on Frank's wet head. He motioned for Mrs. Haney outside. "I asked the doctor if we need to get the priest and he said that would be a good idea."

Mrs. Haney covered her face with her hands and sobbed. He pulled her to him. They both wept. "He's asking for Mattie."

"I'll get someone to go for the priest and maybe Mary Rose can go tell Mattie," he said as he reached for his hat and started out the front door.

******

Wade looked up from his cotton row to see a young girl riding her horse along the edge of the cotton field. He pulled the strap of the sack across his head and holding his hat in his hand, he hurried toward the edge of the field.

"Howdy," he said nodding to her. "You're the Morton girl, ain't you?"

"Yes sir. Could I see Mattie?"

By this time everyone in the field had seen her and Mattie was running toward her.

"Mary Rose, what's wrong?" Mattie yelled to her before reaching her. "Is it Frank?"

Mary Rose slid off her saddle and stood holding her horse's bridle in her hand. "He's mighty sick. He's asking for you. The doctor says he might not make it and all the family should be there." Her voice broke and she clasped her hand over her mouth to quiet her sobs. "They've even sent for the priest."

Mattie felt her heart skip a beat. "Oh no!" she gasped. "What's wrong with him?"

"Double pneumonia."

"I'm going to him." Mattie ran from the field toward the barn.

"Now wait just a minute young lady. You're not going anywhere," Wade yelled to her.

"You don't have a say in the matter. I mean I'm going," she yelled back as she raced toward the pasture and whistled for Prince.

"Mattie!" Wade yelled after her. He felt a hand on his shoulder.

"Wade, it sounds mighty troublesome to me. Maybe its best she go. He may not be long for this worl'." Joshua said soothingly.

Wade put his hat back on and stalked back down the cotton row. "Everybody get back to work! We gotta get this cotton outta the field!"

Mattie managed to put Prince's bridle on, then slung a blanket across his back not bothering with the saddle. She took her foot and tapped the back of Prince's front leg. He knelt so she could pull up on his back by his mane. She straddled the horse, dug her heels into his ribs and he ran full speed leaving Mary Rose behind.

When she arrived at the Haney house she was aware of the ominous crowd of people standing on the porch talking softly, staring at her. She felt out of place in her faded, torn, too small work dress. The neighbor's children were huddled in little groups on the edge of the porch and under the trees.

One of Mary Rose's brothers met her and took Prince. "Just go on in," he said, motioning her toward the front door.

The group of men parted as she pushed her bonnet to the back of her head and walked up the steps.

"Evenin' maam."

"Howdy."

"Come on in."

"That's Wade Posey's girl", voices murmured as she made her way through the crowd.

Mrs. Morton ushered her into the bedroom where all of Frank's family hovered at the bedside. Paul Haney rose from the side of the bed and let go of Frank's hand so Mattie could have his place.

Mattie paled when she saw Frank's ghastly face buried in the white pillowcase. His wheezing, gasping breath was audible even out in the hall. His body shook as he struggled with every asthmatic breath. His hair and face were wet with perspiration and water from the cold, wet cloth his mother used to cool his fever.

The gravity of his condition gripped Mattie. She wanted to collapse on the bed beside him and die with him. Screams, sobs, and tears welled up inside her and choked her. She wanted to scream *"NO, GOD, NO! NOT FRANK! PLEASE, GOD, NOT FRANK! LET HIM LIVE!"* She gulped to squelch the words.

She eased down on the bed and took Frank's hot, limp, sticky hand in hers. She pressed it to her lips. She leaned over him and pressed her cheek to his. "Frank. Frank. I'm here."

Doctor Powell touched her shoulder. "He can't hear you. Try not to upset him."

Mattie pressed his fingers to her lips and held them there as silent tears ran down her cheeks on his hand. "I'm not leaving you Frank. I'll be right here when you wake up."

******

The afternoon sun sank in the west and the sky turned purple and pink. Wade kept watching the road as he finished his afternoon chores. The girls willingly did Mattie's share of the chores and in hushed tones speculated what their parents would do to her when she returned.

"It's getting dark and Mattie's not back yet," Wade said to Annie when he came in the back door. "Guess I'd better go see what's going on."

Annie's eyes glared at Wade through narrow slits. "You should'a stopped her. She has no business over there with them Cath'lics!"

"After I eat I'll wash up, then go over there. The girl talked like it was mighty serious."

"Serious or not, You bring her back home where she belongs!"

******

Wade recognized a somber situation when he saw so many of the neighbors gathered on the Haney's front porch. He slowed his horse to a walk, then stopped and tied him to the hitching post beside Prince. He removed his hat when he started up the front steps and smoothed his hair with his hand.

"Howdy Wade." Jessie Henshaw nodded. He was the nearest neighbor to the Haneys.

"Howdy Jessie. How's the boy?"

"He's mighty low. The doctor is still in there with him. All the family's gathered around his bed."

"Have you seen Mattie?"

"She's in there." He waited for an angry reaction from Wade. There was none. Wade had too much class for that. After all, what threat was a dying boy?

Wade hesitated at the door then opened it and eased inside.

"Evenin' Wade." Mrs. Henshaw spoke softly and opened the bedroom door for him to go inside.

There was a large four-poster bed in the dimly lit room. The Haney children sat huddled together on the floor by the wall opposite the bed. Two oil lamps were turned down low and cast long shadows on the walls and across the bed where Frank lay. Doctor Powell stood at the foot of the bed beside Paul Haney. The only sound was Frank's hoarse, raspy breath. The smell of death overwhelmed Wade.

Wade shook hands with Dr. Powell. When he grasped Paul Haney's hand, he did so with both of his. He said nothing, just looked him in the eye and shook his head slowly. He nodded to Mrs. Haney, then stepped to the side of the bed where Mattie sat, still holding Frank's hand. He put his arm around her shoulder and pulled her against him. She leaned her head against him but never took her eyes off Frank. He stepped away and took his vigil beside Joe Morton.

The door to the room opened and Mrs. Henshaw ushered the priest inside. He shook hands with Mr. and Mrs. Haney, then nodded around the room to the others. Mattie laid Frank's hand gently on the bed and stood up to make room for the priest but he insisted that she stay beside him. Mrs. Haney kept her seat on the bed and Mr. Haney joined her at the bedside. The rest of the Haney family gathered closely around the bed for the last rites.

Father Scott, leaned to Frank's ear, and whispered, "My dear Frank, you have suffered so much. But I know your heart and your love of God will soon be rewarded. I know you can't talk, don't try. Just pray with us as we pray with you."

The priest took a vial of liquid from his pocket and put some on his fingertips, then dabbed it on Frank's head. He said a prayer softly that none but the family could hear, then stepped back and crossed himself as did the rest of the family. He then prayed in a louder voice so all could hear.

"Almighty God, look on this, your servant, lying in great weakness. Comfort him with the promise of life everlasting, given in the resurrection of your Son Jesus Christ our Lord. Amen.

He turned to Mattie and said, "My child, I know you have never seen this before, but it's just like a responsive reading, I'll say something and then everyone will respond.

Mattie, knelt by the bed and held her hand on Frank's cheek. She felt a tear course down Frank's cheek and on her hand. *He does hear.*

Frank's mother watched with a broken heart, and her eyes met Mattie's. In that moment, she knew that she and Mattie would be connected at the heart forever.

Then with unbelievable sighs and breath that seemed to carry pieces of his family's heart with each word, they began with Father Scott's words and then their responses.

God the Father,
Have mercy on your servant.
God the Son,
Have mercy on your servant.
Holy Trinity, One God.
Have mercy on your servant.
From all evil, from all sin, from all tribulation,
Good Lord, deliver him.

By your holy Incarnation, by your Cross and Passion, by your precious Death and Burial,
Good Lord, deliver him.
We sinners beseech you to hear us, Lord Christ: That it may please you to deliver the soul of your servant from the power of evil, and from eternal death,
We beseech you to hear us, good Lord.
That it may please you mercifully to pardon all his sins,
We beseech you to hear us, good Lord.
That it may please you to grant him a place of refreshment and everlasting blessedness.
We beseech you to hear us, good Lord.
That it may please you to give him joy and gladness in your kingdom, with your saints in light,
We beseech you to hear us, good Lord.
Jesus, Lamb of God:
Have mercy on him.
Jesus, bearer of our sins:
Have mercy on him.
Jesus, redeemer of the world:
Give him your peace.
Lord, have mercy.
Christ, have mercy.
Lord, have mercy.
Our Father, who art in heaven, hallowed be thy Name, thy kingdom come, they will be done, on earth as it is in heaven. Give us this day our daily bread. And forgive us our trespasses, as we forgive those who trespass against us. And lead us not into temptation, but deliver us from evil."

"Deliver your servant, Frank Haney, O Sovereign Lord Christ, from all evil, and set him free from every bond; that he may rest with all your saints in the eternal habitations; where, with the Father and the Holy Spirit you live and reign, one God, for ever and ever. Amen."

The priest and all the family made the sign of the cross then each of them kissed Frank goodbye. It took a lot of effort to restrain the sobs but for Frank's sake, they did. They then stood solemnly, silently, waiting.

The priest stood at the foot of the bed with his arms folded and his eyes closed.

Wade was aghast at the ritual he had observed. He had no idea what it meant nor did he hear all the words. It was strange, different. At least different from what the Methodist did. To him different was not necessarily good.

The doctor walked to the bedside saying he needed to turn Frank on his side. Mattie moved back to make room for him. Frank coughed uncontrollably, then, started mumbling. Mrs. Haney put a fresh cold cloth on his face and kissed him on the cheek then sat down on the side of his bed.

"He's asking for you, Mattie," Mrs. Haney whispered.

Mattie hovered near his face. "I'm here, Frank. Can you hear me?" She felt his fingers tighten around hers ever so slightly and he nodded. She leaned her face next to his and whispered, "I love you." He nodded slightly and inaudibly mouthed the words "love you. Come..not...when I..."

Mattie recognized the words he was saying, words to his favorite poem. She knew he wanted her to say them with him. It wrenched her heart to repeat the words but she cherished this precious lucid moment.

"Come not … when I…am dead to drop thy foolish tears upon my grave, to trample round my fallen head to vex the unhappy dust..." Mattie could not say the rest. She put her cheeks on his and let the tears flow. His lips moved. She said the words with him again. "Wed…whom thou…will…go by…go by. She felt his labored breath on her cheek. She was grateful his mother and father let her have the place that was rightfully theirs. The place beside their dying son.

Frank stopped breathing momentarily. His mother frantically shook him and his spasms of coughing began again. He gasped for breath and his breathing started again, course, irregular, labored. Dr. Powell walked to Mrs. Haney's side and spoke softly so Mattie could hear as well.

"Just let him go. When he stops breathing the next time, just let him go. It's more merciful that way."

Frank's breaths became shallow and further apart until they completely stopped.

Ellen Williamson

"Let him go." The doctor whispered. Mattie and Mrs. Haney buried their faces in his shoulders until the doctor gently pulled them away. Mattie reluctantly let go of his hand and backed away from the bed, guided by her father.

The relatives filling the room clung together, crying, sobbing, going to the bed and touching Frank's forehead, hands and cheeks.

Mattie stood alone in a corner with her face to the wall crying. _I must not cry. Frank's last words were – nor drop thy foolish tears upon my grave. Go by, go by. Let me cry Frank. I have to grieve for you but I promise to do it with dignity._ She felt hands on each shoulder turning her around. She buried her face in the softness of her father's chest and sobbed loudly. It would be the last time Wade ever saw his daughter cry.

Is there not an appointed time to man upon the earth?
The Bible – Job 7:1

36

Sunday morning dawned and Mattie was still sitting in a chair in the parlor when she heard the rooster's first crow. At the first hint of light she made her way to the barn loft to read her treasured letters and poems. She climbed the ladder to the loft, scratched in the hay and retrieved the box wrapped in her torn petticoat. The letters and poems tumbled in a pile on her lap. Her hands unfolded each letter until she found the poem Frank had recited to her when she had first fallen in love with him. She could still see him standing tall and straight in front of all the other young people as the girls giggled at his precise demeanor. The memory was so vivid she could almost hear him. Now it seemed almost prophetic.

Come not, when I am dead, ...Go by, Go by.

She clutched the crumbled piece of yellowed tablet paper to her breast, lay her head on the petticoat in the hay and finally slept.

Mattie did not hear her name being called from the house when all the family were wondering where she was – searching and calling.

"I think I know where she is," Pearl told them as she ran to the barn.

Mattie was still sleeping when Pearl climbed the ladder to the barn and called her from the opening in the loft. Pearl crawled on her knees to her side and saw that she was asleep. She pulled Mattie's skirt down around her ankles and quietly left the loft.

"She's sound asleep in the loft. She didn't sleep any last night," she told Wade when she returned to the house.

"Just let her sleep. We'll go on to church without her."

"Well, she needs to be in church and you know it!" Annie snapped.

"I said to let her sleep!" Wade answered harshly.

Mattie awakened to the sound of the family loading into the one-horse wagon to go to church. She gathered her letters and poems, placed them in the box, wrapped it securely and again, nestled it under the hay. Prince came promptly when she whistled for him. He ran to the barn from the pasture where he patiently let Mattie put the saddle and bridle on him. She then led him to the hitching post beside the watering trough at the well and tied him securely.

She went in the house and poured some warm water from the kettle on the stove into a pan then washed her hair and bathed. Resolutely she put on her best dress then brushed her hair until it was dry. She twisted it in a bun on the back of her head then nested it in a soft cloud of hair that fluffed around her face. She put on a black straw hat with white roses around the brim then tied the attached black ribbon under her chin. She took her tablet and pen from the drawer of the bureau then sat in the rocking chair.

My Dearest Frank,

I can't promise not to weep over your grave. I will mourn for you the rest of my life but I will try to be brave and mourn with dignity. You would want that.

I do not regret declaring my love for you and I will always treasure the love you gave me.

Sleep peacefully, sweetheart. I will join you when my time on this lonesome earth is over.

I will love you forever.

Mattie.

She tore the sheet of paper from the tablet, folded it and tucked it in her blouse.

******

Mr. Haney saw Prince coming up the driveway. Mattie sat straight in the sidesaddle, both feet to one side, her head erect, her chin held high. What she had to do she would do with dignity. For Frank's sake she would not cause a scene by unleashing her pent up emotions.

Mr. Haney met Mattie at the edge of the yard. He felt a closeness to this girl - this girl who was little more than a stranger. He had only seen her a few times but the demonstration of her love for his son on his deathbed bonded him to her in a way that could never be broken. He took her hand and helped her from the saddle then tied Prince to the porch post. He noticed the dark circles under her eyes. "Did you sleep any last night?" he asked tenderly.

"No sir."

"Come on inside."

She stoically mounted the front steps. Mary Rose and her mother met her at the door and hugged her tenderly.

"He's in here," Mary Rose said, motioning for Mattie to enter the parlor.

The simple wooden casket sat on the hearth in front of the fireplace. Soft, white, silk fabric had been draped over the inside of it and fell in soft folds around the outside. There was a large pillow with lace on the edge where Frank's head rested. Mattie could see his blond hair from the doorway. Sobs rose to her throat but she swallowed hard and breathed deeply to stop the urge to cry. She felt her lips tighten and her face began to draw. It seemed all the blood rushed from her head. To keep from falling, she gripped the doorjamb to steady herself.

Mrs. Haney stood by the casket and stroked Frank's hand. She turned when Mattie entered the room, walked over to her, embraced her, then led her to the casket.

Mattie seemed to have no tears left. She touched the neatly combed blond hair lightly with her fingers then touched his lips with her fore finger then put her finger to her own lips. She kissed her finger then placed it back on his lips. She then reached in her blouse, removed the letter and put it in his folded hands. She stood there for a long while, saying nothing. She was aware of more people gathering in the room. She felt an arm around her waist, another around her shoulder then another hand gently on her back. She heard the comforting words people spoke but could not bear to face them for fear of breaking her promise to Frank. Their words were simple, sincere.

"I'm sorry."

"He'll be missed."

"He loved you so much."

"Doesn't he look handsome?"

Other words of condolence were expressed - easy words of solace. She never looked to see who was touching her or speaking to her. Mercifully they understood. Hot tears welled up in her eyes. *Oh Frank. My world is turned upside down. How easy it would be to join you.* She felt she was going to cry again so she whispered goodbye then turned, and walked out of the room. The crowd parted for her when she stepped out on the porch, and descended the steps. Someone unhitched Prince and helped her mount him.

******

The subject in the churchyard in Philadelphia was the death of the "The Haney boy" and the fact that "Wade's oldest girl has been seein' him on the sly".

The men shook their heads in shame that she had been taken in by "them Cath'lics." The women expressed the same sentiment but they could not help but be emotionally affected by the sincere love Mattie had shown for him at his bedside the night before.

No one seemed to know what the proper Methodist actions should be with regard to a Catholic funeral. They had been cautioned to stay away from the little Catholic Church, which had recently been built. They were advised to strictly forbid their children from entering it.

The Catholics had cautioned their children, as well, to never marry outside the Catholic faith. Some had been excommunicated from the church when they did. They were urged to convert the Protestants to Catholicism before they considered marriage.

When Rev. Whitley arrived, he was informed of the happenings of the past couple of days and was asked to address the matter. He did so in a rather forthright manner instructing the congregation to keep their children away from the teachings of the Catholics. "Why they just try to pray the dead soul right into heaven regardless of what kind of life they've lived. We don't want our children indoctrinated with all their heathen practices," he declared vehemently.

The ladies nodded affirmation and the men yelled, "Amen", loudly.

"Of course, y'all have to do the neighborly thing and offer condolences. Go visit the family, take food, and the adults could go to the funeral, but WHATEVER YOU DO, PROTECT YOUR CHILLUN FROM THE EVIL INFLUENCES OF THE CATH'LIC CHURCH." The adults nodded agreement. It seemed to Annie he was gazing right at her.

After the service was over Reverend Whitley pulled Annie and Wade to one side. "I heard about Mattie's attachment for that boy. You ain't gonna let her go to the funeral are you?"

"You don't have to worry about that, I don't aim to let her go," Annie exclaimed. Her eyes squinted in determination.

"We'll do as you say, preacher," Wade assured him.

The preacher smiled and nodded as he poked his cheek full of tobacco.

When they arrived home Mattie was solemnly putting lunch on the table. She had decided that it was easier to do something productive than to sit and cry. When they were seated at the table the matter of the Sunday sermon was discussed which was always the subject at Sunday lunch, as well as to gossip about the rest of the congregation.

"Rev. Whitley told us what the proper actions for us Methodists should be - you know about the funeral and all..." Wade said, looking at Mattie.

Mattie raised her head and looked at him questioningly. "What do you mean?"

Annie spoke up. "He said you younguns were absolutely not to go to the funeral."

Mattie felt renewed anger at Annie. "And why not?" She felt her face getting red and anger boiled inside her. "You don't think I'm going to miss the funeral do you?"

"You most certainly are!" Wade informed her.

"But I want to go! I AM going!" Mattie yelled resolutely and got up from the table.

Annie grabbed her by the arm. "You listen to me, young lady! You ARE NOT going if I have to lock you in the smoke house! Do you hear me?"

Fear ran through Mattie. She knew that would mean another beating as well.

"You heard your Ma." Wade spoke firmly as he pushed back his chair and stood beside Annie.

Mattie jerked her arm out of Annie's grasp and went to the bedroom. She fell across her bed and sobbed.

Monday morning, as usual, Wade knocked loudly on the door and announced that it was time for everyone to go to the fields. Mattie knew better than to argue and dutifully dressed and went to the cotton field. The funeral was to be on Tuesday and she tried to figure a way she could sneak off and go but fear of her parents kept her from making any definite plans. Maybe they would change their minds.

Wade and Annie watched Mattie closely to keep her from going to the Haney's. They would be furious if they knew she had gone on Sunday.

Mattie decided to ask kindly at the breakfast table on Tuesday morning if she could go to the funeral. She was told firmly and decidedly that she would not be permitted to go. She went to her room and took her black dress, hat and shoes from the wardrobe. She sneaked out the front door and carried them to the wagon where the cotton sacks were thrown in a pile. She stuffed her clothes in the bottom of her sack and trudged across the cotton field. She laid her clothes in a brush thicket and began to pick cotton.

Wade took both horses and hitched them to the wagon loaded with cotton. Mattie saw him as he left the barn and knew she would have no way to go to the funeral even if she were brave enough to sneak off. Naomi and Pearl joined her in the high cotton at the lower part of the field. Joshua, Louisa and the other children chose to pick at the upper edge of the field so they would not have far to carry their cotton.

At ten o'clock Mattie left her cotton sack and went to the thicket at the edge of the woods where she changed her clothes, then walked to the side of the road and waited. Pearl went with her and waited in the cover of the underbrush. Naomi agreed to stay in the field and cover for them in case someone called them. Fortunately, Annie had stayed home to do the weekly wash and cook lunch.

Mattie's venture to the side of the road did not miss Louisa's eyes. *Po', po' Mattie. Wisht I could jist hold her right now. Po' chile. Uh, uh, uh.*

Mattie heard the clop, clop of the horses hooves before the funeral procession reached the clearing in the road. She stood beside the road and waited. The driver of the hearse, Mr. Bradley, pulled back on the reins. "Whoa, whoa." He tipped his hat. "Morning, Miss Posey."

"Good morning," Mattie greeted the undertaker. "Mr. Bradley, may I see him one more time?"

Mr. Bradley looked back at Mr. Haney for his consent. He and Mrs. Haney climbed from the buggy and joined Mattie. "Let her see him."

Mr. Bradley stepped from the seat to the back of the wagon. He helped Mattie up the side of the wagon and held her elbow firmly to keep her from falling backward. He opened the casket.

The relatives in the buggies following the hearse got out of their buggies and wagons and craned their necks to observe Mattie in her grief. Mrs. Haney dabbed her eyes.

The priest came forward, climbed up in the wagon and stood beside Mattie. Her eyes caressed every curve of Frank's stilled face. *I will not cry. I will not make a public display of my grief.* The sealed eyelids did not permit the deep brown eyes to look back at Mattie, yet she stared at the shuttered windows of his soul and made a promise to him – and to herself. She allowed her cottonburr nicked fingers to caress the blond curls then held her hand firmly against his head to make her resolve. *Just like our love, my tears will forever be our secret – a secret between you and me, but I MUST 'drop my foolish tears upon your grave'. I cannot go by, go by, go by.* She touched his cheek then kissed him on his cold, stiff lips.

Her crumbled note was still tucked under his hand. She stroked his hand, then turned away.

Her hand gripped Mr. Haney's as he helped her from the wagon. She and Mrs. Haney embraced briefly. Mr. Haney tipped his hat and nodded to her.

Mattie waited for the Haney's to get back in their buggy then stood with her head bowed and eyes closed until all the procession passed.

She was humiliated by being denied the opportunity to attend the funeral and having to stand beside the dusty road to say her last goodbye. But with grace and dignity she paid her last respect and watched the procession until it was out of sight.

Mattie walked back to the sweet gum thicket where Pearl was waiting.

Pearl's eyes were red from crying. "You should have been allowed to go to the funeral. It was a disgrace for you to have to stand in that wagon and say your farewell while everybody looked on!" She was fuming with anger as well as pity and humiliation.

Mattie laid her hat on the grass and turned for Pearl to unbutton the back of her dress. "Not a disgrace. It would have been a disgrace if I had not done it."

"Everybody staring at you like that. I wanted to scream 'what you gawking at'?!"

"Gawking or not – I had to do it. I couldn't stand in this cotton patch with him passing so close and just let him go by." Her thoughts echoed, *Go by...go by...go by.*

Pearl's eyes spit fire. "It makes me so cussin' mad! I'd like to tell Ma and Pa a thing or two."

"You can't do that and you know it. Best you let it go. It's over and done with and there's no use in fretting over it."

"Do you mean to tell me you're not mad?"

"I hurt too much to be mad. Nothing can rile me with all this pain inside."

"I'll tell you one blessed thing - if they try to stop me and Bobby, I'll…"

"You'll do just like I did," Mattie interrupted. "You'll be too scared of Ma to do anything different."

Mattie pulled the strap of her cotton sack over her head and started picking cotton. Her grief was dry.

As she picked she determined what was to be her course in life. She would resolutely give the rest of her life to duties around the Posey farm. There would be no pleasure in it but she would do it. What other alternative was there? There was no other life for her.

Nothing to anticipate. Her heart would forever live unfulfilled. Her reason for living was gone. Frank's last wish was that she not cry for him and she resolved that no one would ever see her cry again. If there were any tears they would be in private, then only if she absolutely could hold it no longer. She looked at the trees at the end of the row of cotton and made them her goal. The next row of cotton would have trees at the end of them, then that would be her goal. She would live minute by minute, doing what ever was at hand, saving her love and she would continue to go by...go by.

Pearl and Naomi attempted to offer words of consolation and hope as they snatched the cotton from the prickly, dried bolls. Mattie had no response.

"It be's best if we jist leave her alone in her grieving'."

For the rest of the day they picked cotton in silence.

Tears are not always wet. When the tear ducts are all dried up, the tears go downward to the chest, making it full and heavy. The heart aches and the tears come out as loud, dry sobs.

37

Annie and Wade got word of Mattie stopping the funeral procession beside the road. They were shamed by their family and ridiculed by all that learned of it. Even Reverend Whitley regretted the advice he had offered. His attempt at an apology to Mattie was met with cold, empty eyes. Eyes that were vacant. There is no describing her eyes. Vacant – that was all – vacant. They showed no grief, no sadness, no longing, no desire. Vacant.

Only in her solitude did she let herself give in to her overwhelming grief. In the presence of others, she clenched her teeth giving her jaw line a definite set of determination. She willed her thoughts to replay her resolve, *I will not cry…I will not cry…Go by, Go by.*

The following days were solemn around the Posey house. Mattie's grief was evident to everyone. Pearl felt the bed shaking at night as Mattie cried. She would rest her hand on Mattie's back or head. There were no words of comfort but, at least, Mattie would know she cared, that she was there.

Annie and Wade tried to involve Mattie in things that formerly interested her but she was interested in nothing. She methodically did what was expected of her around the house and the farm but spent every waking moment either in her room or in the hayloft reading Frank's letters and poems.

Ida and Georgia came to visit her regularly and the three of them, along with Pearl sat and talked for hours. They offered words of hope and comfort. Mattie graciously accepted them but they brought no comfort. She pain inside her was almost unbearable.

Louisa and Naomi encouraged Mattie to come to their house as a place of refuge. She would shoo all the children outside and the three of them would talk for hours.

A few days after the funeral Mrs. Haney sent word to Mattie that she would like for her to come to see her.

On Sunday Mattie saddled Prince and rode off to see Mrs. Haney. She didn't bother to tell Wade and Annie where she was going. What did they care? There was no need to watch her any longer. She would not be riding off to meet her lover.

Mattie was extremely apprehensive as she walked up the steps and knocked on the door. She remembered the last time she walked up those steps. Her knees went weak.

"Hello, dear," Mrs. Haney said sweetly to her as she embraced her. "I'm so glad you came. How are you?"

"I'm not doing so good. Just can't sleep or eat. How are you?" she asked in return.

"The same with me. I suppose with time it will get easier. I miss him so much." Mrs. Haney just shook her head sadly.

Mattie kept her eyes on her hands and clenched her teeth. "Me too."

"Can I get you something to drink?"

"I would like a glass of water."

While Mrs. Haney was gone to get the water Mattie walked over to the fireplace where Frank's casket had been and stood with one hand on the mantle board. A dozen questions prodded her thoughts but the main one was, *Why? Why? Why?*

"Here you are, dear," Mrs. Haney said as she returned to the room. "Sit here on the sofa beside me." She patted the burgundy brocade flowers trailing over the padded seat.

Mattie sipped on the water, and swallowed hard to fight back the tears.

"I have something for you," Mrs. Haney said as she reached to the table by the sofa and picked up a book. She handed it to Mattie.

"A book?"

"It's a book of poetry that Frank loved. He read it often. Kept it in his room most of the time so I let him take it with him when he went to school. I found it in his things that he brought from Jackson. I want you to have it."

Mattie took the book. On the well-worn cover were the words: Poetry by Alfred Lord Tennyson. She opened the front cover then slowly fanned the pages, which were dog-eared and worn. She recognized many of the poems that Frank had copied and mailed to her. She closed it and clutched it to her breast.

"I don't know what to say." She whispered. "Are you sure you want me to have it?"

Mrs. Haney nodded and patted her gently.

"Thank you. You don't know how much this means to me." Her moist eyes said more than that to Frank's mother.

Mattie held the book close and closed her eyes as she remembered her resolve. She had to let her thoughts play it over in her head. *I will not cry...I will not cry.*

******

The cemetery beside the little Catholic Church at Tucker was really, not a cemetery – not until two weeks before. The only thing that made the sage brush field look like a cemetery was a single mound of red dirt with withered bouquets of zinnias and marigolds marking the head of the grave. There were no angel wings pointing to the sky - no lamb perched on a cold piece of white marble, only a mound of, rock strewn, red dirt. One day there would be a monument; Elizabeth and Paul Haney would see to that. For now, a mound of dirt, a grave, Frank Haney's grave. There would be others – other members of the Catholic Church to die, but Frank had been the first.

Mattie slowed Prince to a walk then pulled back on the bridle to make him stop. She sat on his back and stared up the hillside at the grave. She had to make only a short detour to go by the church when she left the Haney house. *I won't stop, I'll only...go by. Frank's last words were go by, go by.* The inclination to get closer to Frank was too strong to resist. Her hand gave a tug on the reins and Prince obediently trudged up the hill. The horse halted under the shade of a tree and waited, seeming to know this was close enough. Mattie slid from the saddle and slowly walked to the beckoning mound of dirt. She stood over it for a long while then collapsed on top of it. Her arms embraced the mound and she broke her promise to Frank.

Come not when I am dead,
    To drop they foolish tears upon
    My grave…
Pass on weak heart and leave me
    where I lie. Go by, go by.

Deathbed promises often have to be broken.

38

The crosscut saws sprinkled sawdust on the mulch covering the floor of the forest. Isaac and Elijah each took his turn to pull the end of the huge cross-cut saw. One on each end. When one pulled his full length there was no pause; the one on the other end knew just the precise second to heave the sharp teeth toward him. The tree made a long gap in the underbrush when it fell. Joshua and his sons were a hundred or so feet away waiting to pounce on the tree with axes and saws to remove the limbs.

Wade had gone through and marked the trees to be cut "Don't want'a leave a big gap in the woods." He was particular about his forest where virgin timber flourished. Trees that had been growing for centuries. "Once they've been cut it'll take hundreds of years for the little'uns to grow to the same height. Try not to crush the young saplings". He had marched through the woods giving orders, as he put a hatchet slice in each tree at the exact location he wanted it cut. Not a limb was to be wasted. "Isaac can saw the limbs up for firewood." He wanted the woodcutters to respect the trees as much as he did but to most of the workers they were merely - trees.

"Why he so partic'lar 'bout all these trees. Betcha there be's ten million on this place." Isaac asked his future father-in-law.

Joshua understood Wade's reasoning. He had grown up the same way Wade had and he had come to respect the trees as well. Of course

294

there was a possibility that sooner or later some, maybe all of them, would have to be cut to make more fields to grow cotton.

"You gots a whole lot to learn, boy. You best stick clost t' me and learn some of the Posey ways so's you don't mess up. Wade, got some diff'runt idees than mos' the slave drivers 'round here. That's MISTUH Wade to you." He raised one eyebrow and stared at Isaac.

Isaac had recruited every friend and relative he could find to help saw the logs for his house.

"'Sactly when is this here weddin?" Strawtop Calhoun yelled to Isaac. He was called Strawtop because his hair was more the color of straw and somewhat straight. He did not have the kinky black hair of his siblings. Some said it was because his real Pappy was Red Sawyer who lived across the creek from the Calhoun shack. Seemed he was the only white man that sauntered through the woods near the cluster of shacks nestled in the edge of the swamp.

Strawtop's Mamma had a good explanation for his straw-colored hair. "It be's cause when I wuz totin' him in my belly a bright orange bobcat jumped up outta the sage brush and scairt the bejibbers outta me. Marked 'im, that what it done. Turnt his hair the color a the straw."

"Hey Sic, you gonna answer me?" Strawtop had to yell over the sound of the scraping saw and the axes and yells of the other woodcutters. "When's this weddin' gonna take place?" He leaned on his ax handle.

"Soon's you quit ye yappin' and git enough logs for us to build a house."

"If you 'pendin' on my cuttin' it may be the year nineteen hundert 'fore you git to say yo' I do's to that purty little gal." He threw back his head and laughed loudly.

Isaac grinned and gave his end of the saw an extra hard tug. "My pappy ain't gon' let that happin'. He's ready to git my big feet out from under his table. Ain't that right pappy?" He grinned at Elijah.

"Uh-huh. That sho be's right," Elijah laughed, joining in the banter of his son and his friend.

"When's the dinner bell gonna ring?" Strawtop asked, still propped on his axe handle.

Sometimes recruited workers don't work quite as hard as willing volunteers.

******

The leaves of red, orange and gold fluttered in the crisp fall breeze then drifted lazily to reside forever on the brown grass. For two mornings a sheet of white frost had covered the ground and rooftops of Neshoba County. Any vegetation that had tenaciously held on to its green color gave way to tans and browns. The stately cotton stalks had dropped their leaves revealing scraps of cotton hanging here and there over the field. Heavy ears of corn tugged the drying corn stalks toward the ground. Harvesting the corn had had to wait until the sugar cane was stripped and carried to the cane mill.

Tomorrow was Monday so Mattie and Annie would join Wade and Joshua in the fields pulling the ears of corn and throwing them into the wagon. Then they would have to throw them into the corncrib. The three girls and Tommy would be in school so they would not be there to help until after school. Another week of labor faced Mattie.

But…today was Sunday. It was Methodist Sunday at the church in Philadelphia so she stayed home to cook Sunday dinner while the rest of the family went to church. Since Frank's death she had refused to go hear Reverend Whitley preach. She went on Baptist Sunday but on Methodist Sunday she simply refused to go. No matter how angry Annie became or how long Wade pounded on her bedroom door she refused to come out. After a time she was permitted to stay in bed on Sunday while the rest of the family prepared for church. Annie let her know she was expected to have dinner ready when they returned.

Annie's threats of the pantry or smokehouse no longer phased Mattie. She dared Annie to try again to whip her with the belt or the leather strap hanging ominously inside the pantry. Not that she said it in so many words but the squint of her eyes, her clenched teeth and tightened jaw muscles signaled Annie to stop her threats. Nor did Mattie permit Annie to punish the other children harshly. When Annie would start raving at one of them and take the strap off the nail, Mattie simply stepped between Annie and the child.

Annie's anger and rages were turned inward. She seethed and pouted since she was unable to release her frustrations on her children.

Mattie pushed her chair back from the dinner table. "I cooked - ya'll can do the dishes."

"But Bobby's coming over," Pearl objected.

"Too bad. He can help you do dishes."

Alma and Louella started to object but one glance from Wade told them to squelch it. Annie stared after Mattie as she let the kitchen door slam behind her.

"She's going back to that Cath'lic graveyard again." Annie looked at Wade expecting him to do something about it. "It's been ever' Sunday since he died. It's time for her to stop."

"I tried talking to her about it." Wade answered. "She acted like she didn't even hear me."

Pearl felt she would burst if she said nothing. "I reckon that's all she's got. Just a little mound of dirt. If it helps her feelings to go there, then let her be."

"It's embarrassing, folk seeing her lying across that mound of dirt squawling," Annie huffed.

"Guess it ain't no more embarrassing than her having to say goodbye to him in the middle of the road." There, she had said it! Pearl had wanted to have her say ever since she watched from the sweet gum thicket while Mattie bent over the open casket and kissed Frank. She snatched a plate from in front of Louella and added it to the stack to take to the kitchen.

"I'm not finished eating," Louella whined.

"Pearl!" Wade had to say only one word. He pushed back his chair and went down the hall to his chair on the front porch.

Pearl put Louella's plate back in front of her then whirled in her tracks and went to the kitchen. She was so angry she was livid. "I hate doing these darn dishes." The sound of breaking glass came from the kitchen.

"Smart mouth!" Annie shoved her chair back from the table and started to the kitchen. "I'll put a stop to that." She reached for the leather strap hanging inside the pantry. Pearl ran out the back door and let it slam hard behind her.

"No Ma, no."

When Annie stepped outside Mattie stood beside the door. She caught the swinging strap in mid-air. "Give me the strap, Ma. There's not gonna be any more beatings." She clutched the strap firmly and stared at Annie. Annie released her grip on it then meekly went back inside.

Mattie and Pearl went in the kitchen and waited until Annie made her way to the shade tree in the back yard.

"Alma! Louella!" Mattie called. "You youngun's get in here and help Sister Pearl with the dishes." They obediently came to the kitchen. Mattie was quickly becoming the authority figure since Annie had become so fractious.

Mattie pulled on her Sunday bonnet and draped her crocheted shawl around her then went outside where Prince waited. She took the leather strap with her. *I'll get rid 'a this thing once and for all.*

******

The weeds in the graveyard were dry and brittle. Mattie made her way up the trail to the lonely headstone glistening in the sunlight. Mr. Haney had only recently put it there. It was good to see Frank's name written in the marble. She traced it with her fingers then read the words aloud.

"Thomas Frank Haney
Born January 10, 1878
Died September 4, 1896
Safe in the arms of Jesus"

Mattie spread a blanket on the ground beside Frank's grave, took out her pen and paper and wrote him a letter. It helped her to put on paper all the feelings raging inside her. When she finished writing she folded the blanket then kissed his name on the monument and went back to where Prince was patiently waiting. She unwrapped the leather strap from the saddle horn and threw it in the grass.

Woe is me now! For the Lord has added grief to My sorrow.
(The Bible – Jer. 45:3)

39

"Wade Posey, what the hell do you think you're saying?" Lester Warner shouted as he got up from his desk pushing his chair back hard with the calves of his legs. The chair slammed against the wall behind him.

Wade sat calmly in a chair across from the desk, undaunted by the Chancery Clerk's sudden display of emotion. He was not surprised by the outburst and anticipated more before he finished with his business. "Of course I know what I'm saying. Do you think I walked in off the street and blurted it out without thinking about it? Do I need to repeat it?"

"I think I need to pretend I didn't hear it and walk right out that door leaving you sitting there." He reached for his chair and pulled it back under him.

"I'd still be here when you got back." Wade said in his earthy manner. One heel tapped rhythmically on the wood floor as he waited for Lester to calm down.

"Do you want to start an uprising right out there in the streets around the courthouse square - or worse yet on your own doorstep?"

"Nope. Ain't no need for it to start an uprisin' if you do what I ask and keep your mouth shut. Don't go spouting off to the community."

"If I don't tell it, somebody will. That's something you don't keep a secret very long. You know niggers ain't supposed to own property in Neshoba County."

"Is that right? Show me the law." Wade's piercing unmoving eyes stared deep into Lester's.

Lester averted his eyes to the stack of papers on his desk. "Well, there IS one!"

"Show it to me," Wade challenged.

Lester squirmed in his chair. "I can't put my finger on it right this minute but I assure you it's there."

"Is this a county law? A state law? A federal law? Is it even a law?

"It's a Mississippi law which makes it a county law." Blood vessels bulged on Lester's neck.

Wade looked at him calmly. "I tell you what – you show me the state law forbiddin' colored folk from owning property and I'll find the Federal law saying they can. The Emancipation Proclamation gave them the right to own property and I'm deeding this twenty-five acres to Joshua and Louisa Posey."

"The federal law ain't the ruling authority here and you know it!" Lester leaned back in his chair and crossed his ankles. He locked his fingers across his protruding belly.

"It is if the local law enforcement and the state law enforcement don't uphold the laws." Wade leaned forward and squinted his eyes at the smirking Chancery Clerk. He knew exactly what Lester was referring to but he wanted to make him say it. "Who is the ruling authority?"

Lester grinned. "The Federal law may be the final authority but the "real" county authority can cause a lotta havoc before the Feds can get here." He put his forearms on his desk and started toying with a pen.

"Havoc? Why would the sheriff's office cause havoc?" Wade pretended he did not know Lester was referring to the Ku Klux Klan.

"You know what I'm talking about, Wade Posey. You know the Klan enforces unwritten laws here in Mississippi and you ain't no exception."

Lester Warner knew Wade hated the Klan and usually did things the way he perceived as right, flaunting it in their faces.

Everybody around Philadelphia knew how Wade Posey catered to the Negro man who lived on his place. There was talk they ate at the same table on occasion and at one time at least, Joshua's younguns even slept in one of Wade's beds. No one dared be the least bit abusive to Joshua Posey in any way or they had to contend with Wade Posey. He had a way of getting to a man without punching his lights out. His revenge was subtle and threatening getting into the workings of a man's business and making him wish he'd never crossed him.

The Posey family had been in Neshoba County longer than most and wielded power – power made possible by knowledge. Wade knew the dirt on everybody from generations back and he did not mind using the information to his own advantage. He was no gossip but if he could use his knowledge to quell the threats of the Klan he certainly did not mind doing it. He knew which men had visited their sharecroppers wives, which had made dishonest deals with his neighbor, and who had committed the murder of the young woman found dead in the Pearl River Swamp. He was not telling and he had no proof but the perpetrator did not know that. All he had to do was give him a certain look, a little word here, a comment there. Wade was no blackmailer – not unless it was needed to protect his family.

It was assumed he knew the father of every mulatto in the county and Wade let the sneaky father know that he knew. The threat was always there that Wade would tell his wife and children.

"What do you mean I ain't no exception?" Wade pressed for a more direct threat. Wade's heel had stopped tapping and any congeniality he may have had at the beginning of the conversation was gone. His teeth were clenched tightly together and his lips were pursed causing little wrinkles around them.

"All I'm saying is the Klan don't take no exception to you just cause you're a Posey. They'd just as soon come after you as anybody else." He again leaned back in his chair and smirked confidently.

It was Wade's turn to stand over the desk and show his anger and he did so suddenly. He rested his palms on the desk and glared down into Lester's smirking face. "Is that a threat, Warner?"

Wade had suspected for some time that the distinguished Chancery Clerk was a member of the Klan but had never confirmed it. He had his ways of finding out. He knew most everyone in the county as well as their political stand. There had been veiled threats to Wade before this, so he had devised his own methods of learning their identities. It helped that his brother Stuart ran the blacksmith shop and had marked the horseshoes of suspected members of the KKK. The two often chuckled that they could tell who had been in town that day by the hoof prints in the streets. Each was marked differently and Stuart kept a list of the names and the identifying marks.

Even though the Klan wore hoods while doing their dirty work and issuing their cowardly threats, they could not hide the horse tracks.

Wade and Joshua had done their own investigation at cross burning sites. The secret was safe between the two brothers and Joshua.

"I asked you, 'Is that a threat'?" Wade demanded an answer.

"All I'm saying is just cause you're a Posey and got a lotta relatives in the county don't mean you're immune to retaliation from the Klan." He continued to grin.

"You're right I'm a Posey and I don't take lightly to threats from the Klan or anybody else. I don't need a whole passal of relatives to fight my battles, neither. I'd like to remind you and anyone who might be the least bit curious – I know who is in the Klan and if any of them as much as sets a foot on my place or threatens one of my colored hands they will answer to me. You got that?" His words were caustic. Fire darted from his eyes.

Wade had to sit back in his chair and grip the wooden arms to keep from slugging him. "Now you fix the deed." He pointed to the top of the desk and stared at the face of the elected official.

Lester was no longer smiling. He started to refuse but thought better of it. He opened the desk drawer and removed a notary stamp. He looked over the description of the property Wade had written and reluctantly pressed the stamp into it.

"I got three more copies I want stamped and signed," Wade said as he pulled the papers out of the pocket on the bib of his overalls.

"Three? We don't usually…"

"Stamp 'em!" Wade persisted as he shoved them into Lester's hands.

"Why four deed's? You really don't need…"

"I know the normal procedure," Wade interrupted. "This one is different. One copy of the deed for your records. One copy for Joshua Posey and one copy for Wade Posey." He stopped to let him count.

Lester stopped in the middle of his signature. "That's three. Who's the other one for?"

"The Federal government," he answered smugly.

Wade had no idea how to register the deed with the Federal Government or even if it were possible. He only wanted the County Chancery Clerk, namely Lester Warner, to think it was registered with the Feds.

Lester finished with the papers and slid them across the desk toward Wade. Wade slowly folded them and put them in his bib pocket. He crossed his legs and leaned back in the chair. "I'm waiting," he said.

"Waitin' for what!?" .

"To watch you write it down in that big old book you got stuck under that counter over there." He jerked his head toward the counter.

"I'll do it. You don't have to watch. You can trust me."

"I trust you all right, Warner. I trust you."

The fact was, Wade did not trust him at all. Like most of the outsiders, he had been viewed with suspicion since he first arrived in town sixteen years ago. He had to ingratiate himself to all the locals, which he soon did. Within a few months he was dating the Mayor's daughter and within two years they were married with a baby on the way. He flaunted his education and his suave manner of speaking. After five years his father-in-law was campaigning for him to be the next County Chancery Clerk. It was evident he was more qualified than any of the locals so he was voted in by a landslide.

Wade had nothing against the man – it was just that he was an outsider - so he viewed his sudden arrival as suspicious. Wade made it his business to hang around the depot and chat with the conductors and the engineers who came directly from Memphis. They brought newspapers and verbal accounts of the scandals and mysteries from around the state border. Wade was careful not to voice his opinions or suspicions to anyone, not even his wife. He believed in keeping it under his hat for future use - if necessary.

Wade took the long way home, which, just so happened to go by Lester Warner's place. His riding mare, just so happened, to be grazing near the road. Wade just so happened, to have a large pocketknife with him. Lester's mare, just so happened to be real friendly and nuzzled him through the fence when he called him. The mare obediently lifted his left rear leg when Wade patted it. Wade took his knife and loosened one of the nails holding the shoe on the mare's hoof. This, just so happened, to leave a distinguishable identifying mark on the horseshoe.

40

A cold winter, midnight wind whistled through the bare limbs of the oak tree in the Posey yard. Mattie turned on her side and pulled the cover over one ear to keep it warm. The other was nestled in the feather pillow. Pearl stirred and slung one arm across Mattie indicating that Mattie's movements had disturbed her. Mattie stared into the darkness and listened to the wind, wondering about the time. She waited for the clock in the front room to strike. It was not very long until she was counting the strikes. *One, two, three, four, five, six. It should be getting light back in the east.* She eased from under the cover, careful not to disturb Pearl, and went to the window. She pressed her forehead to the cold glass and searched the sky for any sign of the sun. The sun was not there but dark rolling clouds were. *Snow clouds. Guess I'll have to drive the kids to school in the wagon. Pa will be going to the sawmill.*

Wade and Annie's voices were muffled coming from the front room and the sound of logs being piled into the fireplace signaled the beginning of the new day. Soon the fire would be blazing and the room would be toasty warm. Tommy and the girls would bring their clothes to the hearth to get dressed in the warm glow of the fire. Mattie and Annie would spend their day in front of the hearth crocheting or piecing quilt tops from scraps. If Annie were not in one of her pensive moods the two would discuss the neighbors and their problems. If Annie were depressed she would stay in the bed most of the day and Mattie would crochet and think of Frank. She would take her red velvet box from under her clothes in the wardrobe and read them again. Maybe Louisa or Naomi would join them by the fire and bring their own handwork.

Mattie pulled a quilt snugly around her as she stood at the window watching the morning break. The dark gloomy clouds could not keep the sun from bringing some light to the earth. She could see the outline of trees on the horizon. Naomi and Isaac's house was silhouetted against the northern sky. Mattie had questioned her Father as to why he built their house so far away from Joshua's. It seemed to her it would have been best to build it near Naomi's parents and on the land, which was deeded to them.

"I got no idea what kind of worker Isaac's gonna be." Wade had explained to her. "If I need to run him off and replace him with somebody else I can. I couldn't if he's living on Josh's property."

Mattie noticed a glint of fire coming from Naomi's window and watched as it became a steady glow. She smiled when she saw smoke rise from their chimney then course across the sky. She could imagine Isaac up in his long handles building the fire then getting back into bed with Naomi until the room was warm. She was happy for Naomi but the "if only's" tortured her. *If only Frank and I had not been stopped. If only he had seen a doctor in Jackson. If only he were still alive. If only, if only, if only.* Her eyes blinked rapidly and she shook her head, bringing herself back to reality. A long sigh emitted from inside her as she reached for her dress which lay across the foot of the bed. She slipped it over her nightgown and went to the kitchen where Wade already had a fire in the stove.

She sat on the stack of wood behind the stove until the room was warm. This had been one of her favorite places on cold mornings when she was small. She had felt secure in the warmth of the stove and the smell of meat frying and biscuits cooking. She still found a bit of security and comfort as her head rested on her knees.

The fire snapped and crackled inside the stove and brought Mattie's attention back to the present. "I might as well start breakfast and get the kids off to school. It doesn't look like Ma's gonna get up this morning."

The dogs shuffled under the house then began to bark. They ran across the yard and toward the barn barking at an intruder. Mattie sifted flour into a bowl to make biscuits and listened as the dogs' barking turned to a low whine. *Sounds like somebody's out there.* She tilted her head to one side and listened. There was a sharp rap on the kitchen door that startled her. She jumped. Another knock and a low voice, "Mattie, it's me, Naomi."

Mattie could not help but laugh when she opened the door and saw nothing but a little round, black nose and the whites of Naomi's eyes peeking out from a knitted cap and scarf. A quilt was wrapped around her that touched the floor. Isaac's big shoes flopped on her feet. She was grinning, showing a mouth full of, white teeth.

"I seen it was you through the winder, didn't mean to skeer ye."

"You scared the living daylights out of me, girl! What are you doing out in this cold weather so early in the morning?"

The quilt fell to the floor in a heap along with the cap, scarf, a big coat and the big, floppy, brown brogans. Naomi shivered and spread her palms over the top of the stove to warm them.

"Are you going to answer my question?" Mattie prodded.

"I sho am, soon's I stop shaking from the cold."

Mattie stood facing her expectantly. Flour from her hands sprinkled on the floor around her feet. "Well?"

"I didn't sleep hardly a wink last night I's so excited. Isaac and me talked practic'ly all night."

"What's so exciting here in the dead of winter, way out here in the middle of nowhere on the Posey reservation?" Mattie grinned then a thought popped in her mind. "Are you…are you…"

Naomi had a puzzled look on her face then she realized what Mattie was suspecting. She thought it was hilarious and laughed loudly. Realizing that she may have awakened the rest of the Poseys she clapped her hand over her mouth. "No I ain't in the family way! Sho ain't, but I got 'n idee. You know how you showed me how ta read, then I showed all the little 'uns 'round the house?"

Mattie nodded and waited for her to continue.

Naomi cocked her head to one side and looked at Mattie intently. Her eyes sparkled mischievously. "Why can't I bring some little colored youngun's to my house and teach 'em what you done teached me?"

Mattie reached into the five gallon can and scooped out a hand full of lard. "You mean like a school? You can't be a teacher. You have to graduate from highschool to be a teacher." Mattie squeezed the lard and flour between her fingers then slowly added buttermilk until it became a thick pliable doughy mixture.

"You wadn't no teacher when you teached me! You wadn't no highschool grad'ate neither, you's jist in the first grade. You jist showed me what the teacher showed you. That's all I wanna do. Jist show some po' ole ignert chile what you showed me."

Mattie rolled out the dough into round balls and pressed them in a greased iron skillet. "It might work - at least until they get a school."

"You really thank it would Matt, do ye really? You could be my assistant." Her eyes glared in excitement.

"Your assistant!?" Mattie laughed. You've never been to school and I'm gonna be your assistant?" They both laughed until they had to hold their sides.

"Then I'll be your assistant!" Naomi managed to say through her laughter.

"What on earth is going on in here?" Annie pushed the kitchen door open letting in a rush of cold air from the hall. "What's so funny?" She went into the pantry to get a slab of middling from the meat box.

"Naomi is wanting me to be her assistant school teacher!" This started them laughing again.

"Is this a joke? By the way, what are you doing out so early in the morning?" Annie questioned Naomi.

Naomi composed herself so she could explain to Annie. "Miz Ann, you know how you always wanted us niggers to have a school and ain't nobody started one fer us yet?"

Annie nodded and glanced at Naomi as she sliced a piece of thick bacon off the slab and laid it in the hot skillet.

"Well, me 'n Isaac got the big idee last night to start teachin' 'em right down in our brand new, little house. If'n Matt'll hep me we could do it. Jist show 'em how to read and draw their numbers. That much'd hep the po little ignert chillun." She stood with her hands on her hips waiting for Annie's reply. "What'cha thank?"

"By cracky, it might work! You'd better move back a little before you get splattered with hot grease." Annie turned the sizzling meat with a fork. "It just might lead to a school. If the neighbors see we are serious about educating colored folk they might get a school started."

"Then you be's fer it?"

"Sure. You have my backing. I can't imagine what Wade will say about it. That still doesn't answer my question as to why you're out this early in the morning in this freezing cold weather."

"I jist couldn't wait no longer, Miz Ann. I's so excited I couldn't wait no longer to see if Matt'd hep me."

"I haven't agreed to anything," Mattie quipped as she opened the oven door to check on the biscuits.

"You will, though, won't you?" Annie queried.

"I'll think about it." Mattie's answer was noncommittal.

"They's one mo" thang." Naomi dug her bare toes into the pine boards and fidgeted. "I's wonderin' if'n you's gonna take the younguns to school this mornin' in the wagon – you know like you do when it be's real cold?" She looked up at Mattie.

"I guess I will. Why do you ask?" Mattie turned the pan of biscuits out on a plate and set them on the table.

"I's wonderin' if'n I could go with ye and look 'n see how a school house be's set up. I ain't never been in no school before." She stared at the plate of hot biscuits and the round mold of butter Annie set on the table.

"Well, of course. We might could leave a little early and look it over before the children start arriving," Mattie suggested.

Naomi was jubilant. "It would be a dream come true if'n I could work it out. I'd better go get dressed up like 'my assistant' if'n I's gonna go to the school house." She grinned at Mattie then stuck her feet down in the brogans and put on her cap and scarf. She could not seem to take her eyes off the biscuits. She wrapped the quilt about her and put her hand on the doorknob. "See ye in a little while."

"Why don't you take you and Isaac a couple of these biscuits, then you won't have to cook breakfast?" Annie put the biscuits on a plate and started to cover them with a clean dishcloth.

"Do ye thank ye could put a little pat a that fresh cow butter 'tween 'em?"

"Well of course." Annie ran a knife over the top of the butter and collected a pile on the knife then slid it in a biscuit.

Ellen Williamson

"You might as well take some meat with you as well. We got more than enough for us," Mattie said as she laid some hot slices of fried meat beside the biscuits.

"Um-m-m, I sho 'preciate it. There ain't nuthin' better'n Posey buttered biscuits.

******

Sunday afternoons fit for riding horseback to the cemetery at Tucker were rare during the winter. Mattie longed for just one afternoon warm enough but most of the time she had to be content to sit in front of the fire in the parlor reading Frank's letters and poetry. She read the book of poetry through many times and even committed some of it to memory. She could use her father's wagon but it was big and somewhat bumpy. *I need a little buggy of my own but where on earth would I get the money? Pa sure won't give it to me. He spends all his money on land - more and more land.*

Four girls need a lot of things, pretty things. Things that are in fashion. Wade bought the necessities for his family but he did not consider the latest fashions a necessity. The girls constantly bombarded him with the "I wants". Fashions were not that important to Mattie since she was not in the "courting mode". As long as she had a couple of Sunday dresses and a decent riding skirt she was happy. Mattie did not dare hit him up for a buggy of her own and she had no way to earn money. She pondered how she could finagle it out of him. Mattie would like a little something of her own. A little light-weight buggy to put behind Prince was all she needed.

Prince was getting old and could no longer work like he used to. It pained her to see him working so hard. If she could buy a workhorse for her father, she could put Prince to pasture and use him only for her own purposes. The past spring and summer Mattie had insisted on being the one behind the plow when Prince had to work. She let him walk slowly and pull only a minimum amount of weight.

Spring would arrive in a couple of months and Mattie was anxious to pursue her plan.

The next "Methodist Sunday" Mattie was at home preparing Sunday Dinner when she decided this would be the day she would ask her father. She knew she could do it if he would only let her.

310

The empty platter that held the fried chicken was slid under the bread plate to make room for the blackberry cobbler Mattie had made for dessert. Mattie even took up the dirty plates and put little dessert plates out for every one. She waited until Wade was enjoying his pie.

"When do we start breaking ground to plant cotton?" Mattie decided to lead up to the subject slowly and not reveal her complete plan immediately. Without looking at her Wade knew her question was directed at him.

"Soon's the land gets dry enough, I reckon. Probably be the first of March, depending on how much rain we get. Why do you ask?"

"I was thinking about Prince – you know how old he's getting - and all. He's not really up to plowing another crop year." She peered over her plate of steaming pie at Wade who had not looked up.

"No matter, we gotta use him one more year anyhow."

"But he's really not able." What would it take to get you to consider…" Mattie paused unsure how to continue.

"Consider what?" A spoonful of purple pie was suspended between his mouth and his plate.

"Consider giving me an acre of land."

Annie looked at her suspiciously but did not interrupt the conversation.

"You mean give you a deed to a acre of land, like I gave twenty-five to Josh?" Wade wondered what on earth she would want with a single acre of land. Was she thinking of building a house and moving out? Surely not!

"Oh no! I don't mean like that. What I mean is to let me have it for one crop year and plant cotton on it. I'd work it myself, without asking any help from you and the profit would be all mine." Her heart pounded.

"Ain't no need 'n you doing that. What we make here is part yours. I'll give you what you need. All you have to do is ask me." He put his spoon down in the empty dish and pushed it from the table edge. He tugged on the tip of his moustache to dislodge any food that had gotten on it. "Now tell me, what is it you need with the proceeds from a whole acre of land?"

Mattie knew he was backing down and would never consent if she told him about the buggy.

"I want to buy you a work horse so I can retire Prince. If you let me use one acre for myself I won't ask you or anyone else to help me. I'll do the plowing, planting, hoeing and picking right by myself without asking anybody."

"What about helping the rest of us in my field?"

"I'll work in mine after we quit at night. I'll even buy my own seed and fertilizer. Please, Pa, think about it."

Annie could stay silent no longer. "How you gonna buy your own seed and fertilizer? You got money stashed away we don't know about?" Her question dripped with sarcasm.

Mattie did not bother to answer her. "Will you let me if I can get the money for seed and fertilizer?"

Wade could think of no reason to object. "Sure, if that's what you want to do." He was not too concerned about giving up an acre of good cotton land since he was quite sure she could not get the money.

"Thanks, I'll show you. I'll do it and you'll be proud."

She got up from the table and started stacking the dishes until Wade and Annie were out in the front room sitting by the fire. She then went to the bedroom where the three girls were changing clothes. "I cooked dinner, ya'll can wash dishes."

******

Amos Posey was Mattie's confidant. He had always been a friend as well as a cousin and she could always trust him to keep a secret, even better than his sister Ida. Many times he had made arrangements for her to see Frank. If she told him something she knew it would stay between the two of them. "This is between you 'n me 'n the lot gate," they would say meaning it was not to be repeated. She was sure he could think of some way to help her in this predicament.

The wind in her face was cold as she rode the one-mile to her Uncle George and Aunt Delvine's house. Prince wasted no time in getting her there.

"She pecked on the door then opened it slightly. "Aunt Delvine, it's me," She called then went in and closed the door behind her. The pungent smell of food greeted her. She walked down the cold hall to the kitchen door and knocked again.

The family was finishing their Sunday dinner in the warm kitchen. Delvine and George had ten children and with the exception of Ida they all sat around the table. The majority of them were teenagers or pre-teens. There were two stragglers that came along later than the others.

"Mattie! Come on in," Delvine said as she got up from the table. The rest of the family greeted her warmly. "Let me have your wrap and you can join us for dinner."

"I already ate. I had dinner ready when the rest came in from church."

"We missed you at church today," George said.

"Uncle George, you know I don't go to church on Methodist Sunday. Why don't ya'll get a new preacher, then I could go back."

"Preacher's ain't easy to find in these parts. If Brother Whitley hadn't a moved to Philadelphia he wouldn't a' made it today, as cold as it is." He poured hot coffee from his cup into his saucer then sipped it from the saucer.

"How's Ida and her new husband doing? I haven't seen them in a month or more."

Amos couldn't help but laugh. "Them two love birds don't go much of anywhere in this cold. They stay snuggled up in that little house down under the hill." He stood, then tucked his foot under him and over the bench. "Good dinner, Ma. Think I'll ride over and vist my girl." He winked at Mattie.

The chatter and noise around the table increased as all the children finished their meal and left the table.

"Amos, can I talk to you for a minute?" Mattie said and stood up to follow him out of the kitchen. "I'll be back in a few minutes," Mattie said over her shoulder to Aunt Willie.

"Let me think on it for a couple of days and I'll see what I can come up with," Amos suggested after Mattie told him of her plan.

"Thanks, I knew I could count on you." Mattie smiled.

Amos looked in the mirror over the dresser then took a comb from his pocket and combed his hair. "Does Uncle Wade now what you're planning to do?"

"Oh no! I didn't tell him about wanting a buggy. I only told him that I want to retire Prince."

"Why do you want a buggy of your own?"

Mattie fidgeted and looked out the window. "So I can go to the cemetery in cold weather."

Amos turned quickly toward her. "Mattie Parilee, when are you going to stop going to that cemetery and crying over Frank."

Mattie's eyes pleaded for understanding. "You know how much I loved Frank. You know more than anybody."

"I know, but he's gone. You need to stop going there so often and start seeing somebody else."

She dropped her gaze to the floor. "I will, just as soon as..."

"As soon as what?"

"I don't know!" She was a bit irritated at his insistence. "Will you help me?"

"I'll see what I can find for you. I'll get back to you in a few days. Gotta' run. See ya'." With that he hurried out the door.

******

Willard Johnson's booming voice led the congregration in Amazing Grace then he turned the Sunday service over to the Baptist preacher. He made his way down the narrow aisle to where Mattie sat. Amos moved to the pew behind to let him sit beside Mattie. Willard looked at her and winked. She smiled at him then turned to Georgia and made a face.

Georgia nudged Mattie with her elbow and whispered, "He's flirtin' with you. Flirt back."

"Nope, ain't interested." Willard put his elbows on his knees and rested his chin in his hands. He turned so he could see Mattie and whispered, "I want to talk to you after church."

Mattie looked up at the preacher without answering.

As soon as the last Amen was said, Willard turned to Mattie. "Hear you want to buy a horse." Willard spoke louder than he intended.

"I do but...but I don't," Mattie hedged as she looked out the window at the towering Woodmen of the World monument.

"Either you do or you don't which is it?" He grinned and waved his hand in front of Mattie's face to get her to look in his direction.

314

She turned her back to the window. "I want to buy one in the fall when we sell the cotton, until then I won't have the money." She spread her hands out palms up.

"I understood Amos to say you want to retire your black horse – the one you've been riding for years."

She turned to walk toward the door. "I sure would like to but Pa needs him for plowing for another year, at least."

He fell in step with her. "I have a good work horse I want to sell. Think you would be interested?"

Mattie stopped abruptly and turned to face him. "You have? Can you wait 'til this fall?"

"I really need to get rid of him before summer. We have too many horses. They're eatin' up all the hay."

"I couldn't buy him now. Besides, Pa needs to look at the horse and see if he wants it."

"Why don't I ride him over this afternoon and let your Pa look him over. I need to come callin' on you anyway." He grinned and anticipated Mattie's answer.

She put her hands on her hips and looked at him mischievously. "And, exactly when did I agree for you to come callin' on me?"

"You didn't. I decided to come without you agreeing. See you about two-o'clock." He sprinted down the steps then glanced back at her.

"Smart aleck." She smiled.

Amos grinned and walked over to Mattie.

"How's that for setting you up?"

"Setting me up? She answered indignantly. "He's coming to show Pa his horse."

"Yeah, right!" He teased. "He'll be sitting in the parlor with you before the day is over."

"Will not!" She frowned. "Besides, he thinks he's a ladies' man and every girl in the county wants him to come callin'." She stalked off toward the wagon where the rest of the family waited.

******

Mattie swiped the kitchen table with the dishcloth, then hung it on the towel rack. Annie peered through the kitchen door.

315

"There's somebody out there talking to your pa. I believe it's the Johnson boy." She smiled at Mattie. "Think maybe he's come to see you?"

Mattie snatched her apron off and slung it across the back of a chair. "I hope not!"

Annie touched Mattie lightly on the arm. "I think that would be mighty nice. He's a fine young man."

She glared at Annie "I ain't interested! I want to go to the cemetery."

Annie stood in the doorway. She looked at Mattie tenderly yet fearfully. *You'll keep waitin' and end up being an old maid,* she thought. "Don't you think it's time to get your mind off the dead and on the living."

Mattie flinched and answered harshly. "You just DO NOT understand!"

Annie ignored her harshness. "I understand more than you think! I'm afraid if you grieve much longer you'll miss out on life."

Mattie clenched her teeth and squinted at Annie. "I have already missed out on life. You saw to that!" She squeezed through the doorway past Annie.

"He was a Catholic, Mattie! He was a Catholic!" she yelled as Mattie slammed the door to her bedroom.

Pearl stood before the mirror and tucked strands of hair under the bun on top of her head.

"I see Willard's outside. Do you want me to go ask him in?"

"Nope." Mattie answered curtly. "Let him talk to Pa as long as he will. I'm in no hurry for him to come inside."

"That is some fine horse you got there!" Wade said to Willard as they came through the front door. "How many hands did you say he is?"

"Fifteen and a half," Willard answered proudly. "If you're interested you can take him for a ride."

"I might do that."

Mattie came out of the bedroom door.

"Hi! Did I hear you tell Pa you have a horse for sale?"

"A mighty fine one, too. He's chestnut with a blaze of white on his face," Wade commented.

"Do you like him?" Mattie asked, addressing Wade. "Will he make a good work horse?"

"He's a mighty fine work horse," Willard volunteered. "I've plowed him myself."

Wade tilted his head and looked at Willard. "How much you want for him?"

"I'll give you a good price. Go look him over good and we'll talk money later."

Wade went out the door and left Willard standing in the parlor with Mattie. Willard grinned at Mattie. "Well, it took me three months and a chestnut horse to get to stand here in your parlor. Aren't you gonna ask me to sit?"

"Sure, have a seat." Mattie indicated a brocade chair sitting beside the fireplace.

Willard looked around the room. "I think I prefer that sofa over there." He walked to the sofa and sat in the middle of it. "Here," he patted the sofa beside him. "Are you going to sit or are you gonna stand."

Mattie hesitated but then smiled and sat beside him.

"What are you going to charge me for the horse?"

"I'll let you have him for forty dollars if you'll name him after me"

"Deal. Lets shake on it." Mattie extended her right hand to him.

"Naw," he drawled. "Let's seal it with a kiss."

"I ain't studin' you!" She whirled, turning her back to him. "I ain't tradin' my kisses for a forty dollar horse."

Willard shrugged. "Can't blame a man for trying."

They laughed then decided the horse should be named Willie.

...Nothing ventured – Nothing gained.

41

The dogs raised their heads and perked their ears, then began a low growl. The four of them came from under the house and looked out toward the road. They waited and listened then barked loudly and ferociously as they ran to the end of the driveway. Wade stirred and wondered what they were barking at, then turned on his side to go back to sleep. One of the dogs yapped loudly as though he had been struck with something.

Wade's feet hit the floor with a thud. Annie sat up in bed. "What is it? Is somebody out there?" She asked Wade as he pulled on his overalls and stuck his feet in his shoes. In that instance the entire front of the house illuminated with flickering flames.

"Fire!" Wade ran out into the hall then out on the porch. Flames flickered toward the sky from an object on the ground. It was obvious to Wade that it was a cross though from the porch it was not immediately discernable. He heard the sound of several horses racing down the driveway.

By now everyone in the house was awake and flocked together on the porch watching the fire and the six horses and riders race down the driveway. The unmistakable pointed white hoods and fluttering sheets disappeared at the end of the long driveway and around the curve. With Wade's appearance on the porch the dogs came from under the house and ran down the driveway. "NO!" Wade yelled. "Get back to this house!" he yelled at the dogs.

"Let them catch them, Pa. Let them chase the cowards down," Tommy yelled. "Why'd you call off the dogs?"

"Cause I don't want them messing up the tracks."

Annie stood on the porch in her nightgown and bare feet, crying loudly. "It's the Klan! The Klu Klux Klan! Oh Lord help us. Why'd they come here? She ran down the steps into the yard where Wade was attempting to put out the fire. What you done now, Wade Posey? What you done now? They could have burned the house down."

"It's a cross ain't it?" Pearl screamed.

The five children huddled together in fear. They did not understanding the significance of a burning cross in their own yard. They had often heard of it happening to colored people but never thought there was a reason for it to happen to them.

"Hey what's going on up there?" Joshua called as he ran up the trail.

"It's the Klan! They threw a burning cross in our yard!" Annie screamed. "It's a thousand wonders they hadn't throwed it on the porch. It coulda burned the house down!" She was crying frantically.

"Get back in the house!" Wade yelled at Annie. "All of you get back inside. Get a fire started or something. Don't stand there in the cold gawking at something you can't do nothing about."

Wade dashed a bucket of water on the burning cross then he and Joshua went back to the well for more.

"Why don't ye jist let it burn itself out?"

"'Cause I want some of it left to put in some yards tomorrow – in the daylight."

Sunrise found Wade and Joshua on their knees peering at hoof prints in the driveway. They had no trouble making out the identifying marks in the soft soil.

"How many different sets do you see?"

"I don't much b'lieve there be's mor'n six. What you think?"

"That's all I see," Wade said as he took a piece of paper and pencil and started noting the identifying marks on the horseshoes. "I need to check with Stu about a coupl'a these but I'm dead certain about three of them."

"What you gwin ta do Mistah Wade?" Joshua's eyes were big with fear and anticipation. Until now he was able to mask his fear but the gravity of the situation had to be faced. If the intimidation of a burning cross in a yard didn't get the results they wanted the KKK took other measures. Joshua was all too familiar with what some of them were. He, also knew Wade would not concede to their threats. His pride would not let it go. He would have to confront the culprits and Joshua knew it could mean bad trouble on the Posey farm. Joshua felt it was only right that he go help Wade since he was positive the Klan was retaliating because of him. He did not know why, but he had to be the reason.

"Wade, I axed you a question. What you gwin ta do?" Wade appeared to be concentrating on his drawing of the hoof prints. Joshua persisted. "You got 'ny idee what this is all about? Why they burn the cross in yo yard? Was it sumpin' I done?"

"Nothing you done, Josh. I got a good idea but it was nothing you did."

"Are you gwin ta tell me what you thank their reason be's?"

"The less you know the better."

Wade took an ax and chopped the charred pieces of the cross in six pieces. "Do you mind saddling my horse up for me? I need to make some visits while these sheet flapping cowards are still inside with their wives and chillun."

"You want me to go wid ye? You sho' don't need to ride off by yo'self confrontin' them gun totin' white men."

"Better not. Having a colored man show up on their doorsteps would only make them madder. I don't want you getting involved. You go on about your business today. I'll take care of this in my own way."

"At least tell me 'sactly where you gwin' so if sumpn' happens to ye I'll know where to start lookin'," he urged.

"I told you the less you know the better." Now will you go get my horse?"

******

Mattie pulled her coat close around her and made her way down the frost covered trail that led to Naomi's house. A Negro man with two children riding on his mule with him rode up to the porch. He lifted the children to the porch. They ran to the door as Naomi opened it and let them inside. Seeing Mattie she stepped outside and waited for her to get to the steps.

"How many are here today?" Mattie asked.

"Six so far. Some more could be comin' though. It's still early."

"Did you see the fire up at the house last night?" Mattie asked.

"Fire! No! What was on fire?" Naomi stood with one hand on the doorknob and the other on her open mouth.

"A cross, a simple six foot cross wrapped in kerosene soaked rags," Mattie said matter of factly.

"The Klan?" Naomi's eyes widened with fear. Now both hands covered her lower face. "What'd they want? Did they say anything?"

"Never said a word, left a note or nothing. Pa didn't seem too worried, says he knows who they are. I heard him tell Ma he was going to put the fear of God in them cowardly bas..." She didn't finish her sentence and glanced around to see if any of the children were around.

"Mattie I's skeered. What if'n they takes Mistuh Wade off som'ers and hangs him from a tree like they done some 'a them carpet baggers."

"Don't worry, Pa can take care of himself. When him and his six brothers get together they can pretty well set some neighbors straight. Now, lets get inside and teach these children."

The little Negro school had only been going on for two weeks. Mattie was pleased with the way the children were so eager to learn. Only choice children were chosen to participate - children of parents who vowed to keep the secret. Mattie and Naomi knew it was just a matter of time until the school became common knowledge but for now they had rather not have any crosses burned in Isaac and Naomi's yard. With the coming of spring there would be no more classes since Naomi and Isaac would be helping the rest of the Posey's with the spring planting.

So far, the classes consisted only of learning and writing the alphabet and learning to count. Mattie doubted her ability to teach much more than the simplest reading, writing and arithmetic. Hopefully there would be some definite plans for a Negro school by

October. Meanwhile Mattie and Naomi would teach all who were willing to learn.

******

Lester Warner's house was silhouetted against the sun rising behind it. Two speckled puppies ran from behind the house and yapped at the heels of Wade's horse. He rode up to the well and tied his horse beside the watering trough then reached into a burlap bag and took out a piece of the charred cross. The back door was opened by a teenage boy who looked to be about thirteen.

"Howdy, son." Wade called cheerfully. "Is your pa home?"

"Yes sir but he's still at the barn." He held the door open for Wade to enter.

Wade hesitated not wanting to intrude until he was invited inside.

"Truett, who is it?" Mona Warner called from the kitchen.

"It's Alma Posey's papa," the boy called back.

"Mr. Wade come on in. What are you doing out so early?"

"Mornin' Miss Mona. I need to see Lester for a few minutes, that's all."

"He's still doing the morning chores, should be in the house in a few minutes. Want to have a cup a' coffee while you wait?"

Ordinarily Wade would have gone to the barn to take care of his business with one of his neighbors but for today's purposes the children needed to be present. Wade pulled off his hat and held it in his hand as he went into the warm kitchen. Two little girls appeared in the kitchen doorway rubbing their eyes, still in their nightgowns.

"Good morning!" Wade greeted the two little girls as he feigned cheerfulness. He was anything but cheerful.

"Can you say good morning to Mr. Posey?" Their mother asked as she set a cup of coffee in front of Wade. Neither of them answered. They joined their brother on the bench.

When Wade heard the unmistakable sound of Lester's footsteps on the back porch he braced himself for the confrontation.

Lester did not recognize the horse tied at the well and was curious as to who would be visiting this early in the morning. He pushed the kitchen door open and hesitated for a second before stepping over the threshold. He was startled to see Wade sitting at his table. His knees

322

weakened and he felt the blood drain from his face. Guilt consumed him as well as a fear of what Wade would have to say. *Maybe he doesn't know I was one of the Klan at his house last night.* He recovered quickly and managed a half smile.

"Good morning, Wade. What brings you out in the cold so early in the morning?" He handed the pail of warm milk to Mona. He knew he should offer his hand in a greeting to his visitor but somehow the anger and guilt inside him prevented it. Bad enough he had to fake welcoming him. He dipped water from the bucket on the washstand and poured it in a pan then immersed his hands in the cold water. He rubbed the soap into a lather and washed longer than Wade figured was necessary. Like Pontius Pilate and Lady McBeath, he washed and washed. *'Out these damn spots',* Wade thought. *Reminds me of that story Mattie was tellin' about last year by that Shakespeare fellar. The old woman was guilty of murder and she tried to wash it off her hands. 'Out these damn spots.'*

Lester dried his hands and watched Wade turn a piece of scorched wood in his hand. A small piece of smoked and scorched cloth still clung to it.

Wade did not bother to answer Lester's question as to why he was out so early. He would learn soon enough.

Mona turned a pan of biscuits out on a plate and set them on the table then put a plate and a fork in front of Wade. "You might as well join us for breakfast. There's plenty for all of us, huh, Lester?" She thrust the plate of biscuits in front of Wade.

Lester sat at the side of the table. He refused to look directly at Wade. "Sure. Sure. Help yourself."

Wade held one hand in front of him, his palm toward the plate. "No thank you, ma'am. I already had breakfast."

Truett took the plate and helped himself to two biscuits. His curiosity got the best of him so he asked the question they all wanted to ask. "What's that you got there?" He nodded toward the charred wood Wade was holding.

"A piece 'a wood. A piece 'a burnt wood." Wade held it up in front of him and turned it in the sunlight coming through the window. He turned it slowly as if he were examining it on all sides. "I call it hate wood."

"Hate wood?" Mona laughed. "Why do you call it hate wood?"

The oldest of the girls mimicked her mother in laughter.

"It's hate wood off a cross." His words were slow, drawn out, punctuated with drama. He spoke slowly and paused between each word. "Yep! A flaming, hot, sizzling, crackling, coal-oil soaked, burning cross. Just like the one Jesus was crucified on."

Truett held his fork in mid-air. "You mean like the Kluxers burn in front of nigger houses?"

"Don't you young'uns need to get ready for school?" Lester asked in words that seemed more like a command than a question.

"Let them finish eating," Mona objected. Only they were no longer eating. They were mesmerized by the piece of "Kluxers'" cross Wade was slowly turning in his hand. It seemed that Lester was the only one eating. He stuffed his mouth full before he swallowed the last bite. If his mouth was full he could not comment on Wade's exposition.

Wade was unperturbed by the interruption. "That's ri-i-i-ight! Just the same kinda hate cross." Wade drawled. "Jesus was put on a hate cross 'cause the Jews hated him and wanted him DEAD!" He hit the table with his fist. The children were visibly startled. Wade smiled at them. "Sorry didn't mean to scare you, sweetie." He turned his eyes back to the piece of wood he held up where all could see. "Only this piece of wood is part of a cross that hate filled heathens burned in my yard last night."

Mona gasped. "At your house! Why? Why would anyone burn a cross in your yard?"

"'Cause they hate me, just like they hated Jesus." He turned his eyes toward Lester who had stopped eating and stared at him, his lips pursed with anger. Wade stared back at him.

"'Cause they are sorry, no-good, cowards who ain't got the guts to come to a man in person and talk over their differences. They think their opinion is right and nobody else's matters." He looked intently at Mona then at each of the children.

Mona nodded. "That's what the Kluxers are. Pure cowards!"

"They come in the da-a-a-arkest part of the night just like Judas done to the Christ. They act like they're your friends at church then betray you with their demon friends out in the woods. They have white pointed hoods covering their faces and sheets draped around them trying to conceal their identity." He looked back at Lester. "Too bad they can't conceal the identity of their horses."

Lester was visibly shaken. He was relieved that his family was staring at Wade instead of watching his face change colors.

Wade continued with his eyes fastened on Lester. "They are so full of hate for the black man they take it out on anybody that befriends one of them. They look at the color of a man's skin and judge him by it, when under the skin the black man looks just like me and you." He turned his eyes to the children.

Lester pushed his chair back and stood up. "It's about time..."

"Really?" The youngest of the little girl interrupted him. "You mean they're white under the skin?"

Wade chuckled. "Not white exactly, sorta pink-like. Their blood is red just like yours and they got souls that goes to heaven when they die – or HELL if they are mean like the Kluxers." He emphasized hell and looked directly in Lester's eyes.

Lester sat back in his chair and tried to hold his temper. It was obvious that Mona and his children sympathized with Wade and he would have to be careful not to let his guilt show. He had to put a stop to this exhibition. *How did he know I was with them last night?* "It's time for school!"

Truett was enthralled by Wade's demonstration. If he heard his father at all it didn't show as he interrupted. "What was it like for a cross to be burning in your yard and see them demons ridin' off in the dark?"

"Like HELL! Like the devil was visitin' straight outta HELL." He continued as dramatically as possible. "I could feel the hair on my arms stand on end and the cracklin' of the fire on the cross sounded like the devil cackling in hell's flames. Yep, this here piece of burnt cross is a demonstration of hate filled hell raisers." He put the piece of wood in his lap and grinned broadly. "Looks like I got carried away for a minute there. What was it you was saying, Lester?"

He looked at Lester expectantly but had no intention of letting him say anything. His little bit of drama was going just as he had planned and he was not finished yet.

"I suppose you young'uns are liking school." Wade continued. "I hear it's a lot better than the schools up around Memphis. Ain't that where you come from Lester? Up around Holly Springs and

Memphis?" He stared at Lester with piercing eyes, then smiled when he looked back at the children. "I hear a lot about Memphis from one of my cousins who lives up that way. He told me once about a white woman who was killed up there – she was mistaken for a colored woman and the man who done it..." Wade paused to look at Lester to see if he was on the right track.

Lester turned pale and stood up. "Ya'll go get ready for school!" He spoke sharply at the children.

The girls put their forks down with a clatter and started out of the room. "Bye, Mr. Posey."

Truett sat with his elbows on the table and waited for Wade to continue his story. "Did your cousin know who killed the white..."

"I SAID GO GET READY FOR SCHOOL!" Lester yelled at his son.

"I was just wantin' to... hear..." he stuttered as he reluctantly pushed away from the table.

Wade winked at him. "I'll tell you all about it someday. Thanks for the coffee Missus Warner," he said as he stood up. He left the piece of wood on the corner of the table. "Guess I'd better be going myself. I got about five more places to go before the day's over. Good day, ma'am." He nodded at Mrs. Warner as she cleared the table then he looked at Lester with unblinking eyes and as stern a look as he could muster. He was out the door and on his horse before Lester caught up with him.

Lester's hand trembled as he grabbed the side of the horse's bits to stop Wade from leaving. "My...my...family doesn't know about Memphis."

"Then call off the dogs." Wade said as he jerked the bridle suddenly and the horse pulled from Lester's grip.

Wade wanted to laugh about his little bit of drama but he was too angry to be very amused. He had no cousin in Memphis and had been mostly guessing about the Memphis matter but it seemed to him he had hit the nail on the head. It did help that he occasionally read newspapers from around the state.

Lester was convinced Wade knew about his secret past and shuddered to think of his wife and children learning about it. What he did not know was that Wade had no intention of telling his family

326

anything at all. First of all he knew nothing to tell and second, even if he did he saw no need to hurt innocent children and a trusting wife.

Wade snapped the reins and clucked his horse into a brisk trot. He went over in his mind his plans for the rest of the day. *I need to make it to Red Sawyer's house before his youn'uns leave for school. He needs to know that Strawtop is in bed with pneumonia. Josh tells me he might not pull through. A man's always concerned when he's got a child who's bad sick, ain't he? From there, I suppose I'll have time to make it to the Fancher place. He and his woman need to know that the widow Gebhardt is due to go into labor any day now. That Fancher! He knows how to console a grieving widow.* Wade grinned.

Vengence is mine, I will repay, saith the Lord.

42

"You better get them hands in the air or I'll blow your head clean off your shoulders, you confound Kluxer!" Annie screamed as Wade came through the kitchen door. He froze in his step as he faced the barrel of his own shotgun. Annie had it aimed right at his middle but Wade's observant eye noted that she did not have the hammer cocked. She was trembling and pale, her perspiration soaked nightgown clung to her frail body. Her gray-streaked hair hung limply down her back with wisps of it clinging to her wet forehead and cheeks. Her fear-filled eyes darted from Wade to the porch behind him, then quickly to the open window. The room was cold. Apparently the stove had not had wood in it all day.

With one quick movement he grasped the barrel of the gun and pointed it to the ceiling. Annie tenaciously held on to the stock until Wade took it from her by force. She sank to the floor and dissolved in tears.

"Please don't hurt me and my younguns. Don't burn my house down."

Wade sat on the floor beside her and held her close. "It's me, Annie, it's Wade. Look at me!" He took her face in his hands and forced her to look at him. Her eyes glared at him then darted from him to the door. "Why are you still in your nightgown? What have you been doing all day?"

She did not answer, only rocked back and forth on her knees with her eyes closed. "Where's Mattie? Are the young'uns home from school?" Wade prodded.

"THE YOUNG'UNS!" Wade panicked. He left Annie sitting in the middle of the kitchen floor and ran to the front room. The children were not there and there was not a fire in the fireplace. He went from room to room searching for them then returned to Annie. She still sat in the floor rocking back and forth, moaning. Her limp body draped over his arms as he lifted her from the floor and carried her to the bed. He had the covers tucked snuggly around her and was starting a fire when the front door opened.

"Ma, Ma." Mattie called. She opened the bedroom door expecting a warm fire to greet her, instead she saw her father stooped over the cold fireplace. "Why is it so cold in here? Where's Ma?" She looked closer at the rumpled bed and saw Annie's form outlined under the quilts. "Pa, what's going on?"

"Have you been gone all day?" He blew on the tiny spark of fire on the end of a splinter to make it flame higher then put it under the pile of wood.

"Yes. I left early this morning as usual to help Naomi teach the children. Why?" She rubbed her hands together to try to get them warm as she hovered close to Wade and the little bit of flame on the splinter.

"I've been gone all day too. Was Ann feeling okay when you left?"

Mattie cocked her head to one side and tried to remember exactly what Annie was doing when she left. "She was sitting at the kitchen table still upset over the cross burning - which reminds me - you said you would tell us why they did it."

"I will, but it has to be between the two of us. I don't want to get anyone else upset, especially Josh. When I came in the kitchen door Annie met me with the shotgun and…"

"The shotgun!" Mattie interrupted. "What in the world? Was it loaded?"

"Yes. She thought I was the Klan. It's a wonder she hadn't shot me, she was so scared. She was wet with sweat and her skin was as cold as ice. I figure she had been running through the house for a while trying to defend herself from what she thought was the Klan."

"Oh, no!" Is she having one of her spells?" Mattie walked back to the bed and pulled the cover from around Annie's face and laid her palm on her forehead. "She doesn't have a fever."

"Is she asleep?"

"Uh huh." Mattie looked at the clock on the mantle. "About time for the young'uns to get home from school. What're we going to do, Pa? We're out of that St. John's stuff Doc Powell gave you."

Wade walked back to the bed and stared down at Annie. "Maybe she'll be better when she wakes up. She's stopped shaking. We'll have to wait and see. I'll put a fire in the stove so the kitchen will be getting warm to cook supper." He walked out into the hall toward the kitchen.

Mattie pulled the cover back under Annie's chin and followed him.

"Now, tell me why the Klan burned the cross in our yard."

43

The warm spring sun warmed the dirt covering Frank's body. There were sinkholes around the edges where the winter rains had pushed the loose dirt around the casket. Mattie shuddered to think of Frank's body still lying there through the cold winter. She took her hands and loosened the soil on the pile of dirt beside the grave then scooped up hands full to fill the holes. As she pressed her toe into the soil to tap it firmly in place, the soil gave way and her foot sank into the soil covering her shoe top. She gasped and screamed, thinking she was falling into the grave. It flashed through her mind that Frank was pulling her down to be with him. When she freed her foot she knelt at the headstone and wrapped her arms around it. She cried, sobbing, loud, heart wrenching sobs.

A horse and buggy approached the graveyard and stopped at the hitching post at the front of the church. Mrs. Haney stared at the crumbled figure clutching her son's headstone. "Mattie," she whispered, "poor, poor Mattie." As she made her way to the grave she made as much noise as possible to keep from startling Mattie. She knelt beside her on the ground and put her arm around her shoulder. There were no words of consolation either could speak. It was enough to hold each other and cry.

"I brought some daffodils to put on the grave." Mrs. Haney held them up so Mattie could see. "Do you want to put them in place?"

Mattie dried her eyes with her handkerchief. "They are so pretty. She took them in her hands and held them under her nose. "They smell good." She nestled the vase of flowers in the soil in front of the marble stone then the two of them sat on the dried, crisp grass that surrounded the grave.

"I need to come up sometime this week and put more dirt on it." Mrs. Haney said as she nodded toward the grave.

"I put a little bit on just now." Mattie said.

Mrs. Haney looked intently at Mattie as she tried to say what was on her mind. "I miss him a lot and my whole family misses him...but..." She looked at Mattie tenderly. "You know, I have the rest of my children to keep me going. I have to think of making them happy and try to console them, as well as myself. I know it is probably worse on you. You have no one." She took Mattie's hand in one of hers and patted it with the other. Mattie waited for her to continue.

"I wish you had someone. I wish you would find another boy to love."

"I can't, I just can't bear the thought of somebody else." She looked at Frank's mother, pleading for understanding.

"I know it's hard, but you may have to simply will yourself to tolerate some boy until you can fall in love again. You can NOT go on like this. I don't know if I need to mention this...but..." She wondered whether to betray her niece's confidence. "Mary Rose told me she had heard that the Johnson boy likes you."

Mattie rolled her eyes and managed a smile. "He does, but..."

"But, what?"

"But...he's nice enough, but...he's not Frank."

"Honey, Frank is NOT coming back. There's never going to be another Frank. I don't mean to sound callous - you know I'm not, but Frank is gone and he's never coming back. You HAVE to go on with your life! Find some meaning. What is the last thing he said to you?" She waited for Mattie to answer.

"He said...uh...you know - 'Come not when I am dead, to drop...thy foolish...tears upon my grave...'" She hesitated.

"Go on, finish it. I'll say it with you."

To trample round my fallen head,
And vex the unhappy dust thou wouldst not save.
There let the wind sweep and the plover cry;
But thou, go by.
Child, if it were thine error or thy crime
I care no longer being all unblest;
Wed whom thou wilt, but I am sick of time,
And desire to rest.
Pass on, weak heart, and leave me where I lie;
Go by, go by."

"You know it, too!" Mattie was surprised.

"Sure, I do. Now, you do what Frank asked you to. I'm not saying," she hastened to say, "that you should not come here at all, but don't put your life on hold. Why don't you go with Willard to the spring dance?"

"I might." Mattie managed to smile. "I might just do that."

******

The smell of freshly tilled soil floated across the fields and yards of Neshoba County. The soil had dried enough to be broken up and planted. By late March the corn was in the ground as well as the irish potatoes, cabbage, onions, green peas and other cool tolerant plants. The horses pulled plows and fertilizer spreaders and corn planters. At the Posey farm Prince grazed lazily while the other horses sweated and strained.

"Your time's coming, Prince." Mattie said as she hand-fed him fresh hay and corn. "As soon as the weather is warm enough to plant cotton you and me are gonna get down there on that one little acre of land and plant us some cotton. Then in the fall we'll buy us a brand new black buggy with a fringed top. Won't we be a sight trotting along down to Tucker to visit Frank? You'll work for just me and then only if I think you're up to it. No more pulling a middle buster in that ole bottom land." She stroked his face. "We're gonna let Willie do your work from now on." She smiled as she remembered the day she and Willard had agreed on a price for the chestnut mare. "Gotta get back inside and see about Ma." Mattie said as she gave Prince one last pat.

Annie still sat on the porch in the sunshine where Mattie had left her. She rocked back and forth as she folded and unfolded a dishtowel. Mattie had helped her bathe and braided her hair in one long braid that hung down her back. Her diet consisted of only what Wade or one of the children spoonfed her. She sat in one place and stared at whatever was in front of her. Her catatonic state prevented her from perceiving what was said to her and her only words were random, not pertaining to the subject at hand. She called for Wade or her mama or one of the children and threatened the Klan at times when she seemed to feel insecure.

Naomi had to finish the school year without Mattie's help but she managed fine. It was questionable exactly how much the children learned but at least they could say the alphabet and count to a hundred. That was a lot more than they knew when she started teaching them.

The message came from the State Board of Education that there would be a school for the Negro children in October. The building was already started on the sixteenth section land now occupied by the Cosper family. Old man Cosper was not too happy about forfeiting two acres of the farming land for the school but he had no choice. He knew from the beginning of his lease that the land was set aside for schools. He just didn't think it would be so soon.

The Ku Klux Klan still raged in the County, donning their pointed hoods and flapping sheets, threatening the most vulnerable. But, needless to say, they didn't come near the Posey place.

Mattie had gone with Willard to the spring dance and he continued to come over on Sunday afternoon to keep her company. "Ain't no use in pining away." Mattie had told Prince. "Might as well get out and have a little fun." Still, she made regular visits to the cemetery.

******

"You sit right there, Annie," Wade said as he patted her knee. "While the rain has let up a bit, I'm going out to the barn to check on the new calf and it's mama."

Wade pulled an old felt hat down on his head and took a jacket off a nail on the back porch. "The young'uns are all in the parlor. I'll be right back." He stepped off the back porch and into the rain.

The rain had poured unceasingly for three days and now had slowed to a drizzle. The heavy layer of clouds had stalled up around Noxapater and sent water flooding down the Pearl River and all it's tributaries.

Annie watched Wade disappear through the barn door.

******

Wade stuck his head in the parlor door and was greeted by a room full of teenagers in various stages of courting. Some were serious, some were not. It seemed that this Sunday afternoon every cousin and teenager in the community had made their way through the rain to the Posey house.

"Just looking for Annie," Wade said somewhat apologetically as his eyes scanned the parlor.

"She's not in here," Alma said then went back to the board game she and a friend were playing.

Wade went through the house looking for Annie, then out to all the outhouses. He searched the barn, then went to Joshua's who joined in the search.

"She ain't nowhere to be found." Joshua told Wade. "What we gwin ta' do. She gots to be somewheres."

"I'll start all over from the beginning. Will you get Lou and your kids to do a thorough search around your place? I'll go get that bunch up at the house to help."

Annie's name echoed through the fields, woods, pastures. "Annie!" "Ma!" "Annie!" "Mrs. Posey!"

Willard and Mattie teamed together to search. Mattie cupped her hands around her mouth. "Ma! Ma!" Fear gripped her when she failed to answer.

Ellen Williamson

The search lasted until almost sunset. The water-soaked searchers gathered on the back porch and waited for Wade to decide what to do next.

Wade looked toward the creek below his house and remembered the day he had found her down there with the baby. He shook his head slowly.

"I know we have already looked down at the creek once but lets look one more time. There's no use in you girls going. You stay up here and search the house again. I hate the thought but we might ought to go downstream. Mattie, you and Pearl find some dry clothes for everybody."

44

The stream of relatives and friends that filed past Annie's casket seemed endless. They shook their heads sadly and wondered what made her do such a thing as to jump in the water hole down at the creek, or maybe she slipped, nobody knew. The swollen creek with its swift running water had carried her more than a mile downstream. Few people knew of her mental state but now it was whispered among the crowd of mourners. The Posey family stoically went through the normal procedures of burying a loved one and set aside a reasonable period for mourning.

Now, the ground had dried out from the April deluge and it was time to plant cotton. Life had to go on and go on it did.

Mattie worked her acre of cotton and bought her own little buggy.

Willard looked it over and nodded his head approvingly. "Yep, it's just the right size for the two of us."

"What makes you think I'm going to let you ride in my new buggy?" Mattie teased.

"Please, may I?" He pretended to beg.

Mattie laughed. "Alright, if you're going to beg so pitifully."

She and Willard used the buggy for their Sunday afternoon drives and of course, she used it to travel to Tucker and back at least once a week to visit Frank's grave. Many times when she approached the little Catholic Church on the side of the hill she remembered so vividly Frank's last whisper to her, "Go by, go by". She would smile and make her way to the oldest headstone in the cemetery and place a small bouquet of flowers by it. She would trace his name with her fingers, and place a kiss on the cold, marble stone. Sometimes there were tears but seldom ever, any more. There only remained an unrequited grief, sadness, longing and the ever present "If only...".

******

Being the oldest, it fell Mattie's lot to shoulder the responsibility of the house and garden, which included all the canning and preserving of the fruit and vegetables. Pearl, of course, was there to take some of the responsibility. Mattie ordered the three younger ones around and expected them to do as she said. "I am NOT doing all this work by myself. You need to make them do their share," she told Wade.

Pearl and Bobby Collette planned their wedding for the week before his family was to move back to Gastonia, North Carolina so they could go with them. That left another vacant place in the structure of the Posey family.

Louella decided to marry John Gray, but at least she didn't move very far away. They settled less then a mile from the north end of the Posey farm.

Alma and Tommy didn't turn out much work for the next year or so. Alma didn't take any of the responsibility off Mattie and only did what she had to do. Then it took a stern rebuke from Wade to get her to do very much.

Tommy, of course, was the baby and Wade coddled and protected him. He dawdled at whatever task was given him and that was usually something that was not very strenuous.

It soon became apparent to Wade that without the help of the girls he, Joshua and Isaac would have to cut back on the acres of cotton they planted. He and Joshua couldn't turn out the work they used to and Joshua spent any extra time he had preening his twenty-five acres.

Naomi was busy with four little ones tugging on her and Louisa was plagued with rheumatism. Joshua's and Louisa's two oldest boys decided they wanted to try out the factories in the North and now they were gone as well.

Mattie and Willard became a regular couple at all the social functions around Philadelphia. Many speculated about them getting married but were pshaw- pshawed when they hinted at it to Mattie.

Raymond Whitmire talked Alma into marrying him, or maybe it was the other way around. They moved to a small farm between Spring Creek and Sandtown. At least they were close enough the three girls could get together occasionally.

45

1905

"I'm moving back to Jackson." Willard announced unexpectedly to Mattie.

"Jackson!" she exclaimed. "Why?" Mattie tried to look at his face but he turned it toward the window and sat up on the edge of the sofa.

"Because things aren't working out here - you know, between you and me." He ran his fingers through his hair and shook his head.

"Why aren't they? I thought we were getting along just fine." She tugged on the sleeve of his shirt to get him to face her. Instead, he stood up and walked to the window and stood with his back to her.

"How long have you and me been courting?" He turned quickly to look at her.

Mattie stuttered, at a loss for words.

"Seven years, that's how long," he said sharply. "And how many times have I asked you to marry me?" He stared at her without the tug of a smile she was used to.

"I'll tell you how many!" He sounded angry but Mattie knew it was not anger she was seeing. It was something much more volatile.

"Fourteen! That's how many, maybe more. At least twice a year since we've been courting. And what do you always say?"

Mattie started to speak but Willard interrupted her.

I'll tell you what you always say. 'It's too soon,' or 'Let's wait till spring, or summer, or winter,' whatever season it was not."

"But Willard, you don't understand…" she pleaded as she walked over to him and reached out to touch his arm. He jerked away from her.

"Don't understand? Don't understand!? I understand all right. I understand that you are waiting for me to turn into Frank or for Frank to come back. He's not coming back, Mattie." He thrust both hands outward and sliced the air with the sides of his hands. He's NOT coming back! He is NOT coming back."

Mattie's chin quivered. "I know that. "It's just that…" She started to cry. This was not like Willard. He had always been so patient and understanding.

"Just that what? It is simply that you don't love me. Never have, never will. You don't love anybody but Frank. Never have, never will. You're pining away for somebody you can't give your love to while I'm trying to wait for you to love me. A man can't wait forever, Mattie!"

"I know that, but if you'll wait till…"

"Wait? I am NOT waiting any longer. I'll be on the train to Jackson tomorrow at four-fifteen. I'm leaving all this heartbreak behind. I'm going to find someone that can love me for who I am." He walked to the door of the parlor then stopped to look at her. She thought he was coming back toward her. She would have let him put his arms around her if he had.

"If you would like to go with me, be at the depot tomorrow at four-fifteen." He took his hat off the nail in the hallway and rode his horse down the driveway without looking back.

******

Mattie turned her head and listened then glanced at the clock. The four o'clock train from Louisville was arriving. In fifteen minutes it would pull out of Philadelphia on it's way to Jackson. She looked at the peas in her apron, then resumed shelling. She waited and listened.

She heard the shrill whistle of the train down at the depot and watched as the black smoke huffed above the trees and on down toward Deemer. It would go from there through Deemer, Neshoba, Union and Newton, then to Jackson. Her eyes became moist, sadness flooded her. "I'm sorry Willard, I'm sorry. I could never give myself to anyone but Frank."

46

It is odd how many thoughts can pass through one's mind in a short while. Mattie remembered those days as clearly as if they were last week. Every emotion she had then, came back to haunt her as she sat hunkered under the porch. She wondered how long she had been sitting there. It seemed a long time. Mr. Mayo and her Pa's conversation seemed to ramble on and on. *Have I missed his question to pa?* She wondered. *I suppose not. They're still talking about the weather and the crops.* She heard the back door slam and jumped. She bumped her head on the bottom of the house. *I can't let somebody see me under here,* she thought as she crawled from under the house.

"What are you doing under there?" Tommy said loudly as he came around the corner of the house.

"Sh-h-h," She hissed loudly at him as she brushed the dust off her dress and attempted to smoothe out the wrinkles. She motioned for him to follow her behind the house as she led the way.

"Why in the sam hill were you under the house?" he demanded.

"I was listening to Mr. Mayo ask Pa for my hand."

"Well, what did he say?"

"I don't know. All they were talking about was weather and crops. Pa got to reminiscing and I didn't hear if he asked."

"That's what you get for eaves dropping."

"A lot of good it did me!"

"Mattie," Tommy said, hesitating. "What do you think Ma would have thought of Mr. Mayo?"

"I have no idea. Probably would have liked him. Everybody else seems to. At least he's not Catholic! That would have made her happy." She sounded somewhat sarcastic but didn't mean to, in respect for her dead mother.

"I still miss her. Don't you?" he asked pensively. "I remember the day she died. Seems like yesterday. It sure was sad."

Mattie remembered, too.

"At any rate, I think she would approve of you marrying Mr. Mayo," Tommy added as they went through the back door.

Wade and John walked down the hall toward Mattie and Tommy.

"She'll make you a mighty good little wife," Mattie heard Wade say. "She's been the lady of the house here for a long time and has done a good job. It's time she had a family of her own."

"I sure appreciate it, Mr. Posey," John added as he extended his hand and Wade grasped it firmly.

Mattie smiled. "I don't have to ask what the answer was."

"What did Pa say? What did you ask him? Did he agree to what we talked about?" Mattie peppered the questions at John.

The two of them had gone back into the parlor and sat on the sofa that was now faded and threadbare along the edge of the seat.

John held his hands in front of him, his palms toward Mattie. "Hold on! One question at a time."

"Wade said it was all right with him if I would agree to take you up North somewhere to live," he told her, as he suppressed a grin.

"Then you can just forget it, I'm not moving to Timbucto," she said jokingly. But he knew she meant it, nor did he want to take her far away from her family.

"Seriously," he said, the laughter leaving his eyes, "We did discuss the fact that he dreaded us moving all the way up to Winston County. I told him I was thinking of leaving the farm for my son and his wife and buying a small one here in Neshoba County." He looked at her questioningly and observed her closely for her reaction.

"That would suit me a lot better. I don't care about moving up there. Do you have a place in mind?" Her fingers nervously pleated and unpleating a fold in her skirt.

"Yes I do. There is one just a few miles east of here. A little community called Bloomfield."

"You got it all planned out, haven't you?"

"I sure have. We don't need a big place. Do you want to ride up there and see it? I want your approval before I make the final decision," he spoke hopefully.

"Now?"

"Why not? It's a long time until sundown. Go ask your father if it's okay." He rose from the sofa and reached for her hand.

"Mr. Mayo," she hesitated and tugged on his hand slightly, indicating for him to sit back down.

"You can call me John, I AM going to be your husband," he said somewhat more sternly than he intended.

"I could never do that!" she exclaimed, surprised that he could even suggest it.

She had always called him Mr. Mayo and could think of him in no other manner – husband or not. Even now in her mind she could not conceive of him ever being down on her plane for in her thinking she had elevated him to a much higher status than she. She had far too much respect for him to call him by his first name and could not imagine him being her lover. She respected him and honored him as an older man and would be a faithful, loyal wife but love him? Her heart was – well, elsewhere, but she would try. She shook her head slightly in an attempt to bring her thoughts back to the moment.

"As you wish," he replied. "Were you going to say something?" he asked, still holding her hand as he sat on the sofa beside her.

"Are you sure…" she began slowly, "that you want to marry me? You know that I…well, you know…" she trailed off, not completing her sentence. She could not bring herself to say she did not love him, for in a way, maybe she did. Even more, she could not seem to say the words "I love you". She had only said that to one other person.

"Yes, I'm sure. I know that you don't feel as strongly about me as I do you, but in time you will. Just give yourself some time. You've been through a lot of hurt in your lifetime. I won't rush you. And, yes, I'm sure I want to marry you." He patted the top of her hand, which he held in his.

Am I sure? He thought to himself. *You bet I'm sure! A forty-eight year old man with a pretty young thing like this as my bride. A virgin at that! Where else would I find a beautiful wife like this?* He thought of the others - and there had been others since his wife died. Most of them spinsters – and for good reason. Either they were so homely he could barely look at them or their personality was such that he could not stand to be near them. Some were withdrawn, so much so they seemed mentally deficient and he suspected they were. Slouchy women with their greasy hair stringing around their face. Most had on a dowdy dress. Some were actually dirty, smelling of perspiration or stale clothes. Not Mattie! She always smelled fresh and sweet. Her smile was radiant which spread to her sparkling blue, laughing eyes. Her brow was somewhat furrowed but that was to be expected with her age and the trials she had been through. She was still straight and slim and carried her head with dignity. Her personality was exuberant, always laughing at his silly little jokes.

Then there had been the widows whose husbands had died and left them with several children. They would have made him a good wife, maybe, but he did not feel like raising another's man's children at this time in his life, especially if he could marry Mattie. She was still in her prime and could give him several children of his own.

He had stayed single a long time after his wife died, and raised their only son. He, too, had been heart broken. He knew about Mattie's feelings for Frank but they both had to move on now.

I'll be so good to her she will have to love me.

This time it was he who had to be shaken out of his reverie.

Mattie waved her hand before his eyes. "A penney for your thoughts."

"They're worth more than that. Do you remember when we met?"

"Of course I do. It was over at Georgia's. You came to visit while I was there."

I thought you were the prettiest little thing I had ever seen." He grinned as he looked at her and patted her hand lovingly. "When you agreed for me to come calling I was so excited I couldn't stand it. Just like a little kid!"

Mattie smiled and squeezed his hand. "You know that was only three months ago, don't you?"

"I know but it didn't take me that long to fall in love with you."

Mattie abruptly changed the subject. "We're gonna have a good life, Mister Mayo. If we're going, we'd better go," Mattie said as she pulled her hand from his and got up from the sofa.

"Yes, yes, of course.

******

The house was small but adequate. It sat on a level clearing cut out of the dense forest surrounded by tall, stately pine trees. It had been painted white at one time but was now in bad need of a new coat of paint. The yard was somewhat overgrown with weeds, having been vacant for two or three years but there was evidence that a caring lady had lived there. There were numerous iris beds, their foliage shooting up like swords behind a row of rocks. The daylilies were in full bloom as was a climbing rose bush full of red blooms streaming from its broken trellis. There were perennial petunias surviving nicely around the chimney, which was still standing stately against the house. The house had four rooms with a porch across the front and back. The barn stood majestically against the eastern horizon. Weeds grew in the fertile barnyard. It was evident that all that was needed was some time and effort to get it to looking livable. No windows were broken and no doors were sagging.

John beamed as he showed the house to Mattie. "Just picture two rocking chairs on the front porch. Go ahead, close your eyes while I describe it to you."

Mattie laughed. "I can imagine it without my eyes being closed."

"No, I want you to close your eyes and let me describe it to you. Come on…" he pleaded.

"Okay, if you insist," she agreed as she put both hands over her eyes.

"The house has a fresh coat of white paint. "There are pots of blooming flowers sitting along the edge of the porch. The trellis on the rose bush has been repaired and all the weeds have been cut from the yard and flowerbeds. There are fresh beds of zinnias and marigolds along the edges of the walk from the driveway to the house."

"Who planted the new flower beds?" Mattie giggled.

"You did, of course! I am in the field plowing the corn. Let me continue now. H-m-m-m - I see a buggy in the lean-to at the barn and Prince is in the pasture." Mattie laughed again. "A mother hen with her baby chicks are scratching in the grass."

"May I open my eyes now?"

"Not yet! Oh, I see one more thing. What is it now?" he added as though he were wondering. "I can see plainly now. Yes, yes, there it is – it is Mattie sitting on the porch in the rocking chair and there is something else. She is holding a…a…why yes, its a baby!" he ended excitedly and laughed heartily.

"Oh silly!" She laughed as she slapped him lightly on the arm. "You know, that is probably exactly what it will look like in a few months," she added joyfully with sincere excitement in her voice. She allowed him to put both arms around her and pull her close to him – but only for a second.

******

The wedding was a simple affair, held the last week in August with all the family in their Sunday finery. Wade had ordered a new suit for the occasion and proudly hosted the grand event. Mattie ordered a new white dress from the mail order catalog along with new shoes of the latest fashion. Pearl came from North Carolina with her two small children. She and Ida fixed Mattie's hair with ribbons and flowers intertwined in the soft curls around her face.

The parlor was cleaned and the furniture polished. Fresh flowers adorned the entire house. The mantle board above the fireplace was decorated with ivy and roses. Family and friends brought home-made delicacies. Mattie allowed Rev. Whitley to officiate at the ceremony even though she secretly held resentment against him for what she considered interference with her and Frank's courtship. She did give him the benefit of the doubt, believing he was convinced he was guiding his congregation in the right direction.

John's son, Alonzo was there with his wife and new baby. Mattie cringed to think she was a step-grandma. He was a cute little baby, she had to admit. *Maybe he won't call me granny.*

John had spent hours at the new place cleaning, painting and moving his furniture in the house along with some new pieces Mattie had chosen. The two of them had shared in getting everything in place. They would spend their honeymoon there and then let it merge into the routine of the coming winter and preparation for the coming springtime farming.

47

"Why didn't you just run away again?" Ellen asked as she sat listening to Mattie tell about her love for Frank and her broken heart at his death.

"Oh I couldn't, I was too scared of Ma." Mattie's eyes glowered convincingly.

Ellen was twelve years old, with olive skin, green eyes and straight brown hair. She spent many hours with her Grandma, Mama, as all Mattie's grandchildren called her. When she finished her numerous chores at home her mother sent her to bring firewood into the house for her Grandma Mattie. On the weekends she swept and cleaned her house.

"Why did you always call Grandpa Mr. Mayo and not John?" Ellen questioned her again, as if she had not asked it many times before.

"I just didn't. That's what he was to me - Mr. Mayo, not John." She smiled as if it really didn't matter. "You are just full of questions aren't you?" Mattie teased her as she continued to gently rock and leaned her white head back against the back of the chair.

Mattie was now sixty-five years of age and weighed two hundred fifty pounds with heavy legs and feet. She never exercised - just sat in the rocking chair crocheting or shelling peas when they were in season. Her mind always, at some point, turned to Frank and the love she had for him.

John Mayo died many years before so Mattie moved from Bloomfield to a small house a mile from Philadelphia. They had three daughters, one who died with tuberculosis in her early twenties. The other two gave her ten grandchildren including the one who now sat with her knees under her chin looking up at her with wide questioning eyes, sharing the pain Mattie still felt. Ellen's heart hurt for her grandmother and she determined to never let her true love get away from her.

Ellen had heard the story many times and never tired of it. Mattie always thought of some detail she had not told her before. Ellen listened intently to the story of Frank, as well as the numerous stories of her Grandma's life. She pictured Mattie standing beside the road waiting for the funeral procession and felt her grief as she bent over Frank's casket. A vivid picture was in her mind of a slender Mattie hunkered under the front porch listening to John and Wade's conversation. From Mattie's front porch, Ellen could look across the green turf of the golf course and see the big house, which Wade built for Annie almost seven decades before. It was dilapidated but the tall timbers still held the sagging front porch high off the ground.

Ellen sat now and watched the dying embers in the fireplace and noticed that her Grandma had dozed.

"Mama," Ellen said as she shook her awake. "I need to go to bed; I have school tomorrow. Do you want me to get you some aspirin and a glass of water?"

"I guess so," Mattie answered sluggishly as she attempted to open her eyes. "Help me get out of my clothes and into my night gown."

Ellen tugged at the massive woman's dress and managed to get it off then helped her with her gown.

"I think you still have fever." She helped her to bed and pulled the covers up under her chin. The feather bed engulfed her.

It fell Ellen's duty to stay with her grandma when she was sick - not that she would know what to do if she became seriously ill. She could only run back to her own house and tell her mother to come and check on her. If it were where she could contact her cousin, Jane, the two of them stayed with Mattie.

Mattie often became delirious when she had a little fever, which somewhat frightened Ellen but she was accustomed to it. It seemed the elderly Mattie constantly dreamed about her youth.

Ellen reached up and pulled the string that hung from the single light bulb in the ceiling. Darkness flooded the room. She heard her grandma softly snoring and as usual, talking in her sleep. She listened to try to hear exactly what she was saying. Then she heard her plainly.

"Go by, go by."

Ellen changed into her pajamas in front of the still warm fireplace then sat and watched the red-hot coals, as they slowly turned dark. The heat was overtaken by the cold, which seeped in around the cracks in the front door. She went into the adjoining room and snuggled down in bed. She pulled the quilts around her and over her ears leaving only her nose exposed to the cold of the night. She was soon asleep.

Ellen awoke suddenly, startled by Mattie's voice. She sat up in bed and listened for her to call her, then snuggled back under the covers. *She's just talking in her sleep again.* Then she heard her call again.

"Ma! ... Ma!"

By: Ellen Williamson
Copyright 3/1/02

Postscript

Wade Posey's farm was located where the Philadelphia Golf Course and Neshoba Central School are today. The house was located on the east side of St. Francis Road across the street from the Neshoba Central Elementary School. Tommy Posey built a house where the east parking lot of Neshoba Central School is located today (2003). The house was directly across the street from where the AFLAC Insurance office is located. Mattie Parilee Posey Mayo Gilbert lived her final years in a house that stood on the corner of the Golf Course Road and Williamson Avenue.

The exact location of Frank Haney's grave is in the Holy Cross cemetary.

More of Mattie's story will soon be published in a book as a sequel to this one.

**JOHN A. MAYO AND MATTIE "PARILEE" POSEY
THEIR WEDDING DAY
1906**

JOHN ALBERT MAYO
MATTIE "PARILEE" MAYO
(circa 1920)

WILLIAM WADE POSEY FAMILY
Back row l to r: Alma, Louella, Pearl, Mattie
Front Row l to r: Annie, Tom, Wade
(circa 1900)

Printed in the United States
25675LVS00002B/43-51